P9-BBU-025

ORANGE PUBLIC LIBRARY

3 2159 00061 2677

Withdrawn

DATE DUE

AUG 26 1997			
OCT 16 97			
			•
	261-2500		Printed in USA

GREAT LIVES
World Government

World Government, GREAT LIVES:

William Jay Jacobs

Charles Scribner's Sons · New York

Maxwell Macmillan Canada · Toronto
Maxwell Macmillan International
New York · Oxford · Singapore · Sydney

TOWN OF ORANGE
PUBLIC LIBRARY
ORANGE, CONN.

J
920
J

094538

Copyright © 1992 by William Jay Jacobs

All rights reserved. No part of this book may be reproduced or transmitted in any form or by any means, electronic or mechanical, including photocopying, recording, or by any information storage and retrieval system, without permission in writing from the Publisher.

Charles Scribner's Sons Books for Young Readers
Macmillan Publishing Company, 866 Third Avenue, New York, NY 10022

Maxwell Macmillan Canada, Inc.
1200 Eglinton Avenue East, Suite 200, Don Mills, Ontario M3C 3N1

Macmillan Publishing Company is part of the Maxwell Communication Group of Companies.

First edition   10 9 8 7 6 5 4 3 2 1
Printed in the United States of America

Cover illustration copyright © 1992 by Stephen Marchesi. All rights reserved.

Library of Congress Cataloging-in-Publication Data
Jacobs, William Jay.
   Great lives : world government / William Jay Jacobs.
   — 1st ed.   p.   cm.   Includes bibliographical references (p.   ).
   Summary: Presents biographical sketches of twenty-five world
   leaders from the early nineteenth century to the present day.
   ISBN 0-684-19285-3
1. Heads of state—Biography—Juvenile literature.   2. History, Modern—19th century—Juvenile literature.   3. History, Modern—20th century—Juvenile literature.
[1. Heads of state.   2. History, Modern—19th century.   3. History, Modern—20th century.]
I. Title.
D352.J33   1992   909.8—dc20   91-42368

For Susan Jacobs
With admiration,
with gratitude, and
with boundless affection

Contents

. . . some are born great, some achieve greatness,
and some have greatness thrust upon them.

—WILLIAM SHAKESPEARE

Foreword

In one sense, all people who live are like all other people who ever have lived since the beginning of time. That is because each of us is born and each of us dies. Or as William Shakespeare put it:

> And so, from hour to hour we ripe and ripe,
> And then from hour to hour we rot and rot;
> And thereby hangs a tale.

"Riping" and "rotting" are what happens to every human being. Thus, Napoleon Bonaparte, for all the glory of his military victories at Austerlitz and Jena, tastes no different to the worms who invade his grave than does the humblest street sweeper of Paris.

But there is a difference.

We do not study the life of the street sweeper, though his life may indeed have been fascinating. We know little about it. It is shadowy and unclear. And since the deeds he performed affected few other people, he is soon forgotten.

Instead, we study what are known as "great lives." We want to share the experiences that separate famous men and women from the rest of humanity. We want to know more about such people.

It is not surprising, therefore, that the life stories you are about to read are about the leaders—the shapers of events—in the twentieth century and the century before it.

It is to the deeds of those leaders that we must look if we are truly to understand the world we live in today.

Some of the personalities whose lives we shall explore were born to power: rulers like England's Queen Victoria. Through much of the past it has been such queens and kings, emperors and empresses, who have inherited the reins of power and then succeeded in dictating the course of events. A host of powerful monarchs immediately come to mind: Henry VIII of England, Louis XIV of France, Cleopatra of Egypt, Catherine II of Russia.

But the world of today is a very different place, and the royal figures who once strutted upon its stage would scarcely recognize it. Adolf Hitler, born not to royalty but to the lower middle class, not too long ago plunged six continents into war. Vladimir Ilyich Lenin, the second son of a minor official in Russia, emerged as the sacred hero of the vast Communist empire; his personality—his image—came to dominate the second half of the twentieth century.

We may come to hate such leaders. Or we may love them. Yet we have no choice but to recognize the towering role they have played in the events of our time.

In the years since the end of World War II (1945) leadership has spread even more widely among many nations, old and new. Leaders no longer must be "giants on the earth" to command our attention. Figures like Ho Chi Minh of Vietnam may for a time loom large, although their nations may be small and poor. Certainly that has been the case with such figures in the Middle East as the Ayatollah Khomeini of Iran and Golda Meir of Israel. Similarly, even when the actions of a leader such as Jomo Kenyatta of Kenya do not immediately affect the major powers, we still may be keenly aware of that person's influence in a region.

It is not clear why, either in the past or the present, some few people seek out positions of power while the vast majority of human beings have little desire for such responsibility. Nor are there any set rules, any surefire recipes, for how to get power—or how to keep it.

For the great mass of humanity an even more important question is what people do with power once they have it. Those praised by history as "great" leaders are not necessarily "good." Indeed, some of them clearly have wielded power in ways that could only be described as "evil."

Two figures considered in this book, Winston Churchill of England and Joseph Stalin of Russia, were both—in very different ways—great leaders. But without Churchill, Western Europe today might still be enslaved by the forces of Nazi Germany. Meanwhile, without Stalin, Eastern Europe might have been spared a half century of tyrannical Russian rule.

A great leader, then, is one without whose action an event in history would have been different.

Clearly, such people have made a difference in human existence.

According to an old Chinese proverb, "The great leader is a public misfortune." And there is no doubt that some of history's leaders have climbed to "greatness" by replacing peace and happiness with war, conquest, and bloodshed.

But it is also true that great people sometimes may be good people. Many leaders whose stories are told in this book worked hard to improve life in their countries—leaders such as Mahatma Gandhi, Meiji Mutsuhito, and Kemal Atatürk.

People who hold power, it would seem, make different uses of that power.

Particularly in the world's democratic countries, citizens have a share in choosing their leaders. With care, it is possible to prevent government from falling into the hands of a tiny band of privileged people—an "elite"—who would use power for their own selfish ends.

It is also possible, although more difficult, for historians to judge whether leaders are only busy running their own countries or are working instead toward higher values, higher goals—shared ideals. As President Woodrow Wilson liked to remind citizens of the United States, "Americans must be idealists working in matter."

And what about you in all of this? Leaders of the past—men and women both good and evil whose stories you are about to read—can serve as models for you and for your life. You can learn from them, perhaps even begin to think of your own role in the world of tomorrow. Or, as Henry Wadsworth Longfellow once put it:

> Lives of great men all remind us
> We can make our lives sublime.
> And, departing, leave behind us
> Footprints on the sands of time.

PART I
The Nineteenth Century: Prelude to Our Age

Napoléon Bonaparte

1769–1821   One of history's great military geniuses and conquerors; dedicated, as leader of France, to the unification of continental Europe

Once, on the island of Corsica, off the western coast of Italy, a little child played with his older brother by the seashore.

Later, that child, Napoléon Bonaparte, became one of history's most famous personalities. A general by the age of twenty-four, he has been compared to the greatest of military geniuses—Hannibal, Julius Caesar, Genghis Khan. To some historians, he is a torchbearer, a romantic hero, who spread across Europe the French Revolution's high ideals of liberty and equality. For twenty years he ruled France, producing a code of laws still in use in that country today. Eventually he crowned himself emperor and loomed, a solitary, brooding figure, towering above the life of Western Europe.

At the same time, Napoléon's achievements carried with them a terrible cost. In the bloody wars he fought, some 500,000 young Frenchmen—soldiers in his armies—gave up their lives. Eventually the other European powers combined to defeat him in battle and exile him to the desolate, rocky island of St. Helena, far away in the South Atlantic. And it was there that he died.

In a poem written to honor the memory of Napoléon, the British writer, Rudyard Kipling, wondered about the French leader's extraordinary life and about its bitter ending:

"How far is St. Helena from a little
    child at play?"
What makes you want to wander

there with all the world between?

Oh, Mother call your son again or
else he'll run away.

(*No one thinks of winter when the
grass is green!*)

What, indeed, made him "want to
wander there"? What was Napoléon
looking for in his life? Was it conquest?
Power? Worldly glory? A fame that
would live on forever? Behind the glam-
orous court life, the dazzling costumes
that he loved to wear, what was Napoléon Bonaparte really like, and what
drove him relentlessly to victory after
victory?

When Napoléon's parents married, his
father, Carlo, was eighteen; his mother,
the beautiful Letizia, only fourteen. For
the first six years of their marriage, they
had only two children. First came a
son, Joseph, and then, one year later,
"Napoleone Buonaparte," as it was
spelled on the Italian-speaking island
of Corsica, where the future leader of
the Western world would spend his
early years.

The French had taken control of Corsica only a year before Napoléon's birth,
and for much of his childhood and youth
he bitterly hated France, devoting himself to independence for his island birthplace.

Napoléon's family had little money
to spend but, because they belonged
to the noble class, were able to send
both of their sons, as well as a daughter,
to well-known French schools with
scholarship grants. So it was that at the
age of nine Napoléon was taken to
France by his father and enrolled in
the military school at Brienne.

Already, young Napoléon was known
as a scrapper. Smaller than the other
boys his age, not particularly handsome, he craved attention and insisted
on having his own way. He would strike
back in anger when his French classmates teased him about his Corsican
background and the Italian accent he
would never completely lose. He once
promised bitterly to a French classmate, "I will do you French all the harm
I can." Gloomy and short-tempered,
he kept to himself most of the time.

Yet when he wished to impress others, he could be charming. From the
beginning he excelled in mathematics
and science and seems to have enjoyed
history and geography, as well. What
he especially hated were playground
games, except for the snowball fights
he transformed into miniature wars.

Although young Napoléon was far
from outstanding as a student, his teachers recognized him as someone special.
One teacher wrote of his unusual talent
for planning fortifications, while an-

other described his personality as "granite, heated by a volcano."

In 1784, he was admitted to the École Militaire in Paris, France's outstanding military academy. One year later he graduated, standing only forty-second in a class of fifty-eight. Sixteen years old, he was commissioned as a second lieutenant in the French artillery.

The next seven years marked a low point for Napoléon. With little money to spend he still managed, by skimping on food, to buy books on military strategy, especially about the uses of artillery.

His father had died in 1785. Young Napoléon and his older brother Joseph took on responsibility for their mother and the family's six younger children. Returning to Corsica, Napoléon became an officer in the Corsican National Guard. His primary goal remained the winning of freedom from French rule for the island.

In 1793, the leaders of the French Revolution executed King Louis XVI, an event that Corsicans saw as a chance to declare independence, something they did at once.

By that time, Napoléon had become a firm supporter of the French Revolution, speaking out against the wealthy French nobility and the entrenched religious leaders. In the eyes of Pasquale Paoli, the Corsican governor, however,

the Bonapartes—especially Napoléon Bonaparte—were not to be trusted.

Faced with threats from Paoli, Napoléon helped his mother and the younger children escape to safety in the south of France.

So far, Napoléon's life had been neither pleasant nor successful. Teased by his classmates at school, living in poverty, forced to flee his beloved native land, the future seemed to hold little promise for him.

With few choices of career at hand, he rejoined the French army and, through the influence of a friend, was promoted to captain.

Soon afterward Napoléon unexpectedly got his chance to move toward fame and power. When the French port city of Toulon rebelled against the revolutionary government, it received help from the British fleet. Napoléon, in charge of artillery, saw at once that cannon placed on a high point above the harbor could do serious damage to the British vessels. Although wounded in capturing the crucial hill position, he took charge of a massive artillery barrage on the ships. Finally the British withdrew, and Toulon was recaptured.

As a reward, Napoléon, then only twenty-four years old, was promoted to the rank of brigadier general.

Strangely, the promotion nearly cost

him his life. The decision to make him a general had come directly from the brutal Robespierre, leader by then of the "Terrorist" government of France. When Robespierre was sent to the guillotine in July 1794, Napoléon was thrown into prison, accused of being in sympathy with the Reign of Terror.

For two weeks his life hung in the balance. Then, somehow, he persuaded his captors to release him.

One year later, supporters of the former French monarchy tried to regain control of Paris. A mob of royalists moved to seize the Tuileries Palace. There, as one of those in charge of the palace's defense, Napoléon ordered his arsenal of forty cannons to fire on the approaching mob. Dozens of the attackers were killed, and the building was saved.

For his effort this time, Napoléon was promoted to major general, a victory, as some described it, won by "a mere whiff of grapeshot."

By now young Bonaparte was a popular hero, invited to parties by the leaders of the French republic, often involved with charming, attractive ladies.

In the spring of 1796, at the age of twenty-six, he married the beautiful noblewoman Josephine de Beauharnais, a widow six years older than himself, who already had a twelve-year-old daughter and a fourteen-year-old son.

Two days after the marriage he left for the battlefield, having been appointed commander of forces on the Italian front.

Finding his army poorly equipped, poorly trained, and poorly supplied with food, he held out to them the promise of great rewards if only they fought on to victory. As he put it:

Soldiers, you are naked, badly fed. . . . Rich provinces and great towns will be in your power, and in them you will find honor, glory, wealth. . . . Will you be wanting in courage and steadfastness?

His troops in Italy responded with triumph after triumph. Then, acting against orders from Paris, Napoléon marched directly against France's strongest enemy on the European continent—Austria. In lightning moves he crossed the Alps and advanced to within sixty miles of the Austrian capital, Vienna.

The Austrians, faced with almost certain defeat in battle, asked for a truce. In the Treaty of Campo Formio, dictated by Napoléon, they agreed to give up to France the territories of Belgium, the Rhineland, and a number of islands off the coast of Greece.

Napoléon now dispatched to Paris great storehouses of captured treasures

A portrait engraving of Napoléon Bonaparte striking his characteristic formal pose. *Culver Pictures, Inc.*

and money. Meanwhile, he also organized a government for northern Italy, applying the French Revolution's ideas of liberty. Overnight his name became known across Europe and even in America.

Only England remained to challenge French authority on the continent. At first Napoléon considered an invasion across the English Channel, but after personally inspecting the Channel coast, he decided that the British fleet would prove far too powerful.

Instead, he chose to launch a campaign in Egypt. There he could establish a base of power for France in the Mediterranean while also moving to cut off Britain's profitable trade route to India.

In the spring of 1798 he launched an invasion of Egypt.

Some French leaders, including the wily Talleyrand, secretly were pleased to see the popular, ambitious Napoléon Bonaparte far from Paris, where, or so they feared, he might well decide to seize power for himself.

Quickly, Napoléon captured the Mediterranean island of Malta. Next, he took the ancient Egyptian city of Alexandria. Finally, in the battle of the Pyramids he drove the native Mameluke defenders of Cairo back into the desert and won control of all of northern Egypt.

Once the fighting ended, he moved quickly to set up schools and hospitals for the Egyptian people. He modernized the government. He started irrigation projects. He laid plans for building a grand canal at Suez, thereby linking the Mediterranean Sea to the Red Sea and, from there, to the vast Indian Ocean and to the Pacific.

Before long the team of scholars Napoléon had brought with him from France discovered the Rosetta Stone, the very key to the study of ancient languages. Meanwhile, Napoléon encouraged his soldiers to marry native women and to take on local customs. Never caring much for religion himself, he pleased the people of the region by lavishly praising the Muslim religion. Also, whenever possible, he tried to use the Arab language.

One major defeat, however, doomed Napoléon's Egyptian campaign to failure. The British fleet, commanded by Admiral Horatio Nelson, unexpectedly swooped down upon the French naval squadron lying at anchor at Aboukir Bay, near the mouth of the Nile, completely destroying it. Without ships to help it, Napoléon's army, although superior to British forces, could neither escape from Egypt nor receive reinforcements.

Hoping to fight his way northward, Napoléon launched an attack on Syria, only to be checked by the British.

Encouraged by Napoléon's difficulties, Turkey now joined with Britain, Russia, and Austria in an alliance against the French invaders. Italy, too, turned away from French rule. The situation, Napoléon could see, was fast becoming critical. He decided that in such an emergency something desperate had to be done.

Leaving his army behind him in Egypt, he quietly slipped away to Paris, barely eluding capture by two British vessels on his departure.

Then, once at home in Paris, he joined with Talleyrand, Roger Ducos, and Emmanuel Sieyès to launch a coup d'état in order to take over the French government.

On 18–19 Brumaire (November 9–10, 1799) the plotters succeeded. They set up a new government, calling it "the Consulate," with Napoléon himself serving as "first consul" and holding nearly all the powers of a military dictator.

Shortly afterward Napoléon personally led a French army across the Alps into Italy, where he defeated Austrian forces in the battle of Marengo—a victory he personally considered his most brilliant military success.

The treaty that followed gave France the natural borders first imagined for ancient Gaul in the time of Julius Caesar: the Rhine, the Alps, and the Pyrenees. Shortly afterward, Great Britain, needing a pause following years of bitter warfare, signed with France the Treaty of Amiens. At least for a time, all of Europe was at peace.

Napoléon knew instinctively what to do: he called an election.

All across France, the grateful French people voted overwhelmingly "yes" to the question: "Shall Napoléon Bonaparte be consul for life?"

Following his election Napoléon turned his attention, at least for a time, to problems inside the French nation. To make the economy work better he set up the Bank of France. Always conscious of cultural needs, he gave special attention to the Louvre Museum and the Bibliothèque Nationale (the National Library).

He also improved the quality of French secondary education while giving it a more military tone, all classes now beginning with the roll of a drum. Most important of all, perhaps, he played a major role in producing the *Code Napoléon*, the table of laws used in France to this very day.

At the peak of his power, Napoléon still was not satisfied. He had royalist opponents hunted down and shot. In an act described by some as inhumane he had one royalist leader, the Duke d'Enghien, kidnapped from Germany and returned to France for execution

Napoléon Bonaparte reviewing his troops. *Photosearch.*

by a firing squad. It was a deed that won him praise among people who had favored the French Revolution. It served also to frighten the rest of Europe. Napoléon later dismissed criticism of the Enghien affair with a shrug. "Pooh," he said. "What does the life of one man mean?"

Unsatisfied with the power and glory he had achieved, Napoléon finally decided to have himself named emperor of France. On December 2, 1804, at Notre Dame Cathedral in Paris, he took the crown from the hands of Pope Pius VII and placed it on his own head, crowning himself emperor. Soon afterward he also took the title of king of Italy.

From his humble boyhood on the island of Corsica, Napoléon Bonaparte had risen by genius and hard work to become one of history's most powerful figures.

Yet much remained unchanged from childhood in the personality of Napoléon, the "great man." As before in his life, he seldom laughed. When he did, it was wild, uncontrolled laughter. He was neither courteous nor well mannered. He bragged to others, even to Josephine, about his many triumphs with women. Harsh, impatient, short-tempered, he believed that most human beings were motivated by fear and by self-interest.

Nor did he believe in friendship. As he once said, "Friendship is only a word. I care for nobody." Instead, he used other people for his own purposes. To silence opponents he had newspapers censored, closing down those that dared to criticize him. On a personal basis, he used insults and rage—his harsh temper tantrums usually prepared in advance—to humiliate or frighten lesser people. He was never known to apologize or to say that he had been wrong. Army generals he was afraid of might be imprisoned, or worse. One was found strangled to death in his dungeon cell.

It was not long before Napoléon's new imperial government began to take on the trappings of the old French monarchy. There were public pageants and formal appearances. A nobility was formed, including members of his own family—his brothers and sisters and the children of his wife, Josephine. He had Josephine crowned empress.

On every possible occasion he flaunted his power, encouraging writers, artists, and musicians to make him the subject of their creative projects.

One such artist, the great composer Ludwig van Beethoven, had begun as a passionate admirer of Napoléon, considering him a leader who could transform the Europe of kings and queens into lands that truly cared for the needs of everyday people. In 1804, he had dedicated his Third Symphony, the *Eroica,* or "Heroic," to the dynamic French general. But now, with Napoléon enthroned as emperor, Beethoven changed his mind. Angrily he turned against the French monarch, declaring that he had betrayed his high ideals and was nothing more than all the tyrants who had ruled before him. With ferocious strokes of his pen, Beethoven scratched the name of Napoléon from the dedication page of his famous symphony.

Some of those artists Napoléon invited to portray him took note of his personal habits. They observed his need for very hot baths, sometimes lasting for as long as two hours, and his demand for hotter and hotter water temperatures in times of tension. They noticed his delicate, plump little hands that he so much liked to look at and admire: beautiful pink and white hands, soft, with perfectly manicured nails.

Although fascinated by shows of royalty and by court politics, Napoléon's two great passions remained the same— glory and war. He never was more cheerful than when in an army camp. As he himself put it:

My power derives from my glory, and my glory from the victories I have won. My authority could collapse if I failed to base it on more glory and fresh victories. Conquest has made me what I am, conquest alone can maintain me.

Yet Napoléon's attempts to establish an overseas empire met with little success. On the island of Dominica in the Caribbean, his troops fell victim to yellow fever and hit-and-run attacks by the black Haitian leader, Toussaint L'Ouverture. His plans for renewed French activity in Egypt and in the Indian Ocean also failed. He abandoned his dream of a French empire in America, too, finally selling the enormous Louisiana territory to the United States in 1803 for only $15 million.

Meanwhile, the other nations of Europe grew more and more restless about Napoléon's ambitions for world empire. Great Britain especially found it hard to trade with Europe while France controlled the length of the Atlantic coastline from Belgium to northern Italy. Before long the rulers of Austria and Russia joined with Britain, and later with Prussia, in their opposition to French expansion.

When Austria finally declared war, Napoléon struck back in fury. His army crushed the Austrians at Ulm and then, a few days later, devastated a combined Austrian and Russian force at Austerlitz—according to many historians his greatest victory. When Prussia joined in the fighting, Napoléon won a decisive victory against the Prussian army at Jena.

Some leaders would have gloated over such great triumphs, rubbing the noses of the defeated monarchs in the mud. Napoléon was far too clever for that kind of behavior. Instead, he arranged a conference with Czar Alexander I of Russia, to be held in the Russian city of Tilsit. There, on a raft in the middle of the Niemen River, the two leaders agreed to divide control over the European continent—the Russians to be in command of eastern Europe, France to control the west.

Meanwhile, however, the British admiral, Horatio Nelson, had once again delivered a devastating blow to Napoléon's plans, just as he had done before in Egypt. In a naval battle fought in the Atlantic near Spain's Cape Trafalgar, Nelson lost his life, but not before the British almost totally devastated the French fleet. Without control of the seas Napoléon lost all hope of launching a successful invasion of the British home islands. Trafalgar thus became one of history's most important battles.

With an invasion of England no longer possible, Napoléon set up the "Continental System," a blockade intended to stop trade between Britain and the European mainland. When Portugal and Spain refused to cooperate with him in the blockade, he personally led a French army into those countries and conquered them. Soon after his return to France, however, open revolts broke out against the occupying French forces. With the aid of British troops commanded by the Duke of Wellington, the Portuguese and Spanish inflicted heavy losses on Napoléon's army. Finally, the French were forced to leave the Iberian Peninsula. The Peninsular War had proved to be a failure.

Despite his setback in Spain, Napoléon had managed to establish a great empire across the face of Europe. What he now hoped to do was make that empire permanent by passing control to his own descendants. At the age of forty and without a son, he divorced his wife, Josephine, and in 1810 married the eighteen-year-old Marie Louise, daughter of the Austrian emperor.

In 1811, Marie Louise gave birth to a son. Overjoyed, Napoléon bestowed on the child the title of "King of Rome." There was little doubt that the one-time Corsican schoolboy had future ambitions going far beyond just the leadership of France.

But it was not to be.

When Czar Alexander refused to close Russian ports to British merchant ships in obedience to the Continental System, Napoléon gathered a massive army to threaten him. Alexander still would not give in.

In June 1812, Napoléon invaded Russia. To his surprise the Russian military commander, Kutuzov, did not rush forward to challenge him. Instead, Kutuzov slowly retreated, destroying, as he fell back, all of the crops, all of the shelter—indeed anything that might be of use to Napoléon's army. Today, we call such tactics a "scorched earth" policy.

In September, at Borodino, Napoléon finally engaged Kutuzov in a bloody battle, managing to defeat him and to move on to Moscow, the Russian capital.

Again the Russians fell back, leaving Moscow deserted. The day after Napoléon's troops arrived a fire broke out, turning the city into a sea of flames and almost totally destroying it. Meanwhile, Czar Alexander still refused to meet with Napoléon to negotiate.

In the year 1812, an early winter descended upon Russia. Without shelter, without food, French soldiers died by the thousands in the freezing cold.

Napoléon finally realized he had no choice but to withdraw. His retreat through the snowy drifts proved a disaster, his troops pursued at every turn by Kutuzov's Cossack horsemen. Of the army composed of 450,000 men that had entered Russia in June, only 10,000 still were fit for combat by the time of Napoléon's return to France.

Now, seeing their chance, the subject nations of Europe rose up against their French masters. Prussia and Austria announced a new alliance with Great Britain and Russia against Napoléon. They demanded that he return conquered territories that he had added to the French Empire.

In October 1813, at Leipzig—in the so-called Battle of the Nations—the combined Allied forces decisively defeated Napoléon's *Grande Armée*.

Now Spain and Italy rose up in defiance. So, too, did the Dutch and the Belgians. Within France itself, the French people had grown weary of Napoléon's wars of conquest, weary of his arrogance and pride. They no longer spoke of their undying love for him. Instead, they had come to resent him; many even hated him. They demanded peace.

The Allied armies marched on Paris, and despite heroic resistance by the youthful French soldiers Napoléon had recruited, the city surrendered.

At last, Napoléon realized that the situation was hopeless. In a historic meeting at Fontainebleau (April 4, 1814) he agreed to give up his throne. The Allies named as his successor Louis XVIII, brother of King Louis XVI, who had been executed by the French revolutionaries.

Napoléon tried to poison himself but failed. The victorious Allies exiled him to the island of Elba. So furious with him were the French crowds that for much of the journey there he had to travel in disguise. When he was recognized, people heckled him, taunted him. Some even tried to kill him.

At the age of forty-five, it appeared that his role on life's stage had been played out.

Before long, however, it became clear that the French people had little love for Louis XVIII, put in power over them by foreign armies. Nor could the Allies agree among themselves about the future map of Europe.

Napoléon, bored with life on Elba, saw his chance and took it.

On March 1, 1815, he dramatically landed on French soil. His former soldiers, sent to arrest him, joined him instead. As he marched toward Paris, peasant youths flocked to his side. One of his former commanders, Marshall Ney, had promised to bring him back to Paris in an iron cage. But when they met face to face, Ney fell into Napoléon's arms and pledged his loyalty forever.

Less than three weeks after landing, Napoléon arrived in Paris. There he was greeted by wildly cheering crowds. Louis XVIII had fled the city, and Napoléon found himself once again in command.

He promised a new constitution and free elections. He promised peace, and no more wars.

But the Allies would not trust his promises. They gathered armies on the French border to destroy him. Napoléon did not wait for them to come. Instead, he attacked and defeated the Prussian forces sent through Belgium to capture him.

Then, on June 15, 1815, at Waterloo, Belgium, Napoléon launched a ferocious frontal attack against a British army commanded by the Duke of Wellington. It was Wellington who had hurt the French so badly during years of fighting in Spain. And now it was Wellington, joined at the last minute by the Prussian general Blucher, who finally crushed Napoléon's dreams of triumph.

Beaten at Waterloo, he surrendered. His famous Hundred Days of new glory were over.

This time Napoléon asked to be exiled to the United States. But the British refused. Instead, over his objection, they transported him to the distant, lonely island of St. Helena, in the south Atlantic.

There, he spent his days with a few close companions. Together they read classic literature, played games of cards, and talked well into the night, mostly about the events he had done so much to shape.

He also read history and biography, especially Plutarch's *Lives* (about heroes of the ancient Greeks and Romans). The question of "what history will say" worried him, and he dictated the story of his life to one of the women who had accompanied him into exile.

During his years on St. Helena, Napoléon exercised little, gained weight, and clashed often with the British officials in charge of the island. He found fault with the climate, the food he was served, and his medical treatment. As early as 1817 he showed signs of ill health, especially the same stomach disorder that had caused his father's death.

Gradually his illness grew more serious until, at last, he was unable to rise from bed. Realizing that the end was near, he dictated his will, asking only that "my ashes . . . rest on the bank of the Seine, in the midst of the French people which I have loved so much."

On May 5, 1821, Napoléon died, not yet fifty-two years old.

During the years of his exile, he never once heard from his wife, Marie Louise, or from his son.

In 1840 his body finally was returned to Paris, carried through the Arc de Triomphe, and laid to rest in a circular crypt beneath the beautiful dome of the Invalides, where it remains today.

The question posed by Rudyard Kipling, with which our story began, still
remains to be answered:

> "How far is St. Helena from a little
>   child at play?"
> What makes you want to wander
>   there with all the world be-
>   tween?

It is clear that from an early age Napoléon craved attention, yearned for fame
and glory. Always a soldier, he revelled
in the excitement of battle. Yet he was
also a statesman, as seen in the attention
he paid to creating the Bank of France
and the *Code Napoléon,* as well as to
improving education in French schools.
He opened the way for advancement
in society to poor people of ability and
personally took action to grant full citizenship rights to the Jews of France.
When compared to such ruthless twentieth-century dictators as Joseph Stalin
and Adolf Hitler, he looms large as a
champion of basic moral principles.

It is true that he had little trust in
democracy, believing that government
should remain in the hands of a small
circle of able people. Even in that respect he tended to favor members of
his own family.

Yet whatever our final judgment of
Napoléon's achievements in government and of his motives—especially his
hopes for himself—one thing cannot be
denied. It is that in Napoléon Bonaparte, sprung from the little child of
Corsica, we have one of history's very
greatest lives.

Simón Bolívar

1783–1830   Liberator of much of South America from Spanish colonial rule

Is a seventeen-year-old too young to take on a wife? It was at that age in the city of Madrid, Spain, that Simón Bolívar asked for the hand of Maria Teresa de Toro. She eagerly accepted, only to have her parents hesitate, believing that the couple was too young. Bolívar, they suggested, should return in a year. Meanwhile, they said, since Simón was, like themselves, of the noble class, he had ample money to travel through Europe broadening himself. Perhaps he might even improve his French by studying for a time in Paris.

Disappointed, but deeply in love, Simón agreed. In exchange for a lifetime with Maria Teresa, he reasoned, one year of waiting was not too much to ask. He set out at once from Madrid on an extended tour of Europe.

Until that time, disappointment had not played a major part in the life of Simón Bolívar. True, his father had died when he was only three and his mother when he was nine. But Simón still was well cared for, growing up in one of the very wealthiest families of Venezuela. Simón's distant ancestors had come originally from Spain in 1548, and by the time of his birth in 1783, the family owned silver and copper mines, plantations, and ranches. At San Mateo, their country estate near Caracas, they grew fruits and sugarcane and operated a rum distillery. To help them in those tasks, they owned more than 1,200 slaves.

At the time, Spain owned and governed almost all of Latin America, except for Brazil. Decisions for governing that vast territory came largely from Madrid, with almost no political power given to the Creole class—people in Latin America whose ancestors had come from Spain but who themselves were born in the New World. The Creoles, including such wealthy families as the Bolívars, had prospered. But they were made to pay high taxes and had to obey laws passed for them by officials living three thousand miles across the Atlantic in the Spanish homeland.

As a child, Simón Bolívar cared little for political issues. Instead, he loved horseback riding and games such as racquetball. School interested him scarcely at all. Tutor after tutor attempted to work with him, but none succeeded. He was, they announced in frustration, spoiled and lazy.

Only one book had managed to capture his attention: *Don Quixote*, by Miguel de Cervantes. The hero of that story is an adventurer, a knight who travels about the land fighting against evil to create a better world. Young Simón often carried the book with him, reading it again and again.

When he was nine years old, one tutor finally succeeded in exciting Bolívar about learning. Simón Rodriguez, himself only twenty, believed that education came less from books than from real life. The two rode out into the countryside on horseback. They tamed wild horses. They lived with cowboys.

Bolívar grew up tall and lean, well muscled: tough. He read more and more. He became interested in girls. But he still refused to take formal schooling seriously and remained generally unconcerned about what would become of him in later life. He was what today we would call a "playboy."

At last an uncle and others in the family responsible for him decided that a trip to visit relatives in Spain might help Simón to find himself, force him to grow up. Eager for adventure, he agreed to go.

In Spain, as in Venezuela, Bolívar's money and class standing enabled him to mix with people of the highest rank. Once, at the age of seventeen, he found himself playing racquetball with young Prince Ferdinand, heir to the Spanish throne. Instead of allowing the prince to win as a matter of courtesy, Simón played his hardest. Then, accidentally, his racquet knocked the hat from his royal opponent's head.

Ferdinand stopped the game and demanded an apology. Bolívar refused, insisting that what happened had been only an accident. No apology, he said, was necessary.

Finally, Ferdinand's mother, the queen of Spain, decided to intervene in the quarrel. Simón was right, she told her son, and the two should simply continue to play, which they did.

Neither of the two young men forgot the incident. And two decades later it would be Simón Bolívar who challenged the might of Ferdinand, by then the king of Spain, to continue ruling his colonies in South America.

At the age of seventeen, however, Simón Bolívar was far less interested in political quarrels than in his love for Maria Teresa de Toro. Having promised her family that he would allow a year to pass before asking again to marry her, he soon found himself observing the scene in Europe, particularly in the city of Paris.

There, Napoléon Bonaparte had inherited the gains of the French Revolution, declaring himself completely devoted to its high ideals of "liberty, equality, and fraternity." As Bolívar put it, "I idolized Napoléon as the hero of the Republic." Like many others who began by idolizing the French leader, Simón would later change his mind.

For that time, though, Bolívar's thoughts were mostly of Maria Teresa. When the year's waiting period ended, he returned to Madrid and claimed his bride. They married and returned to what Bolívar was certain would be a life of great happiness in Venezuela.

For a time, his fondest wishes came true.

Then, suddenly, after only eight months of marriage, Maria became ill with yellow fever. The finest doctors of the country could do nothing. In January 1803, she died.

It was to be the turning point of Simón Bolívar's life. As he later put it, "I so loved my wife. . . . If I had not lost her, my whole life might have been different. I should not have been General Bolívar or the Liberator. . . ."

In vain, young Bolívar tried to adjust to life in Venezuela without Maria Teresa, but his unhappiness was too great. Finally he decided to travel again in Europe.

Madrid brought back to him too many memories, so he left. Then, settling for a time in Paris, he found startling changes. His one-time hero, Napoléon, had taken on more power for himself, finally crowning himself emperor. The French Revolution's dream of liberty had been crushed, and in its place was a monarchy, little different from the tyrannies that always before had existed.

While in Paris, Bolívar came to know Alexander von Humboldt, the scientist. It was Humboldt who finally challenged him about the political life of Venezuela, asking whether a leader ever would appear who could free that country from Spanish rule. For the first time, Bolívar began to wonder whether he might play such a role in life—the role

A portrait engraving of General Simón Bolívar. *Culver Pictures, Inc.*

of liberator, fighting for the freedom of his people.

From Paris, Bolívar traveled to Rome, accompanied by his former tutor, the highly idealistic Simón Rodriguez. Together the two climbed Monte Sacro, the "sacred mountain," where two thousand years earlier the Roman plebeians (or common people) had declared their rights to freedom and self-government.

By then Bolívar had learned much about the American Revolution, the war that had secured independence from British rule for his North American neighbors. He knew, too, about the French Revolution and its shining goals of human freedom. Now, on Monte Sacro, he was deeply moved by the hope that once had transformed the history of the ancient Roman state.

As Rodriguez later recalled, Bolívar turned to him, his eyes moist with tears and breathing heavily. "I swear before you," he said, "by the God of my fathers and the honor of my country: I will not rest, not in body or soul, till I have broken the chains of Spain."

From that very moment, Simón Bolívar dedicated his life to the cause of freedom. History would come to know him as the Liberator of South America.

Dedicating one's life to a noble cause is one thing. Achieving victory in that cause is another matter, and often a very difficult one. In the case of Bolívar's plans for revolutionary change, luck at first was on his side. In 1808, Napoléon forced the king of Spain off the throne of that country and replaced him with his own brother, Joseph Bonaparte.

The people of Spain were furious. Refusing to accept a French king, they fought bravely, aided by troops sent against Napoléon's invading armies from Great Britain.

Some leaders in Spain's South Ameri-

A painting by Erwin Ochme shows Simón Bolívar and his colleagues discussing plans following Venezuela's declaration of independence in 1811. *The Bettmann Archive.*

can colonies sided strongly with the Spanish royal family, hoping it would be restored to power. Others, including young Simón Bolívar, saw the European conflict as a chance to win independence—complete freedom from Spanish rule. In his home city of Caracas, Venezuela, Bolívar used his family's money and influence to have the Spanish commander removed from control and sent away. He then headed a delegation dispatched to London to obtain aid from Britain for the cause of Venezuelan independence.

Although Bolívar failed to win British help, he persuaded Francisco de Miranda, an experienced general living in exile in London, to return with him to lead the fight against Spanish forces.

On July 5, 1811, Venezuela declared its independence from Spain, proclaiming itself a republic. In spring of the next year, tragedy suddenly struck the rebel forces in the form of a massive earthquake. The revolutionary strongholds were devastated, with heavy losses of both equipment and lives. To Bolívar's surprise, Miranda quickly surrendered to the Spanish authorities. Bolívar himself barely managed to escape, finally taking refuge in Cartagena, a city in New Granada, the nation known today as Colombia.

It was there that he wrote his powerful essay, the *Cartagena Manifesto,* calling for the total destruction of Spanish authority. "Avenge the dead," he declared, "give life to the dying, relieve the oppressed and bring freedom for all."

Organizing a new army, Bolívar set out on what appeared an impossible mission—to travel more than six hundred miles through territory controlled by the Spanish and recapture Caracas.

Amazingly, city after city fell to his army of peasant volunteers. After each victory, he would send a brief dispatch to Cartagena listing the name of the town he had captured and the word *libertada* (liberated). From that practice he became known as *El Libertador* (the Liberator).

That title became official in August 1813, when he marched in triumph into his home city, Caracas, at the head of a liberating army. There were fireworks and dancing in the streets. For Simón Bolívar, it was a moment of glory he would never forget.

Spain, however, still refused to grant freedom to Venezuela. Reinforcements soon arrived in Venezuela to carry on the struggle. Meanwhile, an even stronger threat faced Bolívar's revolutionary government, a threat from within the country itself—the *llaneros* (cowboys), headed by José Tomás Boves.

Boves himself had once been a revolutionary. But then, after a revolutionary officer dared to strike him with his fist, Boves pledged himself to a life of vengeance. He joined the Spanish forces and raised his own army of llaneros riders. After that, he struck with bloodthirsty force against anyone he even suspected might be a revolutionary.

As prizes of victory Boves promised his men loot and women. The llaneros took no prisoners: they brutally tortured and killed all the men who surrendered to them, sometimes killing all the children of a captured village before the very eyes of their mothers. In one village, Boves made the women dance while his men plunged lances through the bodies of their husbands. Instead of condemning such primitive cruelty, the Spanish government in Madrid openly applauded the methods of Boves and his Legion of Hell.

Finally, Boves and his llaneros captured Caracas itself. He and the Spanish troops cut off the head of the city's commanding general, fried it in oil, and displayed it on a spike erected in the main square of the city. Alongside it flew the flag of Boves's army: a black flag bordered by white skulls.

Shortly after the city's capture, however, a black-skinned revolutionary soldier ran his lance through Boves, putting an end to the life of one of history's most vicious personalities.

Bolívar had meanwhile left the scene—alone—returning to Cartagena. Despite his defeat, many received him as a hero. Others did not, charging him with cowardice in leaving the scene of combat as well as boundless ambition in seeking power for himself.

For a few months Bolívar fought to rid New Granada of Spanish forces. But the jealousy and mistrust of that country's officer corps finally proved too much for him. Giving up his command, he sailed away to the British island of Jamaica, in the Caribbean Sea.

While he was there, Napoléon's forces in Europe finally were defeated by Great Britain and its allies, including Spain. Now, with the French menace removed, the Spanish king could devote his energies to punishing the revolutionaries threatening his power in South America. That Spanish king, it so happened, was none other than Ferdinand VII, the boy now grown to manhood who once had demanded that Bolívar apologize to him for knocking off his hat in a racquetball game.

Ferdinand announced that the spirit of revolution in Spain's South American colonies would be crushed without mercy. He dispatched an army of more than 15,000 men, instructing them to take no prisoners. Cities were burned to the ground, entire families were executed without trial. Suspected leaders were hanged, shot, beheaded.

The result proved exactly the opposite of what Ferdinand expected. Many Creoles who had supported Spanish rule now turned to the revolutionaries for help.

From Jamaica, Bolívar issued his famous "Jamaica Letter," calling for continued defiance of the Spaniards and spelling out his dreams for the future of South America. The nations of the continent, admitted Bolívar, needed stronger central governments than the moderately powered "federal" system of the United States. Nor did he any longer hope for a single nation extending from Mexico at the north to the Cape of Good Hope at the south. But there should still be a common congress, bringing together all the nations of the region to deal with matters that divided them—something like today's Organization of American States—dedicated to preserving the peace.

With supplies and money provided by Alexander Pétion, head of the black Republic of Haiti, Simón Bolívar rushed

TOWN OF ORANGE
PUBLIC LIBRARY
ORANGE, CONN.

to the offensive, challenging the troops of Frederick VII based in Venezuela. Twice his attacks failed, but he would not give up.

Bolívar turned for help to British soldiers, many of whom were without jobs following the end of the Napoleonic wars. He also won the support of José Antonio Páez, a llanero cowboy leader. Bolívar's plan was bold, so bold that in the eyes of most generals it was doomed to failure.

What he proposed to do in the summer of 1819 was to cross the 12,000-foot-high Andes Mountains and attack the Spanish forces in New Granada (Colombia). He would then attack Venezuela from the west, pushing Ferdinand's armies into the sea.

For more than a week Bolívar and his men made their way through mountain passes covered with ice. They waded through swamps, crossed flooded streams with water up to their armpits. With little time for rest or sleep, they pressed on to their goal. In all of history, few campaigns have been so daring or so difficult.

On August 7, 1819, Bolívar's men emerged from the mountains and, in the battle of Boyacá, caught the Spaniards completely by surprise. Most were killed or taken prisoner. Bolívar then entered nearby Bogotá in triumph.

The tide had been turned. From that time onward, the history of South America never would be the same.

Even before launching his attack, Bolívar set forth in detail his future plan of government. It included features that citizens of the United States might not consider democratic. The president was to stay in office for life, while members of the upper house of government, like the British House of Lords, were also entitled to lifetime terms, with their positions passed on to their descendants. Still, it was far more democratic than anything provided by the ruling Spanish government.

One important provision, especially dear to Bolívar, called for an end to human slavery. Although that did not happen at once, Venezuela's slaves still were freed almost ten years before Abraham Lincoln's Emancipation Proclamation declared freedom for slaves in the United States of America.

Bolívar's plan of government was to include the nations of Venezuela, New Granada (Colombia), and Ecuador. He himself proceeded to triumph over the Spanish in Venezuela in the battle of Carabobo. Shortly afterward, his brilliant and faithful follower, General Antonio José de Sucre, conquered Ecuador. In June 1822, Bolívar entered that nation's capital city, Quito, where he was greeted by wildly cheering crowds.

Bolívar had achieved his objectives. The Republic of Gran Colombia was now a reality. But, for whatever reasons, Bolívar decided to press on, expanding his authority southward. The occasion for his decision was a meeting, only one month after his entrance into Quito, with the other great revolutionary hero of South America, José de San Martín.

San Martín, the liberator of Argentina and Chile, met with Bolívar at Guayaquil. It was his hope that the Venezuelan leader would join him in liberating Peru, the last great Spanish stronghold in South America.

What actually happened at the meeting is unclear. But San Martín left the formal ball given for him by Bolívar without even saying good-bye. He immediately retired from public life, spending the rest of his life in voluntary exile in France.

There is some evidence that San Martín considered Bolívar too ambitious, too vain, too hungry for power to work with. Bolívar, in turn, regarded San Martín as a royalist, one who simply wanted to substitute local monarchies for the deposed Spanish king.

One year after the meeting at Guayaquil, Bolívar decided to act. With a nine-thousand-man army, he and the faithful General Sucre invaded Peru.

In the battles of Junín and Ayacucho, they liberated Peru.

The wars of independence now were over. South America was free from Spanish rule. Bolívar, meanwhile, stood at the very pinnacle of his career. He was president of Gran Colombia (Venezuela, Colombia, and Ecuador). He took the title of "dictator" of Peru. One vast area of Peru declared its independence and, choosing to call itself Bolivia, after Bolívar, offered to name him president for life. Some of his followers suggested that he take on such titles as King Simon I, or even Emperor of the Andes.

There was talk, and Bolívar did little to discourage it, that all of the Spanish-speaking nations of South America (most of the continent except for the formerly Portuguese-controlled Brazil) should be united in one federal union. At its head, of course, would be Simón Bolívar.

Bolívar himself boldly put forth such ideas as an "Andean Empire," extending from Panama at the north to the very southernmost tip of the continent. He accepted, too, the notion of an Andean Empire, uniting Venezuela, Ecuador, Colombia, Peru, and Bolivia, with himself as president.

Like the dreams of other great men of history, Bolívar's dreams, too, were not to be realized.

His call, in 1826, for a Panamanian congress to discuss cooperation on many issues resulted in almost total failure. Only England and four Latin American nations chose to attend, and the English delegates refused to participate. The delegate from the United States became ill on his way to the conference and never arrived there.

Meanwhile, bitter conflicts began to reach out within Bolívar's own family of nations. Peru resented the power held over their lives by Colombians. Inside Gran Colombia, factions from Caracas quarreled with those from Bogotá and Quito.

While Bolívar made plans for the whole continent, the other South American leaders were thinking only of their own nation-states. Many, like two of Bolívar's most important generals, Páez and Santander, were concerned mostly with their own ambitions for money and power.

Bolívar tried to bring the conflicting factions together, but he failed. Finally, on the night of September 25, 1828, a gang of thugs armed with guns and knives burst into the room where he was staying, intent on killing him.

Manuela Sáenz, the woman he was with, insisted that he escape by leaping from a window into a ditch some ten feet below. She waved a sword at the attackers and distracted them until Bo-

lívar's soldiers could regain control of the situation.

Eventually, the leaders of the mob were arrested, tried, and punished. But Bolívar never recovered from the humiliation of that night.

Before long Bolivia and Peru went to war. Peru attacked Colombia. Venezuela withdrew from the united republic. So did Ecuador. Leaders of the region were calling Bolívar "tyrant," demanding that he leave. Finally came the deepest wound of all: news arrived that General Sucre, Bolívar's choice to succeed him as leader, had been assassinated.

Bolívar, with only a few trusted friends and servants, left the city of Bogotá behind him. The situation, as he saw it, was hopeless. "Those who fight in South America's revolution," he declared, "only plow the sea."

He boarded a ship bound for Jamaica but, taken seriously ill, returned to the Colombian port city of Santa Marta. There, exhausted, suffering from an advanced case of tuberculosis, he waited for death.

To fill the hours he read and reread the book he had treasured as a child, *Don Quixote*. Like the hero of that work, he had fought for high ideals, grand causes, only to be frustrated, defeated—misunderstood.

On December 17, 1830, at the age

of forty-seven, Simón Bolívar died. His vast fortune was gone, every penny spent to finance the wars he had fought and his attempts to form a broader union of South American nations. He was buried in a nightshirt borrowed from the Spanish army officer at whose home he was staying.

At first, Bolívar's enemies succeeded in discrediting him, both as a leader and as a person. But after a time the tide of opinion turned in his favor. In 1842, his body was removed from Santa Marta and returned in a Venezuelan warship to Caracas. There, with the flags of all the nations he had liberated flying at half mast, his remains were placed in a splendid memorial chapel.

Although bitter and reviled at the end of his life, the memory of Bolívar as the Liberator of South America continues to grow. True, his predictions of continuing warfare, revolutions, and disunity for the nations of that continent had come to pass. There, as elsewhere, the motives that drive people apart have proven stronger than the forces that bind them together.

Yet, even today, the dream of Simón Bolívar remains alive in South America. And the figure of Bolívar towers above all other leaders of those lands.

Otto von Bismarck

1815–1898   The Prussian "Iron Chancellor" who unified the German nation by means of "blood and iron"

How do you choose your friends? What makes you decide that someone will be your enemy? How do you judge whether something a person has done is right or wrong, good or evil?

Most of us enjoy being with people who share the same interests we do, play the same games, laugh at the same jokes. We become angry when others tease us, tell bad stories about us, shake their fists at us. We have friends. We have enemies.

And so it is with nations. Friendly nations join together in alliances to protect themselves. In time of trouble— even in time of war—they try to help their allies and punish their enemies.

But to one statesman, Otto von Bismarck, that kind of thinking made little sense. It was, according to Bismarck, an old-fashioned way of looking at things. In matters of war and peace— the diplomacy of nations—there was no room for such ideas as friendship. Enemies could become allies. Allies could become enemies. Matters of "right and wrong" were always changing and really didn't matter in the long run anyway.

To Bismarck, the world of diplomacy was a chessboard. And in playing the game of chess on a worldwide level, there was only one constant, continuing factor: self-interest—the needs, as he put it, of "*my* king and *my* country."

In the jungle of world affairs, he declared, nations had to look out for themselves in order to survive. In such a dangerous world there could be no friends, no enemies—only interests: national needs.

And those needs could best be satisfied in only one way, through the threat or the actual use of a nation's power. Or as Bismarck put it, through "blood and iron."

During his lifetime, Otto von Bismarck succeeded in uniting in one nation the many separate peoples of the previously divided German states, bringing them together under the leadership of his own native land, Prussia. To achieve that victory, he arranged for Prussia to fight—and to win—three major wars. Then, as the "iron chancellor" of a united Germany, he played off the major European powers against one another.

It is a sign of his genius, but also the great weakness of his world view, that following his death the balance of forces he created proved too delicate to be run by men of more limited intelligence. The balance of powers broke down. The result has been our own "century of conflict," an era marked by history's most devastating, most brutal wars.

Many of the critical events of life in the twentieth century can be traced directly to the ideas and the actions of one man, a man who died more than a century ago, Otto von Bismarck of Germany.

Bismarck was born in Brandenburg, Prussia, in 1815. It was in that year, at the battle of Waterloo, that Prussian troops played a major role in putting a final end to the military career of Napoleon Bonaparte.

Ferdinand Bismarck, Otto's father, was a member of Prussia's aristocratic Junker class, a wealthy landholder. Large-bodied, easy-going, slow-thinking, he would have been willing to leave young Otto alone to do as he pleased. But Wilhelmine, the boy's mother, brought to his upbringing a very different purpose. Not born to the noble class, she was brilliant and ambitious. Because she had married Ferdinand when only sixteen, she was determined to make her mark in life through her children, particularly the quick-witted young Otto.

When Otto was seven, Wilhelmine arranged for the purchase of a home in Berlin. She enrolled him in the city's best private school, one attended not only by the wealthy but also by outstanding children of the middle class. For college, he first attended the University of Göttingen, then known for its openness to liberal ideas.

As a child, Bismarck was known for his wildness, his rudeness, his insistence on reading only what pleased him. An expert fencer in college, he frequently fought duels, carrying with him through life a scar inflicted by a sword blade, the scar extending from his nose to his ear.

He drank much, gambled for large sums of money, played practical jokes, and behaved noisily in the balconies of theaters. For much of his youth, he carried on with one woman after another, caring little for any of them. He made a point of dressing in colorful clothing that would attract people's attention.

Boasting that he studied little, Bismarck actually read widely and grew especially devoted to the words of Shakespeare, Goethe, and the English romantic writers, Lord Byron and Sir Walter Scott. In music he developed a taste for the most passionate works of Beethoven. Although preparing himself for a career in the Prussian civil service, he much preferred reading history to studying law. Never an outstanding student, after transferring to the University of Berlin he managed by intense cramming to pass the examination admitting him to government service.

To Bismarck, the civil service was a bore. He continued to drink and to gamble. As he put it, "I live like a gentleman . . . spend much time getting dressed, the remainder with my old friend the bottle."

One year after beginning work with the government, he simply left, not even bothering to resign. For the next six months he traveled around Europe with a young Englishwoman, only to have her desert him for, in his words, "a one-armed colonel fifty years of age with four horses and 15,000-thaler-a-year income."

Probably a more important reason for Bismarck's sudden departure from the civil service was his unwillingness to take advice from his superiors. "I will play music as I like it, or none at all."

When a friend accused him of being unpatriotic to Prussia by leaving his job, Bismarck responded that few famous statesmen really acted out of patriotism. "Much more frequently [it is] ambition, the desire to command, to be admired, and to become famous. I must confess that I am not free of this passion. . . ."

Barely finished with college, Bismarck clearly knew himself well, understood what interested him most.

For a year he served as a private in the army, satisfying the requirement that all Prussian men must serve for a period in the army. Then, at the age of twenty-six, he became a lieutenant in the reserves. Once, during maneuvers, he dramatically rescued his personal groom and a companion from drowning, plunging into an icy river to save them.

A career in the military, where he was expected to obey orders from those above him, held little appeal for Bismarck. Instead, he returned to the countryside to run his family's large estate.

By then his drinking and gambling

had won him a reputation as "the wild Bismarck" and "the wild Junker." He introduced to his neighborhood a combination of beer and champagne. Sometimes he awoke friends for social activities by firing bullets through their windows while they slept. His appetite for food became legendary, a habit that soon caused him to grow heavy.

Not until he was past thirty did Bismarck decide to change his life-style. It was at that time that he met two women who were to play an important part in shaping his future.

One of them, Marie von Thadden, was the daughter of a Prussian nobleman, living nearby. Deeply religious, she tried to persuade Bismarck that he should come to believe in God and live a Christian life. Until that time he had proudly claimed to be an atheist, taunting with pleasure those people who practiced a formal religion. Beautiful and popular, Marie determined to convert the "wild and arrogant Pomeranian." Bismarck actively pursued her.

Then Marie chose to marry another man, and for the first time in his life Bismarck was heartbroken. Within a year afterward, Marie died of a brain tumor. Not since he was sixteen had Otto von Bismarck prayed to God. Now he did.

Early in their relationship, Marie had introduced Otto to her friend, Johanna von Puttkamer. Not as beautiful as Marie but, like her, a person of deep religious feelings, Johanna agreed to his proposal of marriage.

Johanna's father expressed serious doubts about his daughter marrying "the wild Junker." To ease Herr Puttkamer's fears, Bismarck described in a letter the tearful prayers he had addressed to God at the time of Marie's death. That incident, he said, had changed his life. Now, ". . . daily I ask God to be merciful to me . . . and to strengthen my faith." Convinced, Johanna's father gave his consent.

From the time of his marriage Bismarck liked to claim that God was on his side. When he made political moves, he would argue that he was only doing God's will. "I am now," said Bismarck, "only a soldier of God." God, in turn, could become his ally in the next stage of his life—a struggle for power.

In 1847, at the age of thirty-two, Bismarck was elected to the Prussian *Landtag* (Parliament). He had devoted his youth to pleasure, to "sowing his wild oats." But he also had read much, traveled much. Now he proceeded to plunge into politics. Nor was his goal to be just another politician. From the very beginning he set out to transform the Prussian state and, indeed, to redraw the map of Europe.

At that time, the country now known to the world as "Germany" did not exist. Instead, there were thirty-nine German-speaking states, such as Prussia, Saxony, and Bavaria. There also were many smaller German principalities. But there was no such thing as German law, a German army, or a German government under a German king. True, representatives of a German confederation met for purposes of discussion at Frankfurt, but that group was dominated by the king of Austria.

In 1851 Bismarck was sent to Frankfurt as the Prussian delegate. His loyalty was to the king of Prussia, as well as to his social class, the aristocratic landholding Junkers. But he already had a deeper, long-range purpose: to rid the separate German states of Austrian control and to unite them into one mighty nation.

For seven years he lived in Frankfurt, learning about diplomacy, coming to understand the levers of power—and those who held them. Meanwhile, he increasingly gained the respect of officials in the Prussian government. In 1859 he was appointed Prussian ambassador to Russia. In 1862 he became ambassador to France. As part of his duties he met Czar Alexander of Russia, Napoléon III of France, Prime Minister Disraeli of England. All of them recognized in the one-time "wild Junker" a man

of genius, a person to be watched in future years.

In the summer of 1862 Bismarck unexpectedly got his chance for leadership. When the Prussian parliament refused to grant Kaiser Wilhelm I the money to reorganize and reform the Prussian army, the kaiser threatened to resign.

Instead, the war minister, General Albrecht von Roon, suggested to Wilhelm that he appoint the strong-willed Bismarck to the position of minister-president and see whether he could control the parliament. The kaiser agreed.

In September 1862, Otto von Bismarck was installed as minister-president of the Prussian state. Some Prussians, knowing about his youth, worried that he would be reckless. Others feared that he would represent only the wealthy land-holding class.

His very first speech to the parliament produced a shocking statement, one that would live with Bismarck throughout his career. "Not by parliamentary majorities are the great questions of the day settled," declared the new chief minister, "but by iron and blood."

In Prussian newspapers, and then around the world, Bismarck's words were reported as "blood and iron." How are issues decided? Only by force.

An engraving of the Iron Chancellor, Otto von Bismarck, on the battlefield. From *Great Men and Famous Women* by Charles Horne. New York: Selmar Hess, 1894. *Photosearch*.

Might makes right! According to Bismarck, his remarks had been badly reported, misunderstood. From that time on, however, the words were never forgotten.

Shortly afterward, the Prussian parliament refused to approve Bismarck's request for a large new military budget. But Bismarck, acting against the constitution—illegally—simply had the government continue to collect taxes to pay for the army.

Nor was it very long before he put that army into action to gain his ends.

His first target was Denmark. Trouble long had been brewing in two provinces in the south of Denmark, Schleswig and Holstein, bordering on Prussia. Both German-speaking and Danish-speaking people lived there, producing constant tension. Bismarck, meanwhile, yearned to build a naval base at Kiel, in Holstein, as well as a canal.

He cleverly persuaded Austria's Count Rechberg to supply troops for a joint Austro-Prussian attack on Denmark. At the same time, he kept Napoleon III of France neutral, hinting at the possible expansion of French territory along the Rhine. He shunted aside the danger of British aid to Denmark, suggesting to a friend, "If Lord Palmerston sends the British army to Germany, I shall have the police arrest them."

In a war lasting only two months, the Danes proved no match for Prussian artillery and the well-drilled Austrian and Prussian soldiers. In a peace treaty signed in 1865, Denmark gave up all claim to Schleswig and Holstein. Kaiser Wilhelm, delighted with Bismarck's performance, now made him a count.

The question still remained, however, of who would rule in Schleswig and Holstein: Prussia or Austria. Again, Bismarck maneuvered to keep France neutral. Meanwhile, he tempted Italy with the promise of a right to annex Venetia, then under French control. Through those clever actions he had set the stage for a victorious Prussian war with Austria.

In May 1866, before the war began, a Prussian assassin tried to kill Bismarck, so angry was he at the warlike leader. The youthful attacker fired two shots, both missing, before Bismarck wrested the pistol from his hand and held him by the throat until police arrived.

Two months later Prussian troops under General von Moltke crushed the Austrian forces at Sadowa, a decisive battle ending the Seven Weeks' War. By the Treaty of Prague, Austria agreed to let Prussia annex Schleswig and Holstein, as well as the German states of Hanover, Hesse-Cassel, and Frankfurt. Austria also promised not to intrude in the affairs of the newly formed North

German Confederation. Bismarck, in return, agreed not to take any Austrian territory. It was best, he said at the time, to be lenient with Austria. Germany might need that country's friendship in the future.

In gratitude, the Prussian Landtag forgave Bismarck for financing the army illegally for four years, to which Bismarck replied that, if necessary, he would do the same thing again. The Landtag also voted him 40,000 thalers to purchase for his family a magnificent new estate in Pomerania.

For remaining neutral during the Seven Weeks' War, Napoléon III now claimed France's right to annex Belgium. Bismarck refused. The French soon afterward grew angry when it appeared that a German noble, Leopold von Hohenzollern-Sigmaringen, would be placed on the vacant Spanish throne. Prussia agreed not to move ahead with that plan, but the French ambassador to Prussia demanded a promise that such a thing would *never* happen.

Kaiser Wilhelm, resting in a resort at Ems, sent a lengthy telegram to Bismarck summarizing the French demand. Bismarck then prepared a shorter version of the so-called "Ems Dispatch," making it appear that France was threatening Prussia with war. When he released his own version to the press, the French and German people both were furious.

Napoléon III immediately declared war. On July 19, 1870, the Franco-Prussian War began.

Bismarck's two sons, Herbert and Wilhelm, both served in the Prussian army as privates. Bismarck himself spent week after week at the front, dressed in a cavalry greatcoat and wearing on his head the ferocious-looking Prussian spiked helmet. At one point he was nearly captured. Napoléon III also fought beside his own troops on the battlefield.

Finally, at the battle of Sedan the Prussian army won a total victory, even taking Napoléon III prisoner. At that point a revolution broke out in Paris, the rebels declaring they would never surrender to Prussia. Bismarck ordered that the French capital be put under seige. He ordered, too, that no prisoners be taken and that even women and children should be killed.

On January 18, 1871, in the Hall of Mirrors of the French royal palace at Versailles, Otto von Bismarck personally announced the formation of the new German Empire. Wilhelm I became emperor. Bismarck became chancellor of the empire and was elevated to the rank of prince. In gratitude for his work, the emperor also gave him an enormous country estate near Hamburg.

France was humiliated—made to pay an indemnity of 5 billion francs and to give up the disputed territory of Alsace-

Lorraine, between the two nations. While the French vowed to obtain revenge, the people of the newly united Germany cried for joy in the streets. They applauded Bismarck as the greatest German of all time, a genius who had raised their country to a place of greatness among the nations of the world.

Germany was a nation made up of twenty-five states. There now was a single army, a single capital city, Berlin, and a beloved emperor, Wilhelm I. Prussia held a majority of votes in the *Bundesrat*, the upper house of the national legislature. And Bismarck, as prime minister of Prussia and chancellor of Germany, had become the nation's single most powerful leader.

He used that power to transform and to modernize Germany. By personally writing the new constitution he centralized administrative control. He made certain there was a single code of law across the entire land. He worked to make the educational system serve the technical needs of German industry, hoping to make Germany the world's leading industrial nation.

In domestic affairs, unlike foreign policy, he did not always win. Although faced with the power of the Catholic Church, he had laws passed favoring civil marriages, in contrast to those preferred by the church. He also ended

the practice of having church inspectors visit all schools, even public, non-Catholic schools. But because nearly one-third of the new nation's population was Catholic, he found himself forced to compromise. As a result, his *Kulturkampf*, a struggle to make Germany a united country with a united culture, largely failed.

Similarly, Bismarck failed to crush the nation's rising Socialist party. "I never include Socialists when I use the word German," he said. But despite all of his efforts to prevent Socialists from speaking, from writing, and from holding office, the popular vote for Socialist candidates increased dramatically throughout the 1880s in each national election.

Typical of his actions, when Bismarck saw that he was unable to crush his Socialist enemies in one way, he moved flexibly in another. He had his own laws passed giving the German people exactly what the Socialists promised them—health care, old age insurance, unemployment insurance. Before long, the Socialists, instead of being revolutionaries intent on destroying the system, became loyal supporters of the German nation.

In foreign affairs, Bismarck moved with certainty to achieve his long-range goals. By far the most important of those goals was to insure German safety from foreign attack while the nation grew stronger. His aim, therefore, became that of peace and a balance of power in Europe. To do that, he first organized the League of the Three Emperors, uniting the emperors of Russia, Austria-Hungary, and Germany.

He also concluded a Dual Alliance with Austria, secretly pledging both nations to war if one were attacked by Russia and to neutrality if one were attacked by France. Later, the alliance was expanded to include Italy, in order to give further protection against Russia and France.

Finally, he concluded a treaty with Russia by personally revealing to the Russians the terms of the secret Dual Alliance with Austria! Surrounded on all sides by potentially hostile powers, he acted with subtlety and brilliance to prevent Germany from being squeezed and destroyed.

The result, during his lifetime and for a quarter of a century after his death, was a period of stability and balance among the nations of Europe.

In March 1888, the elderly Wilhelm I died. Three months later, his successor, Frederick III, followed him to the grave, dead of cancer. When Kaiser Wilhelm II took the throne, at age twenty-nine, he soon moved to challenge the great powers of Bismarck, the

chancellor. He himself would be the true leader of Germany. He would build a powerful navy, one equal to or greater than the British fleet. He would acquire lands overseas—in fact, establish a colonial empire.

Eventually the two men could not stand to be in the same room together. Both of them high-strung and temperamental, they found reason after reason to disagree. Should Wilhelm be present, as he demanded, when Bismarck met with ministers or members of the *Reichstag?* Should the treaty of friendship with Russia be extended, as Bismarck wished? Once, according to the emperor, Bismarck appeared ready to throw an inkstand at him.

At last, on March 18, 1890, Bismarck submitted a letter of resignation.

Shortly afterward, departing from a visit to the tomb of Wilhelm I, he was greeted by wildly cheering crowds, singing in his honor the national song, *"Deutschland, Deutschland, über Alles"* ("Germany, Germany over all").

A famous cartoon appeared at the time in the British humor magazine *Punch*, entitled "Dropping the Pilot." It pictured Bismarck, looking experienced and competent, leaving the German "ship of state," while the brash young Kaiser Wilhelm watches him from the deck.

In retirement, Bismarck enjoyed

walking in the woods of his beautiful estate at Friedrichsruh, playing with his dogs. He and Johanna were happy together. Often, distinguished visitors came to honor him, to praise him. So did groups of respectful schoolchildren.

Yet never, in the years left to him, did Bismarck ever forgive Kaiser Wilhelm for forcing him out of office. Instead, he grew ever more bitter and angry. In comments to newspaper reporters and in a continuing series of letters to the press, he criticized the emperor. Finally, he prepared his memoirs—three volumes written mostly to justify the things he had done in his own lifetime and to attack Wilhelm.

Old age finally descended on Bismarck. He grew weaker and weaker, unable to walk the grounds of his estate. On July 30, 1898, he died. The emperor visited, but only long enough to place a wreath of flowers on his coffin.

Bismarck had left instructions that he was to be buried at Friedrichsruh. On his tombstone appeared a message he himself had written that carried his hatred for Wilhelm II with him to the grave. It read: A TRUE GERMAN SERVANT OF THE EMPEROR WILHELM I.

Today Bismarck is remembered as the founding genius of realpolitik—realism in world affairs. Even his critics came to recognize his brilliance, although as one put it, he was "a great man . . . a patriot and a genius, but brutal and cynical."

There is an even harsher criticism to make of him. In order to assure a European balance of power, he had created a complex system of alliances. Yet, lacking faith in others, he failed to train leaders who could, after his death, manage such a system. After World War I, that failure led to the final destruction of the Prussian ruling class and, with it, the empire Bismarck had created.

Similarly, he lacked faith in the great mass of the German people and failed to involve them in the business of government. All that he asked of them was blind obedience. Little wonder, then, that in a time of crisis—the Great Depression of the 1930s—they would place their trust in a man you will read about later in this book, one of history's most brutal and unprincipled dictators, Adolf Hitler.

Ironically, Hitler first came into power following his elevation to the office of chancellor of Germany, a position of great authority created by . . . Otto von Bismarck.

Meiji Mutsuhito

1852–1912   Japanese emperor responsible for introducing Western customs and establishing Japan as a world power

Most people today, at the very mention of Japan, think of Sony television sets, Toyota and Honda automobiles, Toshiba computers. Japan is an industrial society with a highly developed technology. Japanese schools demand of students from the very earliest grades a mastery of science and mathematics, fields essential to success in manufacturing and world trade. Japanese businessmen are based in branch offices around the globe. Many of the great skyscrapers marking the skylines of such American cities as New York and Los Angeles are owned by Japanese investors. The Japanese economy is one of the world's strongest. It is said, "When the Japanese stock market sneezes, the other stock markets pull out their handkerchiefs."

It was not always that way.

There was a time, not so very long ago, when Japan produced no products at all for sale to foreign countries. Japanese travelers never were to be seen, as today, on the streets of the world's great cities. Ships bearing foreigners hoping to visit the Japanese home islands, instead of being welcomed there, were greeted with gunfire from shore batteries. Japan was isolated from the outside world and, for the most part, hoped to remain that way.

Then, beginning in the mid-1800s, events would occur that drastically altered Japanese culture, swiftly thrusting that nation to a position of dominance in Asia and membership in the innermost circle of the world's great powers. Much of what happened is associated with the reign of the emperor Mutsuhito, who ascended to the throne in 1867, at the age of only fifteen. He later was to adopt the reign name of Meiji, meaning "enlightened government," and it was during his rule that the Japanese government would be transformed, along with that nation's industry and the structure of its social classes.

Today, when we speak of the profound changes that took place in Japan at the time, we speak of the "Meiji Restoration," and we have come to describe that entire period as the "Meiji era."

Although Meiji Mutsuhito and the leaders around him truly were responsible for the great changes in Japanese life, they were acting primarily in response to events imposed on them from the outside, particularly by European powers and by the United States.

Westerners long had known about Japan. Before starting out on his historic journey, Christopher Columbus had been fascinated by Marco Polo's exciting accounts of life in the Orient. On first landing in the New World, on islands off the mainland of Central America, Columbus believed he had stumbled upon the fabled "Cipango," the secluded but supposedly wealthy islands close to mainland China—islands known today as Japan. It was the

hope of finding a shortcut to the riches of the Orient that had tempted him to set sail from Spain into the broad, uncharted Atlantic.

The first Western explorers actually to reach Japan discovered none of the fabulous storehouses of gold and silver Marco Polo had been told were gathered there. Rather, they found people who wanted to be left alone. Eventually a few Dutch traders were allowed to establish a trading post near the city of Nagasaki, but they were not allowed to travel about the country without military escort. Japanese citizens were absolutely forbidden to travel abroad, and the Christian religion was not allowed into the Japanese home islands. Europeans, meanwhile, found little to lure them to distant, unfriendly Japan.

Then, in the early 1800s, the situation began to change. British merchants, selling opium and other products to China, hoped for new markets in Japan. The Russians looked to Japanese ports as warm-water stopping points for their newly developed territories in Siberia. To American merchants and to ship captains engaged in whaling, Japan seemed particularly important. If Japanese port cities could be opened up, America would be able to buy much-needed food supplies, as well as coal for the steamboats that increasingly were used in the China trade.

In the autumn of 1852, President Millard Fillmore arranged for four American warships to depart for Japan. Not by accident, their commander, Commodore Matthew C. Perry, was then the highest ranking officer in the United States Navy, a member of one of the most distinguished naval families in American history. His mission was to open the Japanese home islands to American commerce and to assure that ships or sailors in distress would be received with safety in Japanese ports.

On July 8, 1853, Perry's little fleet entered a harbor close to Edo Bay, the city known today as Tokyo. All four ships were metal, powered by steam, and intentionally painted shiny black to contrast with the simple, unpainted wooden craft of the Japanese. There in the harbor, boatloads of Japanese approached the vessels. Artists made hundreds of sketches of what, to them, were incredibly strange-looking ships and their equally strange-looking crews.

The Japanese unfurled a message written in French asking that the ships leave the harbor at once. Perry did not respond. A second message, written in Dutch, demanded that the ships go to the harbor at Nagasaki for formal talks. That, too, was unsatisfactory to Perry.

Finally, on July 14, arrangements were made for Perry to deliver to Japanese officials a personal letter from President Fillmore. On shore, beside a many-colored pavilion made of silk and cotton, five thousand Japanese soldiers in their finest uniforms lined up to welcome the Americans.

Commodore Perry brought ashore with him to the pavilion one hundred sailors, one hundred marines, and all of his officer corps. He himself marched in the lead, flanked by two very tall guards, both of them ebony black in color and heavily armed. In his hands he carried a small wooden box containing the president's letter encased in an envelope of blue velvet.

The letter asked for the opening of trade for a short time, coal and supplies for American ships, and help for American sailors in distress. It was signed, "Your good friend, Millard Fillmore."

Perry announced that he would return for an answer.

On February 11, 1854, he sailed into Edo Bay, but this time with eight ships. Patient and tactful, he remained firm in his demands.

Reluctantly, the Japanese agreed to his conditions. On March 31, they signed a treaty, officially opening relations between the two nations. Before long, the British, the French, the Dutch, and the Russians asked for, and received, the same privileges.

In August 1856, an American diplomat, Townsend Harris, arrived in Japan to represent the United States and to help American merchants who wanted to trade there.

The fact that Westerners had forced their way into Japan angered many Japanese, especially those of the warrior class, known as samurai. Samurai warriors sometimes attacked and killed foreigners they encountered in the streets. They burned buildings used by foreigners. But they were no less angry at the Japanese government that had shown weakness by giving in to the hated outsiders.

The government, too, was made up of warriors, the most powerful of whom were known as the shoguns. For nearly one thousand years the real rulers of Japan had been not the emperors, but the shoguns who governed in the name of the emperor. At the time of Perry's arrival, one group, the Tokugawa shoguns, had ruled the country for two and a half centuries.

Now, because of the presence of Westerners, many Japanese demanded a new government, one that gave the emperors real power once again. They planned to get rid of the Tokugawas and to restore the central authority of the emperors, at least in name. They also demanded that the "barbarians"— the Westerners—be expelled.

On January 3, 1868, soldiers of the revolutionary group seized control of the Imperial Palace in Kyoto. Their forces also won easy victories in the country's outlying provinces. The last of the Tokugawa shoguns gave up his powers, and a new ruling council was formed. It immediately declared that the ancient powers of the emperor had been restored.

The emperor then holding the throne happened to be the sixteen-year-old Mutsuhito, soon known to the world as Meiji. Before very long it became clear that the so-called Meiji Restoration would mark a turning point in Japanese history.

The first change to take place was symbolic. The emperor's castle was moved from Kyoto, where emperors had lived for the past thousand years, to the bustling port city of Edo, now renamed Tokyo. The move was intended to create a sense of unity, built around direct personal loyalty to the emperor.

Previous emperors rarely had been seen by the people. But Meiji now became highly visible. He made frequent public appearances in Tokyo and in the provinces. Handsome and strong, he dressed in a formal military uniform of Western style. Often he was seen in public astride a powerful white horse, giving the impression to his subjects of forceful, firm leadership.

While a tight-knit circle of some

twenty men actually administered the daily affairs of government, the sea of new reform measures that soon began to appear were all done in his name, and in each case his approval was required before anything legally could be done. As he became an increasingly popular public figure, the Japanese people loyally pledged their devotion to the young emperor Meiji.

In April 1868, Meiji signed a statement of principles called "The Charter Oath," presented to him by his advisers. In it, he promised to "search the world for knowledge." Japan was to become modernized, learning from the "barbarians" who had forced their way into Japanese life. In place of the older goal of expelling Western influence, the new government chose as its slogan, "A rich nation, a strong army."

To learn from the West meant visiting there. Notebooks and sketch pads in hand, some of Japan's leading officials traveled to Europe and to America. They saw factories, schools, farms, businesses—everything that had made the West strong enough to have its way with Japan, almost unchallenged.

Meanwhile, they invited visitors from the West to teach them everything from engineering to fancy cooking. Later, they would adopt, with high enthusiasm, such features of American life as baseball.

Modernizing the government itself proved a major problem. Some 260 nobles ruled over separate Japanese states, each commanding an army and collecting taxes. The new imperial council saw that such an arrangement left the country weak and divided instead of strong and united.

Within three years the new government bought—for fair prices—all of the nobles' lands and consolidated them into a few provinces, controlled by representatives sent from Tokyo. Many of the former landowners whose estates had to be taken over were themselves members of the new government.

To decide on the structure of the central government itself, the reformers turned again to the West. They found the government of the United States too loosely organized, too free. Besides, the Japanese had no experience in representative government. Instead, they chose to copy the arrangement created by Otto von Bismarck for the newly united German state. In Germany there was a two-house legislature, or Diet, controlled by Emperor Wilhelm I, with a chancellor—Bismarck—actually holding most of the power. The Japanese, like the Germans, found it worthwhile to set aside the upper house of the legislature for the old nobility while allowing the general population to be represented in the lower house.

Emperor Meiji Mutsuhito at the age of nineteen, five years after he ascended the throne. The one-hundred-twenty-second ruler in his dynasty, he is the great-grandfather of the present emperor of Japan. *Library of Congress.*

In 1889, a new constitution was put into effect for Japan. The role of the emperor was preserved as "sacred" and untouchable.

Meanwhile, the imperial council had struck directly at the privileges of the old samurai warrior class, along with the rest of the rigid class structure of the old Tokugawa form of government. The council made it possible for common people—not just nobles—to adopt family names. People were allowed to choose their own occupations, instead of just being farmers or warriors because their fathers had done that work. The government built 54,000 new primary schools and required all children to attend them. Teachers often were brought from the West to teach subjects until Japanese teachers could be prepared. Before long Japan had the highest literacy rate in the Orient.

For three years, 1874–1877, the two million samurai warriors tried to resist the dramatic changes taking place in Japanese life. But the new government would not allow them to keep their old privileges. At first they were given salaries. Then, when those proved too costly, the government simply gave them a single lump sum payment. Nor were they any longer permitted to carry the vicious-looking swords that had been their trademark. Only the police and the army were allowed to bear arms. In Westernized cities such as Tokyo and Yokohama, the samurai, wearing their oily topknot hairdos, increasingly found themselves to be out of place.

Finally, in 1877, there was a major samurai revolt, lasting for six months. When the samurai leader, Saigo, realized that his forces had been defeated, he asked a comrade to behead him: a deed that was done.

In time, the samurai, like everyone else, began to blend into the new Japanese society.

In place of samurai warriors, Japan created an efficient Western-style army, as well as a modern navy. Beginning at the age of twenty-one, each Japanese male was required to serve in the new army for three years on active duty and for six years in the reserves. Promotion, as well as membership in the officer corps, was based strictly on ability, regardless of social background. In the new Japanese military, soldiers and sailors were taught to work together and fight together for the good of the nation, not just for the good of a special group.

Within a short time after the beginning of the Meiji Restoration, a new Japan had emerged. Factories dotted the landscape, enabling the Japanese to cut down on imported goods. There were railways, a postal system, telephones, gaslights, books. Printing presses introduced the literature of the West. New goods appeared, including beer and even meats. Wages of workers rose.

Japan had become a nation ruled by a modern, streamlined government, boasting a highly efficient army and marked by the dramatic breakdown in privileges previously enjoyed only by the aristocratic classes. Yet, at the nation's head stood Emperor Meiji Mutsuhito, the symbol of Japanese history extending back for hundreds of years, supposedly to the founding of the nation by the gods themselves.

Proud of his nation's progress, Meiji worked hard with the government to keep all social classes in harmony with one another, in sharp contrast to the class competition that had torn apart life in the Western nations. Through the symbol of his own personality, as well as in the teachings of the new public schools, he tried to preserve a strong attachment to traditional values. Since there was no single unifying religion in Japan, reverence for the emperor himself became a unifying force. Schoolchildren were taught the importance of service to the nation, shown by loyalty and obedience to the emperor. In every schoolhouse Meiji's picture occupied a place of honor.

As Japan became industrialized and militarily strong, Meiji and his government turned to questions of national pride and national prestige, especially in relations with other countries. One by one the Western nations that had enjoyed special trading privileges in Japan agreed to give them up. They also surrendered such special privileges as immunity from Japanese laws for their citizens doing business in the Japanese home islands.

Next, as an industrial power needing raw materials and markets for finished goods, Japanese leaders began looking overseas, especially to the nearby Asian mainland. In 1894, Japan became involved in a dispute with China over trading rights in Korea. To the surprise of the civilized world, the Japanese army totally defeated the forces of the supposedly mighty Chinese empire. Japan then imposed on China an embarrassingly harsh treaty, taking for itself the island of Taiwan. Overnight, Japan had become the leading power in Asia.

China's unexpected weakness encouraged Russia to occupy the entire Chinese province of Manchuria. But since neither Japan nor Great Britain welcomed that development, they signed in 1902 the Anglo-Japanese Alliance, hoping to discourage the Russians. When Russia refused to leave Manchuria and also refused to recognize Japan's special interests in Korea,

Emperor Meiji Mutsuhito with the empress and the crown prince and princess in ceremonial dress. *Brown Brothers.*

the Japanese launched a sudden surprise attack on the Russian fleet based at Port Arthur, Manchuria.

In the war that followed, both sides suffered heavy casualties. Japan was victorious, but after a year and a half of fighting, both sides were eager for peace. The treaty of peace (1905) recognized Japan's special interest in Korea and gave Japan the southern half of Sakhalin Island, between Siberia and Ja-

pan. Russia also granted the Japanese special privileges in Manchuria. In 1910, with little opposition, Japanese troops occupied Korea.

The slogan, "A rich nation, a strong army," had indeed come true. The Japanese generals now were national heroes, wildly applauded by the people of the fiercely proud nation. Through victories in its wars with China and with Russia, Japan had emerged from isolation to become one of the world's leading nations. Proud, ambitious, the Japanese people looked ahead to even greater imperial goals—visions that began to raise real concern in the West.

All of these changes had occurred within the lifetime of the emperor Meiji.

Meiji, like his countrymen, no longer wore his hair in a topknot, but cut in Western style. He no longer wore a kimono or pantaloons, but a tight-fitting field marshall's uniform. Heavyset and aging, he had become a father figure to his people. He attended military parades and fancy dress balls, but also wrestling matches. Often he toured the Japanese countryside. His picture appeared in the press, with formal reproductions available to his passionately loyal subjects for mounting in their homes.

True, the nation's real power rested in the hands of ministers such as Ito Hirobumi and Aritomo Yamagata. Yet, to much of the nation, Meiji had become a symbol of what it was that held them together as a people, uniting new ways with old ways.

In the summer of 1912, the emperor became seriously ill. In front of the Imperial Palace thousands of Japanese bent in prayer for his recovery. On July 30, he died.

The funeral took place at night, lighted by torches and by lamps. Meiji's coffin was borne on an ox-drawn cart at the head of a long procession. At the very moment the funeral cortege started from the Imperial Palace, one of the emperor's generals and his wife committed hara-kiri—a ritual suicide done by cutting open the stomach.

In ancient Japanese tradition, those nobles closest to an emperor customarily killed themselves and were buried with him. In that way they would accompany him on his journey to the next world, where they would continue to serve him.

This time, however, instead of the remains of sacrificed nobles, there were buried with the body of Meiji Mutsuhito four sculptured wooden models adorned in full military armor. Thus, without human sacrifice, the symbolism of Japan's ancient ritual tradition still lived on, as in the years of that nation's isolation from the world.

But the Japanese nation and the Japanese people had changed. In a quest for recognition and security, they had joined the competition for world power with the nations of the West. And in that competition they were determined to settle for nothing less than victory; being "second" was not good enough.

It was a course of action that would lead, step by step, to the fateful day in August 1945, when a single bomb—an atomic bomb—was dropped by an American plane on the Japanese city of Hiroshima.

That event led to the surrender of Japan and the end of World War II.

It also marked the beginning of a new era in the history of the world, a period in which the Japanese nation appears destined to play an increasingly important role.

Queen Victoria

1819–1901 Monarch whose reign came to symbolize the unity and strength of the British Empire in the nineteenth century

Until the day she became queen of England in 1837, at the age of eighteen, Britain's Princess Victoria never once had been permitted to sleep in a room of her own, away from her highly protective mother. She never had been allowed to walk down a flight of stairs without an escort.

Yet, when she died in 1901, after reigning for nearly sixty-four years, longer than any other English monarch, the British nation and its empire mourned, for Victoria had been a popular, beloved queen. She also had become a woman of strength and of great personal independence. In time, history would come to identify the age in which she lived as the "Victorian Age."

In 1819, the year of Victoria's birth, her grandfather, George III, reigned as king, this being the very same monarch whose rule had helped bring on the American Revolution and the loss of Britain's colonies in America.

One of George's sons, Edward, the Duke of Kent, had married the princess of Saxe-Coburg, a titled German widow. And it was to that couple that a baby was born, later destined to become Queen Victoria.

Among the group of nobles awaiting the childbirth at King George's elegant Kensington Palace was the Duke of Wellington, the heroic conqueror of Napoleon at the battle of Waterloo. Wellington, along with other British leaders, long had been concerned because of the failure of George's sons to produce children. They feared that, as a result, there might be no legal successor to the throne of England. Now they were relieved. A child had been born.

The child, named Alexandrina Victoria, was known officially from the very beginning as Victoria. "Drina" became her nickname, used by the family.

Only eight months after her birth Victoria's father died. From that time on, her mother took almost complete control of her upbringing. Nobody was permitted to visit young Victoria without the mother's personal permission and without another person being present in the room. For the early years of her life, the future queen lived in virtual isolation, under close protection from any outsiders.

As harsh as such a policy may seem, there was reason for it. On both the English side of her background (the Duke of Kent) and the German side (her mother), the families had been given to heavy drinking and loose sexual practices. Victoria, it was decided, should be brought up with the highest moral principles, producing an unquestionably noble character. Achieving such a goal would be healthy for her as a person. It might also restore trust and respect in the British crown, thus helping the monarchy to survive the

revolutionary spirit then sweeping across Europe. That spirit threatened the very existence of kings and queens, as well as the ancient tradition of government by royal families.

At first, Victoria lived a lonely life. A lively, quick-tempered, outgoing child, she played mostly with Feodora, her mother's daughter by a previous marriage and older by a full twelve years. Then, when Feodora married, the five-year-old Victoria found herself under the care of a German governess, the Baroness Louise Lehzen.

Lehzen played a crucial part in shaping Victoria's personality. Intelligent and caring, but firm, the governess tried to tone down her young charge's stubbornness and short temper. In time, Princess Victoria's temper mellowed, but for the rest of her life she remained stubborn. Once her mind was made up, she did not like to be contradicted and usually insisted on having things her own way.

Speaking German from early childhood, Victoria quickly learned to speak English without the trace of an accent, unlike the children of her grandfather, George III. She also studied French and Latin. Like many other women of the day, she received careful instruction in dancing, singing, and drawing. Special teachers worked with her on the subjects of British history and British law.

At the age of eleven, her academic progress was examined in a special session attended by a panel of bishops. She impressed them with her knowledge. It was shortly afterward that she is said to have remarked, after seeing a chart of succession to the British throne, that she had not realized how close she was to becoming queen. Her response, it is said, was, "I will be good."

Increasingly now she was taken on unofficial trips around the country. There were visits to the homes of noble families, trips to towns where she was greeted with flowers and serenaded by marching bands. Still, the Baroness Lehzen remained her principal companion in what Victoria described in the pages of her daily journal as a dull and lonely existence.

With her seventeenth birthday, a serious search began to find her a husband. From the beginning the leading contender for her hand was Albert, prince of Saxe-Coburg-Gotha, three small German states. To Victoria he appeared far too serious and not nearly as fond of dancing as she would have liked. But he also was very handsome and deeply caring. Like Victoria, he, too, was seventeen years old.

By now Princess Victoria had become plump, a characteristic she would retain through life. Only five feet tall, she had blue eyes, light brown hair, and a silvery clear voice. Her manners had become graceful, her style confident, poised, self-assured. She smiled seldom but with a charm and radiance that during her reign would add greatly to her popularity.

On May 24, 1837, Victoria celebrated her eighteenth birthday. After that, she could legally assume the throne if the situation arose. A few days later, it did arise. On June 19, King William IV died. The next day Victoria became queen of England.

She recorded the events in her journal:

I was awoke at 6 o'clock by Mamma who told me that the archbishop of Canterbury and Lord Conyngham were here and wished to see me. I got out of bed and went into my sitting room (only in my dressing gown) and *alone*, and saw them. Lord Conyngham . . . acquainted me that my poor uncle, the king, was no more . . . and consequently that I am *Queen*.

As queen, Victoria made it a point to become independent of her mother, moving her to a distant set of apartments in Buckingham Palace. In time, Victoria insisted on an appointment in advance when her mother wished to speak to her. She also became less reliant on the advice of her Uncle Leopold

A portrait engraving of the young Queen Victoria, from the painting by Frans Winterhalter. *Culver Pictures, Inc.*

of Belgium, her mother's brother. Of the older influences on her life, only the Baroness Lehzen remained important.

In their place she turned to the British prime minister, Lord Melbourne, for friendship and for help. Handsome, witty, and charming, he became something of a father to the socially inexperienced Victoria. Melbourne assisted her with the enormous burden of paperwork that accompanied the royal office in those days. He taught her about British government. In the evenings the two enjoyed playing chess together or working at puzzles.

Meanwhile, Victoria began to participate in London's social life: the theater, concerts, dancing. Observing her from Germany, Prince Albert noted that, along with her charm and warmth, Victoria "is said not to take the slightest pleasure in nature and to enjoy sitting up at night and sleeping late into the day." Still, Albert wished aloud that one day the two might marry.

For a time, British domestic politics turned Victoria's attention away from the possibility of marriage. As Lord Melbourne's liberal Whig party lost ground to the conservative Tories, Melbourne finally found it necessary to resign. His Tory successor, Sir Robert Peel, demanded that the queen dismiss the ladies of her inner circle, some of whom were hired by Melbourne and married to prominent Whigs. Victoria, reacting angrily to Peel, stubbornly refused.

Melbourne and the popular Duke of Wellington tried to smooth things over, but it was too late. Peel refused to serve as prime minister under Victoria, and Melbourne reluctantly agreed to assume the job again, even though his Whigs now were a minority party in Parliament.

Victoria had shown personal strength in the matter. But the general public, enflamed by the press, expressed great displeasure. Was it right, asked many, that the nation's leadership had been decided by the taste of their young queen for the makeup of her personal staff?

With the so-called bedchamber question behind her, Victoria turned once again to the issue of marriage. Her greatest concern was that, in the event of her death, the line of succession was very short. Unless she married and had children, the monarchy might soon fade into history.

In the two years since last she had seen Prince Albert, he had traveled much, grown more handsome, taken dancing lessons. To Victoria's surprise, when they met once again, she fell in love with him.

Writing in her daily journal, a habit

now so ingrained it would last for her entire lifetime, she described Albert's beautiful eyes and nose, his broad shoulders and fine waist. "My heart is quite going," she said.

Unexpectedly, the self-controlled, conservative Albert also found himself hopelessly in love. It was to become perhaps the happiest match in the history of the British monarchy.

As queen, Victoria was supposed to be the one to propose. She did, offering Albert "her hand and her heart."

After an elegant wedding the couple took a honeymoon of only a few days and then returned to work.

At first, Victoria did not include Albert in the official affairs of government. Before long, however, it became clear that he would replace Lord Melbourne as the queen's chief adviser. Intelligent, serious, and hard-working, he took on more and more of the administrative details of the monarchy. That was particularly true when Victoria was recovering from childbirth or was at uncomfortable stages of a pregnancy.

Nor were such situations rare. The couple had nine children. At the time of Victoria's death she would have forty grandchildren and thirty-seven great-grandchildren.

Increasingly, Victoria took on Prince Albert's life-style, putting aside her habit of staying up late and sleeping late. She began to find happiness spending time in the countryside, mostly at Balmoral Castle in Scotland. Usually, too, she would listen to Albert's advice on important matters, so much so that her critics liked to speak of the "Albertine Monarchy."

Because Albert had established close ties with Robert Peel, Victoria changed her mind and came to value him. She agreed to be more balanced and impartial in her dealings with the major political parties. In the past she had so clearly favored Melbourne's Whigs that in 1841 she had actually contributed a large amount of her own money to their election campaign.

Most important of all, Prince Albert made Victoria aware of how the Industrial Revolution—the dramatic rise of the factory system—was transforming England. He showed her how British farmers had flocked to the nation's cities hoping for jobs, only to find themselves without work, without hope. He brought to her attention the situation of the poor, living in filthy, crowded conditions close to the new factories and mines.

It was Albert who made Victoria aware of the need for social reform—change—in the life of Great Britain. It was he who encouraged such new laws as the graduated income tax, with the wealthy paying much more than

Frans Winterhalter's portrait of Queen Victoria and Prince Albert with their five children in 1846. The children are *(left to right)* Prince Alfred; Albert, Prince of Wales; Princess Alice; the baby Princess Helena; and Victoria, the princess royal. *UPI/Bettmann.*

the poor. Because of Albert, Victoria, reared in seclusion, began to realize for the first time in what truly desperate straits the majority of her people were living.

At the same time, Albert also took pride in the remarkable achievements of British industry, based on the use of science. That, too, he brought to Victoria's attention.

One result was the organization of the Great Exhibition of 1851. Held in a huge glass-enclosed hall near London's Hyde Park, it came to be known as the "Crystal Palace" exhibition. Scientific exhibits from around the world attracted enormous crowds of visitors. As Victoria put it, the exhibition's great sense of pride in achievement and confidence in a better, brighter future for mankind forever would be associated "with the name of my dearly beloved Albert."

Victoria showed pride, too, in the glorious triumphs won by British soldiers in wars overseas. During the years 1854–1856, Britain, France, and Turkey fought against Russia in a particularly bloody conflict, the Crimean War. Although the queen was moved by the success of her troops, she was shocked at the horrors of the war. She warmly praised the work of Florence Nightingale in caring for the wounded. After personally visiting wounded British soldiers she wrote in her journal:

I cannot say how touched and impressed I have been by the sight of those noble, brave and so sadly wounded men and how anxious I feel to be of use to them, and to try and get some employment for those who are maimed for life.

In 1857, the scene of conflict for British troops shifted to India. There, a revolt of native troops, known as sepoys, against the East India Company eventually led Victoria's government to take full control of the administration of that colony. Despite the bloodshed on both sides, the queen urged understanding, reconciliation, and goodwill. In 1877, she was given the title empress of India.

Busy with affairs of state, Victoria also had to deal with childrearing and, by

the late 1850s, with the job of arranging appropriate marriages for her children. In 1858, her eldest daughter was married to Prince Frederick Wilhelm of Prussia. Little could the queen know that one day the first son produced by that marriage would, as Kaiser Wilhelm II, lead Germany into conflict against Great Britain in World War I.

At the time, however, the birth of young Wilhelm was a happy occasion. It meant that—at the age of only forty—Victoria was not only the mother of nine children but also, for the first time, a grandmother.

Then, in September 1861, tragedy struck. Prince Albert, long suffering from typhoid fever, grew more seriously ill. Still, despite icy winter weather he traveled to Cambridge to spend time with young Albert, the royal couple's oldest son. Albert, or "Bertie," as he was known, often had embarrassed his parents by heavy drinking, as well as by his love affair with an actress.

On Prince Albert's return to London, his illness grew worse. The doctors could do nothing to help him. Although only forty-two years old, he died.

Now Victoria's life changed dramatically. Never forgiving her son for his part in Albert's death, she could scarcely bear to be in the same room with him. She refused to give him any responsibilities in the government, scarcely even speaking to him.

Beginning with the day of Albert's funeral, she put on mourning clothes of black, wearing only that color for the rest of her life. All of her happiness disappeared. She withdrew from public view, going into complete seclusion for many months. All that she wanted for herself, said Queen Victoria, was death.

Often the queen would spend hours at a time seated beside Albert's gravesite, praying or simply looking at the place where his body lay at rest. She could not bring herself to deal with the mountain of paperwork that piled higher and higher on her desk. The days of her mourning turned into weeks, the weeks into months, the months into years. The British public, unhappy with her seclusion, began to demand that she abdicate, turning the throne over to her son "Bertie."

Slowly, Victoria began to show herself in public. At first, she would simply take carriage rides, only to be greeted by thunderous applause from her loyal subjects. Then, gradually, her spirit improved. She became more herself, began to come out of her shell.

Astonishingly, the person who proved most important in restoring her confidence, helping her to recover, was one of Prince Albert's personal servants, a Scottish groom and huntsman—John Brown.

Gruff but friendly, and completely honest in his behavior, Brown on several occasions saved Victoria from riding accidents. Once, he courageously saved her life when an assassin tried to kill her. The big, simple Scotsman and the queen of England became closer and closer friends. Victoria listened to his advice, came to trust his judgment, just as she had trusted Albert. Eventually she insisted that nobody but she herself be permitted to give orders to John Brown. He accompanied her everywhere.

Mostly because of John Brown, Victoria in time became more cheerful. She regained her zest for life. Once again she began to care for the daily business that went with being queen of England.

The other person she came to trust completely was the leader of Britain's Conservative party, the brilliant and witty statesman Benjamin Disraeli. Disraeli served twice in Victoria's reign as prime minister. And in those years he managed to come as close to her as any person since the death of Prince Albert. Because he was flamboyant in his style of dress and highly original in his thinking, Victoria at first thought of him as "odd." Increasingly, however, she came to respect him. To Disraeli, she was a woman, and he treated her that way.

On the other hand, William Gladstone, the leader of the Whig party, simply annoyed her. Gladstone, she said, "speaks to me as if I were a public meeting." And besides, she added, "He talks so very much."

Using Victoria's friendship to help him gain his ends, Disraeli worked to strengthen Britain's overseas empire. In 1875, he cooperated with the Rothschilds, the great banking house, to buy a majority interest in the Suez Canal Company. That act gave Great Britain ownership of the canal and a paramount role in governing Egypt, thus protecting the sea route to India.

It was Disraeli who arranged for Victoria to assume the title of empress of India, putting her on an equal footing as empress with two of her daughters then reigning in Russia and Germany.

Because of Disraeli, Queen Victoria, as one British writer put it, no longer was seen as "a neurotic widow" but as the symbol of a great and splendid empire. It was no secret that she felt great warmth and respect for him.

For his part, the aging Disraeli spoke of Victoria as "The Faery Queene" and openly admitted his love for her, knowing full well that the memory of Prince Albert remained the single most important thing in her life. In 1881, when Disraeli was on his deathbed, it was suggested that the queen be invited to visit him. "No, it is better not," he is said to have replied. "She would only ask me to take a message to Albert."

Under Disraeli's successor, Lord Salisbury, the British flag was planted in various parts of Africa—east, south, and west. British influence grew in Asia. Truly it was a time when "the sun does never set on the British Empire."

Victoria herself devoted more and more of her time to the needs of England's poor, especially to provide hospitals and medical care for those who could not afford it. Once, to dramatize her concern for the treatment of women in British prisons, she made a surprise personal visit to the notorious Parkhurst Prison for women.

As the years went by, Victoria became the symbol of British greatness. Everywhere she was greeted by enthusiastic crowds showing their pride in the once discredited national monarchy. Her old age became a time of triumph for her and for her nation.

In 1887, the nation celebrated her golden jubilee—fifty years as queen. Rulers from all over the world came to London to pay their respects. Festivities continued for an entire month. There were banquets, parades, fireworks, and also applause, applause . . . and still more applause.

At home and overseas Great Britain appeared to reign triumphant. And, over it all, summing it all up, sat Alexandrina Victoria, the queen.

Ten years later, in 1897, there was

a diamond jubilee, no less elaborate, marking sixty years of Victoria's reign. By then, at age seventy-nine, she was in a wheelchair, unable to greet the crowds for long. Her thoughts at the time, she declared, were still with her beloved Prince Albert.

On January 22, 1901, Victoria died, peacefully, easily, with many of her children and grandchildren by her bedside. Holding her hand at the end was her adoring grandson, Kaiser Wilhelm II of Germany. Years later, on the very brink of World War I, when faced with fierce British opposition, he thought of his grandmother and declared, "If she had been alive, *she* would never have allowed this!"

During her reign of sixty-four years, Victoria had brought to the throne of England a sense of dignity, stability, calm. Like the British people themselves, she had lived a life committed to duty and honor, hard work, and strength in times of crisis.

At the time of her death, many of her devoted subjects found it awkward to put almost forgotten words to the tune of the English national anthem and to sing once again, after so many years, "God Save the King."

PART II
The Twentieth Century before Hiroshima

Vladimir Ilyich Lenin

1870–1924   Political theorist and fiery leader of the Bolshevik Revolution, which transformed czarist Russia into the world's first communist nation

During the summer of 1990, shocking news began to trickle to the outside world from dozens of cities across the Soviet Union. Statues of Vladimir Ilyich Lenin—the principal leader of Russia's Communist revolt in 1917—were being toppled and defaced. In one case a statue of Lenin was angrily taken apart and the parts put up for sale to the public. Then, in September 1991, the city of Leningrad officially became known once again as St. Petersburg, the name it had carried during the reign of the Russian czars.

For much of the twentieth century the image of Lenin was considered sacred, holy, in the Soviet Union. Likenesses of the revolutionary leader were everywhere. Pictures of him appeared in classrooms and libraries, on huge billboards in public squares, over the entrances to hotels, at railroad stations and airports—wherever people gathered. Hundreds of books were written about him. Children were taught to behave like him: to study like him, to dress like him, even to brush their teeth like him.

From 1917 until his death in 1924 Lenin stood as the undisputed head of the Soviet government. His name came to be joined with that of Karl Marx for shaping "Marxism-Leninism"—a system that eventually dominated the lives of more than one-third of the world's people. Even his enemies, and there have been many, are forced to admit that, more than any other leader, it is the thought and the actions of Lenin that have given shape to many of the major events of the twentieth century.

Now, as that century draws to a close, the once impressive Communist world is crumbling. Still, the shadow of Lenin looms large above our times. There is no question that he will be remembered as one of history's most important figures.

That such a future might lie in store for him hardly seemed likely on the day of his birth, April 22, 1870. Already there were two children in the family when Vladimir Ilyich Ulyanov (his real name) was born in the small city of Simbirsk, along the Volga River. Later, there would be three more children, all but one of them becoming revolutionaries.

Lenin's father, Ilya, had been born the son of a poor tailor. By hard work he had risen to become a teacher and then director of public schools in a large area along the Volga. Fiercely loyal to the czar, the leader of Russia, Ulyanov was also a devout believer in the Russian Orthodox Church. His professional title as a school official made him part of the nation's nobility, although in terms of money the Ulyanov family could best be described as "middle class."

Lenin's mother, Maria, of German ancestry, was the daughter of a doctor. She could speak four languages and cared deeply for history, literature, and music. She brought to the marriage a modest amount of inherited wealth. Feeling isolated from the cultural life of Russia's great cities, she came to play an important role in the education of her children.

Of all the influences on Lenin's early life, though, perhaps the most important was his older brother, Alexander Ulyanov, or Sasha. Sasha, four years his senior, became a model for young Vladimir. Even in such matters as whether he would go out to play or what food he would eat, Vladimir would announce, "The same as Sasha."

The two boys were very different both in looks and in behavior. Alexander, tall and thin, pale, quiet, liked to be left alone. Vladimir, by contrast, was short and sturdy in build. He had high cheekbones and slightly slanted eyes, like his father, a man partially of Mongolian ancestry. Unlike Sasha, Vladimir tended to be noisy, outgoing, aggressive, eager to be with other people. Still, the two boys did many things together: fishing and swimming in the summer, skating and sledding in the winter, and, nearly every evening, chess—the most favored of all Russian games.

Sometimes the Ulyanov children liked to play war games, pretending to be soldiers. And when they did, Vladimir always chose to be Abraham Lincoln, leading American troops against the slave-holding Southerners.

As he grew older, Vladimir became intensely serious about his schoolwork. He gave special attention to the study of Latin and Greek, but also read widely in world literature, history, and economics. He took special care in developing his skills in writing and in public speaking. At the age of sixteen he graduated first in his high school class.

It was at that time, too, that he followed the example of his brother, Alexander, in declaring that he no longer believed in God. As he later told the story, once he decided there was no God, he simply took the cross from around his neck, spat on it, and threw it away.

Shortly before Vladimir's high school graduation, the happiness of the Ulyanov family was shattered by two tragic events. First was the death of Ilya, the father. Young Alexander took on the role of male head of the household. Then, in 1887, word arrived from Russia's capital city, St. Petersburg, of an event that would change Vladimir's life. Alexander, then a student at the University of St. Petersburg, had been arrested for joining with other young rebels in attempting to assassinate Czar Alexander III.

Desperately hoping to win a pardon for Alexander, Maria traveled to the capital. There she pleaded with the czar in note after note to spare her son's life. Her pleas could not change the monarch's mind. Alexander was hanged.

Until that time Vladimir had shown only a passing interest in politics. He had been considering a career as a college professor of classics and humanities. Then, at the death of his beloved Sasha, he is said to have remarked, "I'll make them pay for this! I swear it!"

Instead of proceeding with the study of humanities, Vladimir applied to the law school of Kazan University. To be close to him there and to begin a new life, the Ulyanovs sold the family home at Simbirsk and moved to Kazan.

Only three months after entering the law school Vladimir was expelled. He had been seen attending a student protest meeting there, and in part because of Alexander's attempt to kill the czar, the authorities chose to make an example of Vladimir.

Petition after petition failed to gain him reentry to the law school. Then, grudgingly, the police allowed him to return to Kazan, but not to attend any classes at the university. If he wished to take the law school examinations, he would have to learn the material on his own.

In just one year Vladimir Ilyich Ulyanov mastered the content of a four-year

The Bolshevik leader, Vladimir Ilyich Lenin. *Culver Pictures, Inc.*

program in law. He received perfect scores in every field examined. Kazan University had no choice but to grant him a degree "with honors."

Once admitted to legal practice, Vladimir joined a firm in nearby Samara, where he became a public defender, championing the cause of peasants and other poor people who had gotten into trouble.

Meanwhile, he had been reading intensely about philosophy and politics. The work of one author—Karl Marx— transformed Ulyanov's life.

According to Marx, all of history is the story of conflict, with the rich exploiting the poor for their own purposes. Only through violent revolution could the people, so long abused, throw off the rule of the "capitalist class"— those rich people who owned the factories (the "means of production"). Marx predicted that after the revolution took place—and that was just a matter of time—it would be possible to set up a whole new way of life. Property would be shared, and people would work for the good of the whole country, not just themselves. Ever afterward, the formula for work and for rewards would be, "From each according to his ability, to each according to his needs."

To young Vladimir Ulyanov, Marx's view as described in the classic work, *Das Kapital*, was more than just a beautiful dream. It was a blueprint, a plan, for turning the selfish competition of the marketplace into a way of life that really worked. Around the world the rich would be relieved of the need to clash in ferocious, jungle-like warfare, while happiness and plenty would at last be possible for the poor. For Vladimir Ulyanov, *Das Kapital* became nothing less than a bible.

In January 1889, he formally became a follower of Marx: he began speaking of himself as a "Marxist." He moved to the capital city, St. Petersburg, one day to be renamed "Leningrad" in his honor. There he planned to meet with other Marxists, then known as "Social Democrats." He helped them write pamphlets for distribution to factory workers. He taught classes about Marxism to workers and encouraged them to go on strike against the factory owners for higher wages and better working conditions.

Such activities did not please the Russian government. In 1895 they arrested Ulyanov and, after holding him in jail for several months, sentenced him to three years of exile in distant Siberia. There he was joined by his friend and coworker, Nadezhda Krupskaya, whom he married in 1898.

Together, the two translated into Russian the book *Industrial Democracy*, by the British Socialists Sidney and Beatrice Webb. Ulyanov also wrote the first of his own fifty-five books, *The Development of Capitalism in Russia,* a work arguing that his country no longer was just a land of peasants but an industrial nation. Because of that, he declared, the time at last was ripe for a revolt of industrial workers, the so-called "proletariat."

It was now that Vladimir Ilyich Ulyanov decided to give up his family name. Forever afterward he became known to history as "Lenin."

On Lenin's release from exile in February 1900, he set out at once for Munich, Germany, to help edit a new revolutionary journal, *Iskra (The Spark).* After completing her own sentence, Krupskaya soon joined him there. Together, the two prepared the enormously important new work, *What Is to Be Done?* (1902).

What Is to Be Done? sometimes goes beyond Marx by providing a strategy for victory. It argues, for example, that the coming revolution could succeed only if all power were concentrated in the hands of a small group of professional, full-time revolutionaries. They, working through a single political party, would actually make the revolution happen. Afterward, it was they who would teach the people of Russia—and then the other nations—about socialism.

Then, at last, all the world would be Socialist and free. When that finally happened, according to both Marx and Lenin, there no longer would be a need for government. The state would "wither away and die," and ever afterward there would be equality—and happiness.

But first, there had to be disciplined, strong, highly trained leadership—a small group of dedicated individuals, headed by Vladimir Ilyich Lenin.

In 1902 Lenin moved to London. Like Marx before him, he spent every day working intently in the library of the British Museum. A passionate, intense worker, he churned out a steady stream of books and articles on the need for a Socialist revolution.

While in London he met young Lev Davidovich Bronstein, a brilliant Russian Jew who soon would become one of Lenin's closest, most trusted aides. Bronstein, destined to play a key role in the Marxist seizure of power in Russia, is known to history as Leon Trotsky.

It was in London, too, that Lenin succeeded in gaining personal control of the Russian Social Democratic Workers party (RSDWP). He won out against those in the party who wanted it open to any person who wished to join, not just the small group of professional revolutionaries preferred by Lenin. By a narrow vote Lenin's tougher position was adopted.

V. Serov's painting of Lenin inciting a mob. *Photosearch*.

Ever afterward, those within the party who followed him were to be known as *Bolsheviks* (the majority wing), while those who disagreed and wanted a more moderate organization were to be known as *Mensheviks* (the minority wing).

From that point, the Bolsheviks considered themselves to be the "vanguard of the proletariat," the leaders responsible for giving direction and education to the working class. It was they, said Lenin, who would "overturn Russia." After that, they would bring socialism to the entire world.

People who knew Lenin at the time remember him as a man totally involved in the work of revolution, with little private life of his own. Bald, like his father, he had a reddish beard and mustache. Usually he dressed in an ordinary middle-class suit and tie. Many reported that he lacked the great writing and speaking ability of Trotsky.

Yet those who met him usually were struck by the power of his personality—the piercing look of his slanted eyes, his boundless energy, every ounce of it devoted to his task. He refused to have an easy chair in his room or a soft pillow on his bed. To some, he was a man so intense, so serious, so brooding that even though young he seemed always to have been an old man. It is said that even while sleeping he dreamed of revolution.

In 1905, a revolution did indeed break out in Russia, only to be crushed by the government. Lenin returned to Russia too late to make a difference. But while in his homeland once again, he began to rethink the idea of a revolution based only on the proletariat, the industrial working class. Now he began to speak in favor of the peasantry, too, as a class of its own. The revolution, he said, would be one of workers, peasants (farmers), and intellectuals (thinkers)—all united for victory.

From 1905 to 1914, he became more and more conscious of wars among the various European countries to gain empires—territory—overseas. Drawing his thoughts from Marx, he said that such wars would only make the rich richer, the poor poorer. He also pointed out that the soldiers killed in battle usually were the children of the poor. Thus, when World War I broke out in 1914, Lenin was shocked to see many Socialists proudly supporting their own nations in the conflict. To him, the war was just another example of capitalists getting richer on the blood of the poor.

At the same time, Lenin believed that if Russia was badly enough weakened by the war, the time finally might be ripe for revolution. In his *Imperialism, the Highest Stage of Capitalism*, he argued that only such a Socialist revolution was capable of bringing about a just and lasting peace.

The war dragged on and on, and still there was no revolution against the Russian czar, Nicholas II. For a time, even Lenin grew discouraged. Then, in March 1917, just as he was beginning to lose hope altogether, the hungry, war-weary soldiers of St. Petersburg simply rose up in rebellion. The monarchy was overthrown.

At the head of the new government was Alexander Kerensky, a Socialist but not nearly so extreme in his thinking as Lenin. By a strange coincidence, Kerensky was the son of Lenin's high school principal in Simbirsk, the man whose strong letter of recommendation had won admission to law school for young Vladimir Ilyich Ulyanov.

When news of the revolution first reached Lenin, he was in Switzerland. Quickly, he gained permission from German authorities to travel across their country by train to Russia. The Germans gladly agreed, hoping that Lenin and his fiery group of revolutionaries would overthrow the Kerensky government and cause their powerful enemy, Russia, to drop out of the war. If that happened, they could move all of the German troops tied down on the bloody Eastern Front to the West, to fight against France and England.

Riding in a sealed train, with the window shades drawn, Lenin and his comrades arrived in Petrograd (its name changed from St. Petersburg by the czar) on April 16, 1917.

Since the revolution, councils of workers, known as Soviets, had sprung up not only in Petrograd but all across Russia. Their leaders tended to be moderate Socialists, like Kerensky himself, not like Lenin's Bolsheviks.

Lenin, Trotsky, and the Bolsheviks quickly sprang into action. What was needed, they declared, was an end to Russia's participation in the war. The soldiers must have peace. The peasants must be given ownership of the land they plowed. The hungry factory workers must be fed.

"Peace! Land! Bread!" became the cry of the Bolsheviks. Soldiers, peasants, and workers must unite to make a true revolution, declared Lenin. Then, before long—as he and Marx had promised before—no government at all would be needed. The state would simply "wither away" and die.

Meanwhile, Lenin's slogan became "All power to the Soviets."

Kerensky, angered by Lenin's attacks, tried to arrest him. But shaving his beard and mustache and disguising himself as a Finnish railway worker, he escaped into exile in Finland.

Then, in October 1917, he returned to Petrograd. By that time the situation inside Russia had grown desperate. Soldiers at the front were deserting their posts by the thousands. Crowds of hungry factory workers filled the streets of major cities.

On November 7, 1917, the Petrograd Soviet, under the command of Trotsky, launched an open rebellion against the Kerensky government. The rebels were joined in their activity by a group of armed Bolshevik workers, known as the Red Guards. The Communist Revolution had begun.

By November 8, the fighting was over. The Kerensky government had fallen. Vladimir Ilyich Lenin was elected chairman of the Council of People's Commissars, the ruling body of Russia. Essentially a scholar and writer, never having held a government post in his life, Lenin suddenly found himself head of the world's largest country. Only days before taking power he had been a fugitive, in hiding from the police.

Despite his lack of experience, Lenin acted promptly, decisively. He nationalized all banks, industry, and land. Then, in the Treaty of Brest-Litovsk, he made peace with Germany and the other Central Powers. It was a humiliating peace. Russia lost much territory, but, to Lenin, peace was what the nation needed most to restore its strength. Next, he announced that no foreign loans to the old czarist government would be repaid. He seized all foreign property in Russia and declared that it now belonged to the Soviets.

Angry people, most of them from the wealthier classes, struck back. Calling themselves "Whites," they started a civil war against Lenin's "Red" forces. The Whites had more soldiers, more money, more supplies. Still, they could not defeat the Bolsheviks.

Lenin won the peasants to his side by taking over the landed estates without payment and giving them to the people. He won over the factory workers by promising them food and housing. He won over the various nationality groups within Russia by promising not to force them to remain part of the new government if they chose to leave. Finally, he helped Trotsky organize an effective fighting force, the "Red Army."

By the winter of 1921, the Whites had been defeated. The civil war was over.

During all the years of struggle, Lenin had taken little time for himself. Although in his youth he had loved outdoor activities such as hiking, horseback riding, boating, and hunting, once in power he denied himself such diversions. Even taking time to listen to the music of Beethoven or to play chess now seemed to him distractions from the business of government.

In 1918, a young anarchist, Fanny Kaplan, had tried to kill him, plunging two bullets into his body. He recovered but may have suffered permanent damage from the attack. Then, in 1922, he suffered a serious paralytic stroke. Again, he recovered, but only partially.

All the time, he worked to win formal diplomatic recognition from nations around the world. Most of them, except for the United States, soon admitted that Lenin's new government, by then called the Union of Soviet Socialist Republics (USSR), in fact really did exist. They exchanged ambassadors with the Soviet Union.

Next, Lenin stood up for the rights of colonial peoples, those living in countries dominated by such European masters as France and England. He made such people believe that, in seeking freedom—"national liberation"—they had a friend in the Soviet Union. That belief, even though not always true, lived on into the last decade of the present century.

By 1921, however, Lenin began to see serious problems within his own government. Everywhere, new agencies and bureaus were springing up, staffed by workers looking out for their own interests. Before long there was a vast bureaucracy.

Many of the bureaucrats owed their positions to Joseph Stalin, an ambitious Bolshevik who gathered more and more power to himself. Stalin, in turn, was challenged at every step by Leon Trotsky. As Lenin's health grew worse, Stalin and Trotsky fought bitterly for control of the party.

In December 1922, Lenin suffered a second stroke. Courageously, he struggled to recover while trying to remove the growing abuses in the government he had given so much of his life to create. In Stalin, especially, he saw a man who cared little for the great cause of freeing humanity from oppression. As Lenin wrote at the time, "He is too rough . . . this cook will make too peppery a stew. I propose the comrades find a way to remove him. . . ." Lenin was right. Stalin was destined to become one of the cruelest oppressors in human history.

Increasingly, Lenin became too weak to take part in the daily business of government. Finally, he became an invalid, living with his wife, Krupskaya, in a small house at Gorki, close to Moscow. Although only fifty-four years old, he was barely strong enough to speak. A later stroke deprived him of speech altogether.

On January 21, 1924, he suffered still another stroke. That one took his life.

Joseph Stalin ordered that Lenin's body be embalmed and placed in a red granite tomb of honor, just outside of the Kremlin in Moscow's Red Square. Since then, millions and millions of visitors have stood silently in line for hours, sometimes on bitter cold or blazing hot days, to view his last remains.

In the years between Lenin's death and the beginning of World War II, Stalin may have sent to their deaths in labor camps as many as 7 million people. Nearly a million more were executed by the government. The Soviet Union itself became a place of fear and ruthless terror.

Such a result is far from what Lenin had in mind. His was a dream of people living together in harmony, in a world without poverty and without war.

In place of the dream came a nightmare. And to many of those who lived through that nightmare of tyranny, it was the deeds of Lenin that had made it all possible. Whether they are right or wrong is difficult to say.

But it certainly is understandable that in the waning years of the twentieth century, people in the Soviet Union and its satellite countries around the globe might decide to do what they have done. They have begun to tear down the statues erected in praise of Lenin and to destroy them.

As the statues lie there upon the ground, passersby sometimes remark at Lenin's eyes—intense and piercing—often captured dramatically by the sculptors.

What, we may wonder, might Lenin himself think if, with those penetrating eyes, he could see today's world: a world he did so very much to create?

Sun Yat-sen

1866–1925   Leader of the Chinese revolution against the Manchu dynasty; revered by many today as the father of modern China

China.

Not America, but China. That was the destination of Christopher Columbus in 1492, when first he set out on his fateful journey to find a water route—a shortcut—to the Orient. To him, like most who had heard about the fabled country of the Khan, it was a land of rare spices, of fine silk and satin garments, of stately palaces and temples.

For some two thousand years before Columbus, five centuries before the birth of Christ, high culture had flourished in China. Scholars wrote books and taught the young in schools. Wise men spoke of charity and love, friendship to others, a sense of sharing, of community.

Again and again, conquering armies from the north and west had swept across the peaceful land only, in time, to be absorbed into it, to become part of it themselves. So great was the attraction of China's civilization, the appeal of its people.

All of that was destined to change in "modern times," our own age of factories and rapid communication, of enormous armies and weapons of mass destruction. Merchants from such nations as France and England, Belgium and Germany, Spain and Portugal would descend upon the China coast, demanding special trading privileges, insisting on their right to control rich port cities along the shore.

British traders sold mind-numbing opium to the Chinese people. And when the government of China tried to stop the trade, British soldiers made quick work of armies nowhere near their match in modern weaponry.

The Chinese government itself was soft and weak, rich and corrupt. China at the beginning of the twentieth century, and for more than three centuries before our time, was controlled by Manchus—brutal, ignorant conquerors who had crossed the Great Wall of China from Manchuria, imposing their rule over all the land. Through warlords in the provinces they collected high taxes. They lived lives of splendor, in homes surrounded by beautiful gardens, while in the countryside and in the cities the Chinese people had barely enough rice to stay alive.

Something had to be done. The people of the country cried out for change. More than any other person, it was Sun Yat-sen, the child of humble parents, who would set the stage for a revolution against the Manchu rulers, out of which would emerge a new, unified China.

Although his own life was marked by repeated failures, Sun Yat-sen is a hero to the Communist government that now controls the mainland. Strangely, he is also a hero to the competing nationalists, expelled from China but thriving industrially and commercially today on the offshore island of Taiwan. Both sides have erected statues and monuments in honor of Sun Yat-

sen. To the children of both lands, he is highly respected, and the textbooks they read are filled with pictures of him and with the story of his life.

The life of Sun Yat-sen began simply enough. He was born in 1866 to a peasant family in the south of China, near the Portuguese settlement of Macao. Like other children, he attended the village school. From the very first, however, it was clear that the clever, curious little boy wanted more from life than to repeat the farming experience of his ancestors. Nor did he care much for the long pigtail hairdo that the Manchu rulers insisted all Chinese must wear to show respect.

At the age of twelve he stowed away on a ship bound for Honolulu, Hawaii, where his older brother, Ah-mei, had gone into business as a shopkeeper.

In Hawaii, Sun Yat-sen was enrolled in an English-speaking school, strongly based in the Christian religion. After studying there for three years, he not only had mastered the English language and Western ideas about democracy, but also had decided to become a Christian. That decision caused Ah-mei to send him back to China. It was too late. Sun Yat-sen's life would never again be the same.

Before long, Sun began to speak against the idol worship still practiced in his native village. One day, in front of a crowd, he struck one of the wooden idols with his hand. He broke off the fingers of another. Meanwhile, he often spoke in public about the need for a revolution to topple the Manchu government and bring democracy to China.

Embarrassed, his parents sent him to nearby Hong Kong, where, at the expense of Ah-mei, he enrolled in Queen's College to study Western science. While in Hong Kong, he worked actively to convince his Chinese classmates that they, too, should become Christians.

For a time he seriously considered the possibility of a career as a Christian missionary, converting Chinese people to that religion, a religion that strongly spoke out for individual freedom. But because there was no theological school in Hong Kong, he chose an altogether different career—medicine.

First in Canton and then at the British college in Hong Kong, Sun Yat-sen studied medicine, graduating in 1892 with high honors. The dean of the medical school, Dr. James Cantlie, considered him a doctor of unusual promise and urged him to go on further to become a surgeon. Again, Sun succeeded. He and Dr. Cantlie became close friends.

While Sun was completing his medical studies, his family persuaded him to return to China to marry. It was an arranged marriage, to a woman he had never seen before.

The couple soon had a son, but to Sun Yat-sen life could never again be lived in such an old-fashioned, traditional way. Leaving his Chinese family behind, he set up a medical practice in Portuguese Macao. Sometimes Dr. Cantlie would cooperate with him on surgical operations.

Then came a minor event that, almost by chance, would change his life. The Portuguese authorities in Macao demanded that all foreign doctors had to have a Portuguese certificate to practice medicine in the colony. Faced with the prospect of going back to school for many months, Sun, by then twenty-six years old, decided that perhaps he could help the Chinese people in another way rather than working as a doctor with one sick person at a time. Instead, he would turn to politics. He would devote his life to overthrowing the rule of the Manchus, replacing it with some form of socialism—a government that would *serve* the people instead of tyrannizing and exploiting them.

As a beginning, Sun put in writing his hopes and dreams for a better China. There should be free public education for all children; improvement in farm-

Seated, Dr. Sun Yat-sen, and his protégé, Chiang Kai-shek. *Chinese Information and Culture Center, New York.*

ing methods so that everyone could be fed; the building of new railroads, factories, and mines; and a strong modern army so that foreign countries no longer would be able to do as they pleased with China.

Sun tried to give the summary of his ideas to Li Hung-chang, a prominent reform leader. But Li would not even see him. Disappointed, Sun left for Honolulu. There, he worked with wealthy Chinese businessmen, trying to convince them to help bring about change in their native land. Most important, he organized a patriotic group, *Hsing-chung hui* (the Revive China Society). That society, he hoped, would educate friends of China and the Chinese people themselves about the need for revolution.

In 1894–1895, Japan easily defeated China in the Sino-Japanese War. The war revealed to the entire world just how weak the Manchu government really was, how incapable of protecting the nation against outsiders. In speeches and essays Sun Yat-sen used the lesson of the Sino-Japanese War to urge the Chinese people to rise up against their Manchu rulers.

In such a struggle, he said, the people clearly must have a leader. And because of his love for China, as well as his love of liberty, he could be that leader.

Nor was it best, said Sun, for the country simply to put a new person in charge, a new emperor. Rather, what was needed was a whole new kind of government, one that served the people—a Socialist government.

Traveling to Hong Kong, Sun began to gather guns, ammunition, and explosives for the coming revolution, one he hoped to launch in Canton in 1895. Somehow, the plot was discovered. Five of Sun's closest friends in the revolutionary Hsing-chung hui group were executed. Dozens more were thrown into prison.

Sun escaped to Macao. At the city gate he saw a picture poster of himself, announcing a reward for his capture. He fled next to Japan, where, to disguise himself, he cut off the long Manchu hair knot that, until then, he had still worn.

Finally, he took refuge in Hawaii. There, his brother Ah-mei sent for Sun's mother, as well as his wife and children, fearing that the Manchus would take revenge upon them for the deeds of the family head. Such was the custom in China at the time.

Sun did not remain in Hawaii for long. Still wearing the disguise intended to make him look Japanese, he traveled to the United States. There he tried to organize the Chinese in San Francisco and New York to work for revolution. Learning that the Chinese minister in Washington had given orders for his return to China, where he would be beheaded, he sailed for England.

Only a few days after arriving in London he met a friend, who took him on a tour of the Chinese legation there. It was a trap.

Sun was imprisoned in the legation, prior to being shipped back to China for execution. Somehow, however, he convinced one of his guards, a Christian, to notify Dr. James Cantlie of his situation. Cantlie, by then practicing medicine in London, convinced the British prime minister, Lord Salisbury, that seizing Sun Yat-sen had broken British law. Salisbury agreed. He protested strongly to the Chinese, thus winning Sun's immediate release.

British newspapers gave the incident spectacular coverage. Overnight, Sun became a well-known figure. He wrote a book called *Kidnapped in London*. He spoke to British audiences about the cause of Chinese freedom. He wrote articles in newspapers and magazines. For eight months he studied history, economics, and political theory at the British Museum—in the very library where Karl Marx and Vladimir Ilyich Lenin prepared themselves to play crucial roles in history as revolutionary leaders.

Despite his growing fame, Sun's global wanderings continued. They would drag on for the next sixteen years. During all of that time, agents of the Manchus pursued him, trying to kill him. Sometimes they came close to succeeding. In Nanking, in Canton, on Hainan Island, he narrowly escaped death. In Japan, using the Japanese name Nakayama, he worked for three years with Chinese students and others who had fled China in hopes of a better life.

Finally, in 1905 he became leader of the Alliance Society, a revolutionary group based in Tokyo.

Still, year after year passed without success. Sun encouraged one revolt after another in China, only to see each one crushed—ten in all. Eventually, the Japanese government politely gave him a sum of money and asked him to leave the country. In Hanoi, French Indochina, the French did the same. Even in Hong Kong and Singapore he was made to feel unwelcome.

In 1911, he returned to the United States, discouraged but still hoping to raise funds for his fading cause. After such a lengthy struggle many other leaders would have given up. But Sun did not give up. He spoke to groups of Americans, reminding them of Abraham Lincoln's call for government "of the people, by the people, for the people," as well as Jefferson's statement that "all men are created equal." He reminded them of Christianity—the revolutionary religion—preaching freedom and the equality of all human beings.

Meanwhile, in China, the Manchu empress unwillingly began to give in to the demands of her people for reform. Her brilliant young son, the emperor, leaped at the chance to create a new school system for children, to set up representative assemblies in the provinces, and to reorganize the army. The empress grew to hate her son for the changes he was making. Fatally ill, she had her servants poison him the day before she herself died.

The new Manchu monarch was a gentle young empress, ruling temporarily for the baby prince, her child. To the revolutionaries it was clear that, with such weakness on the throne, the time for rebellion was ripe.

In America, Sun Yat-sen tried to follow the rapidly unfolding events in his homeland. One day, while riding a train from Denver to Kansas City, he was startled to read a brief item in the newspaper. A rebellion had broken out against the Manchus in the Chinese city of Wuchang. The rebels had managed to overthrow the local government. And, continued the article, they intended to set up a new government in China based on the model of the United States of America—with Sun Yat-sen as their president!

Shocked, Sun decided to return at once to China. Stopping in England, he was able to persuade a group of international bankers to grant loans to the new Republic of China, if ever it should take power. The British, committed to democratic principles, also granted him the right to enter Singapore and Hong Kong without fear of arrest.

By the time Sun reached Nanking, the revolutionary armies had set up a national assembly. In America, only months before, Sun Yat-sen had been living in cheap rooming houses, hiding from secret agents of the Manchu government. Now, on New Year's Day, 1912, he formally was sworn in as president of the Republic of China.

Still, the Manchu government in Peking had not surrendered. Strong armies continued to support the old imperial regime. During his many years of travel Sun had planned every detail of what he would do when the day of his triumph finally came. Now he discovered that there was only one way to assure a stable new government—to give up his power to a strong man, General Yüan Shih-kai, hoping that he himself could work closely for reform with the general.

Knowing that Yüan's ideas were not so revolutionary as Sun's, the Manchu ruler finally agreed to give up the throne. As a result, the new republic included all of the Chinese nation.

Before long it became clear that Yüan had little concern for such ideas as democracy, much less the socialism Sun had hoped to establish. Instead, he soon began to call himself Emperor of China. When Sun helped organize a political party, the *Kuomintang* (Chinese Revolutionary party), to oppose Yüan, the general ordered him arrested.

Once again Sun Yat-sen was forced to flee from China, this time taking refuge in Japan. The Japanese, he hoped, would help him in exchange for future trading privileges in China. But by then the Japanese had become more ambitious, hoping for even greater power in China than Sun would ever be willing to give them.

When Yüan died in 1916, Sun Yat-sen once again expected to be president of the entire nation. Instead, he found himself forced to fight a series of bloody battles, civil wars against provincial warlords.

For all of his ability to state high ideals, to stir the people's hopes, it was clear by then that Sun had serious problems in actually using the powers of government. Often he planned badly, failed to act decisively, placed his trust in generals who betrayed him.

The wars continued. The north of China fought against the south. The central government fought against warlords. Once Sun had to flee from the city of Canton, returning to find all of his books and manuscripts burned.

Then, in 1919, the Treaty of Versailles, ending World War I, showed that the victorious powers cared little for the needs of China. Instead, they recognized the interest of Japan in certain key territories on the Asian mainland.

Sun Yat-sen decided that if Britain, France, the United States, and Japan refused to help him, there still might be one nation that would—the new revolutionary Communist government of Russia, by then renamed the Soviet Union.

Sun agreed to admit three Chinese Communists into leadership positions in his own Kuomintang party. In return, the Soviets provided him with money, with arms, and with political and military advisers. With the help of one Russian adviser, Mikhail Borodin, Sun reorganized the Kuomintang along the lines of the Russian Communist party, with power coming from the top down.

Still, Sun insisted on keeping as guiding principles of government his Three Principles of the People. Those three principles were: People's Rule, based on a strong sense of pride in Chinese nationalism; People's Authority, or the idea of democratic government as taught by a small group of well-educated leaders; and People's Livelihood, an economy drawing heavily on Socialist ideas, especially that of heavy taxes on the rich.

Soviet ideas and Soviet money still were not enough to unify China. More and more, Sun relied on an able young Kuomintang general, Chiang Kai-shek, to lead his forces. In 1923, based on Chiang's victories, Sun declared himself "generalissimo," leader of a new government. But all the world knew that the warlords in northern China still did not accept him. The civil wars continued.

Meanwhile, Sun began to suffer from an illness that did not go away. It was cancer. He became weaker. Returning from a trip to Japan, he retired to his bed, too weak even to speak.

On March 12, 1925, he died. His last words were "Peace—struggle—save my country."

In his lifetime Sun Yat-sen had endured failure after failure. Yet to achieve his ends—especially the unity of China—he always had tried to avoid brutal, violent means. He preferred talking to killing. At the same time, he resisted taking the easy path, that of becoming merely a pawn of the Soviet Union, or of the Communists in his own country. Instead, he shook his fist both at the Communists and at the Western world. The path he chose was his own.

After Sun's death, Chiang Kai-shek lost out in battle to the Chinese Communists, led by Mao Tse-tung. Chiang's forces fled to Taiwan.

Today, both the mainland Chinese and the Taiwanese consider Sun Yat-

Dr. Sun Yat-sen at his headquarters in Canton in 1924. *Eastphoto/Sovphoto*.

sen a hero. Both sides agree that he was the most important figure in the long struggle against the rule of the Manchus. By persisting, fighting on against all odds, it was he who wrenched the Chinese people out of the Dark Ages and thrust them into the modern world.

For that deed, he will long be remembered.

Kemal Atatürk

1881–1938   Founder and president of the modern Turkish nation

Once in the land of Macedon, about a century ago, there lived a Turkish schoolboy named Mustafa. He had no last name because most people in his country at the time did not use last names. Macedonia then was part of Turkey, although the ruling Turks received little respect from the Greeks, the Serbs, and the Bulgarians who lived there.

Mustafa first learned to write in Arabic letters, a style sometimes complex, difficult. But he was better off than most Turks, who could not read or write at all. People in the streets wore old-fashioned clothing, including a hat known as the fez. They followed the Muslim religion, often in a superstitious way. Women could not vote and had few personal rights in their married lives.

The Turkish government—inheritor of the ancient Ottoman Empire—was inefficient, backward, and often corrupt.

By the time of Mustafa's death, almost all of those conditions had changed. Turkey had become a smaller country, but a much stronger one. Turks could look proudly at their fine government, no longer in the hands of the Ottoman dynasty. The Turkish language now was written in simple, easy-to-learn Roman letters, often shared with Westerners in commerce, trade, and scholarship. At least in the major cities Turks wore Western clothing, as if they were in New York or London. Women had the right to vote and legal rights close to those of men. The Turkish nation had been transformed overnight—rescued from a state of decay

85

leading almost certainly to its death.

For almost all of the great changes that had taken place, one person was responsible—the Macedonian schoolboy Mustafa, grown to adult leadership. In secondary school he had become known as Mustafa Kemal, only to be dubbed Atatürk ("Father of the Turks") by the grateful people of his nation.

How could this Mustafa, born to a humble family in an outlying province of a dying empire, grow up to make such a profound difference in the affairs of his people?

Even the exact date of Mustafa's birth is uncertain, so unimportant did it seem at the time. We know only that it took place sometime in the year 1881 in Salonika, a bustling seaport city that today is part of Greece but then belonged to Turkish Macedonia.

His father, Ali Riza, worked as a clerk for the Ottoman government, a government so disorganized in collecting taxes that even its own employees never were certain they would be paid. Often Ali Riza received no money for his work. He grew increasingly discontented.

Mustafa's mother, Zübeyde Hanim, came from a poor family that long had lived in lands to the west. She, like Mustafa, had light hair, fair skin, blue eyes, very unlike most of the rough-featured, dark-skinned people on the eastern Macedonian coastline. Although intelligent, she had little education and was able to read and write only a few words. Zübeyde was, however, stubborn, serious, and fiercely proud, qualities she passed on to her son.

Even in elementary school Mustafa proved rebellious, hard to handle. In the traditional Muslim school he first attended, children were expected to sit cross-legged on the floor, writing on pads across their knees. One day Mustafa stood up, saying that it pained him to sit that way. When the teacher ordered him to sit down again, Mustafa defiantly refused. To the teacher's surprise, at Mustafa's command the other children stood up, too, obeying him rather than their own teacher.

Despite the popularity and respect Mustafa enjoyed among his classmates, he refused to join with them in the usual children's games. Instead, he very early became serious, grown-up, proudly standing apart from the other students. He also was sensitive: quick to take offense at what he considered an insult, quick to use his fists.

Meanwhile, Mustafa's father, unhappy over money problems, turned to heavy drinking. He became seriously ill. Then he died.

When Zübeyde moved with young Mustafa to her brother's home in the country, he refused to enroll in another

Muslim school. Zübeyde tried to have him tutored, but he declared that the tutor was ignorant. Nor would he take lessons from one of his mother's female friends, saying that he would not take instruction from a woman.

Without asking his mother's permission, or even telling her, Mustafa took the examination for entrance into the Military Secondary School in Salonika. He passed it. Then, declaring that he wanted to be a Turkish soldier more than anything else in life, he persuaded her to let him go. At the time, he was twelve years old.

Once at the school, Mustafa excelled in his studies, particularly mathematics. While other students of his age still were learning simple arithmetic, he already was working at algebra. It was his teacher, also named Mustafa, who was so impressed that he gave his young pupil the second name of "Kemal," meaning perfection. It was a name he would carry with him ever afterward.

Sometimes when the teacher had to leave the room, he would put young Mustafa in charge of the class, allowing him to teach the others while standing at the blackboard. The role of teacher especially pleased Mustafa. Already more mature than his classmates, he enjoyed the authority that went with teaching them.

At the age of fourteen Mustafa Kemal

enrolled in the Military Training School of Monastir. Much farther from home, he now became almost totally free of his mother's control. It was at Monastir, Turkey's finest military academy, that Kemal first grew concerned with national politics. As Greeks, Serbs, and Bulgarians demanded freedom from Turkish rule, the young cadet became passionate in his loyalty to the Turkish nation. Once he even tried to run away from school to join the combat forces in the field.

It was at Monastir, too, that Kemal began to broaden himself as a person. He came to enjoy poetry and music. He went often to the cafés, where he would dance and sing. Before long he turned to the companionship of women, especially Christians and Jews who, in contrast to Muslim women, wore no black veils and were easier to meet.

Even at that early age he found it difficult to resist the temptation of drinking. Like his father, alcohol would become a problem for him, one that in time became more serious.

Above all else, however, ambition came to govern Kemal's life. He was determined to excel—"to be somebody."

In 1899, he enrolled at the War College in Istanbul, Turkey's capital city. The report that came with Kemal described him as "a brilliant but difficult youth, one it is impossible to know well."

It was in Istanbul that he broadened his political education. He read classic works on government by such authors as Hobbes and Locke, Voltaire and Rousseau. He studied French, meanwhile making Napoleon his personal hero and life model.

Finally, he joined a revolutionary society, *Vatan* (Fatherland and Freedom), pledged to total change in Turkish society, beginning with the overthrow of Sultan Abdul Hamid II, the nation's ruler.

One night, government spies burst into a meeting of Vatan, arresting several of the members, including Kemal. He was thrown into prison, in solitary confinement. Alone, Kemal sulked for week after week, with little hope for the future. Then, suddenly, he was released. His regiment had been sent to Damascus, Syria, to battle Druse forces there, and he was urgently needed.

Holding the rank of captain, he left for Damascus. Once again, he tried to involve his comrades in the work of Vatan, but with little success. Returning to Salonika, he joined a branch of the Young Turk movement.

But, to Kemal, it seemed the Young Turks were not working for real change in Turkish life, only for the replacement of Abdul Hamid by another ruler.

Meanwhile, the group's leader, Enver, personally hated the ambitious Kemal and scoffed at his ideas for the future, describing them as far too extreme to succeed in actual practice.

In 1908, the Young Turk revolution broke out, with Mustafa Kemal playing only a minor role. Enver became head of the new Turkish government. For the next six years Kemal stayed largely in the background: learning, waiting for his chance to come.

Quickly, he advanced to the rank of major, then to lieutenant colonel. In the Balkan War of 1912, he was in charge of defending from Bulgarian attack the Gallipoli Peninsula, at the crucial Dardanelles straits. It was a learning experience that soon would be of major importance to him.

In August 1914, World War I began. Kemal was placed in command of Gallipoli, the outpost he had come to know so well. Wave after wave of British and Australian troops stormed the heights overlooking the Dardanelles, only to be thrown back by Kemal's forces. At nearby Suvla Bay he won again. Because of Mustafa Kemal, the straits remained in Turkish hands. The Turkish nation was saved from defeat. Overnight Kemal became a national hero— "the Saviour of Istanbul."

Next, he moved to the eastern front and defeated an advancing Russian

Kemal Atatürk in Turkish headdress. *Culver Pictures, Inc.*

army. As a reward he was given the rank of brigadier general.

But then his luck changed. Always outspoken, he openly criticized Turkey's German allies for being too defensive, failing to attack. Still bitterly jealous of him, Enver took advantage of the dispute to transfer Kemal to Palestine, where Turkish forces were being badly beaten by the British.

By the time he arrived there, it was too late to turn back the British. Soon afterward word came that the Central Powers, including Turkey, had signed the armistice ending World War I. In fear, Enver had fled the country, leaving it in the hands of Britain and the other victorious Allied powers.

Mustafa Kemal made his way back to Istanbul. On arriving there, he was shocked to see Allied troops tearing down the city's fortifications and giving orders to the local police force. Enemy forces had taken complete control of the community's famous port facilities.

Word soon spread that in the final peace treaty the Allies planned to demobilize the Turkish army. Then they would take away all of Turkey's overseas possessions, thus putting an end to the once great Ottoman Empire.

What was to be done? Many of Mustafa Kemal's friends urged that Turkey should be put under an American mandate to protect it from the other Allied powers, angry with the Turks and greedy for territory.

Kemal himself had a very different idea. He urged that a new Turkish nation should be formed. It would be smaller, with a well-trained army and a highly Westernized economy, complete with factories, highways, and a modern school system. No longer would there be a sultan, but a president, freely elected by the people.

Yet Kemal was still a soldier, pledged to follow the orders given to him. The weak-kneed sultan who had replaced Enver commanded that he go to eastern Anatolia, there to do as the British wished—disband and send home the Turkish forces still stationed there.

Instead, Kemal did just the opposite. He swiftly began to organize the Anatolian Turks as the basis for a new army. He contacted former officers he had worked with, along with governors of the eastern provinces, asking for their help.

Before long it was clear that Mustafa Kemal would not simply obey the sultan's orders. As in the incident with his elementary school teacher, when he refused to sit down and cross his legs, Mustafa was not afraid to disobey an authority figure.

Meanwhile, seeing the weakness of the Turks, their ancient enemies, the Greeks, landed an enormous army at

Izmir. With permission in advance from the Allies, Greece agreed to crush Kemal. In exchange, Greece was to receive Turkish territory both in Europe and in Asia.

Faced with an invasion by the hated Greeks, the Turkish people united in defiance. They rushed to the side of Kemal. When the sultan, furious, dismissed Kemal from his military command, he responded at once by completely resigning his army commission.

Soon he was in open rebellion against the government. The sultan announced that anyone who killed him would receive a reward of money in this world and the blessings of Allah in the world to come.

To dethrone the sultan, Kemal formed a new national government. At the first meeting of its delegate assembly, held at Ankara in April 1920, Kemal was elected president. He also was given the title of prime minister.

At that point, Mustafa Kemal's task was simple: all he had to do was defeat the entire army of the sultan, as well as to expel from Turkey the well-armed troops of Greece and the other foreign countries that had invaded his beloved homeland. Even for so great a warrior as Kemal, the job seemed formidable, perhaps even impossible.

Proceeding at once, Kemal moved to achieve the impossible. In eastern Turkey he defeated the Armenians and the Soviet Georgians, even gaining back Turkish territory lost many years before. In the south he pushed French forces back into Syria. Most important, he repelled a strong Greek attack on Ankara and began to push the Greeks back toward the Mediterranean Sea.

After those victories the British arranged a peace treaty. Turkey once again was given complete control of Istanbul. The Greeks agreed to leave Turkish soil. By the Treaty of Lausanne, signed on July 24, 1923, Turkey became a completely independent nation. The sultan fled offshore to a British vessel, carrying with him bags of gold, as well as the golden coffee cups of the Ottoman Empire.

Six hundred years of Ottoman rule at last had ended.

On October 29, 1923, an election took place. At its conclusion Mustafa Kemal, the rebellious schoolboy of Salonika, stood alone as leader of his people. He had become the president of Turkey.

With his usual energy Kemal moved swiftly to transform Turkey into the dynamic modern state he so long had dreamed it might become. To come into the present, he believed, the most important first step was to separate church and state—to get the Islamic religion

Atatürk abandoned the Arabic script, in which Turkish had been written since the ninth century, in favor of the Roman alphabet. In this photograph, taken in 1928, he teaches the Roman alphabet in Constantinople. *Turkish Culture and Information Office, New York.*

out of the business of government. Like America and the other great nations of the West, Turkey must become a secular state, one concerned with *this* world, not the world to come after death.

Kemal at once closed many Islamic monasteries, turning them into museums. "Science," he said, "is the most reliable guide to life." He made the wearing of the fez, the Islamic hat, illegal, dramatizing the announcement by appearing before a huge crowd while wearing a Panama straw hat. Even more importantly, he threw out entirely the Islamic codes of civil and criminal justice, substituting for them legal systems used in the West. Like his personal hero, Napoléon, he considered the code of justice a good barometer of how democratic a nation really is.

Next, he understood that a modern nation had to be an industrialized nation. And industry requires an educated population. When first he became president, less than 10 percent of the Turkish population could read and write. So Kemal put into place the easy-to-learn Roman alphabet and then personally toured the country, using a blackboard, as in a classroom, to show people how to use the letters.

Under his guidance a whole new system of public schools came into being. He insisted that in these schools there should be special emphasis on the history of the Turkish nation. Nationalism, not religion, he said, would unite the Turkish people, give them a commonly shared sense of purpose and direction.

Finally, he insisted that every Turk should have the dignity of a last name, not simply be known by occupation, as in "Ali the tin worker." The idea of last names became law, leading the National Assembly to bestow upon Mustafa Kemal a new name, too. Beginning in 1933, he became known to the world as Kemal Atatürk (Father of the Turks).

No person in modern Turkish history ever had achieved such popularity as Atatürk. Yet as he grew older, his personal life became increasingly unhappy.

In 1922, he had married. His wife,

Latife Hanim, was a woman of wealth and education. For all of his early life Atatürk, like most men in the Middle East, had considered women as objects to be used rather than as people to be loved. Now, under Atatürk's guidance, Turkish law was changed to make them the equals of men. As in the West, they were to be respected. They were given the right to vote.

Yet in his own life Kemal Atatürk did not want to change his old habits. He still expected his wife to serve him, as in a harem. Although he respected Latife's mind, he insisted on being master of his house.

Latife, proud and tactless, often embarrassed him. When Kemal's guests, many of them old military friends, would stay late into the night, drinking and singing, she would angrily demand that they leave. She grew jealous when any other woman was near to Kemal, her hero turned husband. She nagged him. She taunted him because of his humble background.

Finally, Kemal had enough. He divorced Latife. Then, like his father, Atatürk turned to drink. As a result, for the closing years of his life he almost always was ill with serious liver problems.

At the same time, he grew discouraged that so many of the changes he had hoped to bring about in modernizing Turkish life were affecting only the rich and the people living in major cities. Turks working on farms, especially in the eastern part of the country, continued to live as their ancestors had lived for hundreds of years.

Still, as he grew old and ill he knew that his life had made a difference.

On November 10, 1938, Kemal Atatürk died.

In a frenzy of emotion the Turkish people mourned the man who almost singlehandedly had saved their nation from destruction.

Sometimes cruel, usually domineer-ing and unwilling to compromise, Atatürk had tried to give the people what, in his own mind, he thought was best for them. True, he had offended religious Muslims by his public attack on them and by the wildness of his personal life. Yet he had moved swiftly, if often ruthlessly, to convert Turkey into a free and democratic nation.

And if, as some have said of him, he was incapable of loving other human beings, there is no doubt about what Kemal Atatürk truly did love—the land he had done so much to re-create— Turkey.

Benito Mussolini

1883–1945 Organizer of Italy's Fascist dictatorship and close ally of Germany's Adolf Hitler

From 1922 to 1945 Benito Mussolini ruled the Italian nation with an iron fist. He was a dictator, demanding total loyalty from the people of Italy. Each citizen, he said, must promise blind faith to him and to his government, as stated in Mussolini's famous slogan: *Credere, Obbedire, Combattere* (Believe, Obey, Fight).

Known as *Il Duce* ("the leader"), Benito Mussolini's picture hung in every classroom in the land. Beneath the portrait a statement declared, "Mussolini is always right!" Schoolchildren, like adults, were taught that they must surrender themselves totally to the needs of their nation and its leader. To do what they were told to do eventually would work for the good of all Italian citizens.

Meanwhile, all voices of opposition,

all disagreement, must be crushed. The people were to be disciplined. In casual, lighthearted Italy, the trains were to be made to run on time, and the beggars were to be removed from the streets.

To Mussolini, establishing order inside the country was only a first step. When that had taken place, the people could be mobilized for the real struggle—war. "War alone," shouted Benito Mussolini, "brings up to their highest tension all human energies and puts the stamp of nobility upon peoples who have the courage to meet it." Only a weak nation, said Mussolini, desired peace. And such a nation certainly would be crushed in combat with a strong, vigorous people who welcomed sacrifice and danger.

Such ideas as peace and harmony,

kindness and compassion, declared the Italian dictator, were only signs of weakness. The whole Italian nation, demanded Mussolini, must be militarized, must be "in a permanent state of war."

A humble corporal during World War I, Benito Mussolini rose to power almost overnight as founder and leader of the Fascist party. In the 1930s, some Italians came to worship him almost as a god. For a time he stirred his people to a sense of pride and national purpose. He awakened the image of a new Roman Empire, recalling the glory of the ancient Caesars.

Then, allied with Germany's Adolf Hitler in World War II, he was reduced by military defeats to disgrace and unpopularity. Finally, he died a humiliating death.

Nevertheless, there is much to be learned from the story of Benito Mussolini, the first of the world's modern dictators.

The man destined to govern the Italian nation as its *duce* (leader) was born the son of poor peasant farmers. His mother, Rosa, a deeply religious Catholic, came from a middle-class family. His father, Alessandro, who was very poor, hated all kinds of religions and was a Socialist. Mussolini's father sometimes was thrown into jail for political articles he wrote in opposition to the government, urging people on to revolution and the establishment of a Marxist economy for all of Italy.

Benito himself was named by his father in honor of the Mexican revolutionary leader, Benito Juárez. For the first three years of his childhood, young Mussolini did not speak a word in spite of all that his worried parents did to encourage him. By the age of five, he had learned not only to speak well but also to read.

Throughout Benito's childhood the family remained poor, in part because his father was so much involved in politics. Most of the time the family meals were only vegetable soup and unleavened bread. On Sundays, as a special treat, dinner included a pound of meat. At night Benito shared a straw mattress with his younger brother, Arnaldo, in a room that during the day served as a kitchen.

By the age of eight Benito had become the leader of a gang of wild young boys who roamed through the neighborhood fighting and stealing. Sometimes they swam together in the Rabbi River, near their hometown of Predappio.

When young Mussolini's mother tried to persuade him to attend church services, he refused. Instead, he would climb a tree outside the church and pelt passing church members—sometimes even the priests—with stones and acorns. At a school run by his mother, he enjoyed pinching his classmates until they screamed.

When Benito was nine, his parents enrolled him in a church school in a town about twenty miles from Predappio. There, things were even worse for the mischievous boy. Once, when he was naughty, a priest struck him. In a wild rage Mussolini hit back at the priest and then threw an inkwell at him.

His announced punishment was to kneel for twelve days, four hours a day, on a rough square of corn grain—unless he would agree to beg for forgiveness. Bleeding and suffering great pain, Benito refused to give in to the priests who had hoped to humble him.

The next year, he stabbed a classmate in the thigh with a pocketknife. Finally, he was expelled from the school.

At another school, preparing boys to become teachers, Mussolini stabbed a classmate in the buttocks for causing him to smudge a paper he was working on.

As a teenager, however, Mussolini began to display his very substantial intelligence, especially in classwork demanding writing and speaking ability. He had a powerful voice. He wrote speeches attacking the Italian government and then practiced them aloud

for many hours before presenting them. He read books recalling the achievements of the nation's ancient emperors. But he also read and reread the revolutionary works of such modern radicals as Marx and Bakunin.

At the age of eighteen, Mussolini became a teacher in the town of Gualtieri, in charge of a class filled with forty wriggling sixth-graders. On the first day of school he dramatically appeared before his class wearing a flowing black cape, a black tie, and a black hat with an enormous broad brim.

He was less interested in teaching, however, than in his activities during the evenings: drinking and making love with the women of Gualtieri. At the end of the school year he was told that his contract would not be renewed. Instead of regret, Mussolini felt almost a sense of relief. Rather than teaching, he now had good reason to face "the real world"—and to conquer it.

The fight proved more difficult than he expected. Traveling to Lausanne, Switzerland, he was shocked to find only one kind of work available to him: manual labor. For six days he pushed a wheelbarrow filled with bricks 121 times a day to the second floor of an unfinished building. Then, exhausted, his clothing torn to shreds, he quit.

For the next few days he roamed the streets of Lausanne, hungry and discouraged. Once he snatched the picnic lunch of two old ladies sitting on a park bench. At night he sometimes slept in a packing crate under a bridge or in a public washroom. The police finally arrested him for vagrancy and threw him in jail.

After his release from prison Mussolini approached a group of Socialists in a restaurant. They found him a place to live and then gave him part-time work writing for their local newspaper.

Before long he earned a job working for a labor union in Lausanne. Living mostly on an allowance from his mother, he spoke to meetings of workers and wrote articles on behalf of the working class. More and more, he devoted his time to politics, especially to reading and writing about socialism. In his pocket he carried a medallion bearing a picture of Karl Marx, the founder of modern communism.

Increasingly, Mussolini's speeches were filled with hatred of the rich, along with calls for violent revolution in order to bring down the capitalist system.

After returning to Italy to serve a required term in the army, he established contacts with that nation's Socialists and began especially to champion the cause of Italian farm workers. By the age of twenty-five he was a well-known figure in the Socialist party of Italy.

Before long he was editing his own weekly magazine, *La Lotta di Classe* (*The Class Struggle*). Still urging violence—bloodshed—as the way to solve social problems, he once demanded in the city of Forlì that the mayor have the price of milk reduced for the poor. If not, said Mussolini, he would have the mayor thrown out of a window. The price of milk was reduced.

Meanwhile, Mussolini had fallen madly in love with a sixteen-year-old girl, Rachele Guidi. When the girl's mother opposed the relationship, Benito drew a pistol, threatening to kill Rachele and then commit suicide. Again, through violence, he got his way. Soon the two were married.

As a political leader, Mussolini worked to become a masterful speaker. He learned how to use dramatic gestures, how to arouse the emotions of an audience with bursts of fiery eloquence, how to build a speech to a fiery climax.

By the end of 1912, Benito Mussolini had become a member of the executive committee of the Italian Socialist party. When the party needed a new editor for its national newspaper, *Avanti!* (*Forward!*), Mussolini was chosen. Before long he was writing all of the paper's articles on politics. As a result, the journal's circulation doubled. Then it doubled again.

Benito Mussolini exhorting a crowd. *Culver Pictures, Inc.*

In August 1914, World War I began. Europe exploded in bloody conflict. Nation after nation threw in its lot with the Central Powers (Germany and Austria) or with the Allies (Great Britain, France, and Russia). The Italians, however, stood by, watching and waiting, undecided what their role in the conflict should be.

At first Mussolini used the pages of *Avanti!* to thunder his hatred of the struggle. "Down with the war," he cried. "Down with fighting!" Like most Socialists of the time, Mussolini portrayed warfare as an important way in which the upper class, such as factory owners, managed to stay in power, with poor people doing the actual fighting.

Gradually, however, Mussolini began to change his mind. He feared the danger to Italy if France, a liberal country, lost the war. He also was concerned that an Austrian victory would threaten Italy's northern provinces.

Finally, he came to believe that an Italian victory in the war could mean the addition of important territorial prizes, particularly the cities of Trent, Trieste, and Fiume. His articles in *Avanti!* grew more and more favorable to Italy's entry into the war on the side of the Allies.

Because of that stance most Italian Socialists grew increasingly furious with Mussolini. They demanded that he re-sign his position as editor of *Avanti!* Finally, he was left with no real choice. He resigned.

Soon afterward he began publishing his own newspaper, *Il Popolo d'Italia* (*The People of Italy*). In it, he called for bold action to gain Italy's objectives. His program demanded the use of bayonets and blood, or as he concluded simply—"WAR!"

At the age of thirty-one, Mussolini himself donned a uniform and soon found himself in combat. Surprisingly, he proved to be a hard-working, spirited soldier. He even won a medal for his brave conduct.

Then, in February 1917, a cannon he was helping to fire on the front line of combat became overheated and exploded. More than forty pieces of metal became embedded in his body.

For more than a month Mussolini suffered great pain. He underwent twenty-seven operations, all but two of them without anesthetics. His fever soared so high that he did not know where he was.

Slowly, Mussolini recovered. Then, in November 1918, the war ended. Like other Italian soldiers, he discovered that peacetime brought with it massive shortages of consumer goods. There were few jobs to be had. And to the anger of Mussolini and many of his war-time comrades, the Allies failed to satisfy Italy's claims to such territories as Fiume and the Dalmatian Coast.

On March 23, 1919, Mussolini met in Milan with about fifty men, most of them veterans of the war. The group members organized themselves as a *fascio di combattimento* (a fighting squad). From that first meeting was born the Fascist party, an organization destined eventually to take control of all of Italy.

From the very beginning the Fascists took to the streets. Often they paraded in black shirts and black Turkish-style hats. They sang a wartime combat song, *"Giovinezza"* ("Youth"). In their hands they carried daggers, as well as a black flag bearing the stark white emblem of a skull.

Mussolini himself was known as Il Duce (pronounced doo-chay). Whenever he appeared in public, his followers would loudly begin the rhythmic chant: "Duce! Duce! Duce!"

A growing number of army veterans flocked to join the Fascist party, seeing it as the only group that defended the honor of Italy against other nations while holding out the promise of jobs, lower prices for goods, and an end to the widespread crime wave that gripped postwar Italy.

As their numbers grew, Mussolini had Fascist action squads bomb and set fire to Communist and Socialist head-

quarters offices. The Fascists took over trains and operated them, allowing passengers to ride without charge. More and more Italians came to believe that no matter how violent the methods of the Fascists, anything was better than the continuation of civil conflict. The Fascists promised to end the disorder and to restore peace.

On October 27, 1922, some 50,000 Fascist soldiers gathered for a march on Rome. Fearing a bloody civil war, King Victor Emmanuel III agreed to appoint Mussolini prime minister of Italy.

At 11:15 A.M. on October 30, Benito Mussolini, the total outsider, a man born to poverty and exposed to little formal schooling, took power in the land of classical grandeur where once the lofty Caesars had held sway.

Without any sign of indecision, Mussolini plunged into action. In his office by eight every morning, he rarely left before nine in the evening, usually taking only a few minutes for lunch. He wrote hundreds of letters and telegrams, met with cabinet ministers in sessions lasting five or six hours, and still managed to attend almost every important public ceremony. By Mussolini's order, the year 1922 became the Year I of the Fascist Era, a designation carried on all public documents along with the usual calendar date.

Slowly, Italy returned to normal. Confidence was restored. The value of the lira, the basic Italian currency, increased. Year after year the wheat crop grew larger. Instead of a deficit, the national budget showed a surplus. In his dealings with other countries, such as Greece, Mussolini showed firmness. In exchange for a few concessions he persuaded Yugoslavia to give up to Italy the disputed city of Fiume.

In April 1924, Mussolini called a national election. It was a smashing victory for him and for the Fascist party —four and a half million votes to two and a half million for all of his opponents combined.

Even the assassination of Giacomo Matteotti, a Socialist who had vigorously opposed him, did not destroy the public's confidence in Il Duce. Although Mussolini had not ordered the assassination, he did not resign. Instead, he took full responsibility for the killing.

After the Matteotti incident he no longer tried to compromise with his opponents or allow them to speak out against him. The practice of holding free elections was ended. Now, using brute force, Mussolini moved swiftly to convert Italy into a Fascist dictatorship— one that he would rule with all the power of the ancient Roman emperors.

Step by step, the Fascist government tightened its control. All but the mildest of the opposition newspapers were closed. Local officials were appointed by the Fascist party. The Fascist Grand Council chose the members of the Chamber of Deputies. The power of labor unions was sharply reduced.

In building the Fascist state, Mussolini paid special attention to youth. At the age of six, every Italian boy was given his own black shirt and toy machine gun. Then, step by step, the boy was given military training, drilled in physical exercises, and encouraged to be a loyal Italian Fascist.

In the first ten years of his rule Mussolini transformed Italy. There were hundreds of new bridges and thousands of miles of new roads. Telephone exchanges were set up. New hospitals and universities were built. The Pontine Marshes, malarial swamps since before the days of Julius Caesar, were drained, and new farms and towns laid out on the reclaimed land.

Although the Fascist government seized ever greater control over the lives of Italy's citizens, little opposition developed. Most Italians were content to accept harsh laws and restrictions on free speech as a fair price for the advantages of Fascism that they could see all around them. As one foreign observer put it, "The beggars were off the street and the trains ran on time."

To many Italians, Mussolini became an almost superhuman figure. A likeness of his head appeared on scores of products, including women's bathing suits, soap, and baby food.

Before long, Mussolini himself, like an actor, began to believe his own lines. The pomp of parades and uniforms, Fascist salutes and displays of aerial might—all intended at first to impress the public—eventually became real to him. Forgetting that these spectacles of military strength were all for show, without real substance, he came to regard Italy as a mighty power on the world scene, as he truly wished it to be.

Mussolini's personal vanity and his desire to make Italy a mighty world power led him into an alliance with one of history's most evil figures, the German dictator Adolf Hitler. At first it was Hitler who borrowed from—learned from—Mussolini. Hitler copied Mussolini's use of spectacular military parades, youth organizations, and propaganda. He even called himself *Der Fuehrer* (the leader), the German equivalent of Il Duce.

But there were important differences between the two dictators. While Hitler believed in a "Master Race," Mussolini thought that racial and religious prejudice was "absolute nonsense—stupid and idiotic." Also, while the German

leader was prepared to take any risk to achieve his dreams of military conquest, Mussolini was more cautious, more willing to weigh the cost of military action.

In 1934, with Hitler's encouragement, Mussolini launched an attack on Ethiopia, a nation in eastern Africa. Despite the protests of Britain and France, the Italians succeeded in conquering the militarily weak African country.

From a balcony overlooking the Palazzo Venezia in Rome, Mussolini received the cheers of thousands of Italians packed together in the square below. "Italy," said Mussolini, "has at last her Empire—a Fascist Empire. . . . Will you be worthy of this Empire?" he asked.

"Si! Si! Si!" returned the crowd wildly. "Duce! Duce! Duce!" they shouted, while Mussolini, expressionless, his jaw set firmly, savored the glory of his triumph.

What Il Duce could not know was that the evening he was enjoying would mark the high point of his career. The future, for him, would be increasingly grim.

With each succeeding year Mussolini fell more under the influence—and the control—of Adolf Hitler. Beginning in 1936, the two dictators joined together to help Francisco Franco in his agoniz-

In 1939 Mussolini reviews Fascist women celebrating in Rome the twentieth anniversary of the founding of the National Fascist Party in Italy. *UPI/Bettmann.*

ing, but successful, struggle to establish a Fascist government in Spain. Then, in 1938, he won Hitler's lasting gratitude when he stood by—did nothing— as Nazi troops gobbled up Austria, a neighbor to both of the aggressive Fascist states. Finally, at the Munich conference in 1938, he assisted Hitler in convincing the British and French that Germany deserved to annex the heavily industrialized Sudetenland, then belonging to Czechoslovakia.

In May 1939, Italy signed a formal treaty of alliance with Germany. Known as the Pact of Steel, the agreement pledged each country to aid the other in the event of war.

On September 1, Hitler sent his troops into Poland, triggering the onset of World War II.

At first Mussolini held back, realizing that his army was not prepared for war against such major powers as Britain and France. Then, in June 1940, dreaming of glory and territorial prizes, he ordered his troops into neighboring

France. As President Franklin Delano Roosevelt of the United States put it, "The hand that held the dagger has struck it into the back of its neighbor."

From the beginning, the war against France went badly for Italy. So, too, did Italian military operations in Egypt and in Greece. Italian ships in the Mediterranean suffered high casualties from attacks by British planes.

Finally, in July 1943, British, Canadian, and American troops crossed over from North Africa and invaded Sicily, at the toe of the boot-shaped Italian peninsula. Sicilian villagers welcomed them not as conquerors but as liberators from the rule of Mussolini.

On July 24, 1943, the Fascist Grand Council met. Its members sharply criticized Mussolini for destroying the Fascist revolution by fighting a war that served largely to further Hitler's goals. The council returned a vote of no confidence concerning Mussolini's continued rule. The next day, the king of Italy demanded and received Mussolini's resignation.

When word of their once beloved leader's resignation reached the streets of Rome, crowds of people gathered to cheer the news.

Under heavy guard Mussolini was taken to a hotel in the Apennine Mountains. It was there, in September 1943, that a German commando group, acting under Hitler's orders, crash-landed in gliders and rescued him.

Two days later, with tears in his eyes, Hitler personally greeted his one-time teacher.

Giving in to Hitler's wishes, Mussolini agreed to form a new Fascist government in northern Italy, known as the Salò Republic. By then it was clear to all, however, that Mussolini was attached to Hitler as a puppet, with the Nazi dictator pulling the strings.

In April 1945, while Allied troops began closing in on Berlin, Hitler decided to move Mussolini northward to prevent him from making terms for a separate peace.

At a roadblock near the Swiss border, Italian partisans stopped the truck in which Mussolini was riding. One of them recognized the once powerful Duce, although he had slouched down low in the cab of the truck and was wearing dark glasses, as well as a German combat helmet and a heavy German overcoat with the collar turned up.

Meekly, the Italian dictator surrendered the tommy gun he carried across his lap and the pistol he had hidden in his belt. Pale and exhausted, he resigned himself to his fate.

The next morning, Mussolini and his favorite woman companion, Clara Petacci, were taken to a waiting car and down a twisting country road. After a few miles, the car stopped in front of a lonely country estate, where Mussolini and his companion were asked to stand against a wall.

"No, no, you mustn't!" declared Clara Petacci, throwing herself in front of the Duce to protect him. A single shot rang out, and she fell dead.

Calmly, Mussolini opened his jacket. "Shoot me in the chest," he said.

A hail of machine-gun fire killed him instantly.

That afternoon the blood-spattered corpses of Mussolini and Clara Petacci were thrown into a truck. In the early morning hours of April 29, 1945, they were dumped, without ceremony, on the cobblestones of the Piazza Loreto in nearby Milan.

Later in the morning a mob, crazed for vengeance on their former leader, kicked and stoned the bodies. Then the crowd hung the battered corpses upside down from a construction girder on the side of an unfinished gas station.

So ended, without glory, the life of a man who craved glory above all else. Despite the dazzling parades, the immense gatherings, the heroic trappings of state, Benito Mussolini understood that he had created little that actually was new, or lasting. He dazzled, astonished, hypnotized the masses. But he contributed little toward the solution of the basic problem of politics: how best to govern a people.

Rather than shaping events, he was shaped by them. Or, as Il Duce once put it with the colorful flair that typified his own life, "Sometimes history takes one by the throat."

Joseph Stalin

1879–1953   Succeeded Lenin as ruler of the Soviet Union, eventually raising that nation to rivalry with the United States in world leadership

Once, during the civil war that followed the Russian Revolution, a father and his two young sons were brought to the desk of a Red Army field commander, accused of sympathy for those in power before the revolution. Without hearing the evidence—scarcely even looking up from his work—the commander ordered, "Shoot them!"

That Red Army officer, Joseph Stalin, was destined to become dictator of all Russia and leader of a regime that reached around the globe. To the people of his own country, Stalin's slightest wish was law. His picture, watchful and stern, appeared in the schools, factories, and public squares of Moscow. But it also peered from the walls of dreary huts and hovels in distant Siberia, where in subzero temperatures wretched prisoners struggled to stay alive, condemned for even hinting at criticism of Stalin, the "beloved father" and "savior of the Soviet peoples."

Brooding and cautious, Stalin appeared only rarely in public and was known personally by only a few close associates. Yet, suspicious even of those within his tiny inner circle, he ruthlessly ordered the killing of comrades who had helped him rise to power.

For all of his murderous repression, Stalin achieved incredible successes. To build the industrially backward, militarily weak Russian nation into a world power, he forced millions of Russians to work on huge collective farms and factories. Those who refused were immediately shot to death or imprisoned in Siberia.

In 1941, Adolf Hitler's advancing German armies pushed to the very gates of Moscow. Stalin, as his nation's leader, personally rallied the Russian people to heroic and terrible sacrifices to halt the seemingly unbeatable Nazis, eventually leading his forces to shattering victories over Hitler. In the postwar world he organized the rebuilding of his devastated land. Then, armed with atomic weapons, he set out to challenge the United States, keystone nation in the alliance of non-Communist countries.

Clearly, Joseph Stalin is one of history's great leaders, one whose brutal but no doubt gigantic achievements shaped the lives of millions around the world. Yet, for all of his enormous conquests at home and abroad, there is much about him—especially in his personal life—that, even today, remains a fascinating mystery.

Joseph Stalin's real name was Joseph Vissarionovich Djugashvili. He was born in 1879 in Gori, a small town near the Black Sea in the Russian province of Georgia. His first home was a rented house with only one room and a cellar. For furniture there was a table and four chairs, a bed covered with a straw mattress, and a lamp. All of the family's clothing hung on a few pegs driven into the walls. Cooking was done in the cel-

lar. In later years, that house—Stalin's birthplace—was destined to become a national museum, a shrine attracting tourists from countries around the world.

Before Joseph was born, Keke, his mother, had given birth to three sons, but all three had died in infancy. As a result, when he appeared she hovered over him with great care, lavishing him with love and affection.

His father, Vissarion, a boot maker, could neither read nor write. Unable to support his family, he turned to drink, often returning home to beat his wife and child mercilessly. When Joseph was four years old his father took a job in a shoemaking factory in Tiflis (now Tbilisi), some thirty miles from Gori, visiting his family only occasionally. Eventually he was killed in a drunken brawl in a tavern.

To feed and clothe young Joseph and herself, Keke Djugashvili worked as a dressmaker and washerwoman. She sacrificed everything else in her life for the sake of her son, building in him a strong sense of pride and self-confidence.

When he was seven Joseph (or Soso, as he was called) caught smallpox. For the rest of his life his face was marked by scars and deep pits caused by the disease. Shortly afterward he was struck by a carriage, badly injuring his left arm. It was a wound from which the arm never completely recovered, leaving it permanently two to three inches shorter than the other.

Childhood friends later recalled that Soso, after so many years of severe beatings by his father, seemed to enjoy inflicting pain on others. Once he dropped a brick down a neighbor's chimney onto a lighted fire, badly burning the people in the room. He would have contests with other boys to see who could kill the most chickens. In sports and games he bullied the smaller, weaker boys while patiently waiting for his chance to trick those too big to overpower. Except for his mother, he appears to have shown neither love nor sympathy for any living thing.

Because Soso's mother hoped he would become a priest in the Russian Orthodox Church, he attended church-sponsored schools. He did exceptionally well in school, winning a full scholarship—room, board, and tuition—to the theological seminary at Tiflis, where priests were trained.

Soso had no intention of ever becoming a priest. By the age of thirteen he had stopped believing in God. Instead, his hero became Koba, a storybook hero who championed the cause of Georgian freedom from Russian control. Koba defended the poor and the helpless. He fought for revolutionary change.

By the time he was eighteen Joseph Djugashvili no longer even pretended that he believed in God. As a result he was expelled from the seminary. But he did not mind. Instead of working for God he had decided to give himself over totally to a new cause: the cause of revolution—struggling on behalf of the poor and the oppressed. To do that, he decided to take on a new identity, even a new name. Not surprisingly, the name he chose was Koba (the Indomitable).

Even before he left the seminary young Djugashvili was a Marxist, a follower of the German political thinker Karl Marx. Marx, along with his friend Friedrich Engels, founded the system known to the world as communism. According to Marx and Engels, all of history is the story of the rich oppressing the poor. The two men taught in their writings that, ultimately, revolution would break out and the whole world would be changed. Poverty would end and the world would become a paradise for workers.

Joseph Djugashvili believed that, as "Koba," his special mission was to spread the idea of Marxist revolution to the workers. The czar, the powerful ruler of all Russia, must first be overthrown. Then a Communist state could be set up for the good of all.

To gain those ends Koba tried to get

railroad workers to strike. He organized protest meetings in the city of Tiflis. When Cossack horsemen charged into a crowd of workers and killed many of them, Koba was delighted. The bloodier the street demonstrations, he thought, the sooner the masses would turn against the government and overthrow the czar.

In the years that followed, Koba became a fanatical worker for the cause of revolution. In 1902, he was arrested by the police and sent to a prison in western Georgia. While in prison he learned about a split in the Russian Social Democratic party. One wing of that party, headed by Vladimir Ilyich Lenin, argued that after the revolution succeeded, the new government should be headed by a small group of totally dedicated leaders. Those few leaders, not the masses, said Lenin, should make all the important decisions in organizing the workers' paradise.

From the very beginning, Joseph Djugashvili agreed with Lenin's view and with that particular wing of the Social Democratic party, known ever afterward as Bolsheviks. Lenin, whom he had never met, became his hero—the "mountain eagle," as he called him, of the coming revolution.

Koba was sent to prison in frigid Siberia for his revolutionary deeds. But he escaped. Then he led raids, including a spectacularly successful bank robbery in the main square of Tiflis.

Sometime after escaping from Siberia he married and soon afterward had a son. The woman he married had worked with him in the Tiflis revolutionary movement. She idolized him as "her beloved Soso" and considered him a man of destiny. He, in turn, loved her dearly.

Then, in 1908, about a year after the birth of their son, Koba's wife fell ill with pneumonia and died. She had, as he put it, "softened my stony heart."

With her death, whatever warmth, whatever affection he may have had for other human beings appears to have disappeared. From that point on Joseph Djugashvili-Koba, as one friend put it, became "ruthless with himself . . . ruthless with everyone else."

Following the death of his wife, Koba threw himself totally into the affairs of the Bolshevik party. He attended meetings abroad, in Stockholm and London, finally meeting personally with Lenin. He wrote pamphlets. He edited a secret party newspaper, having personally stolen the printing press.

At this time, to evade the police, he made an important change. While using many names in his professional writing, he most frequently began to call himself by a new name, Stalin (the man of steel).

Many times he was arrested and imprisoned. In one prison, as punishment for rioting, inmates were forced to run between two lines of guards, who beat them with rifle butts. To show his contempt for the guards, Stalin walked slowly and defiantly with a book under his arm between the two lines of soldiers, his head held high. Even afterward, bleeding and battered, he would not allow himself to cry out or to admit pain. Many years later, other prisoners still remembered his icy control over himself.

Between terms in prison Stalin rose higher in the Bolshevik party. Considered crude and ill-mannered by many Bolsheviks, he nonetheless was recognized for his talent. When he was only thirty-three years old, Lenin personally chose him for the party's Central Committee.

In the summer of 1914, when World War I broke out, Stalin was serving a term in the grim penal colony of Kureika, in the frigid Arctic Circle. Since it was virtually impossible to escape from Kureika and return to civilization alive, Stalin feared that his political career might be at an end.

Then, in 1917, with explosive suddenness everything changed. A popular revolution broke out in Russia against Czar Nicholas II, the nation's leader in World War I. Tired of the war, with its enormous casualties, desperate for food, peasants and workers rose in rebellion. Czar Nicholas gave up his throne. Middle-class liberals led by Alexander Kerensky took over the new government.

Kerensky granted amnesty—forgiveness—to all political prisoners, freeing them immediately. Stalin at once left for Petrograd, where he took charge of the Communist party's Central Committee until Lenin's arrival three weeks later.

Lenin called for an immediate revolution to take power from Kerensky and to establish Communist rule, organized through Communist councils of peasants and workers known as "Soviets." Communists marched in the streets of Petrograd. They waved banners demanding:

LAND FOR THE PEASANTS!
BREAD FOR THE WORKERS!
PEACE FOR THE SOLDIERS!
ALL POWER TO THE SOVIETS!

One attempted revolt failed. Then, on October 25, 1917, a second attempt succeeded easily. "All Power to the Soviets!" had become a reality.

Lenin appointed Stalin to an inner circle of seven party leaders, known as the Political Bureau, or "Politburo," responsible for giving direction to the party. He also was one of four men on the Central Committee, with the right to decide on all "emergency" questions.

At first, his assigned job was commissar for nationalities, with the responsibility for bringing together the many diverse national groups that later made up the Soviet Union.

But, like all the other party leaders, he had to play a role in the military struggle to preserve the Communist government against the Allied nations. Those countries, especially Britain, France, and the United States, then were trying to reverse Lenin's revolution and prevent the possible spread of communism to countries around the world.

In a bitter conflict that lasted until 1921, Stalin found himself taking second place in Lenin's regard behind the brilliant Communist general, Leon Trotsky. Once, at the city of Tsaritsyn, Trotsky demanded that Lenin remove Stalin from the battlefront for his strategic blundering. To soften the blow, Lenin had Stalin returned in honor to Petrograd in a special train.

Still, Stalin never forgave Trotsky for the insult of Tsaritsyn. Nor did his jealousy of Trotsky as a person ever disappear. Whereas Stalin had not even graduated from high school and remained distant and withdrawn in public, Trotsky was well educated, a superb public speaker, and an extraordinary writer.

In addition to all that, Trotsky, whose real name was Lev Davidovich Bronstein, was a Jew. Like many Russians, Stalin hated Jews. Long before he met Trotsky, Stalin had grown to regard Jewish Communists as cowards for disliking bloodshed as a way to seize power.

As the civil war within Russia continued, Trotsky covered himself with glory. Victory followed victory for the Red Army. By the end of 1921, Russia was securely in the hands of the Soviets. The revolution at last was complete.

Meanwhile, Stalin had married again. His bride was a sixteen-year-old: Nadya Alliluyeva, the daughter of a Bolshevik leader. Strikingly beautiful, poised, and charming, she contrasted sharply with the coarse-featured and gloomy Stalin, now old enough to be her father. Only five feet four inches tall, Stalin continued to be painfully aware of his pockmarked face and his thick Georgian accent.

Still, young Nadya at first was flattered, then fascinated by the wily adventurer, Stalin. Despite her youth, she worked for Lenin himself, carrying dispatches and decoding secret messages. Because of that key position, she frequently could give Stalin advance information about Lenin's plans. In that way she proved useful to him in the growing struggle for leadership in the Communist party.

In that struggle there was a genuine difference of opinion on how best to build Communist strength in the world. As might be expected, Trotsky and Stalin took opposite sides in the debate. Trotsky argued for greater freedom and democracy inside Russia in order to make the Soviet Union a model for other countries to follow. To him, Russia was just a base for carrying on worldwide revolutionary activities.

Stalin, on the other hand, objected to giving Russians greater freedom. Instead, he believed in organizing and disciplining the people. Communism, said Stalin, should be built up firmly in "one country first"—Russia. Then, other countries would follow the Russian example. Eventually they would encircle the capitalist nations, including the United States, Great Britain, and France, and destroy them.

While Lenin was alive and well, he was able to keep peace between Trotsky and Stalin. But in May 1922, a blood vessel burst in Lenin's brain. Partially paralyzed, he was unable to speak or write. In the next few months he slowly recovered, but he never again was strong enough to give vigorous direction to the nation.

Meanwhile, Stalin maneuvered artfully for power, using well-placed friends to win election as general secretary of the Communist party. Too late, Trotsky realized what was happening.

Lenin planned to speak out personally against "the arrogant Georgian" at a Communist party congress. But in January 1924, another paralytic stroke abruptly ended the life of the brilliant Vladimir Ilyich Lenin.

Before his death Lenin had made it clear to his wife and to other leading Communists that he no longer trusted Stalin. He had written:

Stalin is too rude, and this fault . . . becomes unbearable in the office of General Secretary. Therefore I propose to the comrades to find a way to remove Stalin from that position and appoint to it another man . . . more loyal, more courteous, and more considerate to the comrades. . . .

With Lenin's death Stalin moved quickly to force Trotsky's removal as war minister and then to force him, one of the great heroes of the revolution, out of the country.

Step by step, Joseph Stalin strengthened his control over the Communist party and, soon, over the entire nation.

As leader of the Soviet Union, Stalin began to change it. His goal was to transform that country from a backward agricultural weakling into a modern industrial giant. To do so, he began to create railways, power stations, factories. Partly with the use of slave labor—workers taken from their homes by force of arms—he had whole new industrial cities constructed east of the Volga River and the Ural Mountains.

More than 50 percent of the workers who helped construct the industrial city of Magnitogorsk died of hunger and cold. Others were beaten to death or, as punishment, thrown outside into sub-zero temperatures to die.

At the same time, Soviet farmers sometimes refused to leave their land to work on the new commonly shared "collective farms." Stalin used soldiers to load the protestors into railroad boxcars and deport them to Siberia. There, in the icy wilderness, they were forced to build roads, canals, and railways. Meanwhile, their lands were transformed into collective farms, owned by the state. Some ten million peasants may have died before the remaining farmers finally began to cooperate in trying to make the collective farms succeed.

As a result of Stalin's programs, what had been a backward agricultural society was transformed in the course of two of his "Five Year Plans" into an industrial nation. To speed that process along, he created a vast network of elementary and secondary schools, as well as colleges.

But the cost of victory was high. Once again, as before the revolution, Russia was ruled with an iron hand. Prisons dotted the land. From the window of his office in the Kremlin, Stalin could see the dreaded prison and torture chambers of his secret police—known at various times as the Cheka, the GPU, the NKVD, and the KGB.

In place of the czars, there now reigned a chilling new kind of czar, one drawn from the working class, who concentrated all of his fierce energy and shrewd intelligence on bending the Russian people to his will.

To stay in power, Stalin had to be on guard at all times. Therefore, his secret police lurked everywhere. They wiretapped telephones; they listened in on private conversations in restaurants, on trains, even in washrooms. Children were encouraged with rewards to turn in their parents for criticizing the government.

Beginning in 1934, Stalin regularly had the chief of his secret police prepare lists of possible enemies. Some of those listed who were personally checked off by Stalin simply were arrested and shot without trial.

As the Russian dictator once put it, "Nothing is sweeter in life than vengeance—to identify an enemy, lie in wait for him, and after plunging in the knife to go home for a good night's sleep."

Joseph Stalin with a delegation from a farmers' collective, 1933. *Novosti from Sovfoto.*

In 1936 and 1937, Stalin put on trial, or simply arranged to have executed, almost all of the old Bolsheviks—the men who, along with himself, had made the revolution. At last, in the summer of 1940, an assassin hired by Stalin followed Leon Trotsky to his place of exile in Mexico, splitting open the head of the one-time Communist hero with an iron-pointed stick.

By the end of 1938, Stalin had only to pick up the telephone to order the execution of any person in all of Russia. Stalin's own wife, Nadya, pleaded with him to stop his brutal purge, or "cleansing out," of enemies. When he refused, she threatened to divorce him. Finally, after a bitter quarrel in public about his deeds, Nadya returned to her room, put a pistol to her head, and committed suicide.

For many years afterward Stalin visited the grave of Nadya, usually at night. Standing alone, under floodlights, he would gaze at the sculptured image of her that he had arranged to have placed there.

While Stalin devoted himself to defeating his enemies at home, he never completely forgot the danger of enemies abroad. Until 1933, when Adolf Hitler came to power in Germany, Stalin thought that Russia had the most to fear from such capitalist nations as Britain and France. Hitler, however, made communism—and particularly Russian communism—his special foe.

It was, therefore, a surprise to much of the world when, on August 23, 1939, Germany and Russia signed an agreement not to attack each other for ten years. They also agreed to divide up Poland, the nation that lay between them. On September 1, Hitler launched an invasion of Poland, marking the beginning of World War II.

Needing buffer territories to separate the Soviet heartland from Nazi armies, Stalin quickly sent Russian troops into Latvia, Estonia, and Lithuania. Soon afterward he made those countries a part of the Soviet Union. In bloody fighting he also conquered strategic parts of Finland. Hitler, meanwhile, swept into the Balkans, occupying Rumania and Bulgaria, countries that Stalin had hoped to control.

Finally, on June 22, 1941, wave after wave of German planes launched a surprise attack on the Soviet Union. One hundred and forty-seven divisions of Nazi troops poured across the Russian border. Caught unprepared, the Red Army reeled backward all along a 1,500-mile front.

At first Stalin was stunned that Hitler had betrayed him. Then, speaking to the Russian people by radio, he urged them to fight for the freedom of the "motherland." After the war, he promised them, Russia would be a freer and better place for all of its citizens. But first, he declared, the Nazis must be "hounded and annihilated" at every step.

"Death to the German invaders!" he concluded, with a hatred that clearly communicated itself to his listeners.

Many of the Russians detested Stalin. Indeed, many of them at first had cheered Hitler's invading armies as liberators. But soon they changed their minds. As the Germans entered villages, they burned and looted. They tortured women and children. Trainloads of Russians—considered an inferior race by Hitler—were deported to work as slave laborers in German factories. Special killing squads rounded up Jews and machine-gunned them on the spot.

For several months the Germans steadily advanced. Finally, they entered the very suburbs of Moscow. Still, the Russians refused to surrender.

Then, in December 1941, Stalin threw four hundred thousand fresh troops into battle. He had withdrawn

Stalin with President Franklin D. Roosevelt and British Prime Minister Winston Churchill at Yalta, 1945. *Franklin D. Roosevelt Library, Hyde Park, New York.*

them from Manchuria, where they had been braced for an attack by the Japanese. When, instead, the Japanese bombed Pearl Harbor, bringing the United States into the war, Stalin rushed the soldiers into combat against Hitler's legions.

Those troops—along with the terrible winter, for which the Germans were not prepared—turned the tide. Many months passed, with heavy losses on both sides. But, particularly at Stalingrad and Leningrad, the Nazis suffered horrible defeats. Eventually, the German army found itself in full retreat.

Joseph Stalin—the man of steel—stood alone as the hero of the hour, the man who had inspired the Russian people to turn disastrous defeat into glorious triumph.

As World War II drew to its conclusion, the Allied leaders, especially President Franklin Delano Roosevelt of the United States, hoped that Stalin would give up his selfish goals and, instead, join in establishing a just and lasting peace for the entire world.

But it was not to be. While working

feverishly to rebuild his nation's shattered industries, Stalin pressed hard to expand Russia's influence in Iran, Afghanistan, Greece, Turkey, and Manchuria. Except for Yugoslavia, his troops came to dominate all of Eastern Europe: Poland, Hungary, Czechoslovakia, Rumania, and Bulgaria. He assisted North Korea in its invasion of South Korea in spite of strong American military opposition. At least in the beginning, he supported Mao Tse-tung's newly triumphant Communist government in China.

Meanwhile, although Russian industry flourished, the people of the Soviet Union continued to live in poverty. They ate mostly cabbage and potatoes. In the cities, several people often had to share a single room. The press, radio, and television were closely watched, so that citizens learned only what Stalin wanted them to know. Members of the secret police were everywhere, creating a sense of fear and suspicion.

Then, on March 1, 1953, a blood vessel ruptured in Joseph Stalin's brain. Four days later he suffered a paralytic stroke and, at the age of seventy-three, he died.

On the day of his funeral, happy singing broke out in the streets of Moscow.

Bonfires were lit. Thousands of men, women, and children eagerly pressed into Red Square to celebrate.

Historians, whatever their political beliefs, cannot avoid recognizing Stalin's enormous achievements. He established Russia as a military giant, possessing powerful modern weapons, including a nuclear arsenal capable of destroying much of the world. Because of him, dams, power projects, and factories dotted the landscape of what once was wilderness.

Alongside them, of course, stood the slave labor camps, prisons, and torture chambers that also were living monuments to his leadership. Through the ruthless use of force, he had created a new kind of society.

As Nikita Khrushchev, one of Stalin's successors as head of the Soviet government, once put it, "In everything about Stalin's personality there was something admirable as well as something savage."

"Admirable . . . as well as . . . savage."

Khrushchev's comment may be a fitting summary of Joseph Stalin's contribution to human history.

Adolf Hitler

1889–1945   Leader of Germany's Fascist dictatorship and conqueror of continental Europe in World War II

There are those who say that young people should be shielded from the story of evil people like Adolf Hitler. To write about such people, it is sometimes said, is to glorify evil and make it appealing. But Adolf Hitler really lived. We cannot change history. Shielding our eyes from the reality of his deeds will not erase them.

Rather, it is better to know the story of Hitler, no matter how ghastly it may be. Knowing the past may alert us. Then, when such people seek to be our leaders, to head our governments, we will be able to recognize the symptoms of their ambition for boundless power. Knowing the look of a tyrant—the "face" of evil—we may be ready to defend humanity against its vile curse.

At the peak of his power Hitler proudly boasted that he would build a great new empire for Germany, one that would last a thousand years. The German people—a race of "supermen"—would be supremely happy. The world, boasted Hitler, would be theirs. They would have farmland, beautiful houses, plenty of money.

And any people who dared block the path to Germany's rightful happiness would pay the penalty. Most would be destroyed, and those allowed to live would become slaves for all the loyal Germans who faithfully, obediently, followed the leader of the nation—Adolf Hitler.

Hitler came frighteningly close to doing exactly as he promised. He came close to conquering the world. He very nearly succeeded in winning, for a time, the never-ending battle between good and evil. And if he really had won, our planet could have become a living hell.

Hitler was born in Austria, close to the German border. At the time, his father, Alois, was fifty-two years old. Alois's wife, Klara, was only twenty-nine and more like a daughter to him. Indeed, several years before their marriage Alois for a time had cared for Klara as a foster father.

The first three of the couple's children died in infancy. Adolf was the fourth child. Because he survived he received special attention from his parents, particularly his mother. Whenever Alois, given to fierce temper tantrums, would threaten young Adolf, Klara Hitler would shield him, protect him. She fondled him, spoiled him. Whatever he wanted, she gave him. Adolf, or Adi, as his parents called him, became a "mother's boy."

In school, Hitler's teachers found him bright, lively, good-natured. But then, when he was eleven, his younger brother, Edmund, died of measles. Almost overnight, Hitler's personality changed. Perhaps he had wished for his brother's death and then, when it happened, blamed himself. In any event, he became gloomy and bad-tempered. He snapped at his friends and his teachers.

For two years Adolf attended a Benedictine monastery school and sang in the choir. He dreamed of one day becoming a Catholic priest. Yet, in spite of his obvious intelligence, Hitler did poorly in school. Even in his favorite subjects, history, geography, and drawing, his grades were low. He was considered hard to handle, sullen, arrogant, and lazy. He enjoyed playing pranks on his teachers. Instead of studying, he liked to look at picture books about war or to play war games with his classmates. In those games he always insisted on playing the part of the leader.

In January 1903, when Hitler was thirteen, his father died. Although it is true that Adolf had hated and feared his father, he also had respected him.

For the next three years, until he was sixteen, Hitler continued in school, hoping to become an artist. Then, suffering from a lung disease, he dropped out of school to regain his health. It was destined to be the end of his formal educational career.

The three years that followed, until he was nineteen, remained in Hitler's memory as "the happiest time of my life." Living by then in Linz, Austria, he spent his days roaming the streets or the nearby countryside. At the local library he read books about history. In the evenings he attended the opera.

According to his closest friend at that time, Hitler often would stay out all night under the stars, dreaming of one day becoming a great artist or architect, or perhaps becoming the great "tribune" (defender) of the German people. One villager remembered that he sometimes watched Hitler giving speeches to the trees in the forest.

Although Hitler's mother supported him on her own small widow's pension, he refused to get a steady job. In the morning he would lounge in bed, expecting his mother to wait on him. Then he would stay up late at night, reading or walking. Not until he became chancellor of Germany did Adolf Hitler ever hold down a regular civilian job.

In 1907 Hitler's mother died of cancer. It was, he later wrote, "a dreadful blow." After the funeral he remained by the graveside for more than an hour weeping. Dr. Bloch, the Jewish physician who had treated his mother in her final illness, remembered afterward that in all his career he had never seen anyone so deep in grief as Adolf Hitler.

Nineteen years old, with neither a high school diploma nor a trade, Hitler found himself living in poverty in the Austrian capital city, Vienna. To pay for food and lodging he did odd jobs—shoveling snow, carrying suitcases at the railroad station, even (most humili-

ating to him) laboring as a construction worker. Sometimes he stayed in cheap rooming houses. Sometimes he lived in a charity house. For weeks at a time he did not bathe or shave. His clothes often were filled with lice.

But, unlike the other seedy tramps in Vienna's slums, Hitler neither smoked nor drank. He spent time in the library reading: books on hypnotism, yoga, Oriental religions, history, and politics—especially politics. Often he would sit in coffee houses, talking politics—sometimes angrily shouting and waving his fist at people who disagreed with him.

Slowly he built up a body of beliefs, with necessary evidence from his reading to prove what he already believed. Everything else—and every person who refused to go along with his ideas— he simply cast aside.

During his years in Vienna Hitler's ideas took firm root. For the rest of his life, as he put it, he was to "learn little" and to "change nothing." His "school" of life taught him to lie and to bully. From his intense readings he came to believe, along with many German-speaking Austrians, that the Germans were a "Master Race"—a nation of superior people who deserved to rule the world. For the non-German minorities that made up the Austrian Empire—Czechs, Slovaks, Slovenes,

Croats, Serbs, Magyars—he had nothing but hatred.

But most of all, he hated the Jews. The history of Europe is filled with anti-Semitism. And as a young man in Vienna, Hitler often read about violent attacks on Jews in newspapers and pamphlets, while seeing such hatred in practice all the time.

To him, the Jews stood for everything in the world that was wrong and harmful. They were for equality, democracy, and freedom—ideas that he detested. They favored free speech, a free press, and the free election of representatives, practices Hitler considered signs of weakness and a waste of time. Jews, moreover, were for peace. He personally glorified war, seeing all of life as a struggle.

To Hitler, kindness and humanity were foolishness. Only by brutality, he believed, could one succeed in reaching a goal. For mankind as a whole he had only the deepest contempt. Most people, he came to believe, acted out of fear, or greed, or a desire for power—almost never out of love or compassion.

To achieve his ends, he planned to tell not only lies but "the big lie"—a simple idea repeated again and again in the form of slogans that could be acted upon. All the hatred of the masses, he believed, should be directed toward one enemy—an enemy to be blamed for everything that troubled people in their private lives.

Hitler chose the Jews for that enemy and drummed constantly on his message. He knew that, as in successful advertising, a single thought repeated constantly would eventually sink into the mind of the listener. If told in simple terms—words so simple that any child could understand—almost all the people in society would, before long, begin to believe what they were told.

Along with lies, Hitler came to believe in the importance of force—terror—to convince people that a cause was right and just. Terror, he said, would always succeed in persuading individuals and the masses unless met by equal terror.

These, then, were the lessons Hitler learned during his years in the miserable flophouses of Vienna. Later, as leader of Germany, he would have a chance to put them into practice. And the world would never again be the same.

In the summer of 1914, World War I began. Adolf Hitler joined the German army and, perhaps for the first time in his life, believed that he belonged somewhere. In effect the army had given him a home. Whatever task was demanded of him he performed without a grumble. As a dispatch runner he carried messages from point to point on the battlefront. Even under heavy fire he persisted. His reward was a medal: the Iron Cross, First Class.

In October 1918, Hitler was overcome in a British poison gas attack. While in the hospital he learned of Germany's surrender. Hearing the news, he turned his face to his pillow and cried. Along with thousands of other Germans, he was sure that the army had not lost but had been "stabbed in the back" by traitorous politicians—inspired by Jews and Communists—who had made peace instead of continuing the war. Like so many others, he looked forward to the day when he could take revenge on the "November criminals" who had given up the struggle.

Meanwhile, the war had toughened him, hardened him, and made him feel he was a "somebody" instead of a "nobody." Twenty-nine years old at the end of the fighting, he returned to Munich. Without a job, with no place to live, never enough food to eat, he somehow was supremely confident that one day he would lead the German nation.

Still unwilling to take a steady job, Hitler gained permission in Munich to live in the army barracks. Knowing his political point of view, his army superiors gave him a job spying on Socialist and Communist groups.

One of his assignments took him to the meeting of a small group known as the German Workers' party. Despite its name, it turned out to be a highly nationalistic anti-Semitic organization. Supposedly in attendance to spy on the GWP, Hitler nevertheless spoke up, making a ringing speech against the Jews. The next day he received a letter, asking him to join.

Although Hitler had planned to start a party of his own, he instead cast his lot with the GWP, becoming the seventh member of its executive committee. It was, he later recalled, "the most important decision of my life."

Having finally decided on a course of action, Hitler unleashed all of his energies in a fury of work. To attract new members, he started an advertising campaign in the newspapers. He organized mass meetings in beer halls. He convinced the group to change its name to the National Socialist German Workers' party, or "Nazi" for short.

Under his guidance the party drew up a platform summarizing its beliefs. The platform spoke out against the Treaty of Versailles that had ended World War I. It called for the unification of all German-speaking people, including those in Austria and Czechoslovakia, under a single flag. And it promised to take German citizenship away from all Jews.

Stirred by Hitler's appeal, membership in the Nazi party rapidly increased. As a reward he demanded absolute power over the group, taking the title of Fuehrer. He organized a squad of uniformed street fighters known as Storm Troopers (the S.A.) and then sent them out to attack Jewish shop owners and set fire to their stores.

Soon the red, white, and black Nazi party flag became a familiar sight over all of southern Germany, as did the party insignia, the twisted cross or swastika. Party members extended their arms in the Nazi salute and shouted the familiar German military greeting *"Sieg heil!"* ("Hail victory!"). Some simply declared, *"Heil Hitler!"*

In November 1923, Hitler thought the time was ripe to seize power in Germany, as Benito Mussolini already had in Italy. But the plot failed miserably. Hitler tried to hide in the home of a friend but was captured and, after a trial, was put in prison.

Still, using the trial to express his ideas before an audience including newspaper reporters from around the world, Hitler won widespread popularity. In Germany he became something of a national hero.

Although sentenced to a five-year term in jail, Hitler was forced to serve only nine months. During that time he was confined to Landsberg Prison, which was more like a modest hotel than a prison. He was given excellent food and even allowed to have his personal secretary, Rudolf Hess, visit him regularly.

It was during his imprisonment that Hitler wrote *Mein Kampf (My Struggle)*, a book that frankly told much of what he planned to do when he became the most powerful man in Germany.

Released from prison in 1924, Hitler worked hard at improving his speaking gestures before audiences, as well as his style of dressing and walking. He took lessons in pronunciation. He made it a point to appear deeply serious in all of his numerous public appearances, only rarely smiling.

For five years, from 1924 to 1929, Germany enjoyed prosperity. Much of the people's anger about the war disappeared. Membership in the Nazi party declined. But Hitler remained certain that his chance would come.

Soon, it arrived. In 1929 a great depression struck, first in the United States and then in all of Western Europe. Without loans from America, German industries were especially hard hit. Before long, all classes began to suffer. Seizing his opportunity, Hitler campaigned all across the nation.

To the unemployed Hitler promised jobs. To the middle class he promised order and a stable economy. To the military he promised a massive rebuilding of Germany's armed forces. To businessmen he promised to curb the power of labor unions.

Contributions came pouring into the Nazi party treasury. By July 1932, the Nazis controlled 230 seats in the Reichstag, the German parliament, making them the largest party in Germany.

Finally, in January 1933, members of various opposition parties offered to let Hitler become chancellor. Although they insisted that a large majority of non-Nazis were to hold cabinet positions in the new government, Hitler never doubted that once in power he would know just how to take care of his opponents. On first learning of the offer Hitler is said to have slammed his fist on the table and snarled, "Now I have them in my pocket!"

On the night of January 30, 1933, thousands of excited Berliners cheered as column after column of Nazi Storm Troopers marched down Berlin's beautiful Wilhelmstrasse in a torchlight parade. The crude, vulgar, uneducated "Bavarian corporal," Adolf Hitler, had become chancellor of Germany, one of Europe's most civilized and cultured nations.

Just one month after taking office, Adolf Hitler moved dramatically to make his control over Germany complete and total. First, although the Nazis themselves set fire to the Reichstag building, Hitler blamed the deed on the nation's enemies. He then demanded new powers to crush such people.

Next, declaring an emergency, he took away all constitutional rights from German citizens. From that time on, any German legally could be arrested and sent to prison without a trial.

Step by step Hitler took over the workings of the nation. He savagely attacked labor unions, having the labor leaders beaten or killed. He made all political parties except his own Nazi party strictly illegal. He eliminated free speech and a free press, permitting the German people to read and hear only what he wanted them to. The Nazi party operated all radio stations; it took over any newspaper suspected of being hostile. Hitler took control of the local governments, the courts, and the schools. Only loyal Nazis were allowed to hold public office.

Finally, Hitler moved against those he considered a threat within his own party, including his best friend, Ernst Roehm, head of the Storm Troopers, the party's gangster-type police force. On the night of June 30, 1934, with Hitler himself involved in the slaughter, Roehm and some one thousand other persons were killed. Among them

Adolf Hitler and his officers at a Nazi rally in Buckeberg, Germany, in 1934. *UPI/Bettmann.*

were some of Hitler's old enemies from his days of poverty in Munich.

Nor did the Fuehrer apologize for his cruelty. Now holding total power in Germany, he declared openly, as he once had written in *Mein Kampf:*

Brutality is respected. Brutality and physical strength. The plain man in the street respects nothing but brutal strength and ruthlessness.

. . . If a people is to become free it needs pride and will-power, defiance, hate, hate, and once again hate.

In Germany, the principal target of Hitler's hate and brutality was the Jews. Immediately after taking power, Hitler had laws passed that stopped Jews from holding jobs in the government, as well as in radio, films, journalism, teaching, and farming. Later the ban was broadened to include law, medicine, and the stock exchange. Many grocery stores refused to sell food to Jews; drugstores refused to sell them medicines; hotels would not accept them. Some towns posted signs saying, "Jews Strictly Forbidden to Enter." Thousands of Jews were rounded up and thrown into concentration camps.

But Hitler was saving worse things—much worse—for Germany's Jews. For the time he chose to wait, saying that "the Jews are my most important hostages."

Few Germans dared to speak out against Hitler's deeds. Many were actually pleased. Also, from 1933 to 1939, prosperity returned to the nation. The unemployed were put to work making planes, tanks, guns, and submarines. The size of Germany's armed forces grew swiftly.

Fine new superhighways, the autobahns, stretched across the country, soon carrying Volkswagens, "people's cars," produced with Hitler's personal endorsement. Thousands of workers were grateful to Hitler because once again they had steady jobs, even though strikes were no longer legal and the wages and hours of all workers were decided by the government.

Meanwhile, the powerful industrialists, like I. G. Farben and the Krupp munitions-making family, were delighted that they had chosen to back the Nazis. They now had plenty of cheap labor and enormous new orders for war materials as Germany swiftly rearmed.

In exchange for the confusion and untidiness of democracy—a system demanding that people make up their own minds—Hitler had promised the Germans national order and national glory. In return, they had only to surrender themselves to the Fuehrer. He had made good on a surprising number of his promises. Now he prepared to prove to his followers that with the strength of one will, one discipline, one obedience, one race, one leader, the entire world would be theirs. Or, as it then was said in the opening words of the German national anthem, *"Deutschland, Deutschland, über Alles—über Alles in der Welt!"* ("Germany, Germany, over all—over *all in the world!"*)

Beginning slowly at first, Hitler proceeded to make good on his promises of conquest. In 1935, the Saar industrial district agreed to rejoin Germany. In 1936, he marched troops into the Rhineland and reclaimed that territory for Germany—totally in violation of the Versailles treaty. Then, seeing the League of Nations powerless in the face of Japan's invasion of Manchuria and Italy's conquest of Ethiopia, he decided that the time was ripe for adding still other territories.

In March 1938, he ordered the German army into his homeland, Austria. Thousands of Austrians greeted him as a hero, rather than a conqueror. Next, he persuaded the prime ministers of

Britain and France to let him occupy the Sudetenland, a part of western Czechoslovakia where many German-speaking people lived. But, unsatisfied with that arrangement, in 1939 he gobbled up the rest of Czechoslovakia.

On September 1, 1939, Hitler launched a blitzkrieg (lightning attack) on Poland. By then, Britain and France at last had recognized that Hitler's greed for territory would never be satisfied by giving in to his demands. But where the German dictator easily could have been stopped in 1935, his dive bombers and mobile artillery now slaughtered the courageous Poles. Despite British and French declarations of war against Germany and as much military assistance as the democracies then could muster, Poland was crushed within a month.

The Nazis struck next at Denmark and Norway, easily defeating their helpless northern neighbors. Then, driving quickly through Belgium, Holland, and Luxembourg, German troops forced French resistance to crumble in only six weeks. Now, only Britain held out, unconquered and defiant.

Visiting Paris, Hitler stood for more than an hour silently gazing at the tomb of Napoléon. Like the Corsican Bonaparte, he had made himself the master of Europe. But, unlike Napoléon's soldiers, the German armies carried with

them no bright hope for liberty, equality, and a better way of life. Instead, it was time for the German "supermen" to begin the extermination of the "inferior races."

On June 22, 1941, German troops stormed into Russia, much to the surprise of the Russian dictator, Joseph Stalin, who had agreed to friendship with Hitler. In a message to his troops the Nazi Fuehrer announced that they were engaged in the final struggle against the "Jewish-Bolshevik race of sub-humans." To his military commanders Hitler wrote: "Be brutal!"

Meanwhile, for the territories already under his control, Hitler now ordered a "final solution" to the Jewish problem. All Jews were to be executed without mercy.

At first the task was given to roving squads known as *Einsatzgruppen*. Entering a village, they would gather together all the Jews, including women and children, at the edge of a mass grave. Then, after ordering them into the pit, they would open fire with machine guns and mow down their victims. Those who survived the bullets were clubbed to death with shovels (to save ammunition) or simply buried alive.

Finding that process too slow, Hitler ordered the building of more than thirty new concentration camps—really death

Jews being expelled from Memel, Lithuania, in 1939, after the Memel district was ceded to Germany. *Archiv Für Kunst Und Geschichte, Berlin.*

camps—across the face of the continent. From all over Europe victims were loaded into boxcars and shipped without food or water to the camps—to Dachau, Treblinka, Bergen-Belsen, Buchenwald, and worst of all, Auschwitz.

Before that time, Jews brought to concentration camps were beaten, tortured, and stoned before being killed. Guards sometimes hanged prisoners by the hands and slowly beat them to death with rubber hoses. Babies and young children were thrown alive into fires or into vats of boiling water. Some children were taken by the feet and dashed against trees or walls to split their heads open. There were cases of babies being ripped apart—their arms and legs torn from their sockets before the very eyes of their mothers by laughing guards.

In one camp in France, the eyes of victims were gouged out, live roaches placed in the hollows, and then the lids sewn shut with the roaches inside.

Now, to speed up the killing, Hitler asked German industrialists to invent gas chambers, where as many as two thousand prisoners could be killed at once. Manufacturers competed eagerly with one another for contracts to build the instruments of death. Vast ovens were built to cremate the bodies. Hitler complained, however, that the Jews must not only die; they must be made to die in agony. He personally ordered that quicklime be spread on the floors of freight cars carrying prisoners to the death camps, so they would suffer painful burns on their bodies before being executed.

Never—in all of human history—have such horrible crimes taken place on such a massive scale.

By and large, the German people turned their backs on what was happening in the camps. They also managed not to know that Hitler was killing thousands of non-Jewish Germans—people whose only crimes were that they were insane, or mentally deficient, or sick, or simply old. Instead, the German people were dazzled by their leader's spectacular triumphs on the battlefield.

Slowly, however, the tide of battle began to turn. By the end of 1942, Hitler's empire, which he promised would last a thousand years, was showing signs of cracking. The Nazis' drive to conquer Russia was stopped just short of Moscow. In the Pacific, meanwhile, Japanese planes attacked the American base at Pearl Harbor, Hawaii, drawing the United States into the conflict against the Axis Powers (Germany, Italy, and Japan).

Soon, American troops landed in Africa and then began making their way northward through Italy. Meanwhile, in Russia, German forces suffered defeat after defeat, with thousands upon thousands of soldiers dying. Then, on June 6, 1944, the Allied armies landed in France and began fighting their way toward the German border. Night and day, British and American bombers reigned death and destruction on German cities.

Clearly the war was lost. It was only a matter of time. Still, Hitler refused to surrender. Some of his own generals plotted to kill him, but he survived. He had most of the plotters executed by slow strangulation. They were hanged with nooses of piano wire from butcher shop meat hooks. Hitler had movies made of the agonizing hangings and often ordered them replayed for his personal enjoyment.

With enemy armies closing in on Germany, Hitler's health began to crumble. He took various kinds of sleeping pills but still could not sleep.

His hands trembled. His face twitched. As he grew weaker, he turned to massive doses of Dexedrine, cocaine, and other drugs.

At last, in the closing days of April 1945, he realized that Germany could not win. The German people—the people he claimed to love above himself—had proved themselves weak, he said, unworthy of Adolf Hitler. But if Germany must die, then nothing should be left to the invaders. He ordered the destruction of all German factories, all hospitals, farms, churches, monuments, works of art. The water supply was to be poisoned.

But Germany was not destroyed. The Allied armies were advancing too quickly to permit the destruction Hitler had ordered. Besides, some German officers at last refused to obey the Fuehrer's orders.

Then, on April 30, 1945, with Russian troops only three blocks away from his underground headquarters, Hitler sat on a couch with his companion, Eva Braun, two loaded pistols on a table in front of them. Clutching a photograph of his mother to his breast, Hitler swallowed cyanide poison. Then, according to his instructions, Eva Braun

shot him in the head. She then poisoned herself.

As the Nazi leader had ordered, gasoline was poured over the corpses, and they were set afire. This, Hitler had said, would prevent the Russians from putting his body on display, as had been done a few days earlier in Italy with the body of Benito Mussolini.

So ended the life of Adolf Hitler. With him, too, in the rubble of Berlin, died the thousand-year empire he had promised the German people.

Hitler had raised Germany to dizzying heights of power. His personal authority had been absolute. When he spoke, the entire nation was mobilized to do his bidding. Yet, unlike other "great" leaders of the past, Adolf Hitler did not leave the world—or even Germany—better than when he first appeared on the stage of history. Perhaps that is because his purpose in life was so very limited. Undoubtedly his life goal—the sole purpose he saw in his own existence—was that only he, as leader of the German "Master Race," would subdue and rule the world.

In the end, that goal proved far too narrow to succeed. The rest of the world simply would not permit it.

Winston Churchill

1874–1965   British prime minister who stood firmly and courageously against Hitler's Nazi forces in Western civilization's darkest hour

In the spring of 1940 all of Western Europe lay helpless in the iron grip of the German dictator, Adolf Hitler. Only Great Britain stood in the way of total victory for the Nazi warlord. Englishmen momentarily awaited the peal of church bells, signaling the start of an invasion by the seemingly invincible German army.

Many Britons urged Prime Minister Winston Churchill to make peace with Hitler while there still was time. They pleaded with him to get out of the war before their island kingdom was totally destroyed. The Nazis, predicted one French leader, "would wring England's neck like a chicken."

But Churchill had no intention of quitting. Instead, he stood up to speak in the House of Commons, solid, grim, bulldog-like in his determination. His voice spat defiance at the savage enemy so terribly close to its goal of enslaving the British people. With chin thrust forward he growled a promise to fight on:

. . . We shall not flag or fail. We shall go on to the end, we shall fight in France, we shall fight on the seas and oceans, we shall fight with growing confidence and growing strength in the air, we shall defend our Island, whatever the cost may be, we shall fight on the beaches, we shall fight on the landing grounds, we shall fight in the fields and streets, we shall fight in the hills—we shall never surrender.

The very survival of Western civilization hung in the balance, said Churchill. Britain, therefore, would stand—alone if necessary—against Hitler's tyranny, for if Britain failed, he said, the world would be plunged into "a New Dark Age."

"Let us therefore brace ourselves to our duties," declared Churchill with pride, "and so bear ourselves that, if the British Empire and its Commonwealth last for a thousand years, men will say, '*This* was their finest hour.'"

Incredibly, the British nation did manage to survive. The barbaric Nazis eventually were defeated. And the image of Winston Churchill, defiant and confident in the face of impossible odds, lives on—his courage standing as a high point in the history of humanity.

Again and again in his own lifetime Churchill's most cherished plans had failed. But he continued on, defying his political foes, standing firmly for his beliefs until, in Britain's darkest hour, the nation entrusted its future to him. It was then, speaking to the House of Commons, that he declared with grim resolve and with a determination to succeed that inspired his people, "I have nothing to offer but blood, toil, tears, and sweat."

Winston Churchill was born in November 1874 at Blenheim Palace. But his parents did not live in the palace. They were visiting there for a dance when Winston's mother gave birth to him in a small bedroom, in use that evening as a cloakroom.

Lord Randolph Churchill, one of England's most promising young politicians, was Winston's father. His mother was the beautiful Jennie Jerome of New York City, the daughter of a wealthy American financial speculator and horse racing enthusiast.

In later years Winston often wrote about his parents. "My mother," he said, "always seemed to me a fairy princess: a radiant being possessed of limitless riches and power. She shone for me like the Evening Star. I loved her dearly—but at a distance."

Winston very much adored his father, too, but seldom had a chance to speak with him. In England of the late nineteenth century, parents of the upper class often lived busy social lives: dancing, hunting, horseback riding. They usually entrusted the responsibility for rearing their children to a nurse, or "nanny."

Winston's nurse was Mrs. Elizabeth Ann Everest. He later described her as "my confidante and most intimate friend." When he became one of the world's best-known personalities, it was not his mother's picture that hung on the wall over his desk, but that of Mrs. Everest. Large, fat, and plain-looking, she loved Winston with a fierce, undivided loyalty. He, in turn, trusted her completely.

When Winston was seven years old, he was sent away to St. George's, an expensive boarding school for boys. Winston hated the school, where he was expected to memorize Latin verses and do exercises in mathematics—things in which he had little interest. Stubbornly, he refused to study.

Like many "troublesome" schoolboys in those days, Winston often was flogged and whipped for his behavior. But no amount of beating could make him do work for which he saw no purpose. Rebellious and proud, he became a school hero for his defiance of the headmaster.

When the time came to choose a college preparatory school for Winston, his father ruled out Eton, the school of his own youth, because Winston's Latin—the language of instruction in the finest colleges—still was not good enough. Instead, the choice was Harrow.

For his entire five years at Harrow, Churchill remained at the very bottom of his class, always needing special tutoring in Latin and Greek. Since Winston was considered too stupid for the ancient classical languages, he was given an extra dose of English. His tutor drilled him over and over, insisting on nothing less than perfection. "I gained an immense advantage over the cleverer boys," Winston later remarked:

They all went on to learn Latin and Greek and splendid things like that. But I was taught English. I got into my bones the essential structure of an ordinary English sentence—which is a noble thing.

At Harrow, as before, Winston was a rebel—never afraid to stand up to authority. Once, after taking a particularly vicious beating without uttering a plea for mercy, he turned to the teacher who had flogged him and announced coldly, "I shall be a greater man than you." For that remark he received two more blows.

Unlike most boys at Harrow, Winston disliked the popular team games, cricket and football (soccer). But he excelled at swimming, riding, and fencing. Indeed he eventually became the fencing champion of the British private schools. He also won a school prize for memorizing and reciting 1,400 lines of a book telling of great events in Roman history. Soon, his teachers began to realize that when the strong-willed young Churchill was interested in something, he pursued it with a fierce passion.

Winston's father, Lord Randolph, had noticed his son's intensity, too. Surely, Lord Randolph told a friend, the boy would never be a scholar. But perhaps he could get by in the army, where at that time it was believed that only limited intelligence was needed.

Eager for any sign of concern from his father, who always was cold and distant to him, Winston agreed. Twice he failed the entrance examination to Sandhurst, the Royal Military Academy. On his third attempt he won admission with the lowest possible passing score. Indeed, Winston's mark was so low that he qualified only for the "cavalry class," a group of gentleman cadets wealthy enough to purchase and provide for their own horses.

Always before, Winston Churchill had hated school. But he loved Sandhurst, where there was practical work in constructing field fortifications, as well as instruction in such tasks as blowing up bridges and cutting railway lines.

Sandhurst, Winston later wrote, was "a new start" for him. He finished with honors, standing eighth in his class of one hundred and fifty.

Shortly after his graduation, however, Winston was struck by twin tragedies. His father died, as did his childhood nurse, Mrs. Everest. They were, at the time, the people he admired most in his life.

Joining the Fourth (Queens Own) Hussars, a cavalry unit, Churchill found peacetime army life dull. With his mother's help he won assignment in 1895 as a military observer in Cuba,

where rebels were fighting for freedom from Spanish rule. A London newspaper paid him for dispatches describing the conflict.

Then, rejoining the Fourth Hussars, he was sent to India. While on leave, he traveled two thousand miles to the northwest frontier of India, where the Malakand Field Force was putting down a revolt against British rule among the ferocious Pathan warriors. He distinguished himself in the fighting, killing at least one Pathan and winning praise from an officer for his courage. From his experiences in India he wrote a book, *The Story of the Malakand Field Force*, which became an instant success in England.

Next, he traveled to Egypt, where General Sir Horatio Herbert Kitchener was leading a force up the Nile to take revenge on the famous Dervish tribesmen for their defeat and execution of the colorful English general "Chinese" Gordon.

On the day of his arrival in the Sudan, he rode directly into a line of two thousand Dervish riflemen in one of the last great cavalry charges in British history. Twenty British lancers died in the attack, but the Dervishes were completely routed. Churchill claimed to have "shot five men for certain and two doubtful."

In *The River War*, his book on the

Sudanese campaign, Churchill sharply criticized General Kitchener for ordering that the body of the Mahdi (leader of the Dervishes) be dug up from its place of burial. Kitchener had then commanded that the corpse be cut to pieces.

Following the Nile campaign, Churchill traveled to India to rejoin his comrades in the Hussars. Then, at the age of twenty-four, deciding on a career in politics, he returned to England to run for Parliament. For a young man who had finished hopelessly last in his class at Harrow, Winston indeed had come a long way.

In his first campaign for Parliament Churchill lost. Soon afterward, however, he was offered a generous fee by a London newspaper to serve as its war correspondent in South Africa. There, the British army was engaged in a difficult struggle against Dutch settlers in what is known to history as the Boer War.

Captured by the Dutch, Churchill grew impatient with imprisonment. Boldly, he escaped from captivity, eventually making his way to freedom while posters offered rewards for his recapture, "dead or alive." So great was the publicity surrounding his adventure that Churchill returned to England as a national hero.

Running once again for Parliament in the district where he had been defeated, this time he won.

Churchill's early years in Parliament were filled with controversy. Elected as a Conservative, he was deeply distressed by the poverty of many British citizens and aware of the need for government to play a more active role in helping people in trouble. As a result, he sharply questioned, and then criticized, the Conservative party leadership. Eventually, he "crossed the floor" of Parliament, taking a seat among the Liberal members.

After that, his advance in politics was swift. He became under secretary of state for the colonies; privy councillor (adviser to the king); president of the Board of Trade (a position something like that of the American secretary of commerce); and, in 1910, home secretary—a powerful position concerned with a whole range of questions, including the maintenance of law and order.

Once Churchill had "discovered the poor," as one of his enemies put it, there was no turning back. He urged sharply higher taxes for those with large incomes and a tax on profits from increased land values. He favored government ownership of railroads, canals, and all utilities that were monopolies. The aged, the sick, and children, said Churchill, needed special care, paid for by the government. There should be,

Winston Churchill as a young politician. *Picture Post Library, London.*

he argued, minimum wages and maximum hours for laborers.

Sometimes even Winston's Liberal party colleagues wondered if he was perhaps too eager for attention, too reckless in his policies. Nor did they completely trust his imagination, sharp tongue, and quick intelligence, qualities Englishmen generally valued less in their leaders than sound judgment—even at the risk of dullness. Winston Churchill never was dull.

For all of his hectic activity, Winston still found time to marry and begin a family. His bride was the beautiful Clementine Hozier, or "Clemmie" as he called her. When the couple was married in September 1908, she was twenty-three; he was thirty-three. Some who had observed the unruly Winston from childhood predicted that the marriage would not last. Yet, more than fifty years later, Clementine was standing at Winston's side when he waved to admiring Londoners on his ninetieth birthday. As he once wrote, "I married and lived happily ever afterwards."

Always interested in military strategy and foreign affairs, Churchill found himself deeply involved in those matters beginning in July 1911. It was at that time that the German gunboat *Panther* steamed boldly to the mouth of the harbor of Agadir, on the coast of North Africa. In so doing, the German kaiser announced to the world that he was challenging Britain's supremacy on the high seas. Kaiser Wilhelm also served notice on France, Britain's close ally, that Germany would fight if necessary to stop French expansion to new territories in Africa. From that point on, Churchill awoke to the threat of a powerful new enemy in the kaiser's Germany—a young nation eager for military adventure and conquest.

Before long, Churchill became convinced that war would someday break out between Britain and Germany and that, when it did, Britain must be well prepared. Appointed First Lord of the Admiralty, he was put in charge of the Royal Navy.

Soon he became personally familiar with every important ship in the navy. Much of his time was spent at sea. In 1913, he convinced Parliament to provide money to install fifteen-inch guns on all the battleships in the fleet and to shift from coal power to oil.

Those changes gave Britain a vital edge over Germany in speed and naval firepower. When World War I began in August 1914, Churchill was not taken by surprise. The Royal Navy, modernized and alert, confidently protected the North Sea, defying the Germans to come out and fight. As one general put it, because of Winston "the fleet was ready."

Events in the war itself proved a personal embarrassment to Churchill, nearly bringing his spectacular political career to an end. The most serious blow of all was his leadership in the Gallipoli Campaign. Churchill proposed to send a British force through the Dardanelles and then capture the Turkish capital, Constantinople (now called Istanbul). Arms and ammunition then could be delivered to the landlocked Russians and Russian wheat could be brought out. As a result, Turkey, an important German ally, would be knocked out of the war.

Unfortunately, the British army at first refused to supply troops, arguing that the bloody trench fighting then taking place in France was more critical than Churchill's daring scheme. After the navy first experienced spectacular success on its own, troops were sent— but too late. The arrival of Turkish reinforcements and blundering by British military commanders turned the tide. Following weeks of bitter fighting, the British and French were forced to withdraw, having lost some 55,000 men.

The blame for the disaster in the Dardanelles fell squarely on the shoulders of Winston Churchill since he personally had convinced the British Cabinet to embark on the campaign. Whenever he spoke, his opponents raised the cry "Gallipoli!" Finally Winston resigned from the Cabinet.

For a time he returned to the front lines, serving as a combat officer in France. Then, he was appointed minister of munitions, where he first championed the use of air power as one answer to the stalemate between the warring powers.

But his principal idea was a device he developed and championed almost entirely on his own—the tank. The British used the tank too soon and in numbers too small to win a decisive victory. Still, it was one reason for the Allied victory over Germany and, in November 1918, the signing of the armistice marking the end of World War I.

Despite Churchill's very real contributions to the war effort, the public's memory of the Gallipoli Campaign was long lasting. Prime Minister Lloyd George appointed his promising young friend Winston minister of war and air. He also served with success as colonial secretary, acting as peacemaker between Jews and Arabs in Palestine. Still, in three election campaigns to return to membership in Parliament, he lost each time.

Meanwhile, with the triumph of Vladimir Ilyich Lenin in Russia, Churchill gradually had become convinced that the British Labor party spelled a real threat to Great Britain, possibly even bringing socialism or communism to the British Empire.

Before long, therefore, he rejoined the Conservative party. In 1924, he was appointed by a Conservative prime minister as chancellor of the Exchequer, the person in charge of the nation's finances and, next to the prime minister, the most powerful man in Great Britain.

For Churchill, it was the wrong job. He heartily disliked economics and statistics. He found debate on financial affairs boring. Where in most matters he took chances and invented clever strategies, as chancellor he was cautious and unimaginative.

In 1929, the Conservatives were defeated. No longer a Cabinet officer, Churchill at last found time for his family. He spent weekends at Chartwell, the country estate purchased with royalties from his writings. It was the place he most loved to be. There he took special pleasure in romping with his children. He played games with them, gardened, or just talked with them. He also took up painting, experimenting with watercolors, then switching to oils. His art works, exhibited under an assumed name so critics would not favor them, drew warm praise.

As early as 1932, Churchill warned of the danger in allowing Germany to rearm. The warlike spirit of Adolf Hitler's Nazis, predicted Churchill, would one day "shake to the foundations" all the countries in the world. But, even as Hitler proceeded to build a strong new army and a superb air force, the members of the British House of Commons were only amused by Churchill's warnings. Besides, the threat of Hitler and the Italian dictator, Benito Mussolini, seemed distant and unimportant when Englishmen, thrown out of work by the Great Depression, waited in line for bread.

Winston stood virtually alone in his pleas for action as, step by step, Hitler extended his influence. In 1936, the Nazi leader reoccupied the Rhineland, directly challenging the Treaty of Versailles, which had ended World War I. Two years later, Nazi troops marched into Austria and declared that country to be part of the German nation.

In 1938, at the Munich conference, Britain and France agreed to let Germany take control of the Sudetenland, a region in Czechoslovakia, although Churchill directly warned that the greedy Hitler would not be satisfied with just a piece of that unhappy land. Scarcely six months passed before Churchill's prediction about the Munich agreement came true. Nazi troops gobbled up the rest of Czechoslovakia.

Finally, on September 1, 1939, German forces stormed across the border into Poland. Great Britain responded with a declaration of war. World War II had begun.

Two days later Churchill was appointed to the position he had held when World War I began—First Lord of the Admiralty. Cheers rang out among crewmen of British ships scattered throughout the world as the word was flashed—"Winston is back!"

But the military defeats did not end. Some Englishmen still held on to vague hopes that, somehow, peace could be made with Hitler and that the fighting would stop. Meanwhile, the British people grew more and more disheartened.

Finally, on May 10, 1940, King George VI called for Winston Churchill. He was the choice of all parties to become prime minister.

Winston accepted. It was, he was sure, the moment for which his whole life had prepared him. And now he had his chance.

Day and night, swarms of Nazi aircraft struck at Great Britain. At first they bombed military targets. Then, hoping to break the spirit of the civilian population, they began round-the-clock bombing of London. As bombs rained from the sky, whole sections of the city were leveled. Fires raged, sometimes completely out of control. Thousands of Londoners were killed. Air raid sirens wailed through the night as civilians crowded together in underground shelters.

For Churchill, it was a time of trial. Yet he understood that for the British Empire and for the British people it could be, as he put it, "their finest hour."

It was Churchill's finest hour, too.

Solid, portly, his cigar clenched tightly between his teeth, he was seen everywhere—at the coastal defense positions, in munitions factories, on the streets of London, in Parliament. With his square jaw thrust forward, he would raise his hand in the famous "V for Victory" sign that came to be the symbol of British defiance against the Nazis.

Daily, as British Spitfire and Hurricane fighter planes rose to challenge the enemy bombers, German losses in the sky battle mounted. British bombers ferociously attacked the Nazi invasion fleet massing in the Channel ports, causing heavy damage. In the early days of the war, more than one-fourth of the Royal Air Force's trained pilots were killed. Daring young flight cadets, untrained but deeply inspired, took their places in the air. Weary, bloodied, but unconquered, the Royal Air Force fought on.

Finally, Hitler called off his invasion plan, "Operation Sea Lion." A mere handful of splendid British airmen had turned the tide of battle. "Never in the field of human conflict," declared Churchill, "was so much owed by so many to so few."

Slowly the tide of battle began to turn. After the Japanese attack on the American naval base at Pearl Harbor, the United States entered the war on the side of Great Britain. Churchill, never forgetting that by birth he was half American, was delighted. Then, when Hitler attacked the Soviet Union, Churchill welcomed that Communist nation into the anti-Nazi alliance. In November 1942, British forces won a major victory at El Alamein—at the very approaches to what then was the British-owned Suez Canal.

As the fighting progressed, it was Churchill who worked hardest to make the uneasy wartime alliance of Britain, Russia, and the United States succeed. He traveled repeatedly to Washington and Moscow. He organized major meetings of Allied leaders at Casablanca, Quebec, Teheran, Yalta, and Potsdam.

On June 6, 1944, Allied forces swarmed onto the beaches of France in history's greatest amphibious attack. When British tanks crossed the Rhine River into Germany, Winston himself was only two days behind the lead vehicles, urging his army on. Then on April 30, 1945, Adolf Hitler—"the evil man,"

as Churchill called him—killed himself. A few days later all remaining German forces surrendered unconditionally.

Stepping to the microphone before the wildly cheering House of Commons, Churchill raised his voice in triumph: "Advance Britannia! Long live the cause of freedom! God save the King!"

In August 1945, Japan surrendered. World War II was over.

Shortly after Germany's surrender, to the astonishment of much of the world, the Conservative party was voted out of power. Although seventy-one years old at the time, Churchill decided not to retire. Instead, he spent his time writing history, as well as speaking about the new danger of an aggressive, well-armed Soviet Union. In 1951, just before his seventy-seventh birthday, he once again became prime minister.

As he neared the age of eighty, some of his colleagues noticed signs of a change in him. He walked with more of a stoop than ever; sometimes he seemed to be tired or not to hear a comment; sometimes his mind would wander. But once, when asked by a reporter if he feared the approach of death, he answered: "I am prepared to meet my Maker. Whether my Maker is prepared for the great ordeal of meeting me is another matter."

Churchill crosses the Rhine, March 25, 1945. *The Imperial War Museum, London.*

At last, however, he realized that the time had come for him to step down. Resigning the prime ministry in 1955, he returned to Chartwell. There he lived a quiet life, devoting himself to painting, to writing, to playing with his grandchildren. Honors poured in on him—honorary doctorates from universities, a Nobel Prize for Literature, honorary American citizenship voted by the Congress of the United States. There was a knighthood presented by Queen Elizabeth, so that he became known as Sir Winston.

On Churchill's eightieth birthday he was honored by Parliament. At the climax of the ceremony all the members stood in silence as the band played for Winston, by then in tears, the stirring song of British national pride, "Land of Hope and Glory" ("Pomp and Circumstance").

On January 24, 1965, Winston Churchill died. His coffin lay in state, first in Parliament's Westminster Hall, then in St. Paul's Cathedral, draped with the flag of the great empire he loved. Finally, he was laid to rest next to his father and mother in the small churchyard of St. Martin's in Oxfordshire, within sight of his birthplace, Blenheim Palace.

Churchill will be remembered by history as the leader whose words rallied British pride in the bleak days of 1940. It was he who defied Hitler and successfully guided the grand alliance of Allied nations to victory in World War II.

To the weak, wavering democracies—including the United States—that stood in confusion while the Axis dictators completed one conquest after another, Churchill was the symbol of grim tenacity; he was the confident, inspiring leader who proudly picked up the torch of liberty just as Hitler and his henchmen were about to stamp it out. And in that sense, by a fortunate accident of history, he appeared on the scene at just the right moment to defend the democratic cause.

The quality of Churchill's words and of his brave leadership inspired the British people to stand firm against the storm of tyranny.

And for that deed he will be remembered as long as Western civilization survives.

Mohandas K. (Mahatma) Gandhi

1869–1948   Moral and spiritual leader of India in that nation's struggle for freedom from British rule

"Who am I? What will become of me? What is life all about?"

Like young people since time began, young Mohandas K. Gandhi long had asked himself such questions without finding satisfactory answers. Born to a prominent family in India and educated there, Gandhi had finished a law degree in London. Then, back in India, he had been unsuccessful in his legal career and traveled to South Africa, hoping to turn his fortunes around.

One night in South Africa, an event took place that not only changed his life but also would eventually affect the lives of millions of other human beings. Seated in the first-class compartment of a railroad train, he was asked to leave and to sit in third class with the other Indians and the black-skinned people.

When he refused, Gandhi was put off the train with his baggage and left to shiver in the cold waiting room all night. Shortly afterwards, when he would not give up his seat to a white passenger on a stagecoach, the stagecoach driver beat him badly.

His experience in South Africa led Gandhi to devote himself completely to the struggle for social justice. That struggle would be his personal answer to the question we all ask about our purpose in life.

Gandhi would become known throughout the world, praised by presidents and kings. He would become the single most important figure in India's successful fight for independence from British rule. His people came to speak of him as *the Mahatma*, meaning "Great

Soul," or "The Holy One." Sometimes they referred to him simply as *Gandhiji*, or *bapu* (father).

In the United States, Martin Luther King declared that studying the ideas of Gandhi had inspired the strategy of nonviolence he used with such success during the civil rights movement of the 1960s. Today, the name of Gandhi often is mentioned in the very same breath with Moses, Buddha, Mohammed, and Jesus.

Mohandas, or "Moniya," as he was called in early childhood, was born in 1869, in the small town of Porbandar on the west coast of India. He was the last of four children born to Karamchand Gandhi, a leading government official of his province, and his fourth wife Putlibai, a woman much younger than himself. Although not wealthy, the family belonged to the Indian merchant caste, and young Mohandas never found money a problem in his early life.

One of Gandhi's first teachers considered him "good at English, fair in arithmetic . . . bad handwriting." Writing later about himself, Gandhi said, "It was with some difficulty that I got through the multiplication tables." He cared little for the playground games of his classmates, such as cricket or soccer, but enjoyed taking long walks, a pleasure he would pursue to the end of his life.

It was not the influence of school that shaped Gandhi's formative years, but rather the beliefs of his mother, Putlibai. Although she could neither read nor write, she was deeply religious. Before every meal she would pray. Often she fasted. Once, during the rainy season, she vowed not to eat until she personally saw the sun break through the clouds. Nothing could shake her faith or her good-natured willingness to suffer for her beliefs. Young Moniya watched her and soon began to copy her religious ways.

In the busy port of Porbandar he came into contact with people of many religions: Hindus, Muslims, Zoroastrians, Christians. The Christians, he recalled later, often spoke harshly against the other religions, hoping to convert people to their faith, a practice Gandhi did not like. He very early came to believe, as he later wrote, that "all religions are true, and all religions have some error in them. . . ."

When he was thirteen, Gandhi's family arranged for him to marry, child marriages at that time being commonplace in India. His bride, Kasturba, also thirteen, had not gone to school at all and could neither read nor write. But Mohandas did not mind. Even knowing that Kasturba still would spend most of her time at her parents' home, he considered himself ready for marriage.

Along with the excitement of marriage, young "Mohan," as he now was called, found himself attracted to many tempting but forbidden acts. One of his high school friends persuaded him to sneak away to a secret place and do what religious Hindus never were supposed to do: eat meat. Only a taste of goat meat proved too much for Mohan. For many nights afterward he dreamed that the goat was still alive within his stomach. He would wake up suddenly during the night filled with fear and with regret for what he had done. For the rest of his life Gandhi remained a vegetarian.

The same thing happened to him when he tried smoking cigarettes and when he toyed with the idea of becoming an atheist—not believing in any god. Each time, Gandhi learned from his experience and grew stronger as a person.

Once, young Gandhi stole money from a servant in his house. Then, feeling guilty about what he had done, he wrote a letter to his father, confessing. Instead of punishing him, Mohan's father forgave him completely, believing that no human ever should harm another creature.

That lesson, the practice of *ahimsa*, or nonviolence, was one that Gandhi would follow ever afterward. It was destined to become a central feature of his life. From that time, too, young Gandhi insisted on telling the absolute truth, whatever the penalty might be for himself or for others.

While Gandhi was still a teenager, his father died. Writing about the event many years later, when he already was world famous, Gandhi still expressed guilt for having been away from his father's bedside at the moment of death in order to be with his pretty young wife. Caring for the feelings and the needs of others, sacrificing his own comforts for the sake of truth, and attacking his own weaknesses as a person—these increasingly became the goals of young Mohandas Gandhi growing into manhood.

At the age of eighteen, Gandhi decided to leave India for his college education. In 1888, over the protests of his mother, he set sail for England, enrolling at the Inner Temple in London to study law. Behind him in India he left his mother, his wife, and his infant son, a separation that was to last for three years.

During the early part of his stay in London, Gandhi found himself lonely and ill at ease. Dark-skinned and very thin, he had ears that stuck out awkwardly to the sides. He found it difficult to adapt to English manners, to English

Mohandas (Mahatma) Gandhi as a young man. *The Bettmann Archive*.

clothing, and especially to English food. For a time he did not know about the city's vegetarian restaurants and tried to fill himself mostly with bread and rolls.

Gradually, he adjusted. He became a member of the London Vegetarian Society, even writing articles for the group's publications. He improved his use of the English language. He read the Christian Bible carefully, finding himself deeply moved by the deeds of Jesus. He was especially taken with the ideas of Jesus about caring for the poor and the weak, as well as about nonviolence—"turning the other cheek" when one is struck.

Through the Vegetarian Society he was thrown into contact with prominent English thinkers, including the Fabian Socialist, George Bernard Shaw. He began to think about his own religious views, such as nonviolence, and how they related to politics. He began to understand how competing for profit— the very heart of capitalism—could set person against person and hurt society.

Gandhi found himself increasingly in control of his mind and body. He would not touch meat or fish of any kind, even giving up eggs. He never used tobacco or alcohol. He prayed at regular times during the day. He studied productively.

In the spring of 1891, he passed his law school examinations and was admitted to the High Court of London. The day after the ceremony he immediately set sail for India.

A lawyer now, with an English education, he still was not sure what would become of him, what he would do with his life.

On returning to India, he was shocked to learn that his mother had died. The family had decided not to tell him, fearing that the news would interrupt his studies. Settling now in Bombay, Gandhi and his wife, no longer a child bride, became the parents of another son. Later the couple would have two more sons.

Almost from the beginning, Gandhi's law practice in Bombay proved troublesome to him. Too often, cases were decided through bribery. Guilty people were allowed to go free, and judges traded favors with politicians. Nor was Gandhi comfortable in the courtroom. Once he stood to cross-examine a witness and, painfully shy, found himself paralyzed with fright. He could not even speak.

Unhappy with life in Bombay, Gandhi leaped at an opportunity to practice law for a time in Natal, South Africa, where many Indian citizens had gone to start new businesses. Once again, he left his family behind, expecting to stay for only a year. He could scarcely suspect that, instead, he would remain in Africa for twenty years, an experience that was to shape all of his later life.

Not long after his arrival in Natal, he began to understand what kind of country South Africa really was. The first judge to greet him in a courtroom demanded that Gandhi take off the Indian turban that he wore around his head. Proudly, he refused and promptly left the courtroom.

It was only one week later that the important incident mentioned early in this portrait of Gandhi took place. While riding on a train to Pretoria, Gandhi was removed from the train for refusing to sit in third class with other blacks and Indians, instead of the first-class compartment he had paid for.

That night, sitting alone in a railroad station, shivering from the cold, Gandhi vowed to do something about prejudice in South Africa and in neighboring Transvaal, a former Dutch colony. The cause of racial justice was at stake, of course, but also what Gandhi thought of himself—and his dignity as a human being.

The more Gandhi learned about South Africa's customs, the angrier he became. Indians insultingly were called "coolies." In the Transvaal, they could not vote in elections; could own only limited amounts of property; were not allowed on the streets after 9:00 P.M.;

and had to pay a special tax. Those who signed contracts as indentured servants for a five-year term were little better than slaves. Their employers could abuse them, beat them, do almost anything they pleased, while the servant had virtually no legal rights at all.

When South Africa decided, like Transvaal, to take the vote away from Indian residents, Gandhi swung into action. He was no longer shy. Instead, he began to play a leadership role in the politics of Indian life in South Africa.

He founded an action group, the Natal Indian Congress, to focus the energies of the Indian community, rich and poor alike. He wrote to the newspapers, organized protest meetings, spoke to officials. Although he did not gain the vote for all Indians, he won the attention of officials not only in South Africa but in England and in India.

During a visit to India to bring back his wife and children, he spoke to audiences about the brutal treatment of Indians in South Africa. On his return to Natal a furious crowd of whites, having heard about his speeches, awaited him at the dock, pelting him with stones and rotten eggs. The wife of the police commissioner shielded him with her umbrella and later urged him to take action in the courts. But Gandhi refused to sue, instead accepting an apology from some members of the mob.

During the Boer War between the Dutch and British settlers in South Africa (1899–1902), Gandhi organized an emergency medical corps of Indians to help the British cause. He and his comrades went out onto the battlefields to nurse wounded British soldiers. In the struggle of Britain against the Zulu warriors in 1906, his medical corps helped the wounded of both sides.

For those services he was awarded medals by the British authorities. It was his belief at the time that the British Empire did much to improve the life of the empire's subject peoples. Many years later, declaring that the empire did just the opposite, he returned the medals.

Despite the help Gandhi had given them, Britain's South African leaders passed humiliating laws against the nation's Indian population. In 1906, Transvaal passed a law requiring that all Indians, including children, be fingerprinted and carry an identification paper with them at all times. Gandhi organized an enormous rally against the law at a theater in Johannesburg. He was thrown into prison for his action, the first of many jailings in his lifetime.

In August 1908, he led an even larger rally. This time, thousands of Indians openly burned their registration certificates, many of them considering it an honor to be thrown into prison along with Gandhi.

Gandhi now determined to spend the rest of his life serving mankind. He pledged himself to *satyagraha* (the pursuit of truth), a search to be carried out by means of nonviolent action. That did not mean, he said, just being "passive," just permitting someone to act against a victim. Instead, it meant working creatively, actively, toward agreement with one's opponents in finding solutions to problems.

It also meant that if a person chose to break an unjust law, that person had a duty to go to prison for the act of disobedience.

While in prison in South Africa, Gandhi read the American author Henry David Thoreau's essay on civil disobedience, learning from it, much as Martin Luther King later would learn from Gandhi's writing.

In 1913, another new law was passed that caused Gandhi to use massive civil disobedience. That law stated that only Christian marriages were legal. Hindu, Muslim, and other marriages carried no legal force, so that the women involved in them were no better than prostitutes, and the children of such marriages were illegitimate. This time, even some of the Indian women joined in the protest rallies, including Gandhi's wife, Kasturba. Many Indians, both men and women, were imprisoned as the struggle continued.

Meanwhile, Gandhi and a few friends had set up a special cooperative farming community in Natal, called Phoenix Settlement. It was based on the idea that all people in a communal group should work together at tasks such as farming for the good of all other people in the group. Gandhi had read about such communities in the works of John Ruskin and Leo Tolstoy. At Phoenix Settlement, Gandhi also published a newspaper, *Indian Opinion,* making the case for the rights of Indians living in South Africa.

In 1910, he began a second cooperative community, Tolstoy Farm. Beginning in 1913, many Indians who had been fired from their jobs for protesting against the harsh South African laws came to work in the two communities. There they grew their own food, made their own furniture, and practiced the high moral ideas of Gandhi. Even the leaders in the community were responsible for doing their own cooking and for cleaning the latrines.

Gandhi himself soon was forced to spend still more time in prison. Finally, in December 1913, he was released in order to negotiate directly with General Jan Christian Smuts, the South African leader. Smuts had personally sent Gandhi to prison several times. The two men were opponents. But Gandhi, showing the spirit of love he considered so important, personally made a pair of sandals for the general. Smuts, in time, came to respect Gandhi greatly, considering him "a saint."

Before very long, Indian marriages were made legal. A tax placed on Indian indentured servants was removed. Indians in South Africa were given greater freedom to travel.

Gandhi had won. His use of civil disobedience—protest marches and peaceful strikes—had caused the powerful South African authorities to back down.

Now the skinny little man, Gandhi, with his high-pitched voice, no longer wore formal English clothing. Instead, he had begun to appear barefooted, clad in the ancient Indian dhoti, or cape, of white cloth, as he would for the rest of his life.

True, Indians in South Africa had yet to gain complete equality with whites. But Gandhi had made great strides toward that goal. And in doing so, his name had become familiar to the people of his homeland, India. Indeed, to them he was a hero, the one person perhaps who could achieve the distant dream they were beginning to share—the dream of home rule, independence from the British Crown.

In January 1915, now forty-five years

old, Mohandas K. Gandhi landed in Bombay. At the dock he was greeted by a wildly cheering crowd. Gandhi knew that although their enthusiasm was great, the struggle would be both long and difficult.

He decided to begin by simply traveling around the country, meeting the people. Everywhere, he found large crowds waiting for his blessings, sometimes hoping just to see him. Instead of leaping immediately into politics, he organized a religious community at Ahmedabad, similar to the ones he had begun at Phoenix Settlement and Tolstoy Farm.

Over much opposition, even that of his wife, Kasturba, Gandhi insisted that Untouchables—the lowest of all the Indian social castes—be admitted to the community. Some workers there even feared being polluted by water from buckets used by the Untouchables. But Gandhi persisted. The community survived.

Meanwhile, the British raj (rule) continued to have disastrous results for Indian life. The one thousand or so British officials who governed the country lived in luxury, while millions of Indians suffered. Many of the poorest literally starved to death in the streets while the British, unfeeling, uncaring, exported food from India for profit. Even

when famine or disease struck heavily across the country, the British did nothing to help. They simply looked away.

During World War I, Indian troops had loyally served their British master. At the war's end they expected, as promised, greater home rule in India. Instead, in March 1919, the Rowlatt Acts were passed. Those regulations allowed the jailing of Indians on mere suspicion and their trial without a jury. Gandhi called for a *hartal* (a national day of fasting and prayer with no work).

When a rumor spread that Gandhi had been arrested, some Indians angrily set fires, looted stores, destroyed British property. The city of Amritsar in Punjab province saw particularly severe violence, including the rape of an English schoolteacher.

In response, the British general Reginald E. H. Dyer ordered his Indian soldiers to shoot to kill at a crowd of men, women, and children he had trapped in a marketplace. The result was the horrible Amritsar Massacre, taking the lives of 379 persons with more than 1,000 others wounded.

After Amritsar, Gandhi led the Indian people in a program of noncooperation with the British authorities. He urged Indians not to buy British products. Students were not to attend British schools. Businessmen were not to use British courts or offices. Neither the rich nor the poor were to pay British taxes.

In front of huge crowds of people, Gandhi himself would set afire great piles of British-made clothing, contributed by his audience. Indians, he said, should spin and weave their own clothing. Personally, he made it a practice each day to seat himself for work in front of a spinning wheel, wearing only a white dhoti made of Indian cotton.

It was a striking image, one that soon became known around the world. Here was a man who had made himself the very image of the goodness he wished for others and of the poverty he dreamed of removing. Indians, he hoped, would come to live a simple, happy existence in small villages. Away from cruel cities and brutal machinery, they would produce for themselves whatever they needed.

In March 1922, Indian civil disobedience once again turned violent. This time, Gandhi was arrested and sentenced to six years in prison. In his jail cell he read books. He wrote letters. Often he sat cross-legged and prayed. He fasted. After two years, following an operation for appendicitis, he was released.

For the next few years he tried to persuade the Indian people to develop their own cottage industries, especially spinning and weaving. He worked to bring together Hindus and Muslims, as the nation's two great religions quarreled bitterly over how best to throw off British rule and how India would be organized afterward.

Then, on March 12, 1930, he set out on a mission that would change the course of India's history. Although surrounded on three sides by ocean, the Indian people were not allowed to make salt for their own use without paying a tax to Great Britain. That was true of even the poorest Indians. When British authorities refused Gandhi's gently phrased request to drop the tax, he gathered a group of his followers at Ahmedabad, where they began an incredible march of 241 miles to Dandi, on the Indian Ocean.

History would remember it as the "Salt March," one of the great symbolic acts of Gandhi's life. On arriving, said Gandhi, he would scoop a handful of seawater and make salt, despite the British law.

At every step of the way great crowds cheered Gandhi and his group. Daily, writers and photographers sent a vivid record of his progress around the globe. On April 5, Gandhi and his party walked slowly into the sea for a ritual bath. Then, the beloved "Gandhiji" prayerfully removed a pinch of salt.

Soon afterward Gandhi was arrested.

Without even a trial he was thrown into jail. Because of the acts of civil disobedience that followed, some 60,000 Indians also were imprisoned. But the Indian people would not give in. The salt tax no longer could be collected. Gandhi had made his point. Before long, he and the British viceroy in India reached a compromise on salt.

In the autumn of 1931, Gandhi sailed to London to deal with the British as the sole representative of India's Congress party. Traveling there in steerage class, he walked the streets of the city where once he had studied. Now bespectacled and toothless, with a shaven head, he wore only his familiar white loincloth, a shawl, and slippers. Excited crowds followed him everywhere, warmed by his sense of humor, his wisdom, his love.

To the Western world, Mohandas K. Gandhi, the shy, unhappy, awkward Indian student, had become the Mahatma (a holy person).

While in England he met with virtually every important English leader, including the king and queen. The one exception proved to be Winston Churchill, who would not speak with him. Churchill openly expressed concern that the cleverness of the "half-naked fakir" could very well lead to the loss of India from the British Empire. To Churchill's satisfaction, the London conference held out little hope to Gandhi of Indian independence.

On returning to India, Gandhi was shocked to find the new British viceroy there cracking down severely on the actions of his Congress party. Before long he himself was placed in Yeravda Prison. From there, within the very walls of his jail cell, he launched a new campaign. It had as its goal greater rights for India's most helpless, hopeless people—the Untouchables.

To win the sympathy of other social classes in India, Gandhi began speaking of the poor Untouchables as *Harijans* (Children of God). Beginning September 20, 1932, he announced the start of a fast. It would last, he said, until death if necessary, or until something was done to improve the life of the Harijans.

Six days later the British agreed that never again would there be a formal law that considered a person "Untouchable." Hindu religious leaders now admitted Untouchables to their temples. Some were even allowed to sit in provincial assemblies.

In the spring of 1933, he ended a twenty-one-day fast to gain still more rights for the Harijans. Many of his followers feared that he might die. "If Bapu died," declared his chosen successor, Jawaharlal Nehru, "what would India be like then?"

Gandhi, in traditional Hindu dress, encircled by a crowd at the Simla Conference in India in 1945. *Black Star.*

Gandhi did not die. He lived to see Great Britain and the other Allied nations triumph in World War II over the tyrannical forces of Germany and Japan. Twice he personally wrote to Hitler, hoping to reach the heart of the bloodthirsty dictator. But he received no reply to his letters.

During the war Gandhi demanded a promise from Britain to free India at the end of the war. Instead, the British imprisoned him in the luxurious palace of the Aga Khan at Poona so they could have greater control over him. Across the nation there were angry protest meetings. Violence erupted in the streets. But the British refused to change their minds.

While Gandhi was in prison, his wife, Kasturba, was held there with him. She became ill. Her condition became more and more serious until, finally, it was clear that nothing could be done. She died in her husband's arms. Fearing that Gandhi, now grown old and weak himself, would also die and the world would blame them, the British released him in May 1944. It was to be his last stay in prison. In all, he had spent 2,338 days of his life behind bars—almost six and a half years.

Once free, Gandhi again began to work for Indian independence, something that now began to appear possible. He tried to persuade the Muslim leader, Mohammed Ali Jinnah, that the Muslims should not try to separate from India. Jinnah, however, insisted that a new nation, Pakistan, would have to be created. If necessary, said Jinnah, he would use force to establish it.

In August 1946, the Muslims started bloody riots on the streets of Calcutta. The Hindus struck back. Soon, all across the provinces of Bengal and Bihar there were mass killings, beatings, attacks on holy places, looting. Fires left thousands homeless. Gandhi pleaded for reason and for an end to the violence. He urged that Hindus and Muslims unite to create a peaceful nation.

Finally, on August 15, 1947, Indian independence became a reality. On the same day, Pakistan also was established. Gandhi spent the day fasting and praying for peace. During that one day of happiness, Hindus and Muslims came together in brotherhood.

Then violence again erupted. Hindus fled by the millions from East and West Pakistan to India. Frightened Muslims sometimes crossed paths with them as they left the country. In Calcutta, four days and nights of violence left the city in devastation. Only a fast by Gandhi himself caused guilt-ridden Hindus to stop fighting. Muslims, too, finally became calm, concerned with the terrible vengeance that might descend upon them if Gandhi died.

In January 1948, while living at Birla House in Delhi, Gandhi again fasted for five days to put an end to violence in that city. Gandhi ended his fast with a glass of orange juice. For several days afterward he had to be carried to his prayer meetings.

On January 30, at five o'clock in the afternoon, he walked into the garden at Birla House to address still another prayer meeting. As usual, he leaned for support on the shoulders of two young women.

Then, from the crowd stepped a young man, Nathuram V. Godse. A fanatically religious Hindu, he belonged to a group that was furious with Gandhi for permitting the division of India and the creation of Pakistan. Godse fell to his knees in front of Gandhi. Then, drawing a pistol, he fired three shots into the body of the Mahatma.

"Oh, Ram! Oh, Ram!" cried Gandhi, calling to God for help as he had from the days of his childhood. And then he was no more.

The next day his body was placed atop a pile of sandalwood logs standing near the holy Yamuna River. Millions of people, dressed in white, stood nearby. One of the Mahatma's sons touched a torch to the logs, starting the cremation fire. For fourteen hours the flames rushed upward into the sky. Some people in the crowd groaned. Others cried.

Two weeks later the ashes of Mahatma Gandhi were scattered into the seven sacred rivers of India.

Unlike many religious holy men, Gandhi did not spend his lifetime away in some cave, praying. Instead, he worked—through government and politics—to make a better world for people rich and poor. It was by means of such real tools in a real world, he believed, that human beings could truly serve God.

Caring little for material rewards, he crusaded against the evil of racism and religious bigotry, against the evil of violence, and against the evil of colonial rule—the afflictions that have so cursed our twentieth-century world.

To Viscount Louis Mountbatten, Great Britain's last viceroy of India, Gandhi was destined to "go down in history on a par with Buddha and Jesus Christ."

In speaking of the great Mahatma, physicist Albert Einstein once said, "Generations to come, it may be, will scarce believe that such a one as this ever in flesh and blood walked upon this earth."

PART III
The World
since 1945

Mao Tse-tung

1893–1976   Revolutionary statesman responsible for founding the People's Republic of China and putting into practice his unique model of Communist government

Once, at a time when the 1800s were coming to an end and the twentieth century had not yet been born, there lived in the land of China a boy named Mao Tse-tung. The boy's father was very strict with him and often beat him for failing to jump quickly to what he was told to do.

As the boy grew up, he often rebelled against authority, not just his father, but his teachers, and, later, people in powerful positions in government. He came to believe that people should rule themselves. After reading the works of Karl Marx he became a Communist, declaring that, of all the thousands of truths written by Marx, they all boiled down to one sentence—"It is right to rebel."

On October 1, 1949, Mao Tse-tung, by then fifty-five years old, stood on a balcony at the gate of the Heavenly City in Peking. For many years the Chinese people at that gate had bowed down in fear to the nation's mighty emperors, paying tribute to them in gifts. Now, an enormous crowd gathered to cheer for Mao Tse-tung, wishing that he might "live ten thousand years!"

"The People's Republic of China," announced Mao, "today assumes power. Our nation will never again be an insulted nation!"

Only twenty-eight years before, Mao Tse-tung and eleven others had gathered in Shanghai to form the Chinese Communist party. As Mao once put it, from that small spark had grown a "prairie fire"—the Chinese Revolution, one of the twentieth century's most impor-

161

tant events. Mao Tse-tung himself—philosopher and poet, soldier and ruler—was destined to leave his mark both on China and on the outside world.

How did young Mao, who spent his childhood working with his peasant family in the rice fields of Hunan Province, emerge to become one of the great revolutionary figures of our age, mentioned now in the same breath with such shapers of history as Lenin?

Writing about his early years, Mao remembered vividly that his father "frequently beat me and my brothers. He gave us no money whatever and only the most meager food." Mao's mother, a Buddhist, was much more kind and warm. Quietly, she often took his part. As the family became wealthier because of the father's success as a merchant, Mao's mother often would give food to beggars who came to the door, clearly against her husband's wishes.

When Mao reached the age of six his father sent him to missionary school so he could learn to work with numbers and help keep the account books for the family business. But the boy still had to work in the rice fields every afternoon and well into the evening.

From the beginning, as he later described his school experience, Mao hated learning by heart the ancient Confucian classics. Instead, he would read over and over such stories as *The Romance of the Three Kingdoms* and *All Men Are Brothers*, exciting tales about rebellious heroes. When the teacher approached him, he would quickly hide the stories under copies of the classics.

In his first successful rebellion in a life filled with revolution, Mao once refused to stand up to recite his lesson. He could, said Mao, recite it perfectly well while seated. Clearly, even in elementary school he was what parents and teachers sometimes speak of as a "difficult child."

At the age of thirteen Mao openly challenged his father in front of guests at a family party. When the elder Mao described the boy as lazy and useless, young Mao Tse-tung cursed at him and then fled to a nearby pond, threatening to commit suicide. Finally, and with a firm promise from his father that the beatings would stop, Mao agreed to kowtow (bow down) to his father—but only on one knee.

"From that instant," Mao later wrote, "I learned that when I defended my rights by open rebellion my father gave in, but when I remained weak and submissive he only beat me more."

Shortly afterward he left school to work full-time on the family farm. But at the age of fourteen came one of his boldest acts of rebellion. At that time his father arranged a marriage for him to an eighteen-year-old girl he had never met. Such arranged marriages then were the custom, but Mao Tse-tung absolutely refused to go ahead with it—and never did.

To him, his mother's marriage, arranged in the same way, had virtually turned her into a slave. That, he said, should not be. People should have choices in such important matters. When he became head of the People's Republic of China, one of the first laws Mao put into effect made certain that individuals would have complete freedom in deciding upon a mate.

By the time he reached his late teens Mao was beginning to be concerned with the outside world, especially with politics. In 1910, during a severe famine, his father continued to ship rice for sale at a distant market, even though many neighboring farmers were without food. When some peasants in the village seized a shipment of the rice, Mao sided with them against his father.

Thinking about the whole situation, he began to believe that the problem of poverty was not simple but very complicated, something that might be caused by injustice in the way society was organized.

At the age of sixteen, and against his father's wishes, Mao decided to leave home. He enrolled in a school in a nearby market town. There, he began to read newspapers regularly, learning about the events of the day. He also began to read history, especially a book entitled *Great Heroes of the World*. For the first time he learned about leaders such as Napoleon, as well as George Washington and Abraham Lincoln.

Many of his classmates were children of wealthy landlords. They had fine manners, fine clothing. Mao had only shabby, well-worn clothing. Having left school to work, he was older and taller than the other students, with the rough manners of a peasant. They laughed at him, made him feel awkward and uneasy. Already suspicious of the landlord class, he now began to hate them. With few friends and little concern for team sports, he worked hard at his studies, with outstanding results.

In 1911, he enrolled in a school located in Changsha, the capital city of Hunan Province. There he began to read with greater purpose and direction. At the same time, he worked at toughening his body, especially through long hikes, sleeping in the open air, and swimming in rivers. To Mao, it seemed clear that someone hoping to lead others must be physically strong himself.

When China rose in revolt against the Manchu dynasty in 1911, Mao made a public matter of cutting his hair, then in a pigtail. At that time, the pigtail was a symbol of Manchu rule, and for any Chinese to cut it off was an illegal act, with the penalty of death by beheading. Mao persuaded others to cut their pigtails. Then he proceeded to cut off the pigtails of students too timid to do it themselves.

Soon afterward he left school and joined the revolutionary army of Dr. Sun Yat-sen in the struggle to overthrow the Manchu rulers. For Mao Tse-tung, it was still another act of rebellion against authority.

For five months he served in the army. Then, when the fighting stopped, he spent his time in a library reading such great political classics as Adam Smith's *The Wealth of Nations* and Rousseau's *The Social Contract*.

From the age of twenty to twenty-five, Mao studied at a school in Changsha, preparing to become a teacher. He read still more Western literature, especially books on politics and economics. By the time of his graduation in 1918, he had come to believe in democracy, in reform, and in building what he spoke of as "utopian socialism"—a perfect society based on shared property.

In 1918, he took a job in Peking, working as a librarian at National Peking University. It was there, with the encouragement of the university's head librarian, that he began reading the works of Karl Marx. Soon he became a believer in Marx and the need for China to become a Communist society. He began to organize students on the campus into Marxist study groups. He also tried to organize workers and merchants in the city.

Mao Tse-tung now had launched himself on the highway he would walk for the remainder of his life. He had become a revolutionary.

It was in July 1921 that he and eleven other men met secretly in the city of Shanghai. There, in a school for girls, they officially formed the Communist party of China.

Although deeply involved in politics, Mao still continued for a while to teach children in elementary schools. Meanwhile, he married the daughter of one of his former teachers.

Shortly afterward he decided to give up teaching and devote himself full-time to the cause of revolution. He helped to organize strikes among coal miners. He also worked closely with Dr. Sun Yat-sen's Kuomintang party, serving on the governing central committee of both the Kuomintang and of the Communist party.

Some Communists came to believe that Mao was working too closely with the non-Communist Sun Yat-sen. As a result, they had him removed from his leadership position. Returning to his native province of Hunan, he had time to read and think, but also to meet with the kinds of people he had grown up with, poor peasant farmers.

He came to disagree with Joseph Stalin, the Communist dictator of the Soviet Union, about the best way to seize power in China. Stalin insisted that military control of the cities would bring victory. Increasingly, Mao would argue that by controlling the countryside it would be possible to encircle the cities and then simply swallow them up.

Winning control of the peasantry, argued Mao, was the only answer. Several hundred million armed peasants could never be stopped, he declared. They would rise "like a tornado or tempest" and "send all imperialists, warlords, corrupt officials, local bullies, and evil rich men to their graves."

In 1925, Sun Yat-sen died. The new leader of the Kuomintang, Chiang Kai-shek, feared the power of the Communists and determined to crush them. In a lightning attack Chiang's forces killed most of the Chinese working class that had helped him seize the city of Shanghai. Then he turned for support and friendship to the wealthy, promising them that he would totally wipe out the remaining Communists.

With brutal persistence, Chiang pursued his goal. In 1930, he succeeded

in capturing Mao's wife and sister. He had the heads of both women cut off and placed on spikes to show the peasants of Hunan Province what was in store for them if they followed Mao's Communists.

After four major offensives Chiang launched a massive fifth attack. He succeeded in surrounding the entire Communist army only to have them break out of the trap. Led by Mao and other Communist generals, the troops fled to a remote mountainous area in south central China.

Chiang followed them, but never could destroy them. That was because of tactics of guerrilla warfare that Mao himself developed, summing them up in a slogan:

The enemy advances, we retreat;
The enemy encamps, we harass;
The enemy tires, we attack;
The enemy retreats, we pursue.

In 1934, Mao and Chu Te, the commander of China's Red Army, led the Communist forces on the famous "Long March"—a painful retreat to the far north of China across some seven thousand miles of rugged territory.

Twelve months later, in late 1935, some 8,000 Communist troops of the 100,000 who had set out on the Long March finally arrived in the distant mountains of Yenan Province, just below the Great Wall. There, toughened and strengthened by their ordeal, the survivors united behind the leadership of Mao Tse-tung.

They now had a new discipline and a method of guerrilla warfare that was destined to lead them to victory. Their courage would make the Long March a legend that still lives on today as a glorious chapter in Chinese history, one studied by every schoolchild in that country.

It was in Yenan that Mao began developing the strategies that he eventually would use to govern the nation. He sent Communist party leaders into the countryside to educate the peasant farmers. He established schools for the children. He spread the ideas of sharing work and sharing wealth.

Most important of all, Mao united the people of Yenan, and later of surrounding provinces, in a war against invading Japanese armies. As early as 1931, the Japanese had begun taking advantage of China's weaknesses, especially the war between Communist and Kuomintang forces.

Chiang Kai-shek pledged to defeat the Communists first before defending against Japan. But Mao felt differently. He urged that, for the good of the whole nation, all Chinese people first unite against Japan. Then, after the war, the Chinese could work out any differences that still existed.

In December 1941, Japanese planes launched a devastating surprise attack on the American naval base at Pearl Harbor, Hawaii, causing heavy losses. The United States now joined with Britain and France to help the Chinese defeat Japan. During World War II Mao greatly strengthened his army, gaining control of much of northern China. By the end of the war he had more than one million troops under his command. Meanwhile, the United States had convinced Chiang Kai-shek to fight against the Japanese, not the Communists. Mao and Chiang therefore established a "united front."

After American planes dropped atomic bombs on Hiroshima and Nagasaki in August 1945, Japan surrendered. For a time Mao and Chiang spoke face to face, trying to work out plans for a new government. But the talks failed. In 1946, a bloody civil war broke out in China. As Mao had said several years earlier, "Every Communist must grasp the truth: political power grows out of the barrel of a gun."

The fighting lasted for four years. At first Chiang's forces scored victories, outnumbering the Communists four to one. But Mao had built great trust among the Chinese people. Peasants knew that in Yenan he had divided up the land of wealthy farmers among the poor. Wherever they had fought, Mao's soldiers had shown courtesy to the people, while trying to protect them. Popular support turned the tide of battle in Mao's favor. By 1949, the remnants of Chiang's once mighty army had fled mainland China, taking refuge on the offshore island of Taiwan.

It was on October 1, 1949, standing at the gate of the Heavenly City in Peking, that Mao Tse-tung announced the formation of the People's Republic of China. At last, the civil war was over. China was unified.

Mao began immediately to transform the nation, turning it into a Communist state on the model of the USSR (Union of Soviet Socialist Republics). He took over farmlands, making them the shared property of all the people. Many of the former owners were put on trial before "people's courts." Perhaps as many as a million of those landowners were executed for "crimes against the people." Millions of others, such as college professors, factory owners, and wealthy merchants, were forced to undergo periods of "reeducation." Only when they could show loyalty to group or "collective" ideas instead of their old individualism were they finally released.

In 1950, China's relations with the United States suffered a crushing blow. United Nations troops, mostly Americans under General Douglas MacArthur, had pushed back the North Korean army that earlier had invaded South Korea. As MacArthur's men approached the Chinese border at the Yalu River, Mao sent his forces into Korea to stop them.

Before the Korean War finally came to an end, nearly 900,000 Chinese soldiers had been killed. The Chinese economy had been badly drained. Meanwhile, President Harry Truman had promised that the United States would defend Chiang Kai-shek's island fortress, Taiwan, against any Chinese invasion.

When the Korean War finally ended, Mao speeded up his campaign to take over, or "collectivize," all farmland. At the same time, he had no wish to be a dictator to the Chinese people, as Joseph Stalin had become to the Russians. Instead, he announced a new policy of free speech, allowing open criticism of the government. Or, as he put it, "Let a hundred flowers bloom, let a hundred schools of thought contend." There should be a better balance between discipline and freedom, he said, and now more freedom was needed.

To Mao's surprise, many Chinese, especially the well educated, began to criticize the Communist party bitterly. They demanded sweeping changes. Mao—a rebel from childhood—found it difficult to change his mind, but he declared that sometimes there was such a thing as *too much freedom*. At those times, more discipline was necessary.

He therefore ordered a crackdown on the critics, jailing many of them.

The incident convinced Mao that he could not depend on the nation's brightest thinkers. Instead, he concluded, it was best to rely on the common people of China—to release the energy of the masses. Based on that deep faith in the common people, he launched what is known to history as the Great Leap Forward.

Overnight, hoped Mao, every backyard would become a steel mill. People voluntarily would work eighteen or twenty hours a day in factories or on huge new collective farms, known as communes. Beginning in 1958, the Chinese people began to work furiously to achieve Mao's goals.

The result was almost total failure. Trying to run the nation's farms from the capital city, Peking, meant moving millions of Chinese peasants around the country, wherever they were needed. Instead of rising, agricultural production went down sharply. Many people starved to death. Industrial output also declined.

It took more than three years for the nation to recover from the Great Leap Forward.

Meanwhile, relations between the two great Communist powers, China and Soviet Russia, grew steadily worse. Mao believed that the Russians were giving far too many privileges to their educated class—scientists, inventors, engineers, and scholars. Russian communism, he said, was not communism at all, just capitalism in disguise.

Nikita Khrushchev, the Soviet leader, openly laughed at Mao's efforts, pointing with scorn at the results of the Great Leap Forward. The Russians called home their engineers and others who had been helping to build up China. They cut off all economic aid. Serious arguments also developed about ownership of land at points along the long common border shared by the two nations. Tension continued to grow.

While Mao worried about China's mounting problems with the USSR, he still was concerned that the Chinese people, especially intelligent young people, were becoming too self-centered, too interested, for example, in making money for themselves. Such citizens no longer "served the people." If that attitude continued, he said, the old inequalities surely would come back again. There would be *classes* of people—rich and poor—competing against each other. To be certain that such a situation never would happen, Mao launched the Great Proletarian Cultural Revolution.

One of Mao's first targets in the Cultural Revolution was a powerful figure

Mao Tse-tung, chairman of the Communist Party in China, 1959. *The Bettmann Archive.*

in the Chinese government, Liu Shao-chi, who had begun to reward some Chinese workers with extra money for doing outstanding work. That, said Mao, was only "taking the capitalist road" and was against the idea of equality that should be at the very heart of communism.

Encouraged by Mao, hundreds of thousands of Chinese young people, known as Red Guards, left their classrooms. Many of them dragged their teachers through the streets, laughing at them.

The Red Guards attacked central party leaders. Often they publicly humiliated the officials in front of large crowds of cheering people while wildly waving in their hands "the little red book," *Quotations of Chairman Mao*.

The slogans of the Cultural Revolution could well have been the thoughts of Mao when he himself was still a young man: "Fight selfishness!" "To rebel is good!" Those ideas soon began appearing on the walls of buildings in every city in China. The Red Guards carried them through the streets on posters. Noisy parades and public demonstrations often lasted through the night.

Meanwhile, Mao had thousands of powerful Communist party officials thrown in jail. Even Teng Hsiao-ping (Deng Xiaoping), a longtime friend from the Long March and secretary of the

Communist party, was accused of plotting to bring back capitalism. Such "demons and monsters," declared Mao, "must be punished."

The Cultural Revolution ended almost as quickly as it had begun. When Soviet troops swept into Czechoslovakia in 1968 to put down a rebellion there, Mao grew concerned. He worried that the Russians might leap at the chance to attack China while the nation was weakened by confusion and internal fighting. To prevent such an attack, he ordered the Chinese army to restore order in the streets and put down the Red Guards. By 1969, the Cultural Revolution was over.

The next question, of course, would be how to control the army. Mao feared that Lin Piao, the minister of defence, might use the army to lead a revolution and take over the government.

"The Party controls the gun," said Mao. "The gun must never control the Party." It is not certain whether, as it is sometimes charged, Lin Piao actually was plotting to assassinate Mao. But Mao soon announced that Lin Piao had been killed in the crash of an airplane in Mongolia, supposedly while trying to escape to Soviet Russia. What really happened may never be known.

It is certain, however, that Mao soon decided to improve relations with the strongest rival of the USSR, the United

Chinese farm workers studying Mao Tse-tung's writings, 1968. *China Pictorial.*

States of America. In a move that surprised the world, a smiling Mao Tsetung welcomed America's president, Richard M. Nixon, to Peking in 1972.

For many years Mao had spoken bitterly of the United States as the great enemy of people's revolutions. The Red Guards had made it a point to kick and stab with bayonets cloth-filled dummies labeled "USA." Mao's own son had been killed in active fighting against American troops in the Korean War.

But now it became clear to him that he needed time to rebuild the Chinese economy, to strengthen the Chinese army. Perhaps the Americans would help, or at least keep the Russians occupied.

Long after his trip to China President Nixon claimed that in going there he was "playing the China card." But in reality, the idea of friendship began with Mao Tse-tung. To Mao, it was a matter of "playing the American card." As a result, relations between the two nations slowly began to improve.

Long before Nixon's visit, Mao had begun to slow his personal pace. He no longer worked twelve to fourteen hours a day, followed by nights filled with intense reading. At the age of eighty he knew that the end of his life was near. His speech had become slurred. His face twitched, and he had trouble controlling his hands. More and more, he allowed the diplomat Chou En-lai, another old friend from the Long March, to run the daily affairs of government.

Disappointed in the failure of the Cultural Revolution, Mao worried about what would happen after his death. In a poem written to Chou he said:

Now that the country has become Red, who will be its guardians?
Our mission, unfinished, may take a thousand years.
The struggle tires us and our hair is gray.
You and I, old friend, can we just watch our efforts being brushed away?

In January 1976, Chou En-lai died. On September 9, 1976, Mao Tse-tung died.

After Mao's death there was a struggle for power. By 1981, Teng Hsiao-ping and others who had suffered during the Cultural Revolution had won out. Teng openly welcomed to China some features of the capitalist system that Mao so deeply detested. "It doesn't matter whether a cat is black or white," said Teng, "as long as it catches mice."

For Mao, just accomplishing a task— "catching mice"—was not enough. By the time of his death, China, poor when he first took power, had become the sixth largest industrial nation in the world. It had a well-developed system of health care, serving all of its people. No longer were there beggars on the streets of China's great cities.

But Mao had wanted still more. In 1965, in the midst of the Cultural Revolution, he had encouraged his own niece to challenge her teachers at school. When she admitted her fear of speaking up to them, Mao asked her what the worst thing might be that could happen to her: perhaps being expelled from school? "The school," he supposedly told her, "should allow students to rebel, should even encourage them to rebel."

At that time Mao Tse-tung had stood as the unquestioned leader of a nation containing one of every five people in the world's entire population. Yet, as

so often had shown in his own youth, he still believed in questioning authority.

He knew that, once in power, revolutionaries too often looked out for their own self-interest, not the good of the people—much like the leaders they had overthrown.

To fight against that kind of selfishness, said Mao, was the real job of a revolutionary leader. And because human beings for so many ages of history have been so very selfish, the task of leading a social revolution was never really over.

Having to persist in that difficult—perhaps even endless—task of leadership, said Mao Tse-tung, was the true "price of power."

Charles de Gaulle

1890–1970   Leader of Free French military resistance to the Nazi regime in World War II; president of France 1959–1969

August 25, 1944. General Charles de Gaulle enters Paris in triumph. Adolf Hitler's Nazi armies, in command of the city for more than four years, now have been crushed. As far as the eye can see there is a cheering, swirling French crowd, with the tricolored flag of France fluttering in the sunlight.

De Gaulle joins with the crowd in singing the national anthem, the "Marseillaise." He enters Notre Dame Cathedral for a religious service. Suddenly, shots ring out. People dive for cover. But not Charles de Gaulle. Six feet six inches tall, he walks into the cathedral, proud and straight, never flinching.

"Nothing could be more important," he later writes, "than for me not to yield to the panic of the crowd."

As he leaves the cathedral, the crowd gathered outside greets him with a thunderous ovation:

"Vive de Gaulle!" they shout. "Vive de Gaulle!"

Enormous signs in his honor line the streets of Paris, proclaiming him as the nation's liberator.

It is a time of rebirth for the French people and for the French nation. After the shame of defeat at the hands of the Germans, de Gaulle had refused to give up. He had never surrendered. During all the humiliating years of German occupation he had inspired the resistance forces, promising to return at the head of a liberating army. And now, he has lived up to his promise.

"Vive de Gaulle! Vive la France!"

General Charles de Gaulle in military uniform. *Brown Brothers.*

From the time of his childhood Charles de Gaulle had prepared himself for greatness, prepared himself to lead the French nation. His father, Henri, had fought in the Franco-Prussian War of 1870 and never forgave Germany for seizing the French provinces of Alsace-Lorraine. Charles and the other boys in the de Gaulle family learned early that revenge was necessary.

They came to believe that France must once again be the leading power on the European continent. And they came to see their own lives as having a purpose: that of restoring the lost glory of the French nation.

Although not wealthy, the de Gaulle family lived in considerable comfort. Young Charles was taught very early that his ancestors had played an important role in French history. Some had fought against the English in the wars of the fourteenth and fifteenth centuries. One had continued to defy the British even after France's loss in the Battle of Agincourt (1415).

For Charles's tenth birthday his grandfather, a historian, gave the boy a book of French history that he himself had written. Charles read the book over and over again, memorizing the facts, the dates, and the stories he found in it. Even as an old man de Gaulle would amaze people with his remarkable memory. In his childhood, he applied that special gift to the study of history.

The other influence on his early life was religion. Raised a devout Catholic, he came to believe that God had "chosen" France as a special nation and that the modern Christian French, like the ancient Hebrews of the Bible, were a "chosen people."

Charles soon decided that his life must be like that of France's past heroes—dedicated to resisting foreign enemies. Like Louis XIV, Napoleon, and Joan of Arc, he must be prepared to fight for his nation's safety, but also for its honor and its glory.

His choice of careers, then, was not surprising. In 1909 he won admission to Saint-Cyr, the finest of France's military academies. At home he had already played war games hundreds of times, giving orders to neighborhood children three and four years older than himself.

At Saint-Cyr he quickly became known as a very special cadet. Although he hated the dullness of drill and of barracks discipline, he committed himself totally to learning the skills needed for military leadership.

Because of his unusual height, his classmates spoke of him as "Big Asparagus" or "Mr. Two Yards." And because of his fighting spirit, they also dubbed him "The Fighting Cock" and "The Grand Constable." Stubborn and proud, he never bothered to mix with the other cadets. Still, they could not help but respect him. In a graduating class of more than two hundred students in 1912, de Gaulle finished in the top ten.

Now, as Lieutenant Charles de Gaulle, he began working toward the destiny of greatness that he was so certain lay in store for him. From the beginning, he argued that the way to defeat Germany in war and to win back Alsace-Lorraine lay in technology— particularly those newest of weapons, the machine gun and the rapid-firing cannon. Horses, he said, no longer had a part to play in modern warfare. Nor did it make sense for infantrymen with fixed bayonets to charge into the face of massed artillery and machine-gun fire. That, argued de Gaulle, would simply be a matter of suicide.

He soon got a chance to see how right his views really were. In 1914, World War I broke out. Ordered to lead the charge of his platoon at a German machine-gun nest, he was badly wounded. From his hospital bed he demanded, again and again, to be sent back into combat, only to be turned down.

Finally, to put an end to his protests, he was permitted to lead an intelligence patrol, creeping on his hands and knees at night toward a line of German trenches. Because he understood German, he could lie silently in the dark

beside the trenches and then report back what he had overheard. For that service he later was honored by his commander.

Few of de Gaulle's comrades believed he would survive the war. He took chance after chance, certain that he was destined to live on. Two more times he was wounded, once by stepping on a land mine, only to return again to action.

He volunteered for the most dangerous assignments. In hand-to-hand fighting at the Battle of Verdun, he was pierced in the leg by a bayonet. Then, while lying helpless on the ground, a shell exploded nearby, a fragment penetrating his skull. He was left for dead on the battlefield.

Hours later a German patrol came by, gathering corpses for burial. While riding in a graveyard wagon he awoke, groaning. As de Gaulle later recalled, it was the Germans—the very men he had just been fighting—who saved his life.

For the next thirty-two months de Gaulle was held captive in German prison camps. During that time he improved his knowledge of German. He read. He studied. He came to admire some things about the Germans, to hate other things.

Although still suffering intense pain from his wounds, he tried five times to escape. Once he dug a tunnel only to be caught just as he reached the outside wall of the prison. Angrily, the Germans transferred him to a maximum security fortress, where he spent the rest of the war.

With the fighting over, de Gaulle returned home. During the war he had become a captain. He had been decorated for bravery three times. He had written a book about military strategy. And he had become a personal favorite of General Henri Philippe Pétain, at one time his teacher at Saint-Cyr and, because of the war, known as "the hero of Verdun." At the time Pétain was de Gaulle's special hero, a view that later was to change dramatically.

After the war's end Captain de Gaulle was stationed with the French army in Poland to help defend against Lenin's new Communist government that had seized power in Russia. While hating the idea of communism, de Gaulle could not help but admire the personal strength of some of the Russian leaders—men who refused to give up, even when faced by military forces sent by some of the world's great powers. To de Gaulle, courage, brains, and resistance were qualities to be admired, even in an enemy.

Returning from Poland, de Gaulle married. He taught for a time at his old military school, Saint-Cyr. Then,

looking toward promotion to high rank in the French army, he won admission to the nation's command and general staff college.

As a student there, de Gaulle often criticized his superior officers. He considered them especially shortsighted for failing to see the importance of flexible new weapons used during World War I, especially the airplane and the tank. In magazine articles and in an important new book, he declared that trench warfare never again would work. Instead of digging in to fixed positions, said de Gaulle, it was necessary to have a highly mobile strike force manned by well-trained professional soldiers.

Meanwhile, the commanders of the French army were doing exactly what de Gaulle had warned against. They were busily constructing a network of super trenches, known as the Maginot Line. That line of defenses, they assured the French people, was strong enough to turn back any possible German attack.

Some French politicians eagerly rushed to agree with the military. Remembering French history, they feared that the corps of highly professional soldiers recommended by de Gaulle might one day put an end to the nation's always fragile system of free popular democracy.

If the French would not listen to de

Gaulle's advice, the Germans listened carefully—and followed it. After Adolf Hitler came to power in 1933, German industries began the massive production of tanks and planes. Some German army officers openly quoted the young French officer's writings as a basic source of their new plan for lightning warfare, or *blitzkrieg.*

French military leaders, even Pétain, continued to ignore de Gaulle's warnings. To them, he was still just a "junior officer." They refused to admit that, as he pointed out, France had a smaller population than Germany's. It did not have as good a geographic position for combat. Only modern tanks and planes would give the French an advantage in wartime.

Increasingly, de Gaulle saw his superiors as tired old men who did not want to be bothered. They would not change their ways. And, as a result, they found themselves giving in to the Germans, buying "peace at any price."

And then the war came.

De Gaulle, by then a brigadier general, fought bravely. Personally at the head of a tank column, he repulsed two German offensives. But Hitler's forces were too numerous, too well-equipped.

For a time de Gaulle served in the French government as under secretary of war. When others, including his former hero Marshall Pétain, called for

surrender, de Gaulle would not hear of it. He suggested that, if necessary, the government should be moved to France's colonies in Africa.

But surrender? Never!

Pétain became prime minister. Almost immediately, he surrendered to Adolf Hitler.

De Gaulle left at once for London. From there, on June 18, 1940, he broadcast on BBC radio an emotional radio appeal to the French people.

"Whatever happens," he thundered, "the flame of French resistance must not and shall not die." The struggle, he pledged, would continue.

From that time on, de Gaulle became the rallying point for the Free French movement, pledged to defeating the Nazi invaders. He also became the most hated enemy of the Vichy government, a French puppet regime set up by the Nazis in southern France. That government passed a resolution condemning Charles de Gaulle to death.

De Gaulle moved quickly to strengthen France's African colonies. He also managed to set up close ties with the secret groups of resistance fighters still conducting raids against the German forces within France itself. He worked for a time with General Henri Giraud, the resistance leader favored by President Franklin D. Roosevelt of the United States, who never

General de Gaulle, on French soil again for the first time since the German occupation, walks the streets of liberated Bayeux in Normandy, France, eight days after the Allies' D-day landings. *Globe Photos.*

found it easy to get along personally with de Gaulle.

Gradually, however, the world began to see that Charles de Gaulle was the real head of the Free French government in exile.

On June 6, 1944, Allied troops stormed ashore on France's Normandy coastline, launching their long-awaited attack on Hitler's "fortress Europe." By August 25, the Allies had liberated Paris.

On that day, Charles de Gaulle entered the city in triumph, a hero to the French people.

The French parliament unanimously chose de Gaulle as premier of a French provisional government until a new constitution could be written.

From the time of his childhood he had been certain that such an event would come to pass. And now, at last, Charles de Gaulle stood alone as leader of the French people.

No longer did he have to fear the evil Nazi leader, Adolf Hitler. The threats to French interests now, in his mind at least, came from the nation's allies in World War II: Britain, the Soviet Union, and the United States. Each of those powers, said de Gaulle, would be looking out for its own self-interest in Europe.

At the same time, he had little respect for France's other political personalities, considering most of them selfish bumblers, concerned mostly with making money for themselves. He quarreled often with the members of the various political parties making up the provisional government.

Finally, he became completely disgusted with the pettiness of French politics. In January 1946 de Gaulle resigned as premier. For the next few years he led a group known as the Rally of the French People, which, in the election of 1951, actually won 120 seats in the National Assembly. Like de Gaulle himself, the rally opposed communism and wanted to restore France to a position of greatness in the world.

By 1953, however, de Gaulle and the other rally leaders came to disagree on many issues. As usual, de Gaulle insisted on having his own way. When that proved impossible, he resigned from the group.

For a time he refused even to appear in public. Instead, he retired to his country estate in the tiny village of Colombey-les-Deux-Églises. There, he spent most of his time writing books about his own life and his hopes for renewed French power in the world.

In 1958, de Gaulle once again returned to politics. While he had been away, the French colony of Indochina (led by Vietnam) had won independence in a bloody conflict. Meanwhile, Algerians, too, had been demanding their freedom. When French settlers in Algeria refused to give in, an equally bloody struggle seemed certain. With no other hope, the French National Assembly turned to de Gaulle for help.

He agreed to serve, but only if a new constitution were written, giving him substantial powers in an office to be known as "president." The constitution soon was drafted, and the French people approved it overwhelmingly.

Beginning in 1959, de Gaulle began to use his new powers. He encouraged the growth of French industry. He attacked the problem of an inflated currency. When open warfare broke out in Algeria, he used the French army to restore order there. He arranged for a cease-fire in the war and worked to please both sides. Finally, he agreed to Algerian independence and won approval for it by a vote of the French people. Soon, he arranged for the independence of all of France's other colonies in Africa.

Probably no other French statesman could have brought about such important changes in so short a time.

In de Gaulle's relations with America and the nations of Europe, he tried to show the strength and independence of France. He stopped Great Britain from becoming a member of the European Economic Community (EEC). He completely withdrew French military support from the North Atlantic Treaty Organization (NATO). He demanded that American troops be withdrawn from Vietnam. He spoke in favor of French-speaking Quebec's independence from Canada. He made certain that France began construction of its own atomic bombs.

In the future, de Gaulle predicted, the Cold War would end. There no longer would be two competing groups of nations, one headed by the Soviet Union, the other by the United States. When that happened, he said, France would have a more important part to play. Meanwhile, although he still hated communism, it was important for France to stay neutral, not siding with either of the two great power blocs.

In 1965, he won reelection to the French presidency, an office carrying with it a seven-year term. But his popu-

larity slowly was beginning to fade. By 1968, the French economy was in serious trouble. Inflation returned. Millions of workers went on strike. Farmers organized themselves to complain of hard times. College students demanded the right to share in decision-making on their campuses.

De Gaulle went directly to the people. He dissolved the parliament and called a general election, charging that the French Communist party was trying to take over the country. His own party won a smashing victory in the election, gaining a clear-cut majority in the new parliament.

Then, in 1969, he once again went to the people for a vote, asking for a change in the constitution that would give less power to the French Senate. If he did not win, threatened de Gaulle, he would resign.

This time, the French people refused to go along with him.

True to his word, de Gaulle immediately resigned from office, returning to his country estate at Colombey-les-Deux-Églises. There he spent most of his time writing the story of his life. Brooding, like a child who had not gotten "his way," he refused to take positions on public issues. Almost always he refused to speak to reporters. In silence, he lived out his days.

On November 9, 1970, just before

his eightieth birthday, Charles de Gaulle died of a heart attack.

After his death, much that de Gaulle had worked for was changed. Most important, the European nations moved closer to economic and political unity in something like a "United States of Europe," an idea for which he had shown nothing but contempt.

Always, de Gaulle remained suspicious of cooperation between nations. To the end of his days he remained a "nationalist." The nation-state, to him, was the best way to organize human affairs. For such world organizations as the League of Nations and the United Nations, he had almost no respect at all.

His greatest affection was for France. His goal was that France should stand tall; France should have an exceptional destiny. France, he declared, was only herself when in the front rank of nations. "France cannot be France without greatness."

De Gaulle liked to say that men will give their lives only for their own country, not for some vague set of ideas or beliefs.

He may well have been right. Yet, around the globe during his lifetime, nation fought nation in a seemingly endless series of bloody wars—wars for national power, wars for national "greatness."

As David Schoenbrun, a reporter who knew and very much admired the French leader, once wrote, only one man of the time could have been elected president of a United States of Europe—Charles de Gaulle.

But, above all, de Gaulle was a Frenchman and always remained a Frenchman. His very name, "Charles de Gaulle," may be translated "Charles of France." As a result, said Schoenbrun, he never could rise beyond being *only* a Frenchman."

In our own age and in the century to come, the world may very well need more than leaders of separate national governments, looking out only for the good of their own separate countries.

Instead, we may need leaders who can think in terms of worldwide problems—such as war and hunger—and worldwide solutions to those problems.

Juan Perón 1895–1974
Eva Perón 1919–1952

Nationalist leaders revered by the masses in Argentina for achieving social and economic reforms

When Juan Perón served as president of Argentina, people in that nation often compared him to Simón Bolívar, the great Liberator of Latin America. Others went still further. They believed his wife Eva when she said of him, "He is God for us. . . . We cannot conceive of heaven without Perón. He is our sun, our air, our water, our life."

In the eyes of many, Eva herself loomed as an equally heroic personality—an "Argentine Joan of Arc." Born to poverty, often uncertain where her next meal would come from, she eventually became one of the world's richest women. To her closest followers it was "Evita" Perón, not her husband Juan, who was the real revolutionary, the true shaper of change.

In his childhood Juan Perón certainly was not so poor as Evita. But he was far from rich, something that made him uneasy with the wealthy class that made so many of the decisions in Argentina. Although Juan's grandfather had been a prosperous physician, his own father chose to be a rancher. When farming conditions grew worse in Lobos, close to the capital city of Buenos Aires, Perón moved his family, including young Juan, to distant Patagonia in the far south of Argentina. There, on the cold, windy plains, he tried his hand at sheep-raising.

At the age of ten Juan was sent back to live with relatives in Buenos Aires, where the schools were much better. Welcoming the chance to succeed on his own, he later wrote, "My way of thinking was not as a child, but almost as a man. . . . I endeavored to be a man . . . and to prove myself." From the very beginning young Perón was outstanding as a school athlete and popular with his classmates.

Deciding against a career in medicine, at the age of fifteen he enrolled instead in military school. Many of the instructors at the school were Germans teaching the German approach to military strategy and to discipline. From that time on, Juan always would admire the toughness and the total commitment to duty of German soldiers.

In 1913, at the age of eighteen, Perón was commissioned a second lieutenant in the Argentine infantry. For the next five years he served in port cities in the northern part of the country before being assigned to teach in a school for young cadets.

It was as a teacher that he first won high praise from his superior officers. They, as well as the cadets, spoke of Peron's tremendous energy and "magnetism," his total absorption in his duties, the care he took with students. As one student later recalled, "He stayed in the barracks, only going out on Sundays. . . ." "He taught us good manners . . . and how to eat. . . ." "He was a true father to us. . . ."

Tall and athletic, Perón made it a point to introduce new sports to the school, especially the American sport of basketball. He himself continued to compete in boxing, track, and fencing. While still a teacher, he became fencing champion of the entire Argentine army.

Promoted to the rank of captain, Perón was admitted in 1926 to the nation's most important war academy, the Escuela Superior de Guerra. Military officers were chosen for that school to prepare them for top leadership positions in the army.

Shortly after entering the academy he met a seventeen-year-old girl, Aurelia, living nearby. Before long, she and Juan were engaged. They married in January 1929.

In 1930 Perón played a small part in helping to overthrow President Irigoyen of Argentina. As a reward the new president promoted him to the rank of major, but decided that it would be safest to keep the ambitious young officer away from the official business of government. For the next six years Perón served as a professor of military history at the Escuela Superior de Guerra.

He enjoyed teaching. It gave him a chance to organize his thoughts and learn how to present them to an audience. He learned how to think on his feet and say important things in a simple way. He polished his writing style, publishing books and articles on military history and tactics. From that time on, Perón enjoyed lecturing to groups, whether large or small. Later, as a national political leader, he remained essentially a teacher.

In 1936 Perón was sent to Santiago, Chile, to serve as a military adviser to the Argentine ambassador there. He also was promoted again, this time to lieutenant colonel. What actually happened in Santiago is not clear, but before long the Chilean government asked him to leave. Most probably, Perón was suspected of spying.

Shortly after he returned to Argentina, Perón's young wife, Aurelia, died of cancer.

In February 1939, lonely and unhappy, he eagerly accepted an assignment in Italy to gather information about the growing political tensions in Europe. The experience was destined to become highly important to him.

Based in Rome, Perón soon came to admire the Italian dictator, Benito Mussolini. He was impressed with Mussolini's ability as a public speaker to move great crowds of people to a fever pitch of emotion. He came to believe, along with Mussolini and the Nazi dictator, Adolf Hitler, that the masses of people in a nation could be unified, organized, and mobilized for war. But, in sharp contrast to the two European strong-

men, Perón also came to believe that labor unions, if properly organized, could help bring a nation closer to a vital goal—social democracy.

Yet, to Juan Perón, the more evil features of Mussolini's Fascists and Hitler's Nazis seemed relatively unimportant. What truly fascinated him were the tactics—the methods—used by those leaders in shaping the tone and direction of their nations.

World War II already had broken out when Perón returned to Argentina in 1940. He soon was made a full colonel and placed in charge of training in a school for mountain warfare. In a short time, however, he became involved in politics. He was one of those army officers who formed a political group known as GOU (Group of United Officers). Some of the GOU members hoped to bring Argentina into the war on the side of Germany and Italy. Still others hoped to copy Hitler's aggressive methods and make Argentina the dominant power in South America.

Perón, it appears, saw the organization as having a very simple purpose. It would be a tool to bring about revolution and overthrow the Argentine government. And that, indeed, is what eventually happened.

The Revolution of 1943 toppled the government and brought to power General Pedro P. Ramírez. Although Perón again played only a small part in the uprising, he was appointed under secretary of the war ministry in the new cabinet, as well as head of the National Labor Department.

To Perón, his job in dealing with laborers was critical. Owners of the many new factories then springing up in Argentina made huge profits. But the workers did not share in the good times. Most of them barely managed to survive. Having seen Mussolini's success in gaining support from workers, Perón clearly understood that his own goal of seizing power could best be realized by winning the Argentinian working class to his side.

From the beginning he promised the workers everything, instead of, as he put it, "halfway solutions." The government, he said, must "serve the workers"—or as he often called them, *los descamisados* (the shirtless ones).

In his articles and speeches Perón now began to speak of an "orderly way" to give social justice to workers, not the confusion that he saw in the new Communist government of the Soviet Union. If only the government acted forcefully enough, he said, both employers and workers would gain.

Probably the most imaginative and intelligent member of the Argentine government, he moved quickly to put his ideas into action. Under his leadership, new laws were passed giving the workers higher wages, low-cost housing, paid vacations, and protection in old age similar to Franklin D. Roosevelt's Social Security program in the United States.

Almost overnight Perón became the hero of the Argentinian labor movement. He traveled all across the country, speaking everywhere to large meetings of workers. At one meeting he was received with thunderous applause after being introduced as "Argentina's Number One Worker." Soon, no public figure in Argentina was as well known or as popular as Juan Perón.

In 1944 General Edelmiro Farrell became president. But Perón, as vice president, as well as minister of war and secretary of labor and social welfare, clearly was the dominant figure in the government. Still, many powerful political elements resented Perón's rapid rise to glory. Other army officers were jealous of him. Wealthy industrialists were angered by his struggle to help the workers. And some officials in the government of the United States believed that he secretly favored Nazi Germany and Fascist Italy in the war.

Perón fought back against all of his opponents. At this time, too, he met a woman, Eva Duarte, who before very

Eva Perón distributes gifts to the Argentine people of the interior provinces. Buenos Aires Herald.

long would become his wife, as well as his partner in government.

Eva, or Evita as she was called, had spent her early childhood in poverty. As a teenager she decided to pursue a career on the stage. She read magazines about the stars of movies, radio, and theater. After two years of high school she left home, confidently traveling to Buenos Aires to become a star.

Very pale-skinned, while wearing dramatically dark lipstick, she had light brown hair and dark brown eyes. Evita had neither a good singing voice nor especially good looks. But she was persistent. And she knew how to make friends.

Before long she had won minor roles on radio shows. In one popular radio series, *Heroines of History,* she played the parts of such famous women as Queen Elizabeth of England. She also won small parts in movies. The turning point in her life came when an army officer she was dating took her to a benefit concert to raise money for victims of an Argentinian earthquake. It was there that he introduced her to Juan Perón.

The two instantly were attracted to each other. After that evening the lonely widower, Perón, and the ambitious, quick-witted Evita almost never were apart.

It was not long before their friendship worked to Juan Perón's advantage. In October 1945, some of his enemies in the army and in the big corporations forced him, through threats, to resign all of his government posts. Then, while seizing power in the country for themselves, they had him arrested and thrown into jail. Leading the group that imprisoned him were several army generals, including former president Farrell.

On October 17, large crowds of workers—Perón's *los descamisados*—swarmed through the streets of Buenos Aires. "Long live Perón!" they shouted. Encouraged by Evita, they demanded their hero's immediate release.

Stunned by the size of the crowd and its loyalty to Perón, Farrell and the other generals finally ordered that he be freed.

Standing on a balcony in front of the wildly cheering throng, Perón raised his hands in triumph, like a victorious boxer.

"Workers," he declared in thanks, "I would press all of you against my heart, as I would do with my mother." The victory of the day, said Perón, had

been nothing less than a "festival of democracy," a "triumph of self-awareness for working people."

In the national election that followed just a few months later, Perón was chosen president of Argentina. But even before that, the grateful Juan Perón married Evita Duarte.

During the next four years the Peróns grew more and more popular with the people of Argentina. Their fame also spread around the globe.

As president, Juan Perón took over the nation's privately owned railroads, public utilities, and banks. He shortened the work week to forty hours. He had wages increased. He arranged better retirement pensions for older workers. He arranged for the building of new schools, power plants, and hospitals. To millions of Argentinians he soon became known simply as *El Lider* (the Leader).

Meanwhile, Evita was herself becoming a person of great power. Based in a small office in the Ministry of Labor and Social Welfare, she spent her days visiting hospitals, orphanages, factories, and housing developments. She arranged for distribution of food and clothing to the poor.

Once, when middle- and upper-class women would not allow her to lead a charity organization formerly run by the rich, she set up her own society: The

Eva Perón Foundation. That group, with money taken directly from Juan Perón's treasury, greatly expanded the number of hospitals and schools in Argentina. It set up clinics. It made certain that poor people could get medicines.

To publicize her work Evita bought a newspaper, *Democracia*, and made certain that it carefully reported all of her good deeds. In 1947 the paper described her trip to Europe. In Spain she received a medal from that nation's dictator, General Francisco Franco. While there, she distributed thousands of dollars to cheering crowds of poor people gathered in the streets. In Rome she received a rosary from Pope Pius XII. Finally, she went on to Paris to sign a trade treaty for Argentina with the president of France.

It was also Eva Perón who fought for—and won—the right of Argentinian women to vote. Following that victory she set up a women's branch of the Perónist party. Just as before, when she had attracted many of the "shirtless" class of men to vote for her husband, she successfully won over the women.

Once desperately poor, Evita now wore gowns personally designed for her by the famous Christian Dior. Speaking to the nation's women, she would point out the possibilities that could lie in store for them if they vigorously demanded a fair chance from society, while also supporting Juan Perón.

"You too will have clothes like this someday," she often said. "Some day you will be able to sit next to any rich woman on a basis of complete equality. What we are fighting for is to destroy the inequality between you and the wives of your bosses."

Juan Perón himself also claimed to be fighting for social justice in Argentina. He was not a Communist, said Perón. Nor was he a Fascist, or a capitalist. Instead, claimed *El Lider*, his party stood for a "middle path," one that used the nation's strength to serve poor workers and farmers, but also Argentina's other classes, too. The result, he said, was a new system of *justicialismo* (social justice), combining the Christian religion and the highest of human political values.

Based on his popularity with the people, Perón easily convinced the nation's congress to write a new constitution, one that allowed presidents to serve more than a limited term of office. Then, to no one's surprise, he won a smashing victory in the election of 1951, carrying nearly 70 percent of the votes.

Now, all across Argentina, Juan and Eva Perón came to take on a special role in the nation's life. They became more than just political leaders. They became saints. Statues of them were

President Juan Perón and his wife Eva ride triumphantly through the streets of Buenos Aires after President Perón's reelection in 1952. *UPI/Bettmann*.

erected in public places. Hospitals, schools, and playgrounds were named after them. Their pictures appeared everywhere.

In the early 1950s, however, the nation's economic situation began to sour. Prices of goods rose much faster than wages. Imports skyrocketed, especially from the United States. As a result, much more money was leaving Argentina than coming in. Perón's many building projects left the national treasury empty. The debt grew higher and higher. Even such necessary goods as food became scarce. Meanwhile, there was widespread corruption among officials in the Perónist government. Many officers openly demanded bribes before doing business with private citizens.

Then, an event took place that spelled doom for Juan Perón's control of Argentina. On July 26, 1952, Eva Perón died.

Many people understood that Evita could be greedy, could be vengeful to her enemies, could be proud and arrogant. Still, she also was seen by the great mass of Argentinians as an almost saintly woman, completely devoted to the well-being of the poor. It was Evita who personally had stayed in contact with labor leaders, who personally had managed the day-to-day business of government. She had been for Juan, as one historian put it, "Juan's eyes and his ears."

Now with Eva's death, criticism of Juan Perón's rule increased sharply. Angered, he fought back. He tried to censor the criticism of his government that appeared in the press, actually closing down some leading newspapers. He threw opposition leaders into jail.

More and more, he was seen as a dictator, a tyrant. Student groups, especially in the colleges, began to rise up against him. So did the military. Then, when he made divorce legal and ended religious instruction in the schools, the Roman Catholic Church also turned against him.

Finally, the situation became hopeless. In September 1955, Juan Perón was forced to resign his presidency. First, he took refuge in Paraguay. Then he went to Venezuela, to Panama, to the Dominican Republic. At last he settled in Madrid, Spain, taking up residence in an expensive villa.

For seventeen years Perón lived in exile. Through all of those years, however, he never gave up hope that some day he would return to Argentina, once again becoming the nation's leader. He stayed in close touch with powerful labor leaders. He sent confident messages to his Argentine followers.

In time, as one military leader after another failed to revive the nation's economy, the people grew restless. They forgot their former unhappiness with Perón. Even his former critics, such as student groups and the Socialists, clamored for his return.

In 1973, faced with the possibility of open revolution in the streets, the wealthy classes and the Argentine army invited Perón to come home.

There were wild celebrations. The streets were filled with cheering throngs, eager to greet him. In a special election held in September of that year, he won nearly two-thirds of the total vote.

Once again he had become his nation's president. His new wife, Isabel, became vice president.

"If God gives me health," said Perón, "I will spend the last effort of my life to complete the task entrusted to me."

He tried to end the violence, the political killings, that had spread across the country during the years of his absence. He tried to check the continued rise in prices for almost all consumer goods. He tried to encourage greater trade with Europe, so Argentina would not have to be so dependent on the United States.

But time was not on his side. Despite his winning smile and athletic stride, Perón knew that he was seriously ill. On July 1, 1974, he died.

Juan and Eva Perón still are remembered in Argentina, indeed throughout Latin America. Yet they are remembered far less for their belief in social justice than for their exciting, dramatic personalities.

The Peróns used the methods of dictators. They ruthlessly put down their political opponents. In their speeches they were willing to say whatever seemed most likely to win them widespread public support—and votes.

Today, popular figures like the Peróns continue to be received with high enthusiasm by great masses of people in many countries. Even in the United States of America, some candidates running for office appear to fill such a need, and sometimes manage to win elections.

That such methods are used clearly is a matter of concern to those who believe in democracy. That system—democracy—ultimately is based on trust, on faith in the good judgment of the people. Indeed it is perhaps best defined as "government of the people, by the people, and for the people."

Whether a system based on such idealistic beliefs can long survive is a question that always must be raised. And it may well be that you—the young people of today—will have an opportunity to assist in answering that question.

Josip Broz Tito

1892–1980   Leader of Yugoslav guerrilla forces during World War II
and then head of the Yugoslav government; champion of nonalignment
with the Communist bloc or the West

Josip Broz, or "Tito," as he called himself, was the grandson of a serf, born
on a farm to a poor peasant family. The
seventh of fifteen children, he worked
in his youth as a mechanic, as an electri-
cian, as a waiter. Yet by the time of
his death, he was known throughout
the world. In attendance at his funeral
were 120 of the leading statesmen of
the time, including presidents and
prime ministers. Millions of people
mourned his passing.

Those people understood clearly
that, in his lifetime, Tito had succeeded
in doing what many considered impossible. During World War II his guerrilla
forces had stood up against the invading
armies of Adolf Hitler, the German dictator. Then, after the war, he had united
the fiercely competing provinces, so different in language and religion, that
make up that most unusual of modern
nations, Yugoslavia.

Tito himself realized that after his
death the Yugoslav nation, always fragile, might once again crumble. The
parts might no longer stay together as
a whole. But he was determined that,
while he lived, he would do everything
possible to stop that from happening.

As "Marshall Tito," president of Yugoslavia, the one-time peasant child
found himself in regular contact with
great and powerful figures, such world
leaders as Churchill, de Gaulle, and
Stalin. It was Tito himself who persuaded Nehru of India and Nasser of
Egypt, along with others, to join the
so-called nonaligned bloc of nations.
Those influential countries declared

themselves independent of both the Communist world, dominated by the Soviet Union, and the "Free World," led by the United States.

Although a Communist—a champion of the poor who had survived hunger strikes and frequent brushes with death in battle—Tito eventually took on the life-style of a wealthy monarch, a king. He lived in elegant mansions. He had his own personal train and yacht. He vacationed on his own private island in the Adriatic Sea. He insisted on expensive cigars and the finest of wines and liquors. He courted beautiful young women. Even in his eighties he liked to drive the highways in a flashy convertible.

How did the ambitious young Josip Broz, unknown outside his village, manage to rise from poverty to wealth and fame and to play a starring role on the stage of international politics?

In 1892, when Josip was born in the village of Kumrovec, there was no country known as Yugoslavia. Croatia, his father's homeland, as well as the neighboring Slovenia, where his mother had grown up, were part of the Austro-Hungarian Empire. The whole region was such a mixture of racial groups and cultures that it sometimes was compared to a large fruit salad, with the different ingredients all thrown together.

Nor was the region especially rich. Tito's memories of childhood included times when he would beg for bread to eat, or steal sugar, or perhaps even steal a pig. In the village school there was only one teacher. Tito remembered that it was his job to wash blood from the handkerchief of the teacher, who suffered badly from tuberculosis.

A very good student, young Josip especially liked reading and mathematics. But to help support the family, he was forced to leave school at the age of twelve, going to work on his uncle's cattle farm. Hearing there were jobs and the chance for a better life in America, he thought of leaving Croatia, but his father saw little hope of raising enough money to pay his transportation.

Instead, at the age of fifteen he moved to the nearby town of Sisak, working first as a restaurant waiter, then as helper to a locksmith. He also worked on machinery. Once, while repairing a machine, he badly damaged the middle finger on his left hand. The injury never completely healed, serving ever afterward as a reminder to Tito of his days as an unknown, low-paid worker.

Three years later he moved to Zagreb, the capital city of Croatia. There he joined the Metalworkers Union and, like most members of that union, also became a member of the Social Democratic party (the Socialists). Highly ambitious, he hoped to make money and then return to his native village of Kumrovec in fine clothes, a hero to his friends and family.

It was not to be. Jobs were scarce in Zagreb, forcing him to work at repairing bicycles. When, at last, he was able to buy a new suit, it was stolen. For nearly two years he traveled from city to city—Trieste, Pilsen, Munich—sometimes finding work, sometimes failing.

His greatest success came in Vienna, where he finally won a job as an automobile mechanic at the Daimler factory. With his spare money he joined a gymnasium, where he learned fencing. He also took lessons in formal ballroom dancing, something he hoped would separate him from his humble peasant background. A quick learner, he soon was speaking the local language, German.

In 1913 he reached the age of twenty-one. By law he was then required to serve two years in the Austro-Hungarian army. For that reason he returned home to Croatia and registered for service. Only a year later, World War I broke out.

Young Josip Broz found himself in the front lines, fighting against an invading Russian army. Like most of his Croatian comrades he hated the war. He hoped that Austria-Hungary would lose, thus causing the already shaky Austro-Hungarian Empire to collapse. Croatia then would become an independent nation.

Early in the morning, on Easter Sunday, 1915, fierce Cossack horsemen burst through the Austrian defenses, leaping into the Croatian trenches. One of them thrust a two-foot-long lance into the back of Josip Broz, leaving him for dead.

Before the fierce Cossacks could finish off the wounded, as they had planned to do, soldiers of the regular Russian army put them in carts and took them to a hospital. Because of that, Broz survived.

For more than a year he hovered between life and death. Once, a red tag was placed on his body, and he was taken to a part of the hospital reserved for the dying. Somehow he managed to stay alive.

Taken to a prisoner-of-war camp, his experiences as a mechanic paid off for him. He was put in charge of prisoners repairing severe damage to the St. Petersburg-Siberian railway line. Once he complained to the Red Cross that the Russians were stealing from packages of food and medicine given to the prisoners. For that, he was punished with a severe beating—thirty blows across his back with a whip.

In the spring of 1917, Broz escaped from prison. Jumping aboard a passing train, he hid between sacks of wheat until the train arrived in St. Petersburg, later to become known as Leningrad. At the time it was the capital city of Russia.

Shortly after Broz arrived there the Russian Revolution broke out, with heavy fighting in the city's streets. Once he barely escaped death from a hail of machine-gun fire from the roof of a building.

As the revolution unfolded, Broz went through a series of remarkable adventures. First he was arrested as an escaped prisoner. Then, escaping again, he joined the Bolshevik Red Guard headed by Vladimir Ilyich Lenin. When Czech soldiers came looking for escaped prisoners, he was hidden in the town of Omsk by a young girl—a girl he would later marry.

Finally, he found safety among a tribe of nomadic Khirgiz horsemen. Because of his skill as a mechanic, he knew how to repair their damaged flour mill.

Over several months he learned their language, came to dress like them, broke in horses for them. The nomads liked his sense of humor, liked his toughness. They so completely accepted him that, at last, they invited him to live with them permanently. The tribal chief even offered his daughter in marriage to Broz.

Instead, he returned to Omsk to marry the girl who had hidden him and saved his life.

By then, World War I had ended. Broz and his wife found their way back to his Croatian homeland. During the years of his absence Broz's mother had died, and his father had moved away. Meanwhile, his own personality had changed drastically. Through his adventures he had grown up, matured.

He also had become a Communist.

Why did Josip Broz choose communism? It is difficult to say. His experiences in the war clearly had made a difference. Probably more important, however, was his burning, driving ambition. A mechanic, only roughly educated, he realized there were few jobs to be had in Eastern Europe. The Soviet Communist party offered him money for helping to organize workers, money for enrolling them in the party.

For Broz, like many other intelligent young men of the time, becoming a Communist was one of the few pathways open to advancement. If the party succeeded, he, too, would succeed.

Always energetic, he immediately plunged into action. Working as a mechanic, he moved from city to city in the newly created nation of Yugoslavia. He urged workers to demand higher wages but also eventually to change the society completely through revolution. True happiness would come, he argued, only by setting up a Communist government.

Once, Broz was arrested for speaking against the government but was found not guilty. A second time he was arrested and set free on probation. In 1927 he became an officer of the Communist party of Yugoslavia (CPP) and secretary general of the Croatia-Slovenia region. Shortly after taking office he was arrested again, charged with belonging to an illegal party.

Knowing that he would be found guilty, he turned his trial into a show. As handsome and dramatic as any actor, he sparred with the government's attorneys and with the judge, declaring that the court had no right to try him. The capitalist system, he roared, was corrupt and should be overthrown. He was sentenced to five years in prison.

On hearing the sentence, he turned from the judge to the packed courtroom and, raising a clenched fist in the air, shouted: "Long live the Communist Party! Long live the Third International!"

Prison for Broz, as he later described it, was "like being at a university." The Yugoslav government allowed political prisoners to stay together. As a result, Broz and other Communists formed a study group. They read the works of

Marx, Engels, and Lenin. They read Shakespeare, Upton Sinclair, Edward Bellamy, Thomas Hobbes. A cellmate, the brilliant Mosa Pijade, made a special effort to educate young Broz in the basic ideas of communism, seeing him as a future leader of the party.

Almost all of the time that Broz was not busy as a mechanic, working on the prison's power plant, he was either reading or meeting in regularly scheduled classes with his fellow prisoners, under the direction of Pijade. Often they would end their sessions by linking arms and singing the "Communist International," the party's worldwide anthem.

In 1934, Broz was released. He showed little feeling toward his captors, writing later: "It was only natural that when they caught me they should shut me up. I would have done the same thing in their place." Once in power, he would imprison many people, imposing on them conditions far worse than he himself ever experienced.

After leaving jail he traveled to Moscow, the heartland of world communism. To protect himself from Yugoslav authorities at that time, he began wearing disguises.

He also used many aliases, one of which—"Tito"—was to become the name he would adopt for the remainder of his life.

While Tito was in Moscow, the Soviet

dictator, Joseph Stalin, launched a great purge, bringing to trial and executing many Communist leaders he did not trust. Some 800 Yugoslavs were killed. Somehow Tito managed to survive.

Badly shaken by the experience, he returned to Yugoslavia, vowing that forever afterward he would try to remain as independent as possible of Stalin's rule.

While still using disguises to evade the Yugoslav police, he began gathering around him a small group of loyal followers, including the extraordinarily able writer, Milovan Djilas. Then, in 1937, Tito took on the post of secretary general of the Yugoslav Communist party. At the time, the illegal party probably included some six thousand members, with as many as thirty thousand enrolled in the Young Communist League. Almost all of those men and women operated in secret, not publicly revealing that they were party members.

With the help of Tito some 1,300 Yugoslav Communists made their way to Spain to fight in the Spanish Civil War. Although the Fascist leader Francisco Franco won out in that conflict, aided by Hitler and Mussolini, the Yugoslav fighters gained valuable military experience. Their fighting skills soon would prove of critical importance to the cause of communism in their own homeland.

On September 1, 1939, Adolf Hitler's German armies launched a devastating attack on Poland. World War II had begun.

At the time, Stalin and Hitler were allies. Communists around the world—no matter how much they hated the cruelty of Hitler's Nazis—generally stayed quiet, hoping to give Russia as much time as possible to build up its military strength. Even when German troops invaded Yugoslavia, Tito did not call for open warfare against them.

Then, in June 1941, Hitler invaded Russia. Tito's Communists sprang instantly into action, fighting fiercely against the Nazi invaders, as well as against the armies of Italy, Hungary, and Bulgaria—countries that hoped to win pieces of Yugoslav territory.

Tito's Communists, known as Partisans, were by no means the only Yugoslavs rushing into battle against the invading forces. In the province of Croatia, an army was formed to defeat the Nazis, but also to win independence from Yugoslavia. Another army, called the "Chetniks," demanded a return to power of the old royal government that once had ruled Serbia.

The Chetniks, led by Colonel Draza Mihailovich, gained wide popular support in Great Britain and the United States. To the surprise of Tito, even Stalin considered the Chetniks to be the major resistance force against Hit-

Josip (Broz) Tito, commander in chief of the National Liberation Forces in Yugoslavia, studies topographic maps at Bosnia in 1942. *Eastfoto/Sovfoto.*

ler. Sometimes Mihailovich received credit in the press for victories actually won by Tito's Partisans.

Adolf Hitler, however, soon decided that it was Tito who really was his most powerful enemy in Yugoslavia. From 1941 to 1943, the Nazi leader launched seven major offensives against the Partisans, killing more than six thousand of them. Tito himself was seriously wounded. For days at a time Tito and his guerrilla forces went without food. They hid in the mountains. But they refused to give in. They continued to launch daring hit-and-run attacks against the Nazis.

Gradually, the size of Tito's army grew. By the autumn of 1943 he commanded a force numbering nearly a quarter of a million armed men and women. In response, Hitler ordered the launching of a lightning offensive against the Partisans. This time he used heavy tank divisions and paratroops dropped by planes. Tito himself barely managed to escape the surprise attack.

Yet, despite heavy losses, the Partisans still fought on.

In 1943 Italy surrendered to the Allies. Shortly afterward, Tito formed a new government for all of Yugoslavia, naming himself "field marshall" of the new nation. Both Winston Churchill and Joseph Stalin wanted Mihailovich's Chetniks to share equally in ruling the country, but in meetings with the two leaders Tito made it clear that he alone would be in charge when the war finally ended. Stalin, cold and hostile, openly showed his displeasure with the Yugoslav leader. Tito, however, stood his ground, refusing to give in.

In the spring of 1945, Nazi Germany fell. Hitler committed suicide. Meanwhile, Tito took complete power in Yugoslavia.

His first dramatic moves enraged people around the world. First, he had Mihailovich put on trial for treason and then had him executed. He ordered Aloysius Stepinac, a Catholic archbishop from Croatia, thrown into prison for cooperating with the Nazis during the war—an act that angered Catholics in Europe and in America. Finally, Tito demanded that Yugoslavia be given the Italian city of Trieste, along the Adriatic coast.

Most importantly, Tito refused to knuckle down to Stalin's Russia. Yugoslavia had been devastated by the war, losing more than 10 percent of its population and almost all of its industry. Still, Stalin refused to help reconstruct the country. Instead, he demanded that Tito supply him with raw materials to help rebuild Russia's own war-ravaged industries. Tito absolutely refused.

In 1948, Stalin lost his patience. He expelled Yugoslavia from the Cominform, the world Communist organization. Russian troops were placed menacingly on the Yugoslav border, as if in readiness to launch an invasion. Russian ships blockaded Yugoslav port cities. Russian secret agents sabotaged Yugoslav factories.

Many Yugoslavs had been angered in 1945 when Tito first declared the nation Communist, like the Soviet Union. He had nationalized industry, agriculture, and banking, while taking over much private property. But in the face of Stalin's threats, the Yugoslavs eagerly rallied in support of Tito. Young people were carefully trained for membership in a strong, well-equipped army. Even the United States provided assistance to the small nation that dared stand up to the mighty Soviets.

Stalin, faced with such opposition, decided to back down. He withdrew his pressure on Tito.

Then, in 1953, Stalin died.

Nikita Khrushchev, the new Soviet

President Tito reviews troops upon his arrival in Moscow, 1956. *Sovfoto.*

leader, tried to heal the wounded relationship with Yugoslavia. For a time, the two Communist nations warmed to each other. But in 1968, when the Russians used force to put down a revolt in Communist-controlled Czechoslovakia, they made it quite clear that Yugoslavia could be next.

Tito did not hesitate. He quickly mobilized his entire army, answering that, unlike the Czechs, Yugoslavia would meet any Russian invasion with total war. All men up to the age of

sixty-five were ordered to prepare for battle. All women, ages nineteen to forty, were assigned to emergency units.

Again, the Soviets backed down.

Long before that confrontation, Tito quietly had begun working to organize a new group of nations. In his planning it was to be a group independent of both the Russian-led Communist bloc and the Western or "Free World" bloc, headed by the United States.

Because of Tito, there emerged in the late 1960s and early 1970s the so-called nonaligned bloc of nations, including some twenty-five countries. Along with Tito, the group was headed by such leaders as Jawaharlal Nehru of India and Gamal Abdel Nasser of Egypt.

Often the members of the nonaligned bloc were themselves deeply divided. Some of them, such as Cuba, clearly were tied closely to the Soviet Union. Still, primarily because of Tito, the group continued to warn the two major powers, Russia and the United States, to stay out of the affairs of Third World, or developing, nations.

By the mid 1970s most of the great national leaders who had fought in World War II had died. Tito lived on, still physically strong, still alert. He had married three times, none of those marriages proving particularly successful. Yet he still enjoyed the company of young women. He liked to dress in fashionable clothes and to drive in his convertible, with the top down. He still enjoyed hunting and fishing, playing the piano. Occasionally, as in his youth, he made things in a machine shop.

Even such former comrades as Milovan Djilas, who had turned against him, could not help but admit that Tito continued to be a man of strong character,

a flexible leader who could adjust to changing events without giving up his deeper principles. It was for those qualities that the people of Yugoslavia continued to admire him.

In 1974, realizing that he was growing old, Tito developed a plan for a new form of Yugoslav national government to take over after his death. In his plan, the presidency would be rotated—shared in turn by representatives of each of the nation's provinces.

On May 4, 1980, three days before his eighty-eighth birthday, Josip Broz Tito died.

Writing several years later, Milovan Djilas remembered Tito as a person of great courage, great energy, with a fine sense of humor. He was a man whose drive and ambition had carried him to a position of leadership in his own nation, as well as to worldwide fame.

Yet, as Djilas recalled, Tito also had limited the personal freedom of Yugoslav citizens, something that had happened, too, in the other Communist nations.

Instead of transforming Yugoslavia into an open society, with free speech and free press, Tito had imprisoned many of his opponents. He had taken people's property away from them.

It was true, said Djilas, that Tito had brought to Yugoslavia, a nation composed of many diverse religious and ethnic groups, more than three decades of order and stability.

But to do so, he had used force. He had used power.

Always, in the affairs of government, we are faced with a choice. As Djilas put it, we must decide which is more important to us—the "power of law" or "the law of power."

There is little doubt that, for Tito, like so many leaders in human history, the law of power is what really counted most.

Eamon de Valera

1882–1975   Central figure in the struggle for Irish independence from British rule; prime minister and president of Ireland

Napoléon Bonaparte, born on the island of Corsica, always spoke French with an accent. Yet he is known to history as perhaps the greatest of all French leaders. Adolf Hitler, born in Austria, always will be remembered as the head of an aggressive, conquering German nation.

So, too, Eamon de Valera, although born in New York City, in the United States of America, devoted his life to the people of Ireland. As he once put it, "If I wish to know what the Irish want, I look into my own heart."

De Valera loved Ireland with a deep and lasting passion. It was he, probably more than any other person, who helped that country win freedom from British rule and then shaped its history well into the twentieth century.

De Valera's mother, Catherine Coll, usually known as Kate, came to America in 1879, at the age of twenty-three. Like so many other Irish immigrants of the time, she had suffered from poverty, indeed even hunger, in her native land and saw America as a place where she could get a fresh start. She took a job as a maid with a wealthy French family living in Manhattan. It was there that she met Vivion Juan de Valera, a Spanish sculptor who came to the home of her employers to give music lessons to the children.

In 1881, the couple married. A little over a year later, while living at 61 East 41st Street, Kate Coll de Valera gave birth to the couple's only child. His name was Edward, or Eddie, but he would become known to the world by the Irish variation of that name, "Eamon."

Always in bad health, Vivion de Valera left his young family behind him and traveled to Colorado, hoping that perhaps the healthier air would help him. Within a few months he died.

Now a widow, Kate went back to work, leaving Eamon in the care of another woman who also had come from the tiny Irish village of Bruree, in County Limerick. Later in his life Eamon would remember occasional visits from "a woman in black"—his mother.

Kate de Valera decided that Eamon would be better cared for by her family in Ireland. Before long he found himself away from noisy Manhattan, living in Bruree in a one-room house with mud walls and a thatched roof. Living with him were his grandmother, his twenty-one-year-old uncle, Pat, and young Hannie, his fifteen-year-old aunt.

Shortly after Eamon arrived, the family moved to a cottage built by the government for farm workers, but it was only slightly larger, made up of two rooms, most of which were given over to kitchen space.

After a year Eamon's mother visited briefly—long enough to announce her marriage to an American, Charles Wheelwright, known ever afterward to Eamon as "Uncle Charley." Kate soon returned to America. She thought it best that four-year-old Eamon remain in Ireland.

Eamon's childhood was typically Irish. He worked at farming with his family, went to school, played Rugby football, and starred as a runner. At the age of fourteen, after eight years of school, it was time to decide what to do next. He considered returning to America and even wrote to his mother about it. But it was not to be.

Instead, he enrolled at the Christian Brothers' School, some seven miles from his home. Since the family could not afford to buy him a bicycle, he had to walk the entire distance—both ways every day—carrying a heavy load of books.

Eamon proved so strong a student that after two years he was admitted with a scholarship to Blackrock College. That school, located near Dublin, was run by the Holy Ghost fathers. Eamon entered the college unsure of his future career but inclined either to teaching or to the priesthood.

It soon became clear to him, however, that his greatest interest, as well as his greatest academic strength, lay in mathematics. After five years at Blackrock he became a mathematics teacher at a school in Tipperary while completing his college degree. In 1904 he graduated from the Royal University in Dublin.

Very tall and thin with dark hair, dark

eyes, and pale skin, like his Spanish father, what struck people immediately was his seriousness. Just as he had been passionate about Rugby football and track as a youngster, now he was passionate in his devotion to the Catholic Church, to the study of mathematics, and to the cause of freedom from British rule for Ireland. Yet, as always, he remained a private person, seldom smiling, seldom revealing his emotions. Whether he was happy or unhappy was hard to tell.

He taught Latin, French, and mathematics at various secondary schools, but also at colleges, training teachers. Finally, he became a faculty member at St. Patrick's College, an outstanding Irish seminary, responsible for preparing men for the priesthood. At St. Patrick's his involvement with Catholicism became even more intense.

As part of his concern for Irish independence, de Valera plunged into the study of Gaelic, the language of ancient Ireland. It was at a meeting of the Gaelic League that he met an extraordinarily beautiful young actress, Jane Flanagan, then only eighteen years old. Jane soon changed her name to the Gaelic Sinéad Ni Fhlannagáin. Soon, both she and Eamon became fluent in the ancient language.

They also fell in love and, after a courtship of two years, were married. It was a marriage destined to last for more than sixty years and to bring the couple great personal happiness, along with six children and many grandchildren and great-grandchildren.

By 1910, the year the de Valeras were married, the struggle for Irish independence from Great Britain had grown more bitter. That struggle was by no means new. Long before Eamon de Valera's birth, such leaders as Michael Davitt and Charles Stewart Parnell had championed the cause of poor Irish farmers, forced to leave their homes when they could not pay the rent to British landlords. In time, many Irish leaders came to see freedom from British rule as the only answer.

At first, Eamon tried not to involve himself in politics. Instead, he devoted himself to the Gaelic League. But as the situation with England grew more tense, he joined both the Irish Republican Brotherhood and Sinn Féin (We Ourselves)—groups pressing for Irish freedom. He was even more active in the Irish Volunteers, a group that was arming itself and preparing for open rebellion. He became commander of the Third Battalion of the Volunteers, a force of about 125 men.

In April 1916, the bloody Easter Rebellion broke out in Dublin. De Valera and his men seized the railroad station there, as well as a large bakery. They defeated British reinforcements sent to recapture those positions. But after nearly a week, the British, armed with artillery and heavily outnumbering the Irish, finally forced the exhausted rebels to surrender.

As the British troops closed in on them, de Valera is said to have declared to his troops, "You have but one life to live and but one death to die. See that you do both like men." He and his battalion were the last to give in.

In the weeks that followed, the British put the leaders of the rebellion on trial. Sixteen of them were hanged. De Valera's wife, as well as his family in America, pleaded that his life be spared. They argued that to execute a person born in America would stir great anger among the American people.

At the time, Britain desperately needed American help in World War I, the momentous conflict then being fought in Europe against the Germans. It was decided, therefore, not to hang de Valera. Instead, he was sentenced to life in prison.

In June 1917, the British announced a general amnesty, setting free all the Irish prisoners they were holding. On his release from jail Eamon de Valera was greeted by the Irish people as a hero. Of all the major leaders of the Easter Rebellion, only he had survived. He was elected president of Sinn Féin. He was elected president of the Irish Volunteers. Everywhere he went people cheered him. He was their favorite, their very own "Dev."

A serious person, a scholar in the world of politics, de Valera now threw himself completely into the struggle for Irish independence. Never again would he be a soldier, fighting in the front lines. Instead, with dignity and with careful, almost mathematical planning, he set forth a strategy that, he was certain, would lead to victory.

Meanwhile, British losses on the European battlefields of World War I had been climbing rapidly. In 1918, hoping to fill their badly depleted ranks with Irish soldiers, the British put into effect a program of conscription—a draft.

The Irish refused to serve.

Furious, Great Britain declared a state of martial law in Ireland. Soldiers, known as "Black and Tans" because of the uniforms they wore, were sent there to force the Irish to do their patriotic duty by serving in the British army. One of the first acts of the Black and Tans was to arrest the leaders of the Irish resistance.

Without even a trial, Eamon de Valera was thrown into Lincoln Prison in England.

For nearly a year he languished in jail. Then, one day, during a Catholic religious ceremony, he saved the wax from a candle used in the service. With that wax he made an impression of a prison passkey and managed to smuggle it to Michael Collins, another Irish leader. From that impression Collins had a key made, cleverly returning it to de Valera in a fruitcake disguised as a gift.

On February 3, 1919, de Valera saw his chance. Using the key, he made a daring escape from prison.

In Manchester, England, he hid in the house of a priest. Then, pretending to be a seaman, he managed to board a ship bound for Ireland. To avoid discovery he hid below decks between sacks of potatoes.

While the police still hunted desperately for him in England and Ireland, he made his way to America, working as a coal stoker on a merchant ship.

Once in America, he was well received by the large Irish population, people generally in favor of Irish independence from Great Britain. Politicians in New York's Tammany Hall organization were especially helpful, arranging many public speaking appearances for him. In eighteen months of campaigning, he raised some $6 million for the cause of Irish independence.

Meanwhile, in a free election held in Ireland, the Sinn Féin party had won a tremendous victory. It was decided to set up a Dáil (parliament) and to run Ireland as if British rule did not exist.

Even though Eamon de Valera was not even in the country at the time, he was elected president of the assembly.

During all the time he was raising funds in America, a bloody civil war raged between British and Irish forces. Many private citizens, including women and children, were killed in the vicious street fighting.

Shortly after de Valera's return to Ireland, both sides, drained by the costly struggle, arranged a truce.

Formal peace talks then followed, supposedly intended to bring a final settlement between Ireland and England. De Valera himself decided not to go to London to attend the talks. Later, he explained that delegates to such conferences become too involved in bargaining and lose sight of the really big issues at stake.

Instead, he sent Arthur Griffith and Michael Collins to present the Irish position. Winston Churchill and Prime Minister David Lloyd George—two of the leading figures in British life—represented England.

After nearly two months of talks the Irish delegates finally agreed to a treaty and signed it.

When de Valera saw the document, he was furious.

Under its provisions, the twenty-six largely Catholic counties of southern Ireland gained certain limited freedoms

Eamon De Valera (*center*) with members of his staff after having left in revolt the session of the legislature in which the Irish Free State Treaty with Great Britain was ratified. *Times Wide World Photos.*

from British rule. At the same time, however, the six largely Protestant counties at the north were to have their own separate government.

Thus, as the so-called Orangemen of Northern Ireland had wished for many years, they were to become citizens of a nation completely separate from the south. Yet their nation would still be very closely tied to Great Britain—and under the protection of the British army. In effect, Ireland was parti-tioned—divided into two countries: the Protestant north, now to be known as Ulster, and the Catholic south, now called the Irish Free State.

Furthermore, at least for the time being, both parts of Ireland were to stay very much within the British Empire. Britain was to keep the right to use naval bases in both Ulster and in the Irish Free State. Members of the two Irish parliaments were to swear an oath of loyalty to the king of England.

De Valera angrily rejected the treaty. Even today people still ask why he had not led the Irish delegation in the first place instead of sending a "second-string team." Whatever the reasons may have been, he and the Irish leaders of the south were bitterly disappointed with the result. They declared that in signing the document, Griffith and Collins had gone far beyond the powers given to them. To de Valera and his followers, there could be only one solution—one Irish nation, completely united and completely independent of British rule.

The result was civil war.

In 1922 brutal fighting began. Irishmen—north and south—who favored the treaty fought those who did not. The British, meanwhile, struggled to restore order, especially in the rebellious south.

De Valera enlisted as a private in his old battalion, never playing a leadership role in the actual combat. During the war Michael Collins was ambushed and killed by Sinn Féin fighters who refused to forgive him for signing such a humiliating treaty with Great Britain.

For nearly a year the fighting continued. Thousands of lives were lost. By the spring of 1923, however, British troops had won the war, crushed the rebellion. Then, to maintain order, those forces began regularly to patrol the streets of Dublin and other Irish cities.

During the following summer the British arrested de Valera, claiming that he was an agitator, stirring up the people. Without even a trial they threw him into prison. There he remained for a year, mostly reading about mathematics, playing chess, brooding about what seemed to many Irish leaders a hopeless situation.

Still, de Valera refused to give up. On his release from prison in 1924, he started at once to organize those who still dreamed of an independent Irish nation.

Hoping to rally support in Ulster, he illegally crossed the border to the north, only to be arrested and once again thrown into prison. For one month the British held him in solitary confinement. It was, in de Valera's memory, the worst treatment he ever received in any of his many experiences behind bars.

Always a realist, seeing things as they actually were—not as he wished they might be—de Valera decided on a new strategy. Military force, he now understood, would not win Irish freedom. Clever politics might.

He urged the Sinn Féin leaders to swear to the oath of allegiance demanded by Great Britain and to take

Eamon De Valera addressing a crowd in Dublin in 1925. *UPI/Bettmann.*

their seats in the Irish Free State parliament, the Dáil. That oath, he declared, was nothing more than "an empty formula."

When a majority of the Sinn Féin leaders refused to accept his strategy, de Valera formed a new political party, Fianna Fáil (Soldiers of Destiny).

He himself dramatically signed the oath. First he removed the Bible from the table, so he would not have to swear upon it. Then he covered the words of the oath with a piece of paper so he would not have to see them.

Some of the Irish never forgave de Valera for that act. To them, military action—violence—was the only way to a free, united Ireland. Today's Irish Republican Army, the IRA, still is convinced that such action is necessary. Even now the IRA uses terrorism in an effort to bring Northern Ireland into union with the south.

To de Valera, politics, not violence, was the way to a single, united Irish nation. As leader of Fianna Fáil he joined with the Labor party to form a new government for the Irish Free State. For five years, from 1932 to 1937, he personally held the office of both president of the Cabinet and minister for external affairs. Then, in 1937, he took on the new title of prime minister.

By then the British had agreed not to require the oath of allegiance. They had agreed to give up their rights to use Irish ports as naval bases. But they did not agree to the union of Ulster and the nation of Ireland to the south—the nation known officially in the Gaelic language from that time on as "Eire."

In September 1939, World War II broke out. Ireland declared itself neutral, siding neither with Great Britain nor with Adolf Hitler's Germany. Clearly though, de Valera favored the British cause. He even sent firefighters from Dublin to help fight fires caused by an attack on Belfast, Northern Ireland, by Nazi bombing planes.

By 1944, de Valera was so popular that Fianna Fáil held twice as many seats in the Irish parliament as any other party. De Valera himself held not only the titles of prime minister and minister for external affairs, but also minister of education.

The political situation then changed. By 1948, three years after the war's end, de Valera's party had lost its majority. It was defeated by a group of smaller, moderate parties headed by John A. Costello, who now became prime minister. The newly elected parliament soon voted to separate completely from the British Commonwealth, officially becoming "The Republic of Ireland" in April 1949.

De Valera, growing old, refused to retire. While out of office he traveled to America, to Australia, to India, always speaking eloquently on behalf of Irish unification. In 1951, he became prime minister once again, only to lose to Costello in 1954.

In 1957, at the age of seventy-four, he once again won election as the leader of his nation. His victory came in spite of serious problems in the Irish economy and, as a result, the loss of many people through emigration to the United States and other countries.

To de Valera's followers he still was referred to affectionately as Dev. He still was giving long speeches, or as one admirer put it, "Marching on Dublin at the head of twenty thousand words."

But age had begun to take its toll. Despite a successful operation, his eyesight, never very strong, was all but gone. He spent many hours alone with his wife, listening to the radio or having her read to him.

In 1959 he resigned the office of prime minister, serving in the largely ceremonial post of president. While holding that position, he visited the United States at the age of eighty-one, speaking to a joint session of Congress. Americans, he said, deserved the thanks of the Irish people for having helped so much in winning freedom for that nation from British rule. But the task would remain unfinished, declared de Valera, until northern and southern Ireland at last were united.

Whether that union will ever occur still remains unclear. And de Valera must have known it would not happen in his lifetime.

In 1973 he and his wife retired to a nursing home near Dublin. And it was there, one year later, that she died.

Then, on August 29, 1975, Eamon de Valera himself followed her to the grave.

For nearly half a century he was the dominant figure in Irish political life. Despite economic hard times, the continuing failure to unite the partitioned Irish nation, and the bloody violence of civil strife, de Valera remained a symbol of hope to the Irish nation.

John Costello, the political opponent who for so long had competed against him, once declared that de Valera would leave behind him "nothing of permanent use." Yet even Costello once described him grudgingly as "a great man with great courage."

To the editor of *The Irish Echo*, a newspaper published in the United States, Eamon de Valera ranked considerably higher. "He was probably," said the editor, "the single Irishman who influenced history most in this century."

And that is, indeed, no small tribute for a child born on the streets of New York into a life that appeared to offer little, if any, hope of success.

Golda Meir

1898–1978   Born in Russia and an immigrant to the United States;
later played a crucial role as prime minister of Israel

To be a child. To be a Jewish child. To be a Jewish child in Russia at the dawn of the twentieth century.

Those three experiences were to shape the life of Golda Meir, a woman destined later to become the leader of Israel—the Jewish homeland she helped to establish.

As a child she knew cold and hunger. She knew fear. And she was determined that other Jewish children should not have to endure what she had endured. Because of her achievements in working toward that goal she is remembered today as one of the truly outstanding leaders of modern history.

One of Golda's earliest memories was that of being hungry, yet having her mother sorrowfully take food from her plate to feed her younger sister, Zipke. Even more frightening was the vivid memory of her father trying to nail a board across the door, fearing a "pogrom"—one of the frequent attacks against the Jews by crowds of angry Russians.

She knew that in many pogroms the Russians, shouting "Christ killers," had stormed into the Jewish quarter of a city or village. They stole what they wanted from the homes. Some of them drove nails into the heads of Jews. They threw Jewish children from upper-story windows onto the streets below. Women were raped, and then their stomachs ripped open. Some had their breasts cut off with knives.

Meanwhile, the police usually stood by, refusing to help the victims. Only if the Jews dared to fight back would the police step in, arresting not the attacking rioters but the Jews who dared to defend themselves.

Sometimes the Russian monarchs, the czars, would personally order the beginning of a pogrom. By blaming the Jews for the nation's problems, a czar could divert popular attention from his own failings.

Some Jews thought the violence would end if, by revolution, the czars were overthrown and a new kind of government established. Other Jews held little hope for such a change. Instead, they argued that the terror, the hunger, the beatings would end only when Jews had a country of their own in Palestine, the ancient "Zion" of biblical times.

Golda was born in 1898 in the Russian city of Kiev. Her parents, Moshe and Bluma Mabovitch, had eight children in all, four boys and four girls. All of the boys and one of the girls died in childhood. Only Golda, her younger sister Zipke, and an older sister Shana managed to survive the poverty and disease that was then the lot of Jewish children in Russia.

Golda later remembered how her father, a carpenter, once had borrowed money for materials to build a chess table that he entered in a competition. His table won the competition. But when he came forward to claim the prize money, the judges knew from his name that he was a Jew. They refused to pay him.

Moshe Mabovitch later moved his family to the city of Pinsk, hoping that in that city there would be more work to be done by a skilled carpenter such as himself. Day after day he went out looking for jobs. But there were no jobs. The family was hungry. They lived together in a tiny room. Their situation grew desperate.

At last Golda's father made a decision. He would take his family to the *goldene medina* (land of gold)—America. There, it was said, there was work for everyone. Even poor people from Russia could become rich. Furthermore, in America there would be no need to live in fear. In America there were no pogroms.

Moshe Mabovitch borrowed money to pay his way to the United States. He promised that as soon as he saved enough money, he would send for his wife and children. Meanwhile, they were to live with Moshe's father and mother.

Three years passed. Finally Moshe, by then living in Milwaukee, was able to put together the money needed to bring his family to America. Their home, in a section of Milwaukee where poor Jews lived, was a cramped two-

bedroom apartment with a small kitch-
enette and no bathroom.

Golda's father took whatever carpentry work he could find in order to support his family. To add to their income,
Golda's mother, Bluma, opened a small
grocery store in the neighborhood. At
first she spoke almost no English. Without money, she had to buy all of her
stock on credit. Shana, the older daughter, found work in a tailor shop, sewing
buttonholes by hand.

By the time the Mabovitches arrived
in America, Golda was eight years old
and immediately began attending
school. At dawn every morning, however, her mother had to buy items to
sell in her store. So she would leave
Golda in charge of opening the store
and running it until she returned with
her purchases.

As a result, Golda almost always was
late for school. Once a truant officer
tried to warn Mrs. Mabovitch that she
was breaking the law by keeping Golda
away from school. But, speaking only
Russian and Yiddish, she could not understand him.

Golda hated working in the store.
Sometimes she cried. But, as in most
matters, once Bluma Mabovitch made
up her mind about something, nothing
could convince her to change it. Later
in life that would be true, too, of Golda.

Golda worked in the store not only
in the morning but also until ten o'clock
every evening, as well as all day on
Sunday. Somehow, however, she still
managed to become an excellent student. Soon she was making straight A's
in all of her subjects and was recognized
as one of the brightest children in the
school. English came easily to her, and
she quickly mastered it.

Making high grades never was the
only goal for Golda. By the time she
was eleven years old, in the fourth
grade, she already was beginning to
show an interest in broader matters
rather than in just academic success.
One issue was textbooks. Because textbooks were not free in the school, some
families were too poor to buy them.
Golda strongly believed that it was un-
fair for some students to have books
and others to be without them. As a
result, she organized a public meeting
for a group she herself had created, the
"American Young Sisters Society." On
her own, she hired a hall for a Sabbath
(Saturday) evening.

On the night of the meeting she described the problem to a large crowd
of adults. As Golda put it, she was confident that if people only knew how important it was that all students in the
Fourth Street School had textbooks,
somehow they could be found.

She was right. The audience contributed enough money that night to help

buy books for the poorer students of the school. At the age of eleven, Golda Mabovitch already was making a difference, helping to improve the lives of others.

At the age of fourteen, Golda graduated as valedictorian of her class, the student with the highest grades. Her mother then expected her to begin working full-time in the store or to get a paying job as a typist. Going on to high school seemed an expensive luxury. When Golda still insisted on enrolling in a high school, her mother instead tried to interest her in marrying a well-to-do neighbor, a man who already was more than thirty years old.

Firmly refusing, Golda ran away to Denver, where her older sister Shana, now married, had gone to live.

Many of Shana's friends were Jews who, like the Mabovitches, had come to America hoping for a better life. Most of them were Socialists—people who believed that all workers had the right to live in a democratic society and to have decent jobs. Many of them, too, hoped that someday there might be a national homeland for Jews in Palestine: a place where Jews from around the world could set up a nation of their own. Those people were known as Zionists.

One evening a quiet young man named Morris Meyerson joined the usual discussion group at Shana's house. Less political in his interests than the others in the crowd, he especially loved music, art, and poetry. He and Golda soon came to enjoy each other's company. They went to concerts together, read poetry to each other, took long walks in Denver's beautiful parks. Before long, the two were in love.

Golda attended high school classes in Denver. She also worked in a shop, measuring the linings for skirts. She spent time with Morris. And she talked politics, becoming more and more interested in the idea of Zionism. She could not accept the Communist beliefs of Karl Marx, but she did become a follower of the American Eugene V. Debs, who believed that "democratic socialism" was the way to build a better society.

After about a year, Golda's father wrote to her, insisting that she return to Milwaukee to be with her mother, who missed her greatly. It was understood that if she came home, she could enroll once again at North Division High School, where she had been studying before running away. Morris Meyerson sadly agreed to put off any plans for marriage until Golda finished her education.

Readjusting quickly to life in Milwaukee, Golda became vice president of her high school graduating class. She

Golda Meir as a young woman. *The Golda Meir Library/University of Wisconsin, Milwaukee.*

next enrolled in the Milwaukee Normal School or, as it was then called, the Teacher's Training College, preparing to become a teacher. Meanwhile, she worked regularly as a librarian. She also worked at a school that taught Jewish folk culture to young children.

Most important of all to her, however, was her involvement with the movement to free Palestine from Turkish rule. Because there was an active, energetic Jewish community in Milwaukee, many Jews from Palestine came there to speak. Golda learned from them about the new city of Tel Aviv that had just been founded in desert sands along the Mediterranean coast. She learned about the kibbutzim (agricultural settlements) where Jews were trying to set up model communities, based on sharing and caring for each other. She learned about the Labor Zionist party in Palestine that was working to make the dream of a Jewish homeland a reality.

As Golda later put it, "Zionism was beginning to fill my mind and my life." She still attended college. She still corresponded with Morris and intended to marry him, even though he did not share her great enthusiasm for a Jewish homeland in Palestine. Yet, for Golda, both her academic studies at school and her love for Morris were becoming less important than her passion for Zionism.

Often she spoke on behalf of the Jewish cause to crowds of people on street corners or in front of synagogues. Golda's father, himself a Zionist, did not approve of a woman speaking in public, especially in front of a synagogue. To him that was a disgrace. Once he went to hear her speak, intending to pull her off the speaker's platform "by her hair braid" and bring her home.

When Golda returned home that night, her father already was asleep. But her mother, smiling, reported that after listening to her he had been very proud. He had gone to bed shaking his head and saying, "I don't know where she gets it from." Golda later declared it "the most successful speech I ever made."

In 1917 Golda became Mrs. Morris Meyerson. Not until 1921, however, did she finally persuade Morris to leave America and to sail with her to Palestine to start a new life. As much as Golda truly loved the United States, she later declared that she was never to experience a moment of "homesickness" for it, or ever to regret leaving it for Palestine.

To Golda's surprise, her sister Shana decided to take her own two children and go with the Meyersons to live in Palestine. Shana's husband, Sam, joined them later, as did Zipke, Golda's younger sister.

While Shana and her children remained in the city of Tel Aviv, Golda and Morris applied for membership in Kibbutz Merhavia—a communal farm located ten miles south of Nazareth. For Golda, living in a kibbutz was important. People who lived in such communities owned no personal property. There was to be no individual profit from the farm's activities. Instead, people were to work together, sharing their faith as Jews, sharing all the work, and—as a group—meeting the needs of the community.

At first the Meyersons' written application for membership was rejected. Golda demanded an explanation. The answer, it turned out, was that the members of the Merhavia group did not believe that an American girl could—or would—do the hard physical labor needed on the kibbutz. By living in America, they thought, she would have become "spoiled."

Golda insisted on the right of Morris and herself to visit Merhavia personally. They did. And the members of the kibbutz changed their minds. The Meyersons were accepted. Golda later joked that the only reason for their acceptance was that they promised to bring along their record player and some records.

As a member of the kibbutz Golda busily plunged into its work. During the day she picked almonds, worked in the kitchen, took care of children,

raised chickens. In the evening she learned Hebrew and Arabic. As hard as it all was, she loved farm work, believed in the ideals of the kibbutz. Morris, on the other hand, simply hated the situation at Merhavia.

Finally, to please Morris, Golda agreed to move to Tel Aviv. She became a secretary in the office of Histadrut (the Israel Labor Federation).

Next they moved to Jerusalem, where Golda gave birth to a son, Menachem. Then came a daughter, Sarah. To support the family, Morris brought in a small salary as a bookkeeper, while Golda took in laundry.

For four years, from 1924 to 1928, the couple struggled to make ends meet. For Golda, it was the hardest time in her entire life. She later admitted to wondering whether this was all that life was all about.

But then one day, just when she was feeling at her lowest, she visited the Wailing Wall, all that remained of Solomon's Temple from ancient biblical times. There she saw people on their knees, praying, and she determined that her life did indeed have meaning after all.

The wall had uplifted her sights and made her want to keep working for the high ideals of a homeland in Palestine for the world's Jews.

In their married life, Morris and Golda slowly began to drift apart, although they were not formally divorced until 1945. To divert her mind from such personal problems, Golda took on more and more work on behalf of Jewish causes.

She once again began working for Histadrut. There, people began to notice her, to recognize her great ability. In time, she was chosen as a delegate to the World Zionist Congress. She served on the executive board of Vaad Leumi, a council that represented Palestine's Jews in dealing with the nation's British rulers. She became chairman of a group that arranged medical services for much of the Jewish population.

In 1939, when war with Germany began to seem probable, the British feared that Palestine's Arab population might side with Hitler. To assure Arab support, Great Britain issued what was known as a white paper, sharply limiting the immigration of European Jews into Palestine.

That single act cut off the escape of thousands of Jews from the bloodthirsty Nazis. Golda joined with the Jewish leader David Ben-Gurion in trying to fight the white paper. But nothing could be done. As a result, many lives were needlessly lost.

When World War II finally ended in 1945, the Zionist leaders decided to act as if a Jewish nation already existed. In response, the British government arrested many leading Jews, including Ben-Gurion.

With almost all the other major figures of the nationalist movement in prison, Golda took over the leading position in Palestine's Jewish community and began to deal personally with the British.

Meanwhile, a committee of the United Nations had been investigating the situation. On its recommendation, the United Nations voted to divide Palestine into two nations, one for Arabs, the other as an independent homeland for the Jews.

The Arabs of the Middle East refused to permit such an arrangement and immediately began to prepare for war.

The Jews, without money to buy arms, turned desperately to the outside world, especially to America, for help. David Ben-Gurion, freed from prison, sent Golda to America to do whatever she could, but with little hope for her success.

Remarkably, in a whirlwind tour of the United States she quickly raised a total of $50 million.

Then, almost immediately after returning to Palestine, she set out at Ben-Gurion's request on a highly daring secret mission. Her purpose was to assure King Abdullah of Jordan that a Jewish nation, when it was finally formed, would not harm his country.

Wearing black robes to pass as an Arab woman, she crossed the Jordan River and tensely made her way by car to the Jordanian capital, Amman, passing safely through several military checkpoints.

Once she had arrived in Amman, King Abdullah asked her, among other questions, why the Jews were in such a hurry to have a nation of their own.

"We've been waiting for two thousand years," Golda later remembered answering him. "Is that really a *hurry?*"

Jordan, it soon became clear to her, would certainly join with Egypt, Syria, Lebanon, and Iraq in making war on the new Jewish nation. Still, Golda believed that the time for independence had come, and David Ben-Gurion agreed with her.

On May 14, 1948, Golda and twenty-four other Jewish leaders declared the formation of the nation of Israel. Meeting together, they signed a declaration of independence, much like that of the United States of America.

In the bloody war that soon followed, the Israelis, although badly outnumbered, surprised the world by defeating the attacking Arab armies. Israel had won its independence.

After the war, Golda served first as Israel's ambassador to the Soviet Union. Next she was elected to the Knesset, the Israeli parliament. Then, from 1949 to 1956, she served as minister of labor and social insurance. In that position she organized Israel's generous housing program for refugees flocking to the country from around the world.

In 1956 David Ben-Gurion chose Golda to be his minister for foreign affairs. At Ben-Gurion's suggestion she began to call herself Golda Meir, the Hebrew version of Meyerson. Because of her strong will and firm character Ben-Gurion once described Golda as "the only man in my Cabinet." During Israel's spectacular victory over the Arab nations in the war of 1956, it was Golda who, along with Moshe Dayan and Shimon Peres, was mostly responsible for winning the cooperation of France and Britain.

In 1965, ill and growing old, she resigned her position in the Cabinet.

By then she had become a grandmother with five grandchildren and, like any other Israeli citizen, proudly would push a baby carriage along the crowded streets of Tel Aviv. She did her own cooking and laundry and went from place to place without a guard, often riding on the city buses. Yet, although semi-retired, she still stayed active in the affairs of the Labor party.

In 1967, the Arabs once again tried to destroy Israel, only to be spectacularly defeated in the Six-Day War. To protect itself against further Arab attacks, Israel occupied the Gaza Strip, the Golan Heights of Syria, and the West Bank of the Jordan River, as well as East Jerusalem and the Sinai Peninsula.

Two years later, when the prime minister of Israel unexpectedly was stricken with a heart attack, Golda Meir was chosen to replace him.

Seventy years old, she had become the leader of the Jewish nation.

What Golda wanted most was peace with Israel's neighbors. She offered to speak with Arab leaders anywhere—in their capital cities, at the United Nations, in neutral countries such as Switzerland. But they would not meet with her.

Meanwhile, for refusing to give back Arab lands taken in the Six-Day War, the enemies of Israel—even in such supposedly friendly countries as the United States—spoke of Golda as "intransigent," meaning that she would not change her mind.

Once, she met in Rome with the Pope, who also asked why she did not give in to some of the Arab demands. Her answer may have surprised him.

"Your Holiness," she said, "do you know what my earliest memory is? It is waiting for a pogrom in Kiev. Let me assure you that my people know all about real 'harshness' and also that

we learned all about real mercy when we were being led to the gas chambers of the Nazis."

Similarly, as Golda Meir was asked many times, what would happen if the Jews simply went back to the pre-1967 boundary lines? But that, she reminded people, is exactly where things stood when the Arabs last attacked them. The Arabs, she pointed out, keep on trying to wipe out the Jews. "But do they really expect us to cooperate?"

In 1973, on Yom Kippur, the holiest of Jewish holy days, the Arabs launched a massive surprise attack on Israel. Caught off guard at first, the Israeli armies were thrown back with heavy losses.

Eventually they rallied and once again went on to win a spectacular victory. Still, Mrs. Meir never forgave herself for accepting the advice of those military commanders who, on the eve of the war, had assured her that no attack was coming.

By then seventy-six years old, she finally retired from office. But she continued to speak out, continued to defend the right of Israel to exist. Her private life was given over to her children and her grandchildren. She loved to read, to listen to classical music, and to cook traditional Jewish foods, such as gefilte fish.

Once, following Israel's victory in the

Israeli Prime Minister Golda Meir arrives in New York to meet with President Richard Nixon, 1970. *UPI/Bettmann Newsphotos.*

1967 Six-Day War, Iraq's foreign minister had addressed her personally from the rostrum of the United Nations. "Mrs. Meir," he had declared angrily, "why don't you go back to Milwaukee—that's where you belong!" Now, in retirement, Golda decided on her own to do just that. She arranged to visit the school in Milwaukee where, as eleven-year-old Golda Mabovitch, she had raised money for children too poor to buy their own textbooks.

Much had changed since then. As prime minister of Israel, Golda was known throughout the world. Over the years, the school had become mostly black, rather than Jewish. But the students welcomed Golda, in her words, "as though I were a queen."

They sang songs to her in Hebrew and in Yiddish. When they sang the Israeli national anthem, "Hatikvah," her eyes filled with tears. There were large posters saying SHALOM (peace). Two little girls, wearing headbands with Stars of David on them, presented her with a white rose made from tissue paper and pipe cleaners. She wore it through the day and then carried it back with her to Israel.

Golda Meir had accomplished much in her lifetime. And if Israel still had not persuaded its Arab neighbors to make a just and lasting peace, it was not because she had failed to try. President Anwar el-Sadat of Egypt, her foe in the Yom Kippur War of 1973, praised her as "a first-class political leader." It was Mrs. Meir, declared Sadat, who deserved credit for starting the peace talks that ended the conflict between Israel and Egypt over the Sinai Peninsula.

On December 8, 1978, at the age of eighty, Golda Meir died.

World leaders, including former enemies like Sadat, expressed sorrow at her passing. She was, they said, an "extraordinary woman," an "extraordinary human being."

To those who knew her, Jews and non-Jews alike, Golda was, as they so often put it, "unforgettable." And, truly, that is the way history remembers her.

Fidel Castro

1926– Revolutionary leader and longtime president of Cuba

Why is it that most leaders, including even famous and powerful figures, so often pass quickly from the stage of history, soon to be forgotten, even by their own people? On the other hand, what enables a very few men and women to advance into greatness—to join that small handful of personalities known to the world for their influence and their importance?

Fidel Castro came to power on the tiny island nation of Cuba on New Year's Day, 1959. In his role as a national leader he outlasted eight presidents of the United States and five rulers of the Soviet Union.

To Castro, his survival was no accident, no surprise. From early in his youth he always believed that a person of faith and determination could move mountains. With the right ideas—high ideals that the person in charge genuinely believed in—the people would continue to follow. But the leader, he said, must also be genuinely determined to succeed and must never give in. According to Castro, a battle . . . or an entire war . . . must always be fought under the principle of "victory or death." Never give in. Never compromise. Hold to your beliefs, with complete certainty.

"Victory or Death!"

"Never give in!"

It was with that kind of faith, that kind of persistence, that Fidel Castro first rose to power. And it is also how he became one of the major personalities of the twentieth century.

Fidel Castro was born on August 13, either in the year 1926 or 1927. To gain Fidel's admission to a school his parents preferred, they may well have changed his birthdate on official documents, making him appear one year older. His father, Angelo Castro, was born in Spain and had come to Cuba with the Spanish army when the island still was a Spanish colony.

After the Cuban war of independence in 1898, he stayed on in the new nation, becoming a farmer in Cuba's Oriente Province, near the city of Santiago. Through hard work and persistence, Castro then became wealthy.

Angelo Castro had two children by his first wife. When she discovered, however, that he also was fathering the children of a cook on the estate, she divorced him. In the years following that divorce, Lina Ruz González, the cook, bore him four children, including Fidel and his brother Raúl, who was himself destined to play an important role in the Cuban government led by Fidel. Angelo and his companion later married and had four more children.

Growing up in a rigid, conservative Catholic society, Fidel could not help being sensitive to his illegitimacy in a family that had experienced divorce. Often he defended himself from teasing by using his fists. Strongly built, he soon became known as wild, unruly,

hard to handle. He came to love the nearby seashore, taking a special interest in swimming and, later, in skin diving.

From an early age he was aware of his family's wealth. His classmates and teachers flattered him, expected him to behave like a member of a privileged class. In the small public school in his community, he was the first student to learn how to read and was physically stronger than the other children. Before long he came to see himself as outstanding, with a pride and self-confidence that eventually was to shape his attitude toward the outside world.

When Fidel was six, his parents sent him, along with a brother and a sister, to a Catholic boarding school in Santiago. Under the tough discipline of the Jesuit priests Fidel began to do well in his classes. His brother Raúl remembered, however, that Fidel was in a fistfight with other boys at the school almost every day.

As early as 1940, Fidel showed an interest in politics, writing a letter in that year to Franklin Delano Roosevelt to congratulate him on his successful reelection to the American presidency.

At the Colegio Dolores, another Jesuit school, Fidel began to excel at sports—soccer, basketball, jai alai, baseball. He was good at all of them.

When he was fifteen, Fidel enrolled at Belen, an outstanding Jesuit college preparatory school in Havana. There, he developed a special love of history, with a deep fascination for the heroes of the past—the great figures who had exercised personal power in shaping events. It was an interest that would continue even after he himself had become a leader known throughout the world.

At Belen, Fidel excelled in public speaking and debate. He also was recognized for his stamina and endurance on mountain climbing trips. In 1944 he was awarded a prize as the outstanding school athlete in all of Cuba, having been a star in baseball, basketball, track, and soccer. For a time, the Washington Senators, then an American League baseball team in the United States, considered him a likely prospect for a pitching contract.

His yearbook entry at the school predicted that with all of his physical and intellectual strengths, Fidel Castro would "make a brilliant name for himself."

During his formative years, influenced especially by the Jesuits, Castro had learned how to study hard. He had learned to depend on himself, rather than on others. He had acquired self-discipline. Finally, too, he had come to understand the way Jesuits looked at society and their view of how best to govern it.

By the time he left Belen he already had rejected the Catholic religion, but the habits he formed there would stay with him for life. According to one Cuban Communist leader, when once in power, Fidel Castro was far more a Jesuit than a revolutionary or a Marxist.

In 1945 Fidel enrolled in the faculty of law at the University of Havana. From the day of his arrival on campus he immersed himself in politics, expressing strong views on world and national affairs, as well as on college matters.

Tall, aggressive, well spoken, he usually wore a handsome dark blue suit and tie, helping him to stand out from the other students. Before long he had attracted a large following at the college, friends who eagerly backed him in his campaigns for campus offices.

But even as an undergraduate Castro had broader political interests. In 1947, he left school to take part in an attempted invasion of the Dominican Republic, an unsuccessful effort to overthrow the ruthless dictatorship there headed by Generalissimo Rafael Trujillo.

In 1948, while participating in an international student congress in Bogotá, Colombia, Fidel found himself joining a military revolt against the Colombian government. In that incident, he finally managed to escape by seeking refuge in the Cuban Embassy.

Returning to Cuba, he threw himself into national politics, actively supporting the candidacy for president of Eddy Chibás, the leader of the Ortodoxo party, a liberal reform group. Often young Castro appeared on the speaker's platform with Chibás, as well as campaigning for him on radio. Chibás, although possessed of a brilliant mind, failed to build strong support among the people and therefore lost the election. It was an important lesson for Fidel.

Still enrolled in law school, Castro took time out to marry Mirta Díz Balart, the sister of a fellow law student. The newlyweds honeymooned in Miami and then in New York, where Fidel drove his bride around Manhattan in a white convertible.

It was on that trip that he bought his first copy of Karl Marx's work, *Das Kapital*, a book expressing the political position that later would change his life.

In September 1949 the couple's only child, Fidelito, was born. By then Castro had fallen far behind the other members of his class in law school, both because of his marriage and the time he had spent in politics. Still, through hard study he managed to receive an A on most of his final exams. To graduate with his classmates, however, he had to enroll as an "irregular student," completing all the courses he had missed. In 1950 he graduated from law school.

Immediately afterward, Castro, along with two of his classmates, formed a law firm in Havana. They received little money in legal fees since most of the firm's clients either were poor themselves or members of political causes championing the poor. But, for Fidel, the money he earned meant little and was only a tool for staying politically active. Still, both Castro's father and his wife's father had to help out the young couple with money.

In early 1952 Fidel began to campaign feverishly for membership in the Cuban congress, with elections scheduled for June.

The elections never took place. On March 10, General Fulgencio Batista, with the help of the army, seized power and established himself as the nation's dictator.

Hearing the news, Castro was furious. From that moment on he pledged himself to destroy the political system that had allowed such a corrupt leader as Batista to rise to a position of authority. But to change the system, Castro soon concluded, would require force—an armed rebellion against the government. Only in that way, he reasoned,

At his revolutionary base in Sierra Maestra, Cuba, guerilla leader Fidel Castro teaches a young recruit to shoot. *China Photo Service/Sovfoto*.

could Cuba ever hope to achieve true democracy and social justice for the nation's people.

Working with a few friends in the strictest possible secrecy, Fidel gathered a force of some 165 men and women. It was his plan to use them in an attack on the Moncada Barracks, near Santiago, where an important group of Batista's troops were housed.

On July 26, 1953, he launched the assault.

It was a miserable failure. More than half of the attackers were killed. The rest, including Fidel and his brother Raúl, were thrown into prison. In the trial that followed, Fidel conducted his own defense, concluding his deeply moving speech with the memorable phrase *"La historia me absolvera"* (History will absolve me). The speech was a summary of Fidel Castro's political beliefs, explaining, as he saw it, the reasons for the great suffering of the Cuban people.

That defiant address, made into a beautifully illustrated book once Castro actually came to power, did him little good at the time. He was sentenced to a prison term of thirteen years on the Isle of Pines.

Still, the Moncada Barracks attack—and even the date of its launching, July 26—were destined to become landmark symbols in the history of the future Cuban revolution.

While in prison Fidel read widely, including works by Shakespeare, Victor Hugo, and Dostoyevski, as well as books on political theory by John Locke, Thomas Paine, Karl Marx, and Vladimir Ilyich Lenin.

Castro also read carefully about the steps President Franklin Delano Roosevelt had taken to fight the Great Depression in the United States, especially in dealing with unemployment, job shortages, and problems relating to agriculture. By no means was Castro a Communist at the time. To him, political theory was primarily a practical tool to be used in winning victories against injustice to a nation's people.

In May 1955, after arranging his reelection without any opposition, General Batista decided to gain public support by setting free the imprisoned *Moncadistas*, the survivors of the Moncada attack, as well as by pardoning all of those Moncada fighters who had escaped to other countries.

Castro and his comrades promptly returned to Havana. Greeted by cheering crowds, they tried for a time to carry on a peaceful campaign of opposition to the government. But Batista refused to allow Fidel to be heard on Cuban radio, while personally condemning him on radio and in the newspapers and magazines.

Daily, the government's pressure against Castro mounted. Finally he decided to leave Cuba. In a statement to the press he proclaimed that he and his followers no longer would "beg" or "plead" for their rights. Instead, they would fight for them.

Taking refuge in Mexico City, Fidel began to plan a revolutionary expedition to overthrow the Batista government. It was in Mexico City that he met a dynamic young Argentinian physician, lately turned radical: Ernesto "Che" Guevara. The two immediately became best friends, and before long Che agreed to join Castro's movement. Eventually he would become one of its heroes.

Once again acting in great secrecy, Castro began to organize a new invasion force. This time he called his group the "26th of July Movement," in memory of the date of the earlier Moncada attack. Despite the attempts of Batista to kill him, or at least have him arrested, Castro persisted in his planning.

On December 2, 1956, Fidel Castro, accompanied by a force of eighty-two men, landed the yacht *Granma* on the coast of Oriente Province in Cuba.

The landing itself proved close to disastrous. In a shipwreck, all of the group's heavy weapons and food were lost. So was the only radio transmitter. Three days later the conspirators were caught in a deadly ambush by Batista's troops. Before long, only twelve men

from the original landing force remained, including Fidel, his brother Raúl, and Che Guevara.

Still, Fidel somehow remained remarkably confident. "Now," he told the others, "we are going to win."

Taking refuge in the Sierra Maestra mountains, the survivors soon began to conduct surprise guerrilla attacks against nearby military outposts. They ambushed government patrols, being careful to treat all captured soldiers with respect and to give them food and medical care.

Soon, many volunteers from the Sierra Maestra area began to join Castro's force. Peasants, resenting the corrupt Cuban government, learned of Fidel Castro's revolutionary goals and made him a local hero.

As word of Fidel's deeds spread to the outside world, Herbert L. Matthews of the *New York Times* journeyed to the area to interview him. Matthews reported in the *Times* that Castro was a man of high ideals and great courage, a leader, moreover, who was working for democratic socialism, not for communism.

Despite a heavy offensive launched by Batista's combat forces, Castro persisted. The 26th of July Movement soon had much of the nation's population on its side, even though it was badly outnumbered on the battlefield. Church leaders, businessmen, even some highly placed military officers, eventually came to believe the nation would be better off with another person as president.

Finally, Batista realized that his situation was hopeless. On New Year's Day, 1959, he boarded a plane and fled the country, taking refuge in the Dominican Republic.

That afternoon the Cuban people filled the streets of Havana. Caravans of cars, their horns blaring, streamed through the city. Music filled the air. Crowds of people shrieked with joy, crying *"Libertad!"* ("Liberty!") at the tops of their voices.

The next day, Fidel Castro arrived in Havana.

Still only thirty-two years old, he was greeted as the nation's greatest hero. As he spoke to the cheering crowd, thousands of white doves were released into the air.

"Fidel! Fidel! Fidel!" chanted the people, regarding him as their liberator from tyranny.

In the weeks that followed, Castro arranged for the arrest, trial, and execution of many of Batista's supporters. They were guilty, claimed Fidel, of crimes such as torture and murder, and therefore they must be punished. Some of the trials, however, became public

spectacles—held in athletic stadiums with hawkers selling ice cream and soda pop to the spectators. Especially in the United States, the public reaction to such show-trials became increasingly hostile.

After officially becoming prime minister, with a figurehead serving in the higher office of president, Castro visited the United States. He assured Vice President Richard Nixon that he would not interfere with the American naval base at Guantanamo Bay, nor with the large property holdings of American corporations in Cuba.

According to Castro, he was firmly committed to the Western world in its struggle against international communism. On American college campuses in the East, such as Princeton, Fidel was greeted with wild enthusiasm by the students.

With each succeeding month, however, it became clear that Cuba's new relationship with the United States would not be friendly. Castro began to set limits on the size of landholdings, badly hurting such huge American interests as the United Fruit Company. He also began to distribute land held by large companies to landless peasants. Soon, Fidel came to realize that his ideas of reform in such fields as agriculture would put him in direct conflict with the United States.

To protect himself, Castro increasingly turned for support to Communists within Cuba and to such Communist nations as China and the Soviet Union. By 1960 Fidel had made a deal providing for the purchase of oil from Russia and the sale of Cuban sugar to the Soviets. Always influenced by personal relationships, Castro became especially friendly with Premier Nikita Khrushchev. At the same time, he gradually took over almost all American-owned property in Cuba.

Meanwhile, Communist revolutionaries from throughout Latin America flocked to Cuba. Some of them then used it as a launching base for unsuccessful attempts to overthrow the governments of Panama and the Dominican Republic.

With Communist support, Castro himself arrested loyal aides, including the brilliant Hubert Matos. Matos, although strongly anti-Communist, had been one of Fidel's most faithful followers during the campaign for control of Cuba. Castro now jailed him for twenty years, allowing the proud Matos to be tortured and humiliated during the entire time.

A lawyer himself, Fidel showed from the beginning of his rule a willingness to use the law primarily as a tool of power for achieving his political ends.

Seeing what was happening in Cuba, the United States struck back, angrily cutting off formal diplomatic relations with the island nation in January 1961.

Finally, under pressure from Vice President Nixon, President Eisenhower authorized the CIA (Central Intelligence Agency) to begin arming and training a strike force of Cuban exiles for an invasion of their former homeland. On April 17, 1961, with John F. Kennedy by then serving in the presidency, an invasion force of some 1,400 men landed at two beaches in the Bahia de Cochinos—the Bay of Pigs—some one hundred miles southeast of Havana.

Within a day, however, Castro had surrounded the invaders with more than twenty thousand soldiers, along with heavy artillery and tanks. Those rebels who were not killed were captured by Castro's army. After negotiations, the survivors later were freed and sent to the United States in exchange for some $53 million worth of food and medicines.

Now completely in control, Castro canceled the forthcoming Cuban elections. He was, he now declared, a dedicated Marxist-Leninist, committed to making his country a model for—and a defender of—the so-called developing (or poorer) nations of the world. Soon afterward he sent his only son, thirteen-year-old Fidelito, to school in the Soviet Union to show just how dedicated he was to friendship with the Communist bloc.

Step by step, Castro now moved toward total control of his nation. Thousands of people who had dared even to question his acts were rounded up and put into prison. Writers were forced to side with the government. Local "Committees for Defense of the Revolution" soon organized citizens on every block in every city, with neighbors often terrorizing neighbors. Before long, Cuba became a tightly disciplined, well-organized nation. But fear was everywhere.

In 1962 Premier Nikita Khrushchev decided to place Soviet offensive missiles in Cuba, a gamble posing a direct threat to the United States. Castro long had been eager for short-range defensive missiles to discourage an American invasion, but he had serious concerns about Khrushchev's decision and the possible reaction by President Kennedy.

On October 22, Kennedy declared in a television broadcast to the American people that Khrushchev's move could possibly lead to nuclear war. He announced a naval and air blockade of Cuba, prohibiting the shipment of all offensive military equipment to the island.

For six days, the possibility of nuclear war sent a chill through much of the world. American troops gathered in Florida, poised for an invasion. American ships established a defensive line in the sea, refusing to let Soviet vessels pass to Cuba.

Finally, Khrushchev backed down. He agreed to remove the missiles already in Cuba, while Kennedy agreed to end the blockade. The Cuban Missile Crisis was over.

Fidel Castro was furious. During all the heated negotiations between the two superpower leaders, he never once had been contacted by either of them. He felt overlooked, insulted. According to Che Guevara, who was with him when he heard the news of Khrushchev's decision to pull back, Fidel began kicking a wall in anger. He cursed, speaking of the Russian leader in the foulest of gutter language. Finally, in disgust, he broke a mirror.

Always before, Fidel had trusted Khrushchev, admired him. Now, in a speech at the University of Havana he accused the man he once had regarded almost as a father of having no courage. Nor would Fidel even meet with the highly placed Russian official Khrushchev sent to Cuba to soothe his ally's hurt pride.

In the long run, however, the Missile Crisis of 1962 worked to Castro's advantage. As part of the agreement with the Soviets, President Kennedy agreed to give official recognition to the right of Cuba, a Communist nation, to continue to exist in the Western Hemisphere. Also, the United States did nothing when Castro refused to allow on-site inspection of the nuclear missile stations there. Because of those actions it became understood, without a formal treaty, that the United States really was giving up the right, dating from the Spanish American War, to send troops into Cuba whenever it seemed necessary.

In the years that followed, Fidel Castro worked to transform his nation. Rejecting a luxurious life-style for himself, he made certain that the majority of his people would live better lives. Cuba's health care system became one of the best among developing-world countries. In the cities and in the countryside there was a new network of health clinics, serving every citizen. The death rate for infants was brought to a rate lower than in some large cities of the United States.

Meanwhile, hundreds of miles of roads were built. There were new children's nurseries and day-care centers, as well as mental hospitals. In the schools, every child was entitled to free basic education. Fidel also introduced free education at the college level, open to all, and based entirely on ability.

Sometimes it is said that Castro saw his role in the nation as similar to that of the principal in a Jesuit school, with all the citizens as his pupils. Once, when visiting an order of nuns in Santiago, he declared to them that they were "the true Marxists." It was a statement showing just how very different his view of communism was from that of governments which, until the 1990s, ruled the Soviet Union and the nations of Eastern Europe.

In actual matters of religion Fidel greatly shifted his policy. In the 1960s and 1970s, he was, like most Marxists, openly hostile to organized religious practices. Then, during the 1980s, he met with visiting delegations of Methodist and Catholic clergy. He openly invited the Pope to visit Cuba. He once again allowed the celebration of Christmas. And he spoke often of the importance of religious influences in shaping his own life.

From time to time serious discussion took place between officials of Cuba and the United States about ways to improve relations between the two countries. That was particularly true during the presidency of Jimmy Carter. However, the open use of Cuban troops and money to aid Communist causes overseas always prevented any real progress. Cuban influence was especially strong in Africa (both in Angola and Ethiopia) and also in Nicaragua, follow-

President Castro escorts President Mikhail Gorbachev through an exhibition commemorating the thirtieth anniversary of the Cuban revolution, 1989. *Sovfoto*.

ing the 1979 Sandinista victory in that country. Cuban military advisers also served in Grenada prior to the American invasion of that island nation.

In the 1990s, with a decline in Soviet economic aid to Cuba, the Cuban people began to suffer greatly. Chicken, eggs, and beef were tightly rationed. Clothing and shoes became hard to find, as did gasoline and medicines. Even bananas and sugar, major Cuban export products, were in short supply.

Still, Castro continued to insist that communism was the proper path to fol-

low. He remembered how, following the disastrous landing of his yacht, *Granma*, he had fought on with fewer than twenty men, bearing only rifles, against Batista's well-equipped army of more than 20,000—and still managed to win.

To him, determination was the key factor in his success. According to Fidel, if only Russia and China had been as strong in backing Iraq in 1991 as he himself had been after Moncada, the Iraqis would have defeated "the United States and Zionism."

Castro thus continued to hold fast to his Marxist faith even as communism waned in the Soviet Union and in Eastern Europe. He also continued to exercise total power in Cuba, claiming to do so for a noble cause—communism—and not just for his personal pride and wishes.

After thirty years in power Fidel Castro clearly had achieved his youthful goal of becoming one of the twentieth century's most important leaders. Yet his use of dictatorship to stay in power prevented him from winning the love and admiration that he also had craved from the days of his childhood.

In a sense then, Castro was similar to President Charles de Gaulle who could rightly say, "I am France," since Fidel quite rightly could say, "I am Cuba." But there was a difference. Unlike de Gaulle, the enemies aligned against Fidel were not tyrants—like Adolf Hitler—but rather the world's democracies, including the United States of America.

Facing the future possibility of war with such a powerful bloc of nations, Fidel increasingly found himself returning to the promise of his earlier life, the hard commitment that any struggle in which he was involved must end decisively.

It must end only with . . . "Victory or death!"

Jomo Kenyatta

1894?–1978   Central figure in winning independence from Great Britain for the African nation of Kenya and afterward that nation's president

"*Uhuru!*" ("Freedom!")

"*Harambee!*" ("Unity!")

Those two words—*Uhuru* and *Harambee*—became dramatic watchwords for the people of the African nation of Kenya as they fought to free themselves from British colonial rule and to emerge into the twentieth century.

The leader who one day would make it possible for Kenyans to achieve both freedom and national unity over tribal differences was Jomo Kenyatta, among the most admired and respected figures of modern times.

At his birth he was known simply as Kamau wa Ngengi, or "Kamau, the son of Ngengi." Since his native tribe, the Kikuyu, did not bother to record the dates of childbirths, Kenyatta, as he later called himself, could only guess

that he was born in the year 1894. His birthplace was the village of Ichaweri in the highlands of East Africa, to the south of the fabled Mount Kenya.

It was in that tribal village that young Kamau spent his childhood, tending sheep, gaining the skills of a hunter, and learning the magical secrets of medicine from his elderly grandfather, a witch doctor.

Then, when he was about ten years old, Kamau became ill with a disease that his grandfather could not cure. Parasites had entered the feet of the barefoot boy. The illness spread upward into his legs. Animal sacrifices did not help, nor did the singing of sacred songs.

Finally, fearing that he might die, Kamau's family took him to Fort Hall, near the city of Nairobi, where the

Church of Scotland operated a missionary hospital.

Never before had Kamau seen white men or white women. At first he was paralyzed with fear at the strange people who worked over his body, trying to help him. But as his health returned, he grew less fearful. He asked question after question. The missionary doctors were impressed with how bright the young Kikuyu boy seemed to be. He, in turn, was fascinated by the strange language they spoke and by their books with so many pictures and symbols. He wanted to know more. He wanted to learn.

At last Kamau was well enough to return to his village. Once again he herded sheep. He worked in the fields. He hunted with a bow and arrow. But he had not forgotten his experience in the Fort Hall missionary hospital.

When he was about thirteen and almost old enough to take on adult responsibilities in the village, he ran away, returning to the mission. There he claimed to be an orphan and asked to stay, working as a servant while he learned to speak and to write the English language. The missionaries accepted him.

Kamau learned quickly. Before long he began to dress like the English, to copy the table manners of the English, to do reading, writing, and arithmetic as well as almost any English schoolboy. He also learned carpentry and was put to work as a houseboy in the missionary kitchen.

Then, for a time, he returned to his village. He married. Once again he farmed the land and hunted. But by the time he was about twenty, it had become clear that village life was not enough to satisfy him.

In August 1914 the Fort Hall missionaries welcomed him back, formally baptizing him as Johnstone Kamau. He polished his English language skills and also learned Swahili, a language spoken by many African tribes when they traded with each other.

Before very long, young Johnstone Kamau decided he was ready for the next step in his journey of self-improvement. Leaving Fort Hall, he traveled to Nairobi, where he won a job as a clerk in the Public Works Department.

The bustling city of Nairobi was more to his liking. Although he had to live in a black section of town and blacks were not allowed in many hotels and restaurants, Johnstone Kamau did not mind. He was earning a good salary. He dressed well. He drove his own motorcycle at breakneck speeds along the highways. He went to parties and drank alcohol. Since, among the Kikuyu, it was considered proper to have more than one wife, he married a second time, with the full approval of his first wife who had remained behind in their native village of Ichaweri.

As a final symbolic act to show that he had matured into manhood, Kamau changed his name. He now became Johnstone Kenyatta. *Kenyatta* was the Kikuyu word for a belt—the dramatic belt of white, black, red, and green beads, with an enormous copper buckle, that he always wore around his waist.

For a time, Kenyatta simply enjoyed himself. He began to raise a family. He took a job with the Nairobi Town Council. According to friends, he showed no interest at all in politics.

Then, slowly, the situation began to change for blacks in Kenya. After the end of World War I, Great Britain altered the status of the country from just a protectorate to an actual colony. The British greatly increased taxes. They cut the wages of Kenyan farm laborers. But, most importantly, they set aside larger and larger amounts of land for settlers from Great Britain itself. Before very long the Kenyans were reduced to poverty in their own country, while the British grew ever more rich.

Unlike other African nations dominated by colonial powers, the Kenyans decided to do something about their situation. Their first leader was a well-educated Kikuyu tribesman, Harry Thuku. It was Thuku who, in 1921, founded the East Africa Association (EAA), which demanded the return of Kenyan farmland taken over by the British.

The British government responded to Thuku's protests by arresting him and throwing him into jail. When an angry crowd gathered around the jail, British troops opened fire, killing fifty-six Kenyans, including many women and children. Thuku then was deported to a desert village.

It was not long after Thuku's deportation that Johnstone Kenyatta, the young Kenyan who most enjoyed going to parties and speeding down the road on his motorcycle, made a decision. Previously uninterested in politics, he now joined the EAA. His life would never again be the same.

Because of his fine education, Kenyatta immediately became the propaganda secretary of the EAA, although as a government worker he was not supposed to become involved in political matters. Three years later, in 1925, the British government ordered the EAA disbanded. The group quickly reorganized as the Kikuyu Central Association (KCA).

After three more years, in 1928, Kenyatta quit his job with the Nairobi Town Council and became the leader of the KCA.

In planning for change, the first target he chose was the missionary movement in Kenya, including the very group at Fort Hall that once had saved his life and then had taught him English. By 1928 the British missionaries had begun to attack sharply such Kenyan practices as multiple marriages and what they considered "un-Christian" songs and dances.

Kenyatta responded by speaking out for the right of Kenyans to their own culture, their own ways of living. He founded a monthly journal, *Muigwithania* (the *Unifier*), which in gentle terms described native Kenyan practices, such as farming techniques. Without ever attacking the foreigners directly, its real message was clear: "Kenya for the Kenyans!" Still, Kenyatta was careful never to insult the British Empire or the British government of Kenya.

In 1929 Kenyatta traveled to London. His purpose was to win back for the Kikuyu their title to certain lands taken by British settlers. He failed to achieve the goal. But he did convince British authorities that the Kikuyu at least had the right to run their own schools for children of the tribe. He also convinced Parliament not to outlaw certain tribal religious ceremonies, as the Christian missionaries were trying to do.

The one group in Great Britain that rose up strongly in defense of Kenyatta's claims was the League Against Imperialism, made up mostly of Communists.

The league sent him to Moscow, where he was received with honor as a leader representing a nation made up of African blacks. After two months in Moscow he visited briefly with Communist party officials in Berlin and Hamburg, Germany. There, too, it was his skin color that won him favor and respect. How very different from the daily humiliation of living as a black in Nairobi!

In 1931 Kenyatta once again traveled to England. That visit, however, was destined to be a much longer one. He would not return to his native land for fifteen years.

At first he testified before various committees of Parliament, defending Kikuyu land rights. Then he began to study in earnest, improving his English and writing letters to newspapers about the mistreatment of Africans by European colonial powers.

For nearly two years Kenyatta attended Moscow University, while also studying at a revolutionary institute in the Soviet capital city. For a time he actually became a member of the Communist party.

On returning to London, he wrote magazine articles demanding "self-rule" for Africa and expulsion of "the imperialist robbers from the land."

While in London he met the famous American singer and movie star, Paul Robeson, a black who himself had become a believer in communism as a path to racial justice. For a time the two shared an apartment. Robeson once arranged for Kenyatta to play the part of an African chieftain in a movie.

Always pressed for money, Kenyatta also helped write a textbook on the Kikuyu language. With some of the money from that textbook, he enrolled in a college, the London School of Economics and Political Science. There he became a student of the great anthropologist Bronislaw Malinowski.

Working under Malinowski's guidance, Kenyatta eventually wrote a book describing the tribal life of the Kikuyu natives, calling it *Facing Mount Kenya.* In it, he cried out against colonial misrule and praised traditional Kikuyu culture.

With the appearance of that book Kenyatta decided to modify his personal image, emphasizing his African background. One change related to his own first name. Instead of using the British-sounding Johnstone, he now insisted on being called Jomo, which in the language of his tribe means Flaming Spear.

Although Kenyatta was still a member of the Communist party, his writings dealt almost entirely with the needs of the Kikuyu, not the broader issues relating to communism and capitalism.

In 1935, when the Italian dictator, Benito Mussolini, invaded the African nation of Ethiopia, Kenyatta joined with other African leaders in protesting the invasion. Through the 1930s and during World War II he met with such figures as Kwame Nkrumah, who later would lead the nation of Ghana. His main purpose was to speak out against the colonial rule of European powers and to champion the cause of independence for all the African nations.

Thus, African freedom, not communism, continued to be Kenyatta's real interest.

To support himself while living in England, he sometimes gave public lectures for the Workers' Educational Association, but most of his income came from his work as a hired farm laborer. In his free time he continued to write articles and pamphlets. His theme, always presented with politeness, with tact, still remained unmistakable: "Africa for the Africans!"

In September 1946, Jomo Kenyatta returned to Kenya. He became head of a college whose purpose was to prepare people to teach native children. The schools the children attended, he hoped, would be completely independent of those operated by the British-run government. Before long there were some 300 such schools, enrolling some 60,000 students. In the classrooms young people learned tribal languages, but they also learned the pan-African language, Swahili, and the international language, English.

By that time it was clear that Kenyatta saw himself not just as a leader of the Kikuyu tribe, but rather of all Kenyans in standing up for their rights against the British. No longer would Kenyans accept the teaching of Christian missionaries that African civilization was inferior to the civilizations of the West. More and more, they grew proud of their own culture.

Kenyatta soon became the best-known defender of the rights of native Kenyans. He spoke to huge public rallies, sometimes numbering as many as 50,000 people. Always a dramatic, exciting speaker, he would greet audiences with a rousing cry of "Eeeeeeh!" Then, shaking his fist in anger or using humor, he would bind his listeners together in calling for freedom from British rule. He was a dynamic, electric personality, one the British understood had great influence over the people.

For some Kenyans, the organization that Jomo Kenyatta headed, the Kenya African Union (KAU), was moving too slowly. Beginning in 1948, there were more and more incidents of violence—murder and torture—against white peo-

ple and their African followers. The terrorists, impatient with the slow pace of progress toward freedom, united. They began to call themselves the Mau Mau.

Kenyatta denied that he himself was a Mau Mau. He tried to separate the KAU from the Mau Mau's bloody deeds. But in October 1952, after a particularly ugly series of Mau Mau killings, the British arrested him. When the British police arrived at his home, he already was dressed and waiting for them. Extending his arms for the handcuffs, he is supposed to have smiled and said, "What kept you so long? I've been expecting you."

After Kenyatta's arrest some 50,000 other Kenyans were thrown into hastily built prisons. The independent Kenyan schools were shut down. British authorities imposed an iron discipline throughout the country.

Although Kenyatta denied having any connections with the Mau Mau, he was tried and found guilty of leading the terrorist organization. The court sentenced him to seven years in prison.

When word of the sentence became public, the Mau Mau unleashed savage reprisals. Many of their opponents, black and white alike, were found dead in the streets. Often the bodies had been badly mutilated. So angry were

After nine years of prison and exile, Jomo Kenyatta returned to his home and posed in a monkey skin presented to him by Kikuyu tribesmen. *UPI/Bettmann*.

the Kikuyu and other Kenyans at Kenyatta's imprisonment that many of them now united against the British by joining the Mau Mau organization.

For Jomo Kenyatta, the years 1952 to 1959 were the hardest of his entire life. Confined to a prison cell, he had nothing to do but read and play checkers. His cell was filled with snakes and insects. Sometimes he fought with other prisoners. Often he lost himself in bouts of drinking—he was actually encouraged to do so by his British guards. Already more than sixty years old, there were times when he lost hope of ever again playing a role in the life of his nation.

On the outside, however, Kenyans still considered him their leader. For that reason, perhaps, when the end of his term came, the British continued to hold him. The Kenyan people cried out for his release, demanding, "*Uhuru na Kenyatta!*" ("Freedom for Kenyatta!").

Finally, in 1961, the British set him free.

By then nearly seventy, he managed to stop drinking altogether. He also began at once to cooperate with the younger black leaders of Kenya for the nation's freedom. All Kenyan tribes, declared Kenyatta, now must come together in unity.

"*Harambee!*" he cried out. The one goal of all Kenyans of all tribes must be freedom for Kenya—"*Uhuru!*"

Finally, in December 1963, the conflict ended. The British, exhausted by the struggle to maintain their empire around the world, gave in. In a deeply moving ceremony, they lowered their flag and joined with Jomo Kenyatta in raising the flag of the newly independent Kenyan nation.

Kenyatta became the first prime minister of Kenya. One year later, with a reorganization of the government, he became the country's president.

Some Kenyans urged that he take revenge on his black opponents and on the British. But Kenyatta refused. Instead, he kept in their old jobs many white officials of the former British government. He did the same with members of the army and the police force. He appointed cabinet ministers from tribes other than his own Kikuyu tribe.

"*Harambee!*" he repeated over and over. "We must all pull together in unity!"

Calling his movement "African socialism," Kenyatta totally rejected the rigid dictatorial models of communism seen in the Soviet Union and China. Why, he asked, should Kenya "exchange one master for a new master?"

In handling the nation's economy, he refused to have his government take over industry and agriculture. Instead,

The tower of the Jomo Kenyatta Center dominates the skyline of the city of Nairobi, Kenya. *Karkkainen/Sipa.*

he had self-help groups of people build schools, hospitals, and roads. Many whites continued to operate their own businesses and farms. Kenyatta insisted on such democratic institutions as a free press and free public schools.

Because of Kenyatta's leadership, foreigners felt it safe to invest money in his nation's businesses, confident that he would not take them over for his own gain. Agriculture prospered. So did tourism, as people from Western countries flocked to visit the African country that had not only beautiful scenery and a fine climate but also had become stable and prosperous.

Kenyatta himself became wealthy. He owned a Rolls Royce. He owned thousands of acres of land. He dressed in well-tailored British suits. But he also wore on his head the native crown given to him by the minority Luo tribe. And, always, he wore around his waist the beaded kenyatta belt with its enormous copper buckle.

At last, well past the age of eighty, nearly all of the nation's power came to rest in Kenyatta's hands. His rivals, such as the ambitious Tom Mboya, sometimes died mysterious deaths. Yet the people remained fiercely loyal to the clever Kenyatta, speaking of him with affection as *Mzee* (Grand Old Man). Throughout the world, too, his name was honored, revered.

On August 22, 1978, Jomo Kenyatta died in his sleep.

At his funeral, thousands of Kenyans waited for a final view of the shepherd boy who had risen to be their leader.

At the time of his death the nation of Kenya, which he had done so much to create, was a model of prosperity and peace for all the former colonial nations of Africa.

Anwar el-Sadat

1918–1981   Leader of Egypt in the Yom Kippur War with Israel; later a cosponsor of the dramatic Israeli-Egyptian peace treaty

Yom Kippur, the "day of atonement," is the holiest, the most sacred day in the Jewish calendar. On that day in October 1973, as leader of the Egyptian nation, Anwar el-Sadat launched a massive surprise attack on the state of Israel. Thousands of lives were lost, both Egyptian and Israeli. Sadat himself had planned the attack and supervised every detail of its execution.

Only four years later, in November 1977, the very same Anwar el-Sadat stood at the rostrum of the Knesset, the Israeli parliament, and urged that the two nations, foes since ancient times, should work together for a lasting peace—a permanent peace based on justice.

Sadat admitted his role in starting the 1973 Yom Kippur War. He admitted that the Arab people always had refused even to talk with Jews about the right of Israel to exist in peace and security, without fear of attack. But now, he declared, Israel *does* exist. It was an accomplished fact. There must be peace.

As nation after nation in the Arab world learned of Sadat's journey to Jerusalem, people shook their fists in anger. Some Arab leaders vowed never again to do business with Egypt. Arab terrorists announced that, given the chance, they would kill the traitor Sadat, who had dared to propose peace with the hated Israelis.

How dare he, they demanded, laugh and joke with Israeli leaders such as Golda Meir—even exchange gifts with her? How dare he quote the holy Muslim book, the Koran, and ask for "love, right, and justice" for the Jews? "*Salam Aleikum*" ("Peace be upon you"), Sadat had told the members of the Knesset.

"Never!" declared other Arabs. "*Death* be upon them. And *death to Sadat!*"

Who was this tall, dark-skinned man, Anwar el-Sadat, dressed usually in an elegantly tailored European suit and smoking a pipe? Speaking perfect English and German, was he truly an "Arab"? And how had he come to believe that peace—instead of war to the death—was the way to deal with the Israeli "intruders" in the Middle East?

In the story of his own life, *In Search of Identity*, published not long after his historic visit to Jerusalem, Sadat began by stating that he was "a peasant born and brought up on the banks of the Nile—where man first witnessed the dawn of time." The events of his own life, said Sadat, closely matched the painful history of Egypt since the time of his birth.

While serving "the cause of right, liberty and peace," Sadat declared, his life always had been lived for the good of Egypt. That image of himself as an Egyptian, he said, was one that had grown inside of him ever since childhood.

Clearly, Sadat's childhood had shaped his later life. In 1918, when he was born in the quiet village of Mit Abul-Kum, on the Nile Delta near Cairo, Egypt was part of the British Empire. Anwar's father had received a General Certificate of Primary Education (GCPE) from a British school, one in which English was the language of instruction. Because in those days few Egyptians could read or write, he was treated with respect in the village and referred to as effendi, meaning a man of education.

Anwar, too, was sent to school. First of all he learned Arabic and managed to memorize all 114 chapters of the Koran. Next, he attended a Christian school, where he began to learn English.

During much of Anwar's early childhood his father, serving in the Egyptian army, was stationed far to the south, in the Sudan. Anwar's mother, herself of Sudanese birth, chose to be with him. As a result, the most important figure in shaping Anwar's first years was his grandmother. Although unable to read and write, it was she who had insisted that her own son and then her grandson, Anwar, become educated.

"How I loved that woman!" Sadat later recalled.

It was his grandmother, too, who convinced Anwar to be a deeply religious Muslim. Like other Muslims, he often fasted, not eating for entire days. Five times a day he touched his forehead to the ground in passionate prayer to God, eventually causing a permanent blister to develop there, something known in the Muslim world as a "prayer knot."

Finally, Anwar also learned from his grandmother to love the land and the history of Egypt. She often told him bedtime stories about Zahran, a local peasant who, condemned to hanging by the British army for a minor crime, had gone to his death with heroic pride. Often, said Anwar, "I wished *I* were Zahran."

Meanwhile, he came to love the games he played with the other boys, the carrots and onions that he himself was growing on the land, and the songs that the villagers would sing together by moonlight along the banks of the Nile. All of those things, he believed, were part of life in Egypt, the nation he adored.

When Anwar was seven, his father moved the family to Cairo. Instead of the joys of outdoor life in Mit Abul-Kum, they all were crowded together in a small apartment. New children were born until, eventually, Anwar found himself cramped together with twelve brothers and sisters.

In 1930, Anwar and his older brother, Tal'at, finished primary school. The cost of sending even one of them to secondary school amounted to one whole month of their father's yearly salary. But he paid the first installment for both boys anyway.

Tal'at took the money given to him for the second installment and spent it on pleasure. He hated school and did not want to go. Then he dropped out.

Probably there would not have been enough money for both sons to further their educations, and Anwar, as the younger one, would have had to stop going. Without schooling, his chances for a career in politics would have been slim. Thinking about the incident later, Anwar wondered if it had all been a matter of fate, or "destiny."

Young Anwar el-Sadat soon discovered that the other students in his school had money for fine clothing while he had but one suit. They filled themselves with candy and chocolates while each day he could afford but a single cup of milky tea.

In one way, however, Sadat was like the other students. He, too, hated the British who ruled the nation and who looked down upon the Egyptians as inferior. One day he joined a student demonstration in the streets of Cairo, helping to overturn a streetcar and set it on fire. He and the other boys also broke dishes in the school kitchen to show their dislike of the British.

It was at that time in his life that young Anwar el-Sadat acquired a hero—Mahatma Gandhi of India. Gandhi was struggling against British rule in South Africa and India, and Sadat hoped to lead the fight to expel the British rulers from Egypt. Sometimes he went as far as to strip to the waist, as Gandhi often did, and to spin yarn. His other hero was Kemal Atatürk of Turkey, a military leader working to rebuild his nation after its defeat in World War I.

Increasingly, Sadat began to believe that Gandhi's method—nonviolence— would fail to win freedom for Egypt. Instead, the situation would require military might—warfare. With that conclusion in mind, after finishing his secondary education and receiving a General Certificate of Education (GCE), he applied to the Royal Military Academy in Cairo. In 1936, he was accepted at the academy as one of fifty-two new cadets.

It was in military school that Sadat first met Gamal Abdel Nasser, a fellow student. After their graduation in 1938, Nasser and Sadat both were assigned to duty at a fortress located in Mankabad, close to the Sudan. There, along with ten other young Egyptians, the two military school comrades formed a secret society—the Free Officers Committee. It later became a revolutionary group whose purpose was first to overthrow the Egyptian monarchy and then to liberate Egypt entirely from British rule.

In September 1939, war broke out between Great Britain and the forces of Adolf Hitler's Germany. Before long, German troops and tanks under General Erwin Rommel were storming across the North African desert. Their goal was Cairo.

Many Egyptians were openly pro-German. Sadat, along with others, hoped that the Nazi threat would encourage Britain to grant independence to Egypt. At the same time, Sadat appreciated the British respect for law and for people's rights. The Nazis, he feared, might be far more cruel. Dark-skinned because of his Sudanese mother, he knew that Hitler condemned all black people as inferior to the blond-haired, blue-eyed Germans.

Still, Sadat considered Egyptian independence more important than anything else. He began working directly with two German spies. Unfortunately for him, the two proved more interested in whiskey and women than in their mission as spies. They were arrested by the British. Winston Churchill, the British prime minister, then visiting his troops in Egypt, personally questioned the two, offering to spare their lives if they would tell about their mission.

When they did, Anwar el-Sadat promptly was arrested. He was stripped of his commission as an officer in the Egyptian army and thrown into prison.

With nothing else to do in his jail cell, Sadat learned to read and speak German from another prisoner. He improved his English. Finally, in 1944, he managed to escape.

Until the war ended in 1945, he disguised himself, finding work as a cab driver, a tire salesman, or whatever odd jobs would enable him to stay alive. By then he also had a wife and two small children. All through his imprisonment they had received money from members of his revolutionary action group.

At the end of World War II the British lifted martial law, and Sadat once again was free. But he still was an angry young revolutionary, intent on putting a stop to British rule.

He proposed to blow up the British Embassy and kill all of the people in it. But Gamal Abdel Nasser refused to go along with the plan. Instead, Sadat cooperated in the killing of Amin Osman Pasha, a pro-British cabinet minister.

Once again Sadat found himself in prison. But this time it was Cell 54 of Cairo's infamous Central Prison. He was placed in solitary confinement in a cell with no bed, no lamp, no table, no chair. Unlike his previous prison confinement, there were no pleasant companions to keep him company and no books or writing materials. Water dripped from the prison walls onto the floor. Bugs were everywhere.

According to Sadat, it was during the two years he spent in Cell 54 that he came to know himself, to decide what was important in his life. It was in Cell 54 that he found, as he called it, "peace of mind."

When finally he was brought to trial, he was declared not guilty of murder and was given his freedom.

Although free, he had no job and no money. He no longer had a commission in the army. His future looked bleak.

Meanwhile, during his time in prison, affairs in the region had changed dramatically. Israel, under a 1948 United Nations resolution, had declared its independence as a nation. The small but well-trained Israeli army then had inflicted a humiliating defeat on the far more numerous forces of Egypt and other Arab countries that had combined to crush the newborn Jewish state.

Anwar el-Sadat, still intensely political, unhappily watched the handling of the Israeli situation by the Egyptian leader, King Farouk. But much of his time was spent trying to deal with his personal life. He divorced his first wife and, at the age of thirty, married a beautiful, highly independent fifteen-year-old, Jihan Raouf, who was half British.

Then, to help support the children of his first marriage, he went into business supplying drinking water to villages near Cairo. He tried working as a newspaper reporter. Finally, he won back his military commission and, as a captain in the Egyptian army, was stationed in the Sinai Desert.

By 1952 the Egyptian people had lost faith in King Farouk. Once, during a bloody riot in the streets of Cairo against British control of the Suez Canal, Farouk busied himself as host of a luxurious banquet in the royal palace.

Finally, on July 22, 1952, the Free Officers Committee—the revolutionary group that Sadat had helped to form—moved to oust King Farouk and seize power in Egypt. Gamal Abdel Nasser notified Sadat to return to Cairo for the event.

On the night of the planned attack, Sadat had taken his wife and children to the movies. However, he arrived at Nasser's headquarters in time to announce to the Egyptian people on radio that Farouk no longer was their king.

Sadat later recalled his pleasure when, some three days afterward, he watched Farouk sail into exile. "From the bridge of a destroyer," he said, "I watched Farouk pass into the twilight of history."

For several years after the victory, Nasser gave his good friend, Anwar, responsibilities of relatively minor importance. Sadat worked at public relations, served as editor of the semiofficial government newspaper, and represented Egypt on visits to several countries overseas, including the Soviet Union and the United States.

It is sometimes said that Nasser refused to entrust Sadat with major jobs because he considered Anwar too "inefficient." More probably, the Egyptian leader was following his shrewd personal policy of not allowing anyone else to gain too much power in his government.

Then, in the Six-Day War of 1967, Israel won a tremendous victory, seizing from Egypt the entire Sinai Peninsula and the Gaza Strip. Nasser, whose effort to crush the Israelis in 1956 also had been a failure, once again was humiliated.

Soon his physical health began to decline. Unable to trust other Egyptians around him, he turned to his old friend, Sadat. Sadat became his vice president.

In September 1970, Nasser suffered a fatal heart attack.

President Anwar el-Sadat with his wife and daughters in 1974. *Stern.*

Anwar el-Sadat became president of Egypt.

From the very beginning he pledged himself to the recovery of "every inch of Arab territory conquered by Israel." Many observers considered Sadat tougher than Nasser, less willing to use peaceful means to gain his ends. His public statements often were filled with threats of war. He placed missiles along the banks of the Suez Canal, facing the Israeli-occupied Sinai Peninsula.

Yet quietly, behind the scenes, he promised that if the captured lands were returned, he would recognize Israel's right to exist and would guarantee permanent peace in the region. The promise, as he put it to Israel, was that of "land in exchange for peace."

Meanwhile, Sadat worked hard to improve conditions within Egypt. He allowed greater freedom than Nasser ever had, even permitting newspapers to criticize his operation of the government. He allowed opposing political parties to organize. He encouraged the growth of the economy, especially of new industries.

Before long, Sadat had become highly popular with the Egyptian people.

Still, the matter of Israeli control of

the Sinai troubled him, in part because of the profitable oil fields there. The Egyptian economy still was in serious trouble. More important, though, was his belief that Egypt must continue to be the leading nation in the Arab world. The shattering defeat in the Six-Day War of 1967 had badly shaken the confidence of other Arabs in the power of Egypt. That confidence, he believed, had to be restored.

At 2:00 P.M. on October 6, 1973, Sadat launched a surprise attack on the Israeli positions along the Suez Canal. By pre-arrangement, Syria attacked Israel at the same time from the north. To the astonishment of most of the world, the Egyptian forces succeeded at first in overrunning the Israeli defenses and breaking into the Sinai Desert. The Egyptian people were overjoyed.

So was Sadat, although his pleasure was tempered by sadness, too. One of the first attacking planes to be shot down by Israeli defenders had been piloted by Sadat's younger brother Atif, whom he had brought up from childhood.

By October 10, the tide of battle had begun to turn. In a brilliant maneuver Israeli troops crossed the Suez Canal to the south of the original battlefield, as if driving toward Cairo itself. Then they suddenly turned back to surround

the Egyptian Third Army in a tight circle. In effect, the Egyptians were prisoners.

Complicated negotiations followed. Finally an agreement was reached. The fighting stopped. Both sides pulled back.

Egypt had not won the war, but in the eyes of most Egyptians Sadat was a hero. He had inflicted heavy casualties on the Israelis. For a time he had pushed back the Israeli armies.

Now, supported by most of the Egyptian people, Sadat began working for lasting peace in the region. With the help of United States Secretary of State Henry Kissinger, Egypt and Israel signed two agreements. The first moved their forces farther apart. The second led to the withdrawal of Israeli troops from the western part of the Sinai Peninsula, near Egypt. Israeli ships once again were given safe passage through the Suez Canal and the Red Sea.

Then a deadlock developed in the discussions. Neither side would give in. It appeared that a final peace treaty never could be achieved between the two neighboring countries.

It was at that point that Anwar el-Sadat proposed to do what no other Arab leader ever had been willing to do. He offered to meet directly with the Israelis to talk about peace. Even

Presidents Anwar el-Sadat and Jimmy Carter with Prime Minister Menachem Begin of Israel after the signing of the Egyptian-Israeli peace treaty on the White House lawn March 26, 1979. *UPI/Bettmann.*

more startling was his announcement that he himself was willing to go to Jerusalem for the talks.

Sadat's speech to the Israeli parliament, the Knesset, remains one of history's most dramatic moments. His personal talks with Golda Meir and with the new Israeli prime minister, Menachem Begin, opened the way to serious negotiations. Both sides still held firmly to their positions, but Sadat's courageous jour-

ney to Jerusalem had provided new hope for peace.

In September 1978, Sadat and Begin met for twelve days with President Jimmy Carter at Camp David, in Maryland. The talks were stormy. But, in the end, the Egyptian and Israeli leaders reached a historic agreement.

Israel agreed to withdraw in stages from the Sinai Peninsula. Egypt, in turn, agreed to total peace with the Jewish national state, including full diplomatic relations, open trade, and even tourism. Soon, the two nations signed a formal peace treaty.

To show just how important the peace agreement seemed to the rest of the world, in 1978 Begin and Sadat were jointly awarded the Nobel Prize for Peace, the most significant of all international honors.

Through the long and difficult negotiations Anwar el-Sadat had gained much for Egypt. The Sinai Peninsula had been returned to his nation. The United States had begun to provide billions of dollars in aid to rebuild the devastated Egyptian economy. Sadat now was able to attract foreign investment to his country. Money came in from the sale of oil from the Sinai fields. Foreign tourists once again visited Egypt's ancient historic sites, such as the pyramids.

At the same time, however, many Muslims refused to forgive Sadat for signing a peace treaty with the hated Israelis. Some Egyptians considered him too democratic, too Westernized. They disliked his friendship with the United States. They even criticized his wife, Jihan, for behaving like a liberated Western woman in her dress and her habits.

Sadat tried to crack down on his opponents, especially the Muslim religious fanatics who by then were openly threatening to kill him. In September 1981, he had more than sixteen hundred suspects arrested. For a time it appeared that he had won out. The vast majority of Egyptians appeared to support him. He appeared on television to assure the nation that opposition to him had ended.

Then, on October 6, 1981, he attended a parade honoring the Egyptian soldiers who, exactly eight years earlier, had fought in the Yom Kippur War with Israel. As president, he sat in a place of honor in the front row of the reviewing stand as the troops passed in front of him.

Suddenly, four Muslim fundamentalists, dressed as soldiers, rushed toward the reviewing stand, throwing hand grenades and shooting machine guns. When the shooting finally stopped, Anwar el-Sadat and several other officials had been killed.

Many world leaders attended Sadat's funeral, including three former presidents of the United States and Menachem Begin of Israel. Henry Kissinger spoke of Sadat as one of the greatest statesmen of the past century. The Japanese, the British, the Germans praised him greatly. Yet only three member nations of the Arab League even sent representatives to the funeral. In Cairo, daily business proceeded almost as if nothing had happened.

Meanwhile, in other Arab capitals, there was dancing in the streets as word came of Sadat's assassination. Guns were fired into the air. People cheered and shouted with joy. In Damascus, Syria, the official government radio station announced with enthusiasm that "at last, the traitor is dead!"

Anwar el-Sadat, the peasant boy from a small village in the Nile Delta, had grown to manhood and led his nation into battle.

For that, he was seen as a hero.

But when he dared to act on behalf of peace—peace in the Middle East as a step toward peace in the world—he was put to death.

The pyramids of ancient Egypt have survived in the lonely desert sands for thousands of years. Perhaps, some day in the future, they will be seen as symbols of the lasting peace among nations for which the courageous Anwar el-Sadat gave his life.

Ho Chi Minh

1890–1969   Vietnamese Communist leader in a victorious revolution against French rule as well as in an extended war against South Vietnam and the United States

"Ho, Ho, Ho Chi Minh!"

"Ho, Ho, Ho Chi Minh!"

"Ho, Ho, Ho Chi Minh!"

In 1969 and 1970, as American soldiers battled for victory in the jungles of Vietnam, students on college campuses across the United States held anti-war protest rallies. With fists raised in pride above their heads, they swayed together, chanting the name of America's enemy, the Vietnamese leader, Ho Chi Minh.

It was Ho Chi Minh who had convinced many Americans that they were fighting the wrong war. He had persuaded them that, in reality, they were not stopping the spread of Russian and Chinese communism in Asia. Instead, they were only putting down poor Vietnamese peasants, struggling for final freedom from Western colonial rule. Ho Chi Minh also showed many American blacks that he was fighting for the same thing they so desperately craved—a chance for equal justice.

Finally, it was Ho Chi Minh who first caused American policy makers to pause—to wonder whether, with all of the economic and military might at their command, they actually had the power, or the right, to shape events in underdeveloped nations around the world.

Who was this tiny, frail old man with the scraggly, wispy beard who had so influenced American life? How had Ho Chi Minh, born to poverty in an out-of-the-way country in Southeast Asia, risen from obscurity to a place among the world's leaders?

As a young man he had been forced

to leave high school without even graduating. Later he had been drawn into service as a cook, a busboy, a street sweeper, spoken to by his haughty Western masters only as "Ba." How could such a person emerge as a major figure of the twentieth century?

And what, in the end, can we learn about the dynamic, moving force of nationalism in our time by studying the life of this dedicated, sometimes mysterious Oriental patriot, known to his respectful, adoring people as Uncle Ho?

There is much about Ho's life that even today remains lost in shadows. It is uncertain whether he ever married or had children. He used anywhere between twelve and fifteen names for himself as he traveled around the world, with whole periods of time in his life unaccounted for. Even the date of his birth is uncertain.

What is certain is that he was born in the province of Nghe-An Ti in central Vietnam. His father had been the child of peasants who worked on a farm and tended buffaloes. Later, his father married the daughter of the farm owner and thus was able to spend time studying, later becoming a scholar.

Ho himself probably was born in the year 1890 as Nguyen That Thanh, the youngest of three children. In his boyhood he learned from his father to hate the French colonial masters who controlled the country. So bitter was the father toward French rule that, although well educated, he refused even to learn the French language. Ho's sister later was sent to prison for life after stealing weapons to fight against the French. His brother became a guerrilla fighter, totally dedicated to winning freedom from French domination.

By the age of nine, Ho had become a message carrier for the anti-French underground. Everywhere around him he saw the French, considering themselves superior to Orientals, seizing Vietnamese boys and young men, putting them to work in the fields, almost as if they were slaves.

After going to village schools and learning from his father, Ho was enrolled in the Lycée Quoc-Hoc, a famous high school in Hué, a city designated for a time by the French as the nation's capital. Among other young people to study there were Vo Nguyen Giap, who later would be the leader of Vietnam's anti-French army, and Pham Van Dong, destined to be Ho Chi Minh's assistant.

Before arriving at Hué, Ho briefly had attended a high school at Vinh but was expelled, according to some because of low grades, according to others because of his anti-French views. Nor did he graduate from Lycée Quoc-Hoc.

Leaving that school, he briefly became a teacher of young children in the fishing village of Phan Thiet.

In 1911, at the age of twenty-one, he traveled to Saigon, in the south of Vietnam, enrolling in a trade school. There he learned how to cook and to be a busboy, practical skills that would assure him a job with the country's French ruling class.

Instead, he decided to leave Vietnam altogether, signing on as a kitchen helper on a French steamer bound for Africa and for the city of Marseilles, in the south of France. For three years he sailed the seas, visiting such port cities as London, Boston, and New York. In his spare time on shipboard he read classic works of literature by Shakespeare, Tolstoy, and Zola, as well as the writings of the Communist theorist, Karl Marx.

With the outbreak of World War I, Ho went to live in London, working as a street sweeper. Because of his knowledge of French cooking, he eventually won a job as a kitchen helper at London's famous Carlton Hotel.

Then, in 1917, he moved to Paris, where he lived for six years. He first supported himself by working in a laundry, then as a gardener, a waiter, a cook, and a photo retoucher.

Sometime during those years he visited the United States, living in New York's black community, Harlem. He later wrote bitter attacks on racial prejudice against blacks in America, targeting especially the bloody deeds of the Ku Klux Klan in such states as Georgia and Mississippi.

During the Versailles Peace Conference of 1919, Ho rented a dark suit and a bowler hat and tried to arrange a meeting with the president of the United States, Woodrow Wilson. But Wilson refused to see him. What he had planned to discuss with the president was an eight-point program, guaranteeing equal rights for the Vietnamese people with their French rulers.

Gradually, Ho became convinced that the true path of freedom could be found only in a Communist revolution for Vietnam, just as the Russian Revolution had overthrown czarist rule and established the Soviet Union. As a result, Ho joined the Communist party.

Ho soon began to edit his own French language newspaper, *Le Paria* (The Outcast), demanding the end of colonialism around the world. At that time he took the name Nguyen Ai Quoc ("Nguyen the Patriot"). He came to know most of the revolutionary Communist leaders in France, speaking often to meetings of militants around the country. Word of his activities found its way back to Vietnam where, before long, he became a hero in the eyes of his countrymen, who longed desperately for independence.

Late in 1923 Ho Chi Minh traveled to Russia. Shortly after his arrival there, Vladimir Ilyich Lenin died. For Ho, the writings of Lenin had been crucial in shaping his view of the world. In honor of the great Communist leader, whom he had come to know personally, Ho wrote a moving tribute, published in the official party newspaper, *Pravda*.

In 1924, he played an important role in the meeting of the Communist International, championing the role of peasant farm workers from underdeveloped colonial areas in spreading communism. At that time, most radicals thought in terms of industrial workers rather than farm workers as being most important in the revolutions they were hoping to encourage.

During a two-year stay in Moscow, Ho Chi Minh met often with Joseph Stalin and Leon Trotsky, along with Lenin the two most important figures in the early development of Russian communism. He also attended classes and studied intensively at the University of Toilers of the East, learning techniques there for using propaganda and political agitation as tools of revolution.

In 1925, Ho was sent to Canton, China, supposedly to serve as a translator for Mikhail Borodin, a Soviet aide

to the Chinese leader, Chiang Kai-shek. Actually, Ho busied himself organizing Vietnamese refugees in China into a revolutionary youth organization. He also set up the League of Oppressed Peoples, whose purpose was to encourage revolution in the nations of Asia dominated by colonial powers.

In 1927, Chiang Kai-shek and his Kuomintang party turned against the Communists, trying to kill as many of them as possible. Ho Chi Minh managed to escape to Moscow, where he became responsible for organizing efforts against conservative governments in China, Japan, India, and all of Southeast Asia. In 1929, he formed the Indochinese Communist party, aimed especially at independence for Vietnam.

When the French authorities in Indochina (Vietnam, Cambodia, and Laos) found out what he was doing, they passed a death sentence on him, threatening to track him down and execute him. During one visit to Hong Kong, British officials arrested Ho as a Communist agitator and were about to turn him over to the French when friends won his release. They helped him to escape in disguise to Shanghai and, from there, once again to the Soviet Union.

During the 1930s, despite very real suffering from tuberculosis, Ho Chi

Minh continued to make his way from city to city in Southeast Asia and China, organizing for revolution. Sometimes he would disguise himself as a merchant, sometimes as a peasant or as a beggar, sometimes even as a Buddhist monk. He also found time to attend the Lenin School in Moscow, becoming a specialist in colonial matters. By that time he was fluent in Russian, as well as in French, English, German, and Japanese. He also spoke several Chinese dialects.

After Japan attacked China in 1937, Ho journeyed to Yenan, the headquarters of the Chinese Communist leader, Mao Tse-tung. Then, with Germany's defeat of France at the beginning of World War II, Ho returned to Vietnam in 1940. Working with his old friends Vo Nguyen Giap and Pham Van Dong, he organized the League for the Independence of Vietnam, destined to win lasting fame as the Viet Minh.

Under his leadership some ten thousand Vietnamese soldiers launched fierce guerrilla attacks against the Japanese in the jungles of Vietnam. It was at this time, too, that Ho took on the name he would use ever afterward—Ho Chi Minh (He Who Enlightens).

Encouraged by American generals, Ho traveled to China, hoping to unite with Chiang Kai-shek in fighting the Japanese. Chiang, however, still did not trust him, considering him more a Communist than a Vietnamese patriot. When Ho arrived in Kunming, Chiang had him arrested and thrown into prison. There he remained for eighteen months during 1942–1943, spending most of his time writing a deeply moving collection of poetry, later published as *Notebook from Prison*. When Ho agreed to support China against the French in Vietnam, Chiang finally released him.

Until 1945, the occupying Japanese forces permitted French officials to continue administering Vietnam. Then, with the war nearly over, they either imprisoned or executed the French and took complete control of the country.

In August 1945, the United States dropped atomic bombs on the cities of Hiroshima and Nagasaki, forcing Japan to surrender and bringing an end to World War II. With both the French and the Japanese removed from the scene, Ho Chi Minh and his comrades proclaimed the independence of Vietnam.

On September 2, 1945, speaking to an enormous crowd in the North Vietnamese city of Hanoi, Ho Chi Minh read a statement based largely on the American Declaration of Independence: "All men are born equal," it stated. "The Creator has given us inviolable rights to life, liberty and happiness . . . !"

Independence for Vietnam would not come that easily. Chiang Kai-shek's Chinese forces soon crossed the border and occupied North Vietnam. From France, Charles de Gaulle dispatched French troops, who quickly made their way northward from Saigon. Before long, France persuaded the Chinese to leave the country, and just as before World War II, French forces once again controlled Vietnam.

In June 1946 Ho Chi Minh went to Paris. During talks that lasted until September, he worked out an agreement with the French government. Vietnam, under Ho, was to be a free nation within the French Union with its own finances and its own army.

By the end of 1946 the agreement had broken down. Both sides were angry. Then, a French cruiser in the Vietnamese port city of Haiphong opened fire on the civilian population, killing as many as six thousand unarmed people.

Open warfare broke out between France and Vietnam.

For Ho Chi Minh it was not a war to spread communism in Asia. Rather, it was a struggle to expel at last the white colonial power that for so long had drawn large profits from the labors of the Vietnamese people. Often Ho went to the front lines to be with his soldiers. When French bombers appeared, he would take cover with the troops. When food ration supplies ran low, he gave up most of his own share, living on practically nothing.

Always the French were confident, certain. They won victory after victory. But, somehow, the Vietnamese fought on. After eight years of bloody fighting France still had not won, although their field commanders assured the French people at home that "there is light just at the end of the tunnel."

At last, with opposition to the war mounting in France, the French generals planned a trap that would draw out of the jungle the elusive Viet Minh guerrillas. At the fortress city of Dienbienphu, in a valley in North Vietnam, they gathered a large force of French troops. According to the plan, when the Vietnamese came to destroy the garrison, French airpower and artillery would devastate the guerrillas, and the war would be over.

Instead, Ho's close friend, General Giap, had Vietnamese peasants carry a supply of Chinese artillery, piece by piece, down the murky "Ho Chi Minh Trail" from the north. Assembling the cannons, the peasants pushed them to the peaks of the hills surrounding the Dienbienphu fortifications. The

Vietnamese, controlling the heights, steadily pounded away at the French troops, cutting them to ribbons.

In the spring of 1954, after fifty-six days of fighting, Dienbienphu surrendered. At the Geneva Conference a treaty was signed. France at last agreed to withdraw from Vietnam. But the Russians, French, and Chinese Communists persuaded Ho Chi Minh to settle only for control of North Vietnam. The country was partitioned—divided between north and south—at the Seventeenth Parallel, until elections, scheduled for 1956, could be held for the entire nation.

Rather than entering Hanoi, the new capital of North Vietnam, in a formal victory parade, Ho Chi Minh rode in with his soldiers, seated in the front seat of a captured French truck. It was not, he said, a victory for him, but for the people of Vietnam.

Again and again the promised national elections were postponed by the South Vietnamese. They remained fearful that Ho Chi Minh would win and unite the country under Communist rule. Soon, guerrilla supporters of Ho, known as the Viet Cong, were launching regular raids against the troops of the South Vietnamese leader, Ngo Dinh Diem.

Meanwhile, the United States feared a Communist victory. In 1961, President Dwight D. Eisenhower began to supply South Vietnam with sophisticated helicopters, tanks, and artillery, along with some eleven thousand American military advisers and many millions of dollars in economic aid.

When Diem's forces failed to put down the Viet Cong, the United States decided to take stronger action.

Beginning in 1964, American heavy bombers began to attack such North Vietnamese cities as Hanoi and Haiphong on a regular, systematic basis. A greater tonnage of bombs was dropped on Vietnam than on Germany and Japan combined in all of World War II.

Also in 1964, large numbers of well-armed American soldiers began to arrive, trying just like the French to search out and destroy the stealthy Vietnamese guerrillas. According to General Giap of North Vietnam, the Americans killed perhaps as many as a million of his troops. Beyond that, an even greater number of civilians were killed in American bombing raids.

Still, Ho Chi Minh would not surrender. As month followed month and year followed year, opposition to the war steadily began to grow in the United States. Again, as in the case of the French, the light of victory seemed "just at the end of the tunnel." But,

A 1957 photograph of Ho Chi Minh, president of the Democratic Republic of Vietnam. *UPI/Bettmann.*

somehow, that final victory never seemed to come.

Meanwhile, opposition to the war reached new heights on American college campuses. As more and more body bags returned to the United States filled with the remains of American servicemen, protests grew louder in the halls of Congress.

Then, suddenly, in February 1968, Ho Chi Minh launched what became known as the Tet Offensive, featuring massive attacks on such Vietnamese cities as Hué. North Vietnamese and Viet Cong troops suffered enormous losses at the hands of well-trained, well-equipped American troops. But coverage by American television crews vividly brought home to the viewing public the horrors endured by both sides in the war.

The demand for peace became too loud for President Lyndon B. Johnson to resist. In a surprising statement on national television, he announced that he would not run for reelection as president of the United States in 1968. He also announced that he was ending the bombing of North Vietnam.

His decision to stop the bombing signaled the beginning of peace talks in Paris between the Americans and the Vietnamese. Still, the fighting went on. President Richard Nixon pledged that the United States would never give up.

Ho Chi Minh, on the other hand, declared that although the Americans were much stronger than the French and the war might last another ten years, Vietnam, in the end, would win.

Sometimes American newspaper reporters visited with Ho. Close to eighty years old, he always wore a simple Mandarin-style cotton suit with no tie and, on his feet, rubber sandals, made from used tires. Small and frail, his beard more scraggly than ever, his cheeks sunken by old age and disease, he still spoke with deep feeling about the need for Vietnamese independence.

On September 3, 1969, Ho Chi Minh died.

But the war continued. Finally, after long negotiations in Paris, President Nixon began to withdraw American troops, declaring that South Vietnam at last was safe. Before long only a small force of Americans remained.

When fighting broke out again, the North Vietnamese easily conquered the South. In April 1975 the South Vietnamese capital city, Saigon, formally surrendered. Soon it was renamed "Ho Chi Minh City." Vietnam—North and South—at last was united as one nation, with the colonial powers completely gone.

Ho Chi Minh, the humble peasant boy, grown to the stature of world leader-

President Ho Chi Minh speaking at a banquet in honor of Premier Chou En-lai of China, 1956. *Eastfoto/Sovfoto.*

ship, had won. Intelligent, persistent, single-minded, he had put to shame the seemingly invincible French and the even mightier Americans. Meanwhile, he had balanced off the two competing Communist giants, the Soviet Union and China.

Rejecting glory for himself, Ho had won victory for his people and for his nation, Vietnam.

The cost of that victory, however, had been enormous, both in lives lost and in destruction to the country. Nearly two decades after the war, Vietnam still found itself one of the poorest of the world's nations. Boatloads of desperate Vietnamese civilians often risked their lives in hopes of somehow reaching such neighboring locations as Hong Kong.

In the 1990s, the Vietnamese leaders realized that they no longer could expect help from their ally, the greatly weakened Soviet Union. Instead, they hesitatingly began to reach out for friendship with their former enemy, the United States of America.

For the two nations the process of healing wounds from their painful conflict has been slow. Yet, like two boxers in the ring at the conclusion of a bitter fight, the day may come when the American and the Vietnamese people look with favor upon each other. And then, perhaps, they will reach out, touch hands—and smile.

Ayatollah Ruhollah Khomeini

1900?–1989   Fanatical Muslim religious figure who first led a
successful revolutionary movement in Iran and then headed the Iranian
government

It was sometime in the late 1950s that a middle-aged scholar, Ruhollah Khomeini, was honored with the title of *ayatollah*, a word that in Arabic means "mirror image of God." For most of his lifetime, the Ayatollah Khomeini was a man of religious faith. He was also destined to become a political leader of Muslims in the land of Persia, the country known for much of our present century as Iran.

Living in an old one-story house in the Iranian holy city of Qom, Khomeini wore a black turban on his head, a symbol to show that he was a descendant of the prophet Muhammad. He ate only cheese, toast, fruit, rice, and yogurt. Every day he spent many hours alone in prayer and meditation.

Yet, for ten years, the Ayatollah Ru-hollah Khomeini ruled Iran with an iron fist. His every word could mean life or death for citizens of that land or for other people—including Americans—who came under his unchallenged power.

At his command thousands of Iranians were executed. He fought a bloody war with neighboring Iraq in which young children and teenagers sometimes made suicide attacks on the enemy lines. Sometimes, too, such young people were sent running barefooted into minefields to blow up the explosives, clearing the way for advancing Iranian soldiers.

Meanwhile, in Khomeini's own nation the ayatollahs would not allow men and women—or boys and girls—to swim together. Nor could boys and girls

273

go to school together. In the name of religion those people caught drinking alcoholic beverages sometimes were executed. Couples showing affection in public—even just holding hands—were severely beaten. No music could be broadcast on Iranian radio or television because, said the Ayatollah Khomeini, music dulls the mind of those who hear it and makes them silly and lazy.

During the years of his rule, Khomeini poured words of abuse onto the United States, a superpower, and managed to humiliate two American presidents, Jimmy Carter and Ronald Reagan. He used acts of terror against his enemies in other countries. Iran, a huge exporter of oil, became isolated from much of the world, including the other superpower of the 1980s, the Soviet Union.

Claiming to be the great champion of the Islamic religion, Khomeini earned the hatred of most other leaders in the Muslim Middle East. Those leaders—if not their people—united in opposition to the Islamic Republic of Iran, which Khomeini himself had founded.

And what of the Iranian people themselves? Ten years—an entire decade—under such a ruler! Yet, when he died, despite all the suffering he had brought to his nation, his funeral was a scene of passionate sorrow and of grief. In the streets of Teheran, the Iranian people wept openly. Wailing aloud, they stretched their arms toward the heavens. They fought each other for the honor of touching his corpse, an object they were certain was sacred, holy. The memory of his reign, they were certain, would last forever.

Who really was this man Khomeini? What did he stand for that made him one of the most loved—and most hated—figures of modern times? What can we learn from his remarkable life about the world's people—and what it is they may be searching for in their leaders?

The child who one day would lead his nation "in the name of God" probably was born in the small town of Khomein on May 27, 1900. But the date, even the year, is uncertain. His parents, Hajar and Mustafa—last names seldom were used in those days—chose to call him Ruhollah, or "soul of God." He was the last of their six children.

Although not wealthy, Ruhollah's father and his grandfather both were mullahs (religious leaders). For that reason they were held in much respect in the community. When Ruhollah was only five months old, his father was murdered for reasons that even now remain unclear. Eventually, the killer was brought to trial, convicted, and executed, mostly because of testimony given in court by Ruhollah's mother,

Ayatollah Khomeini in exile in France in 1978. *UPI/Bettmann.*

something unusual for a woman to do in the ancient land then known as Persia.

It was his mother who brought him up, she along with an iron-willed sister of his murdered father. The two women first taught him to be unbending, rigid, in defending the sacred Muslim religion against competing faiths.

Like the other boys in Ruhollah's town of Khomein who were to receive an education, he was sent to a religious school. Each day he would read aloud a portion of the Muslim holy book, the Koran. By the age of seven he had completed it, for what would be the first of many readings during his long lifetime. Bright and quick-witted, he was an excellent student. He also enjoyed playing soccer.

When he was fifteen, both Ruhollah's mother and his aunt died. But he still continued in school, with the family now directed by his oldest brother.

By the age of nineteen it was clear that he would be a religious scholar. With such a purpose in mind, he arranged to study with the Ayatollah Abdul Karim Haeri, one of the country's leading students of the Koran. Soon he became Haeri's prize pupil.

In 1922 Haeri moved to the city of Qom. There he began to organize a national center for Islamic studies. Ruhollah, too, wanted to live in Qom, and it was in that city he would remain, as student and as teacher, for most of his career.

As the years went by, Ruhollah's life slowly began to take shape. He took on the surname "Khomeini," from the city of his birth. He studied logic and law, as well as Islamic philosophy. He learned to live simply, eating little and furnishing his quarters with only a few Persian rugs on which he both ate and slept. He wrote poetry about nature and about his religious faith. At the age of twenty-seven he went on a pilgrimage to the holy city of Mecca in Saudi Arabia, the journey expected of all devout Muslims.

When Khomeini was twenty-eight, he was married, by arrangement, to the daughter of an ayatollah from the city of Tehran. According to some accounts she was only thirteen years old at the time. Khomeini's first son died. His second son, named Ahmed, would one day become his chief political assistant. He also had three daughters who lived to adulthood and as many as fourteen grandchildren.

Gradually, Ruhollah Khomeini's reputation as a religious scholar began to grow. He wrote book after book, eventually producing twenty-one. In his writing and in his teaching he was greatly influenced by the ancient Greek philosophers, particularly Aristotle and Plato. From his reading of Plato's *Republic* he began to think seriously about the ideal state—the perfect government—one ruled, as Plato believed, by a philosopher king. But, to Khomeini, the philosopher had to be first of all a man of religion, a person finding his vision of life—his sense of purpose—in God.

Religion, he came to believe, was not just a matter of ceremonies. It was to be a way of life, lived day by day. The religious person must fight passionately against evil wherever it existed, even in the government of his own country. Nothing could be more holy, said Khomeini, than to give up one's life fighting against tyranny and injustice. And, given the chance, men of religion had a duty to enter politics in order to create a more perfect society.

As he grew older, Ruhollah Khomeini

worked ever harder at disciplining himself to serve the Islamic religion. His life became regimented, orderly. Three times a day he walked rigorously for exactly the same length of time, twenty minutes. Every day he ate his meals at exactly the same time. Every evening he went to bed at exactly the same time. Every morning he arose at exactly the same time. He never missed the proper moments for saying his prayers. He fasted even when nobody else was fasting.

Gradually, Khomeini became a person of indomitable strength and willpower. His eyes carried a fierce and piercing gaze. Tall and thin, clothed always in formal robes, he soon became a famous scholar and a man whom, already, many had grown to fear.

During the years of Khomeini's youth and his development as a religious leader, great changes had begun to take place in the land of Persia. Most importantly, a new line of rulers took power, the Pahlavi dynasty. From the beginning, the Pahlavi shahs (kings) set out to transform Persia—to modernize it and to break down the ancient social and religious customs that they believed were holding the country back.

The religion of Islam proved a special target for Reza Shah, the first Pahlavi monarch. He had mosques torn down.

He transformed religious schools into government-run schools with no religious teaching allowed. Like Kemal Atatürk in Turkey, he had women remove their veils and urged people to dress in Western style, like the British, French, and American tourists he encouraged to visit.

The shah also refused to support religious leaders with public tax money, thereby taking income away from such men as Khomeini. The old Arab calendar, based on the moon, was replaced by a calendar based on the sun, like that of the Western nations.

As in Western countries, too, people were expected to choose family names. Ruhollah was registered by the government as Ruhollah Mustafavi, taken from his father's name, Mustafa.

Finally, the very name of the country was changed. No longer was it to be known as Persia, but "Iran," to call attention to the ancient "Aryan" race from which most of the nation's people were descended, in contrast to the neighboring Arabic states.

To Ruhollah (Mustafavi) Khomeini, the dramatic changes pushed through by the shah were a betrayal of everything he stood for—everything to which he had devoted his life. At first, Khomeini said little. Then, in 1941, he published a book, *Unveiling the Mysteries*.

In that book, he declared that the

shah's government was without value. All of the new laws that had been passed, he said, should be burned. The only true government, stated Khomeini, must be based on Islam. It must take a form decided by the religious leaders. And religious leaders must supervise all of the government's activities. They should be the real power behind the throne.

Because the shah believed the Aryan race was superior to all other races, he strongly supported Adolf Hitler's Nazis, who claimed to be pure Aryans. Great Britain, then at war with Nazi Germany, toppled the shah from power and replaced him with his son, Mohammed Reza Shah.

Once, in 1953, Mohammed Reza Shah visited the Muslim holy city of Qom. When he appeared before the religious leaders there, all but one of them rose to greet him. That one cleric was Ruhollah Khomeini.

All across Iran, Khomeini's name was becoming well known. Young Muslims, in particular, came to admire his courage, his defiance. Like him, they believed that Islam should be not only a religion but a way of life.

Before the 1950s ended, Khomeini had been honored with the title ayatollah, shared with fewer than a thousand other Muslim leaders of Iran. In 1962 he was named "grand ayatollah," a title held by only six other clerics.

It was also in 1962 that Khomeini led a general strike to protest the shah's order that witnesses in courts of law no longer were to swear an oath upon the Koran, the Muslim holy book.

Tension rose even higher in 1963 when the shah, with the encouragement of the United States, announced his "White Revolution." According to the shah, the time already was overdue for Iran to modernize itself, to leap into the twentieth century alongside the Western nations. Now, women were to have equal rights. Lands owned by the clergy were to be seized. Iran would cast its lot with the West.

The Ayatollah Khomeini proceeded to launch a fierce attack on the White Revolution. On the campus of Teheran University students joined in support of Khomeini. They held marches. They distributed pamphlets. When the Ayatollah was thrown into prison for demanding that the army remove the shah, rioting broke out in the streets.

For several months Khomeini remained in jail. Then he was released but required to remain in his house. Still, his verbal attacks against the shah continued. In 1964 he spoke strongly against a new agreement with the United States, one that exempted American soldiers stationed in Iran from trial by Iranian courts.

The Iranian government responded by expelling Khomeini from the country. He fled first to Turkey, then to a Muslim holy site in Iraq. Even from his place of exile he attacked the shah, sending tape-recorded sermons to be played in Iranian mosques.

As the years passed, Iran became prosperous, mostly because of the sale of oil to Western countries. But the prosperity did not filter down to the great mass of Iranians—almost never to the poor. If anything, they were even poorer than before.

Increasingly, those who hated the shah turned to the clergy for support, and especially to the exiled Ayatollah Khomeini.

In 1978, when Iraq expelled Khomeini at the shah's urging, he took up residence in France, on the outskirts of Paris. From there, he stayed in close touch with his Iranian followers. At his command there were work stoppages, enormous public rallies, days of silent prayer. None of the shah's many efforts succeeded in stopping Khomeini.

Meanwhile, the economic situation inside Iran grew more serious. Because oil workers stayed away from their jobs, the economy ground slowly to a halt. The country soon was in desperate straits.

In January 1979 the shah left the country for a trip to Egypt, saying it was only a vacation. But the Iranian people knew that he would never return.

Millions of people jammed the streets of Teheran and other Iranian cities, calling for the Ayatollah Khomeini to return from France, loudly demanding that he take over the reins of power.

On February 1, 1979, to thunderous applause, Khomeini entered Teheran. Never again, he promised, would he allow the United States to force the rule of the shah upon them.

Soon Khomeini proclaimed an Islamic republic in Iran. Now at last, he said, the nation had a "government of God."

Within days, the executions began. Supporters of the shah were killed. So were those who offended traditional Muslim values, such as homosexuals, prostitutes, and adulterers, as well as users of drugs and alcohol. Newspapers that dared even to question "the *Imam*" (Khomeini) were shut down. Many Iranians convicted of criticizing their new leader discovered that the price of that act was death.

Within a few months, thousands of people had been shot, hanged, or stoned to death.

Khomeini attempted almost at once to export his revolution. His agents tried to stir up trouble in Egypt, Saudi Arabia, Kuwait, Bahrain—all across the Arab world. The Ayatollah's picture began to appear on the walls of shops in cities of the Soviet Union with large Muslim populations, such as Baku, and

Khomeini greets frenzied followers in Tehran, Iran, in 1979. *Setboun/Sipa Press*.

even in Jerusalem, the capital of the Jewish nation, Israel.

In November 1979, after President Jimmy Carter allowed the shah of Iran to enter the United States for medical treatment, Iranians exploded in rage. Many of them climbed the walls of the United States Embassy in Teheran. Once inside, they made hostages of American diplomats and soldiers.

For 444 days, until the day that Jimmy Carter left office and Ronald Reagan was inaugurated as president of the United States, the Americans were held captive, often blindfolded and publicly insulted by the Iranians. Again and again the Ayatollah spoke of his hatred for the United States— the enemy of the Islamic world.

Despite that hatred, President Reagan secretly sent diplomats to Iran. Their mission was to offer military supplies in exchange for the freedom of Americans then held hostage by the Ayatollah's supporters in such Middle Eastern countries as Lebanon. Eventually, an arrangement was worked out.

When word of the "arms for hostages" deal at last became public, President Reagan—who often had spoken with passion against Khomeini's cruelty— was deeply embarrassed.

Some of the arms supplied by the United States were used by Iran in its eight-year-long war with neighboring

Iraq. Although Iran had far more soldiers, Iraq, led by Saddam Hussein, had a powerful air force and guided missiles. Nor did Saddam Hussein hesitate to use such inhuman weapons as poison gas against his Muslim brother, Khomeini. Finally, in 1988, both sides, by then exhausted by the terrible and costly years of bloodletting, agreed to a truce.

The Ayatollah Khomeini had long been in ill health. When first he took power in 1979, he had promised the Iranian people that "the remaining one or two years of my life I will devote to you to keep this movement alive." Ten years later he still had not won victory for his movement—the struggle to make belief in Allah (God) a way of life for the world.

What he had done, however, was to transform his country. Where, before, Iran had been a busy crossroads of trade between East and West, it had become isolated.

By the time of his death, on June 3, 1989, the once prosperous land was a place of poverty and devastation.

Veterans of his ferocious war with Iraq, many of them blind and crippled, begged for bread on the streets of Teheran.

Yet many of Khomeini's followers still revered him—still loved him. They continued to believe firmly, like the Ayatollah himself, that Islam must be not just a faith—a religion—but must be a "way of life" for all the world.

To such people, governments are merely tools to achieve a much broader, more universal goal—the goal that someday everyone on the planet would finally join them in becoming "true believers."

Mikhail Gorbachev

1931–   Leader in the restructuring of the Soviet Union at home and also in ending the Cold War with the United States

"Arise ye prisoners of starvation! Arise ye wretched of the earth!"

The words of the "Communist Internationale" have been sung by millions of people around the world during the twentieth century. For the hungry, the poor, the distressed—not only in the Soviet Union, but also in Eastern Europe, China, Cuba, and a host of Third World countries—that anthem has held out the hope of a better life, a life filled with happiness instead of misery.

The Communist dream of a world based on equality, a world in which the rich no longer oppress the poor, has not come to pass. Instead, Communist governments, which were supposed to be the tools for shaping an ideal future, too often turned the dream into a nightmare.

They frightened, jailed, tortured, and killed those citizens who refused to show loyalty—total loyalty—by obeying orders without question. In that sense they were little different from Adolf Hitler's fanatical Nazi followers, demanding the same kind of obedience the Nazis demanded of the German people.

For a time, in the years following World War II, it appeared that ambitious, well-disciplined Communist leaders might actually succeed in their hope of organizing the political affairs of the entire planet Earth. Wearing the costume of liberators, it seemed they might actually become the world's masters.

Instead, during the 1980s the tide began to turn. In Eastern Europe, one after another of the Communist nations threw off the yoke of the powerful Soviet Union. Poland, Hungary, Czechoslovakia, Rumania, Bulgaria, and East Germany declared independence from Soviet control. In Africa, Asia, and Latin America such nations as Angola and Nicaragua no longer chose to model themselves on the Marxist governments first structured by Lenin and Stalin of Russia.

Remarkably, the Soviet Union itself did virtually nothing to halt the crumbling of its world empire built up at such great cost over so many years. Instead, to the wonder of most, the leading figure in the Communist empire openly applauded what he called *perestroika*, or the restructuring of the international community. In time, that leader predicted, the entire world would become a place of peace, governed by "reason and logic" in place of war. "Neighborly relations, openness, and mutual trust," he said, "would replace brutal instincts" and aggressiveness until, finally, there would be "universal security" for all the "peoples and governments of our planet."

The man who uttered those words was Mikhail Gorbachev, the president of the USSR, as he accepted the Nobel Prize for Peace in December 1990.

During Gorbachev's childhood and youth, Joseph Stalin, the leader of the USSR, may have killed as many as twenty million Soviet citizens. Even Stalin's closest aides lived in fear of him. Yet, under Gorbachev, crowds of citizens in cities such as Moscow, Leningrad, and Minsk felt it safe to gather in massive public demonstrations. They dared to complain to Gorbachev that he should allow them still greater freedoms and provide them with economic prosperity—things that, partly because of him, they had come to expect.

How had life in the Soviet Union changed so swiftly? Why had Gorbachev done virtually nothing to prevent the breakup of the Soviet overseas empire? And, finally, who was this man, Mikhail Gorbachev, and how had he come to play so critical a role in matters affecting the entire world?

Mikhail Sergeyevich Gorbachev was born on March 2, 1931, in the Caucasus area of the Soviet Union, a region not far removed from Georgia, where Joseph Stalin had spent his youth. The Gorbachevs were a family of peanut farmers, and in his childhood Mikhail worked in grain fields on the collective farms near his home.

Gorbachev was still in grade school when Hitler's German army launched its surprise attack on Russia in June 1941. It was not until the autumn of 1943 that Mikhail was able to return

Mikhail Gorbachev talking with crowds in the city of Minsk in 1991. *Novosti from Sovfoto.*

to his education. Even then, with the men still in combat, he and the other children sometimes were asked to work all summer in the fields, often for eleven and twelve hours a day. A new school year did not begin until the harvest was complete.

From the earliest possible time, young Mikhail played an active role in the Komsomol (the Communist Youth League), a group whose task was to educate young people in the "spirit of communism." At the age of eighteen he was one of the very few in his village

to be awarded the Red Banner of Labor for his contribution to a successful harvest. In the same year, he applied for membership in the Communist party and also for admission to Moscow State University—the most distinguished college in the Soviet Union.

Those who knew Mikhail in his boyhood and youth remember him as outgoing and friendly but also exceptionally hard working, ambitious—eager to succeed. A high school girlfriend recalled how once he became so angry that he corrected a history teacher in front of the entire class. When he believed he was right, she said, he would argue stubbornly with anyone.

Stubbornness, persistence, intelligence: those were his outstanding traits. For a time, Mikhail considered a career as a professional actor. He also enjoyed mathematics and physics, as well as history and literature. But he finally chose law school and, in 1950, became a student at Moscow State University.

Once in Moscow, Gorbachev expanded his activities for Komsomol, becoming the group's leader for his class. All Soviet young people were considered members of Komsomol, but as *komsorg* (leader) Mikhail was responsible for publicizing and supporting the policies of the Kremlin leadership itself, at that time a government still headed by the vicious tyrant, Joseph Stalin. *Komsorgs* also were expected to keep watch over the political ideas of their classmates and report any hints of disagreement with official Communist party belief.

In 1952 Gorbachev was chosen as *komsorg* for the entire law school. He also was formally admitted to membership in the Communist party. One of the duties of *komsorgs* at the time was to spread Stalin's vicious statements against Jews and even to organize campus meetings to criticize Jewish professors and writers.

Some of Gorbachev's friends said later that although he then went along with official Stalinist policies, he already was beginning to work toward a broader purpose in life: to win power in order to bring about democratic change in Soviet society. Meanwhile, however, he did whatever was necessary to advance within the Communist party.

As a student, Mikhail, a farm boy, at first lagged behind his better prepared classmates from the city. But in his second year at the university, his grades earned him the Kalinin Prize, next to the highest position in his class. He worked to discipline his mind, consciously reading and absorbing all of the required materials. He also tried to bring order and discipline to his daily life, even winning an award for neatness in his dormitory room.

Always, however, young Gorbachev went beyond the expected concerns of a college student. In addition to works by Marx and Lenin, for example, he read such diverse political and religious philosophers as John Stuart Mill, Thomas Aquinas, Thomas Hobbes, and Jean Jacques Rousseau—men whose ideas often disagreed with those of the ruling Communist party.

While in college, Mikhail also met his future wife, Raisa Titorenko. The two studied together. They went to the theater together. Raisa translated books written in English for the ambitious "Misha," as she called him. Finally, during their last year at the university, the couple was married.

In June 1955 they both graduated from college and returned to Stavrapol, Mikhail's native province in the Caucasus, where he began working for the party as a Komsomol youth organizer. Soon they had a daughter, Irina, their only child. The self-confident Raisa began working on a doctoral degree in psychology, which she completed in 1967. At the same time, Mikhail also took a second degree, this one in agricultural planning.

Mikhail came to rely on Raisa's advice and her ability to make a favorable impression on crowds, especially later, in their overseas travels. Always confident of himself, Gorbachev made no secret of the fact that his wife was one-quarter Jewish.

For twenty-three years Mikhail Gorbachev served as a Communist party official in Stavrapol. During that time he continued to believe in some form of socialism as the best way to help the great mass of humankind. But, with the lesson of Stalin's tyranny in mind, he grew more and more fearful of what evil leaders could do, when once in power, to destroy the benefits of social-

ism. He saw every day how Russia's Communist party officials looked out for their own self-interest, their own personal privileges.

To Gorbachev, it became clear that the high ideals—the dream—of a Socialist state could become a reality in his nation only if the system were changed to become more democratic. That would not be easy. But always a practical man, one who used politics as a means to achieve broader ends, "Misha" was certain that he could, indeed, reform the system. First, however, what he needed to achieve that goal was power.

Bright, inquisitive, friendly, known as a loyal worker for the Communist party, Gorbachev rose step by step within the party ranks. Advancing quickly as an official of Komsomol, he moved to increasingly responsible positions in agricultural planning. Soon he became party chief for his district. In that role he allowed farmers to own more land of their own, pointing out that crop production was much higher when profits went to those who actually did the work. He also allowed workers on collective farms to become more involved in planning.

Before long, Gorbachev's work and his outgoing personality won him favor with important local and national figures in the Communist party. They became his mentors, teaching him about politics, helping him to move ahead. He gained the attention of Mikhail Suslov, who eventually rose to high office in the government of Premier Leonid Brezhnev—head of state in the Soviet Union for many years. Fyodor Kulakov, in charge of agriculture for the entire nation, took a special liking to him. But perhaps his strongest supporter became Yuri Andropov, chairman of the KGB, the powerful Soviet secret police.

By 1971, while still specializing in youth education and agriculture, Gorbachev had worked his way to a position on the vitally important Central Committee of the Soviet Union. Then, in 1978, his friend Kulakov died. Gorbachev was chosen to replace him as the agriculture expert reporting directly to the Central Committee of the Communist party.

In his new position Gorbachev tried to give more authority for decision making to local farming officials instead of having all the decisions made in Moscow. He also tried to give higher rewards—more money—to individual farmers who produced more food.

Harvests still remained far too low. Yet, despite that failure, Suslov and Andropov helped Misha in 1980 to become a member of the Politburo, the small inner circle most responsible for policy-making in the Soviet Union. Not yet fifty years old at the time, he was the Politburo's youngest member.

In 1982 the elderly Brezhnev became seriously ill and then died. Yuri Andropov, Gorbachev's friend and supporter, replaced Brezhnev as general secretary of the Communist party, then the nation's most powerful position.

To bring about much-needed changes in the Soviet system, Andropov increasingly counted on young Mikhail. He encouraged his vigorous young aide to replace some of the Communist party officials in Moscow who had come to look out more for themselves than for the people. With Andropov's approval, Gorbachev also arranged to give greater authority for planning to regional and local managers of industries. That move, the two leaders hoped, would make industries more efficient.

But Andropov, too, was an older man, in poor health. Probably he was planning to have Gorbachev succeed him as general secretary of the party. Before he could make that choice certain, however, he died.

Once again, party leaders turned for leadership to a member of their tight inner circle of friends, a man who had served with them for many years in the government. Their choice was Konstantin Chernenko.

Although disappointed, Gorbachev

gave his complete support to Chernenko. His loyalty paid off. Before long the elderly leader put the energetic, efficient Gorbachev in charge of major responsibilities of government, including economics, party organization, and ideology (political ideas). Eventually, Mikhail even became involved in the field of foreign affairs.

In March 1985 Chernenko died. This time there was no question of who would inherit the leading position in the Soviet Union. A few hours after the public announcement of Chernenko's death, Mikhail Sergeyevich Gorbachev became general secretary of the Communist party.

Now it was he who held supreme power in a nation covering one-sixth of all the world's territory, stretching across eleven of the world's twenty-four time zones. It was a nation that had in its possession an enormous stockpile of nuclear weapons. Its armies commanded virtually every government in Eastern Europe, as well as client states in Africa, Asia, and Latin America.

At the same time, the Soviet Union also was a nation in deep trouble. Supplies of coal and iron, once great, were dwindling rapidly. Because of that, industrial machinery had to be bought from other countries. The production of Soviet industry had slowed down. So had its agricultural output.

Meanwhile, the United States and its allies in the North Atlantic Treaty Organization (NATO) were pouring billions of dollars into modern weapons— expensive new guided missiles, new bombing planes, new ships—all of them using advanced scientific equipment. With every passing day, the Soviet Union was falling farther behind.

Gorbachev understood that unless he took action—truly drastic action—the USSR could not hope to hold its position alongside the United States as one of the world's two leading powers.

First, Gorbachev moved to change things at home, opening the Soviet Union up to contact with the outside world after many years of isolation. He allowed citizens to read books that had been banned. He allowed criticism of Communist party officials to appear in Soviet newspapers. He even allowed Soviet television coverage of life in the wealthy United States.

To describe the new "openness" in Soviet life, Gorbachev used the Russian word *glasnost.*

Along with *glasnost,* Gorbachev also moved quickly to change the Soviet economy and Soviet politics. He called those changes *perestroika.* First, he introduced to the agricultural system of the USSR the idea of privately owned farms, run for a profit. In industries, he encouraged the idea of paying more

President Gorbachev with British Prime Minister Margaret Thatcher. *Rex/Sipa.*

to those workers who produced more.

Meanwhile, he set free from prison such well-known critics of the Soviet government as Anatoly Scharansky and Andrei Sakharov. Thousands of other political prisoners still suffered in Soviet jails, but at least Gorbachev had shown his willingness to risk personal freedom for a few.

Before long, Gorbachev's ideas caught on in the Soviet satellite empire. They were greeted with special relief in those countries of Eastern Europe threatened before by almost certain So-

viet invasion for daring to disobey. In 1989, freedom movements swept like wildfire through the satellite states— Poland, Hungary, Czechoslovakia, Rumania, Bulgaria, East Germany.

Then, in the autumn of 1989, one of the greatest symbols of previous Soviet tyranny—the Berlin Wall—came tumbling down. At a rate of more than two thousand people per day, East Germans poured into West Germany, to freedom.

Gorbachev made no attempt to send in troops. He stood by and even sent his congratulations as non-Communist governments began to appear in countries that for more than forty years had lived in fear behind the "Iron Curtain." Meanwhile, Soviet troops were withdrawn from Afghanistan, where they had suffered bloody casualties over many years in supporting that country's pro-Communist government.

Within the Soviet Union itself, citizens demanded—and were given— greater freedom. That was so even in the Soviet Baltic republics, Latvia, Estonia, and Lithuania—eager for independence since first they had been taken over by Stalin at the beginning of World War II. Other parts of the USSR, long uneasy with Russian domination, also spoke up, especially Georgia, Armenia, and Azerbaijan.

By late 1990 it had become clear that the economic problems of the Soviet Union truly were severe. Even with a master politician like Gorbachev at the helm, those troubles would not simply disappear. Indeed, they were getting worse.

At the same time, Gorbachev himself had opened the way to even more revolutionary forces among the Soviet people. It was he who had first encouraged workers to demand more for themselves. The result was strikes of coal miners, bus drivers, farmers, dock

workers. It was Gorbachev who had opened the way for newspapers and magazines, finally freed from censorship, to criticize him. It was Gorbachev himself whose talk of *glasnost* had initially encouraged the various Soviet republics to think of freedom until, at last, they began to demand independence.

By the spring of 1991 Mikhail Gorbachev was faced with huge public demonstrations against his continued rule. Even in Moscow and Leningrad there were shortages of such products as tobacco, meat, and bread. Crowds cried out against continued Communist control. In one crowd a man was observed holding a large sign declaring, "Women! Don't give birth to Communists!"

What was to be done?

On the one hand, the army, the KGB, and such hard-line critics as Yegor Ligachev pressed Gorbachev to return to the strong, highly centralized control of previous Communist governments, beginning with Stalin.

On the other hand, Boris Yeltsin, the president of the Russian Federation, demanded that Gorbachev move rapidly toward a completely free economy. And if he refused to do so, said Yeltsin, he should resign at once as leader of the Soviet Union.

Gorbachev worked hard at balancing

off the two positions—those Soviets demanding that he become tougher in his handling of affairs; the other side urging him to grant still greater freedom and move toward a more capitalistic economy.

It was then that Gorbachev's own foreign minister, Eduard Shevardnadze, resigned from office, warning his close friend Mikhail of the danger of dictatorship if he gave in too much to the army and to the KGB.

Gorbachev decided that Shevardnadze was right. He began to fight back against the hard-liners. Speaking to a meeting of the Communist party's powerful Central Committee, he lashed out at those who wanted to reverse the many reforms he had made in Soviet life. Some people, said Gorbachev, were asking him to resign. But, if he did, there would be violence in the streets. Law and order would break down. There would be no authority, leading to a situation that political scientists describe as a "power vacuum."

To fill that vacuum, warned Gorbachev, there would not be democratic institutions. Instead, there would be a new dictatorship, controlling the people with armed force.

Suddenly, on August 18, 1991, a small group of hard-line Communist leaders seized power, taking over the Soviet government. While Gorbachev was on vacation in the Crimea they placed him under house arrest, announcing that he had been removed from office for "health reasons."

To be sure that the takeover, or coup, would succeed, the Soviet vice president and other formerly loyal aides to Gorbachev rushed troops and tanks into Moscow and the Baltic republics. They rigidly censored the press, radio, and television. They announced that public demonstrations against the new government would not be allowed. It was the hope—the firm belief—of the coup leaders that the Soviet people would not dare do anything to stop them.

They were mistaken. In Moscow, great crowds of demonstrators poured into the streets. Unarmed civilians surrounded the tanks. Boris Yeltsin, the Russian president, climbed onto one tank and defiantly addressed the wildly cheering crowd. Instead of trying to stop him, many of the soldiers and tank crews joined the demonstrators.

During the next three days, public rallies in Moscow, Leningrad, and other cities grew even larger, even more angry. Finally, the leaders of the coup fled from Moscow, realizing they could not possibly control the nation. On August 22 Mikhail Gorbachev triumphantly returned to the capital, once again taking over his duties as president of the Soviet Union.

It was too late, however, to turn back the course of history. In the months that followed, the once powerful Communist party found itself deprived of its leadership role. Gorbachev himself resigned his position as head of the party, while staying on as leader of the nation. With that act Gorbachev ended seventy-four years of rule by the Communist party.

Meanwhile, one after another of the Soviet Union's fifteen member republics declared their independence. Leading the way in August was Ukraine, next to Russia the most powerful and populous of the states. In December 1991 the Ukrainian people voted overwhelmingly to support the decision of their parliament and to form their own nation.

As the republics broke from the mother country, President Gorbachev's power swiftly faded away.

Finally, on December 25, 1991, Gorbachev addressed his nation—and the world—on television. Declaring that he disagreed with the idea of a badly divided nation, he announced that he was resigning his office.

According to Gorbachev, much had happened since he first became his nation's leader in 1985. During those years, the people of the Soviet Union had ceased to be moral and political serfs. Under his direction the nation had eliminated the totalitarian system that had prevented citizens from flourishing. Yet, as he put it, the old system had collapsed before it was possible to put a new one into place.

Shortly after the conclusion of his speech, the flag of the Union of Soviet Socialist Republics—bearing the hammer and sickle of communism—was lowered from the flagpole atop the Kremlin in Moscow. The Communist regime no longer was in command. The Soviet Union no longer existed.

In place of the USSR there now was a loose union of the former Soviet republics, known as the Commonwealth of Independent States, the CIS. President Boris Yeltsin of the Russian republic took command of the vast supply of Soviet nuclear weapons.

"I did all that I could," declared Mikhail Gorbachev in his farewell speech. Now, however, he was out of power.

Still, there was no denying that it was Gorbachev who first had launched the dramatic period of change in Soviet life and in the history of the twentieth-century world. In large part it was Gorbachev's idea of *perestroika* that first had brought about greater friendship between the Soviet Union and the United States. It was Gorbachev who had opened the way to independence for the nations of Eastern Europe: Hun-

gary, Rumania, Bulgaria, Czechoslovakia, East Germany.

In a larger sense, it is unlikely that,
without the vision and cooperation of
Gorbachev, such leaders as President
George Bush and others could even
have begun thinking about—dreaming
about—the possibility of a "new world
order," with lasting peace in the world.

Clearly, such a dream is hard to
achieve, not only for the world but for
the people of a single nation. In biblical
times, Moses led the Jewish people out
of captivity in Egypt. But Moses, much
like Mikhail Gorbachev, discovered
that it is one thing to lead a people
out of trouble; it is still another
thing to lead them into the Promised
Land.

Nevertheless, Gorbachev's eventful
career, including his dramatic attempts
to improve the Soviet system of government, undoubtedly has earned him a
place in history among the most important world leaders of the twentieth century.

Further Reading

What if you were to walk down the streets of the world's great cities and, at random, ask people passing by the name of the secretary general of the United Nations? Most of those you interviewed would not be able to answer your question. But ask those same people about the leaders of their own country today—or even the names of great national leaders in past times—and they would respond at once.

In this book you have read about some of the best-known leaders of the last two centuries. Some, like Gandhi, have been good, and they are revered, even loved. Other national leaders, like Hitler, have brought suffering, misery, destruction, and death.

Through most of the world's history the great drama of human life has been played out with *national* leaders as its stars. And those stars have seen themselves as leaders of *national* causes. To maintain world peace after World War I, the League of Nations was organized, and then, following World War II, the United Nations took its place. But even in our own era today, little serious thought has been given to the possibility of what President George Bush has described as a "new world order"—a system calling upon all nations to work together to form a free, united world—a true community of nations.

Despite the spread of great arsenals of atomic weapons to distant corners of our planet—weapons that could put an end to all human life—the idea of world government still looms as only a distant dream.

We do not know what will happen in centuries to come. And it is not, of course, the task of historians to predict the future, no matter how deeply they may feel about what *should* happen. Thus, in telling the story of the human past, they do so by describing what actually happened, whether they like it or not.

One way to tell about human history is to describe the lives of national leaders, such as those whose deeds you have read about in *Great Lives: World Government*. If now, therefore, you would like to know more about these important leaders—men and women both good and evil—you might like to examine some of the historical works that have been useful in helping to make this book possible.

And, as you do, you may also wish to keep in mind the words of William Shakespeare with which the book began, for Shakespeare, like the following authors, understood that, among the great figures of the human past:

". . . some are born great, some achieve greatness, and some have greatness thrust upon them."

Part I: The Nineteenth Century: Prelude to Our Age

NAPOLÉON BONAPARTE

Maurois, Andre. *Napoléon.* New York: Viking, 1963.

Savant, Jean. *Napoléon in His Time.* Translated by Katherine John. New York: Thomas Nelson & Sons, 1958.

SIMÓN BOLÍVAR

Madariaga, Salvador de. *Bolívar.* New York: Pellegrini and Cudahy, 1952.

Masur, Gerhard. *Simón Bolívar.* Albuquerque: University of New Mexico Press, 1948.

OTTO VON BISMARCK

Snyder, Louis, and Ida Mae Brown. *Bismarck and German Unification.* New York: Franklin Watts, 1966.

Taylor, A. J. P. *Bismarck: The Man and the Statesman.* New York: Random House, 1967.

MEIJI MUTSUHITO

Beasley, W. G. *The Meiji Restoration.* Stanford: Stanford University Press, 1972.

Hall, John Whitney. Japan: *From Pre-History to Modern Times.* New York: Dell, 1970.

QUEEN VICTORIA

Shearman, Deirdre. *Queen Victoria.* New York: Chelsea House, 1986.

Strachey, Lytton. *Queen Victoria.* New York: Harcourt, Brace, 1921.

Part II: The Twentieth Century before Hiroshima

VLADIMIR ILYICH LENIN

Trotsky, Leon. *The Young Lenin.* Translated by Max Eastman. Garden City: Doubleday, 1972.

Ulam, Adam B. *The Bolsheviks.* New York: Macmillan, 1965.

SUN YAT-SEN

Schiffrin, Harold Z. *Sun Yat-sen and the Origins of the Chinese Revolution.* Berkeley: University of California Press, 1968.

Wilbur, C. Martin. *Sun Yat-sen: Frustrated Patriot.* New York: Columbia University Press, 1976.

KEMAL ATATÜRK

Kinross, Patrick Balfour (Lord). *Atatürk.* New York: Morrow, 1965.

Lengyel, Emil. *They Called Him Atatürk.* New York: John Day, 1962.

BENITO MUSSOLINI

Collier, Richard. *Duce!* New York: Viking, 1971.

Mussolini, Benito. *My Autobiography.* New York: Charles Scribner's Sons, 1928.

JOSEPH STALIN

Deutscher, Isaac. *Stalin: A Political Biography*. New York: Oxford University Press, 1967.

Hyde, H. Montgomery. *Stalin: The History of a Dictator*. New York: Popular Library, 1971.

ADOLF HITLER

Bullock, Alan. *Hitler: A Study in Tyranny*. New York: Harper, 1964.

Shirer, William L. *The Rise and Fall of the Third Reich*. New York: Simon and Schuster, 1960.

WINSTON CHURCHILL

Churchill, Winston. *My Early Life: A Roving Commission*. New York: Charles Scribner's Sons, 1930.

Cowles, Virginia. *Winston Churchill: The Era and the Man*. New York: Harper, 1953.

MOHANDAS K. (MAHATMA) GANDHI

Erikson, Erik H. *Gandhi's Truth*. New York: Norton, 1969.

Fischer, Louis. *Gandhi: His Life and Message for the World*. New York: New American Library, 1954.

Part III: The World since 1945

MAO TSE-TUNG

Schram, Stuart. *Mao Tse-tung*. Baltimore: Penguin Books, 1974.

Snow, Edgar. *Red Star over China*. New York: Grove Press, 1968.

CHARLES DE GAULLE

Crozier, Brian. *De Gaulle*. New York: Charles Scribner's Sons, 1973.

Schoenbrun, David. *The Three Lives of Charles de Gaulle*. New York: Atheneum, 1966.

JUAN PERÓN and EVA PERÓN

Frazer, Nicholas, and Marysa Navarro. *Eva Perón*. New York: Norton, 1980.

Page, Joseph. *Perón*. New York: Random House, 1983.

JOSIP BROZ TITO

Auty, Phyllis. *Tito: A Biography*. New York: McGraw-Hill, 1970.

Djilas, Milovan. *Tito: The Story from Inside*. New York: Harcourt Brace Jovanovich, 1980.

EAMON DE VALERA

Fitzgibbon, Constantine, and George Morrison. *The Life and Times of Eamon de Valera*. New York: Macmillan, 1973.

Longford, Lord, and T. P. O'Neill. *Eamon de Valera*. Boston: Houghton Mifflin, 1971.

GOLDA MEIR

Martin, Ralph G. *Golda: Golda Meir, the Romantic Years*. New York: Charles Scribner's Sons, 1988.

Meir, Golda. *My Life*. New York: G. P. Putnam's Sons, 1975.

FIDEL CASTRO

Bourne, Peter. *Fidel: A Biography of Fidel Castro*. New York: Dodd, Mead & Company, 1986.

Franqui, Carlos. *Family Portrait with Fidel*. New York: Random House, 1984.

JOMO KENYATTA

Delf, George. *Jomo Kenyatta: Towards Truth about "The Light of Kenya."* New York: Greenwood, 1961.

Wepman, Dennis. *Jomo Kenyatta*. New York: Chelsea House, 1985.

ANWAR EL-SADAT

Rosen, Deborah Nodler. *Anwar el-Sadat: Middle East Peacemaker*. Chicago: Children's Press, 1986.

Sadat, Anwar el-. *In Search of Identity: An Autobiography.* New York: Harper & Row, 1977.

HO CHI MINH

Fall, Bernard B., ed. *Ho Chi Minh on Revolution: Selected Writings, 1920–66.* New York: Praeger, 1967.

Halberstam, David. *Ho.* New York: Random House, 1971.

AYATOLLAH RUHOLLAH KHOMEINI

Rajaee, Farhang. *Islamic Values and World View: Khomeyni on Man, the State and International Politics.* Lanham, Maryland: University Press of America, 1983.

Wright, Robin. *In the Name of God: The Khomeini Decade.* New York: Simon and Schuster, 1989.

MIKHAIL GORBACHEV

Doder, Dusko, and Louise Branson. *Gorbachev: Heretic in the Kremlin.* New York: Viking, 1990.

Medved, Zhores. *Gorbachev.* New York: Norton, 1988.

Index

TOWN OF ORANGE
PUBLIC LIBRARY
ORANGE, CONN.